D1501270

BARELY Breathing

KATERINA BRAY

BARELY BREATHING
Copyright © 2017 by Katerina Bray.

All rights reserved. Printed in the United States of America. No part of this book may be used or reproduced in any manner whatsoever without written permission except in the case of brief quotations embodied in critical articles or reviews.

This book is a work of fiction. Names, characters, businesses, organizations, places, events, and incidents either are the product of the author's imagination or are used fictitiously. Any resemblance to actual persons, living or dead, events, or locales is entirely coincidental.

For information, visit: WWW.KATERINABRAY.COM

Book Edited By: Kathy (Kate) Smith

Cover Design By: Dawid Boldys

Dedication Image By: Maria Zogu

ISBN: 978-0-9985247-0-2

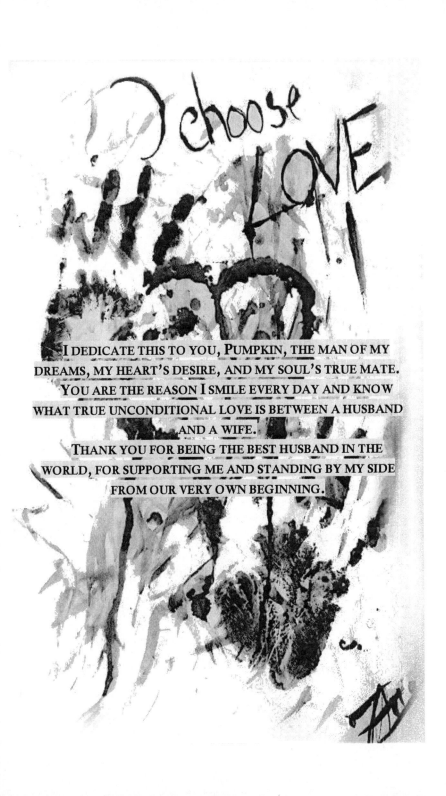

I DEDICATE THIS TO YOU, PUMPKIN, THE MAN OF MY DREAMS, MY HEART'S DESIRE, AND MY SOUL'S TRUE MATE. YOU ARE THE REASON I SMILE EVERY DAY AND KNOW WHAT TRUE UNCONDITIONAL LOVE IS BETWEEN A HUSBAND AND A WIFE.

THANK YOU FOR BEING THE BEST HUSBAND IN THE WORLD, FOR SUPPORTING ME AND STANDING BY MY SIDE FROM OUR VERY OWN BEGINNING.

THANK YOU

First and foremost, I must thank a dear friend and partner in novel writing crime, Author Kate Smith. If it wasn't for you coming along when you did, I'd have given up. For that alone, I'll forever appreciate you. That isn't all you've done, is it? Nope! You went deep into the minds of each character alongside me by entering the dark zone madness until it was perfect. To go even further, after seeing my despicable first drafts you taught me how to fix the problems rather than discouraging me from pursuing my dream. Kate, you'll always be my first and last writing buddy. So, to you my friend, I say THANK YOU for absolutely everything you continue to teach me.

Also, a huge thank you—to my amazing sister, brother-in-law and the most loving parents a girl could ask for. You gave me that extra push I needed to take a chance on this endeavor. To all of you, thank you for the unconditional love and believing in me and my abilities. I will forever be grateful! I love you all so much more than words could ever describe.

To my dear Maia (Grandmother), I thank you for continuously believing in your grandchildren. The pride you felt for us was always visible in your eyes and even though I can't see it anymore, I feel it deep within the depths of my soul. I love you so much and I miss you even more, but I know you're smiling down on us all. You will forever be in my heart and soul.

THE BEGINNING

"Remember, there are times that even those who are beautiful are broken inside. Tread carefully." - Katerina Bray

GROWING UP I HAD THIS idea true happiness meant being married, having kids, buying a big house with a picket fence, and of course, being rich. You know, all those things you see on television.

My mom would tell me it's all fake and life is very different when you're an adult. To this day, I remember her exact words to me, *"Not every fairy tale consists of two perfect people who are destined to fall in love. In the real world, perfect doesn't exist, especially to those who have bled and are scarred by the thorns that pricked them."*

But how could I believe her over the many commercials and sitcoms that made it look so easy to a ten-year-old? So, of course, I did what every kid does… refuse to listen to a word her parents say.

Well, turns out the TV and its ads, all flat out lied. My time in foster care should've proven that to me, but I couldn't give up on the things I'd watched as a child. A Happily Ever After had to be out there for me too, right?

Wrong.

Three weeks ago, my entire life changed, breaking my soul into a million unfixable pieces. The proof of how wrong I was is now slapping me across the face. I look back and question it all; search for answers, even though it's too late now.

Giving up has never been a part of who I am, but as I lay helplessly in this stark white room, the memories flourish in my mind. They're a never-ending burden on my soul.

It all ended differently than I expected. I thought I would end up dead—but didn't. He stormed out of the room, leaving me all alone, letting my sorrow take hold of me. At first, I was fine with how he'd left me. His departure brought forth tears of joy, if only for a little while. Later that night, I found out the tragic fact which broke my heart.

As the medication wears off, pain grips my insides, again. I throw my head back and scream, letting the tears fall like a never-ending waterfall. Never-ending tears for him. Never-ending tears because of the men who've destroyed me. Never-ending tears for the fairy tale I wished for—but would never have.

At the sound of my hysterics, the nurses come rushing in with my saving grace. Too weak and powerless, I don't fight them, I accept and simply let myself fall into the welcoming darkness.

-1-

Ruby

TWO UNBELIEVABLY LONG AND DREADFUL months have passed since my admission into the psychiatric ward. Today is finally the big day. As excited as I may be to leave, there's a nagging question lingering in my mind—where am I going? The idea of returning to that place, into that nauseating apartment, where it all ended, brings a sick feeling to my stomach.

A crazy plan forms in my mind—*sell it all!* Every single, solitary stick of furniture! Along with it, I hope to dismantle every horrible memory. My top priority is to erase the past, to have absolutely nothing to do with any of it—the townhouse, the furnishings, or the deeply painful, and gut-wrenching memories.

A fresh new start, that's exactly what I need. It's the only thing that can save me.

I sit at the edge of the bed, legs swinging, and ponder my future as my psychiatrist slips into the room.

His wrinkled face creases as if in pain and he lowers himself carefully into a chair. "Okay, Ruby, all the release paperwork has been filled out." Dr. Miles smiles, folding his hands in front of him. "Before you go, do you have any questions for me?" He hands me the two sheets of paper clipped together, which turn out to be my copies of the discharge and prescription.

Dr. Joseph Miles has been my doctor for the last five years and seems to be a compassionate man with that ready smile. However, it never quite eases my nerves whenever we have our one on one sessions. Just the sight of this place throws me into a cold sweat.

Today is no different. I glance at the papers, his warmth and kindness doing nothing to comfort the anxiety deep in the pit of my stomach. I'm lucid enough to leave this prison, but I cannot even feel happy about it. I've longed to return to the real world for almost my entire stay, yet I can't help worrying about the future, this frightening new life I'm embarking on all *alone*.

Again.

The thought of this newfound ability to do whatever I want, whenever I want is overwhelming.

What if I make the same mistakes again?

I can't even imagine the damage that would cause me this time around.

I might never recover!

"I don't have any questions. Thank you for your time, but I'm ready to go." Even though externally I appear calm and happy, inside I'm screaming.

Maybe this whole thing is a bad idea? What if I screw up, and I lose what's left of my sanity?

I take a deep breath to calm my nerves. "No offense, Doc, but I want to get out of here. There's nothing left for me here but bad memories."

Smiling sadly, Dr. Miles nods and rises from his chair. "I understand. Well, Ruby, please take good care of yourself. If you ever feel yourself slipping, please call us, or... call me directly, anytime at all."

He extends a business card, which I take and stick in my

pocket. "Thanks, but I don't think I'll be needing this."

"Ruby, can you do me a favor?"

I nod ever so hesitantly. I can tell what's coming.

"Can you try to keep out of, and away from trouble? You and I both know you've been through enough. Stay strong, and remember, if you're overwhelmed, just stop and take a deep breath before moving forward." He takes off his glasses, rubbing the bridge of his nose wearily before he shakes my hand. "Ruby? I want to help you through this, so... there are going to be days when you will think everything is fine, but I want to caution you. You absolutely must keep up with your medication."

"Thank you, Dr. Miles. I will, and I appreciate everything this facility has done for me."

He nods, and leads me to the room where my few belongings have been kept safe; my purse, my phone, my wallet, and my jacket. The sum and total of what I will take into my new life.

The doctor clears his throat. "This is where I leave you, Ruby. Remember, you are a very strong person, and if there is one thing someone can't take from you—it's that inner strength."

His gentle reminder of the only thing that's kept me going all of these years means so much to me. Words are impossible to form and I simply nod as he leaves the room.

My freedom starts now.

The realization has me frozen in this spot, unable to proceed. Taking a few moments to myself, I wait until my body relaxes enough to approach the door. Forcing myself into motion, I take short halting steps toward the front door of the facility, every step is an enormous effort.

Deep breath. Am I ready for this? Deep breath.

I pause, and slowly extend my trembling hand, and rest it lightly on the handle.

Am I prepared to take on the real world?

My heart swells with fear.

Ruby, once you step outside, your whole life is going to change.

Am I okay with this?

I have to be. I can't stay here forever and I have nowhere else to go.

I push through the door, the bright June sunlight kissing my face as I lift it toward the sky.

Oh, how I have missed this!

I inhale the fresh sweet air and smile. My confidence grows with each step I take, further and further from the door, my heart pounds as if it's trying to escape my chest. I savor my new-found freedom, it feels amazing to be here in this moment, and suddenly, I can't wait for another second to move on with my new life. All of my fears dissipated the moment I stepped outside, and somehow, I know it will all be okay.

Strength, Ruby. You have it, you always have.

Approaching the nearest bench, I sit on the warm, hard surface, and dig out my phone. First order of business is to find a realtor and sell my current apartment. My hands shake in excitement at this momentous step forward. I emphasize the need to have it sold as fast and efficiently as possible. Once I leave, I don't want to come back here... ever!

No one will miss me, or even look for me.

Managing to accomplish this task without too much trouble boosts my confidence even further.

I can do this!

Now for the hard part.

Where do I want to live?

Money isn't an issue, so my possibilities are endless. With all that free time I had in the ward, I spent hours upon hours dreaming about all the places I could go, and I managed to narrow my list to three major cities—Los Angeles, Dallas, or Chicago. Google soon becomes my best friend as I research the pros and cons of each area, narrowing it down further. Dallas, Texas.

Yes!

That's where I believe I'd be the happiest. The slogan speaks to me: *'Everything's Bigger in Texas.'* Definitely sounds like the perfect place to start my new life. Plenty of room to get lost, and go unnoticed.

Now I need a realtor in my chosen area of Dallas, and a phone call later, I'm listening to a sexy Texan southern drawl.

"I'm relocating and in need of an apartment in the Dallas area." I introduce myself to the agent.

"Howdy, Ruby! I'd be happy to help you out." His deeply accented voice is like a bite of sexy ear candy. "I can show you our available listings. You in town?"

"No, I'm not. Is it possible for you to email them to me? I need to get this sorted out before I arrive in Dallas next month."

"Why certainly, little lady! Give me all your information and I'll get them off to you this afternoon?"

"Perfect! I appreciate your time, sir." I'm truly grateful that he's so willing to accommodate me and I spend a few more minutes relaying the wish list for my new home.

After the call, I expect to be refreshed and excited but instead, I'm greeted by nervous butterflies fluttering in my belly. Anxiety begins to take its now very familiar control over my body. Doubt and fear cloud my mind, and the hope I felt minutes before fades into the background. My palms are a sweaty mess and I can barely breathe. I try to inhale but all I can manage is a painful ragged breath. Exhaling is even worse, it's as if knives stab their way up and out of my throat.

How is this possible? A panic attack over what exactly? What is wrong with me?

The idea of leaving everything behind is more than appealing, but when awareness kicks in and an actual action takes place— I freak?

When did I change so much? When did the effects of my past start to mark me in such a permanent way? Was it when I was ten, fifteen, or twenty-one years old? Or maybe the worse it got and the longer I stayed, the deeper my scars became?

No matter how much time I spent away from the real world, it won't change how hard it is to come back from what has transpired. Closing my eyes, I let the still raw emotions and very vivid memories wash over me.

Why can't I forget? Someone help me erase it all from my mind…

please?

I shake my head in a meager attempt to clear my mind enough to call a cab. I have no other option for transportation since I was taken to the hospital by ambulance all those painful weeks ago.

In less than twenty minutes, I find myself standing in front of the oh-so-familiar townhouse. While I stare up at the structure where my whole life changed, an unexpected memory hits me.

* * *

As I'm peering up at my new apartment, I can't stop fidgeting with my hair because of all this excitement bubbling through me. My parents would be so proud of me. I can clearly picture them with their proud smiling faces, and their welcoming arms wide open. My heart swells at the image in my head. I wish they could be here and witness the first place I can really call home since they've been gone.

From the time my mom passed on, to this moment, I was placed in the care of foster parents who took me in solely for access to the monthly stipend from my trust fund.

Lowlifes who took advantage, using the funds my parents worked their whole lives to save! My mom and dad tried so hard to ensure I would never have to worry after they left me behind. But it didn't work out that way. I often went hungry and was mainly ignored, abandoned in a broken system. Just thinking about that family makes my skin crawl.

This apartment is a new beginning, my new beginning. It has freedom written all over it, a safe place where I no longer have to beg for scraps to eat or ask permission to take a shower.

Those people don't own me anymore. I am free, exhilarating free of them.

A smile spreads across my face as I take the stairs which lead to my front door. When I put the key into the lock, my independence opens before me.

Looking around the bright and open space fills me with a delirious amount of happiness! I bounce from room to room, stopping in each one to jot down the items needed to furnish it. My fingers tremble as I stare down at my first ever detailed list of items for my... home.

Mom? Dad? Are you listening? If you are... please know I'm happy. I've found a safe home to live in now. And know, I don't blame you for what those people did to me. You had no way of knowing how bad they would turn out to be. I love you both so much, and today is a fresh start. The past is just that... the past.

Closing the door behind me with a contented sigh, I head out into the bright sunlight. Glancing over my shoulder, a sense of peacefulness washes over me for the first time in years. I skip the last few feet to the bus stop, happy to the bottom of my very core, knowing the adventure of living alone in my own home has started.

* * *

RECENT EVENTS ASIDE, RECOLLECTING THE day I bought this place gives me the hope I need. I've felt true happiness before— though it's better described as mere flashes—it doesn't stop my optimism at feeling it again.

The first ten years of my life were filled with so much love and joy, well... until my parents lost their battle to cancer and the happiness I once knew disappeared. Losing my mom was the final straw. I thought my life was over.

It felt like it was. At times, I wished it was, at least then I would be with them in heaven and not in this shit hole of a world.

Yet, somehow, I found this hidden strength deep within me that helped with overcoming the grief of their loss. That anguish turned into an ache, but the space in my heart, which used to be filled by their love, remains empty. I look down at my bared arm and my eyes automatically focus on my wrist.

Strength. Hidden within me for the last fifteen years and counting.

Unfortunately, after losing my beloved parents, I also had to grow up fast. The need to learn how to be stronger than I appeared became inevitable. It was the only way to stop kids from bullying me for being in foster care.

'Nobody loves you' was the term most used by my classmates.

It was impossible to hide the fact that I was a foster child, especially when I came into school with filthy clothes and unkempt hair.

That sure didn't help.

In order to protect myself, I was forced to become someone else, to change everything about the girl I once was. All the while knowing deep inside doing so would alter me forever.

That tough, strong and unemotional girl had to resurface many times in the past. Most recently, she emerged to keep me sane while I was in the hospital. Having survived all of that and then some, I believe I can do it once more.

Can a third time be my charm?

All I need to do is keep my guard up, and not show my true colors... to anyone.

Should be easy... right?

-2-

MAESON

MONDAYS. THE BANE OF MY existence. Words can't express how much I detest them; they're at the absolute top of my shit list.

I drag my ass into the elevator, leaning in a daze against the wall while it descends to the first floor. Damn convenient having my office on the first floor of the same building where I reside.

Thank fuck for small mercies. I don't have to face commuting on top of the dreadful hangover I'm dealing with on this not-so-fucking-lovely morning.

I glance at the reception desk as I step toward my office door. Molly's nowhere in sight, but she's definitely around here somewhere. That woman is always here before me. Which doesn't upset me one bit, because her dedication over the course of the past five years has made her irreplaceable to the daily function of my business.

"Fuck!" I instinctively lift my hands, covering my eyes as the blazing sun assaults them.

I forgot to shut the fucking shades!

The floor to ceiling windows face the rising sun, and on days like these, I regret installing them. This morning the light reflects harshly against the stark white walls, the expanse broken only by a couple of black and white paintings. I yank at the cord, shielding my face until the shades cut off the agonizing glare.

A massive dark cherry wood desk dominates the spacious room, but I avoid even a glance in its direction. There is no need, I can picture the sky-high pile of paperwork, folders, and who knows what else stacked on it, and buried underneath it all is my precious laptop. Of course, if it wasn't for the corner of it peeking through, it would be lost in the abyss of the massive disaster happening around and over it.

Everything in my life has order. Except for my desk.

Most people surround themselves with plaques and lame photos, that bring sappy smiles to their pathetic faces. I have none of those things, nor do I need them. My smiles are reserved for those deserving of them. Although, lately, it seems I rarely smile.

There's work to do, quit moping around.

Before I can face the mountain covering my desk, I need the biggest cup of coffee I can find. The pile's been screaming my name for the last fucking month, it can wait for a few more minutes. Or days... Whatever.

When did I become so lazy?

Perhaps it's the boredom? Same God damn routine gets mighty old after so many years.

Work? Check!

Booze? Check!

Sex? Double check!

Sleep? Check... mate?

I drop my briefcase on the floor and stick a finger into my collar giving a yank on my red Giorgio Armani tie. The worthless two-hundred-dollar scrap of silk is currently strangling the fuck out of me and chafing the shit out of my neck.

I need to get my shit together.

The aroma of fresh coffee wafts in from the kitchen, and my

nostrils flare as I inhale the delicious scent. My hands are shaking, reminding me of my severe caffeine deficiency. I'm in desperate need.

"Morning, Molly," I grumble as I stomp into the kitchen.

My assistant stands by the Nespresso machine. Her long shapely legs are crossed as she leans against the cabinet and smiles. She's gorgeous as fuck, but there's no sexual spark. The temptation to sleep with her is literally nonexistent, making her the perfect assistant.

"Mornin', Boss!" Her southern drawl is way too cheery this morning.

"Down a notch, buttercup. My head hurts." Rubbing my pounding temples, I yank off my glasses, squeezing the bridge of my nose. Her cup fills, and I stare longingly at it, wishing the machine weren't so fucking slow.

"Another bender?" She shakes her head in displeasure, and her long dark hair swirls around her face. Her pale blue eyes lift to mine, anger blazing in them. They're tinged with something else... Sadness? Disappointment?

A throbbing ache surfaces in my chest. I rub my left pec and wince. I haven't felt that kind of pain in years. She's the last person I want to disappoint. When I look at Molly, I see the sister I wish I had in my life.

I rub my beard and smirk, then slice my head to the right in an upward motion.

She sits at the nearest table. "Is that a yes? Quit with your sexy little moves and speak."

"Yes. A wee one."

Her lip curls in disgust. "I can tell." Molly's glower expresses her opinion on my questionable lifestyle choices.

I doctor up my coffee with a touch of cream, two packets of raw sugar, and take a long grateful sip. "What gives it away?"

The message in her baby blue's rings loud and clear.

She needs to stop that bullshit. It messes with my mind.

"Your face and hair look like shit and you're wearing glasses. Dead giveaway, you *only* wear them on hangover days." She abruptly stands and turns away from me. An awkward moment of silence passes before she faces me again, tears staining her face. "And who the fuck says 'wee' before anything, boss?"

She let tears drop for me? Why?

"I do, la—" *Fuck!* Crying women gut me. I compose myself. "Mo. I do." Damn! I'm starting to let go around her. "Why are you crying?" I enunciate each word perfectly.

I can't keep slipping.

Her glassy eyes widen. "Why?" She raises the mug to her lips and sips the remaining liquid. "I'll tell ya why, Maeson. You're reverting to the guy I met five years ago, and it makes me sad for *you*." She sniffles. "You've made such progress, now you're getting wasted again. You're the only man I have left in my life. I don't want to lose you, damn it! Who's gonna walk me down the aisle, if I *ever* find a man?"

Damn it! I can't handle sniffles for fuck's sake!

"I'm not going anywhere. I promise you. It's been a rough few months and I'm getting old. Like you, I have no one in my life. At long last I'm ready, and no one worth a damn comes a knockin'. I'm tired of one night fucks. At some point, you want more. You know?" I run a hand through my hair and notice I'm in major need of a haircut; this shit is becoming obnoxiously long.

Sex God Fabio, eat your heart out!

"I know, Mae Mae, but don't overdo it or maybe take me with you? I promise I won't cock block, just block your drinkin'!" She runs her fingers through my hair. "And I'm so amazing that I will give ya free friendly advice, without you askin' for it." She tugs at my long strands. "Like trim that wanna be sexy beard, and get a fucking haircut, it looks like a dirty brown mop." Her joyous laugh fills the room.

I hate that damn childish nickname!

"First off, don't call me *Mae Mae* in public, or you're fired! Second, you're an automatic cock block. You're a beautiful young woman, which deters other young beauties who want to fuck me. And lastly, for now, the hair and beard stays. So, fuck off, buttercup." I wink and stun her my with dazzling dimpled smile.

It helps me get away with everything.

"*Mae Mae*, how about you fuck off with those damn dimples, or I'll quit." She wags a finger in my face. "I know what you're doing! One day you're going to need me as wingman and I'll make you beg. Remember that shit, Mae." She lightly sweeps her hand across her shoulder and winks.

"Like that'll ever happen," I scoff. "I have my secret weapons." I broaden my smile.

"You're *too* cocky. But I'm not worried because eventually, you will get yours, *Buddy*. One day, *real soon*, you'll meet that girl who'll put you in your place. Teach ya a lesson ya won't soon forget." She unceremoniously dumps her empty mug into the sink. "Clean that shit, I've got work to do." She dismisses me with an uppity wave as she struts out the door.

My brows furrow in annoyance.

The damn woman knows she's indispensable to me.

The corner of my lips rise into a smirk. I'll get her back real good because little does she know I'm planning a big surprise. I'll show her by offloading all these fucking day to day details right onto her lap. Of course, I'll call it a promotion to butter her up and reward her a hefty raise to close the deal.

"Boss, stop here on your way back!" Molly calls down the hall.

"Coming," I grunt and arm myself with another massive cup of coffee, needing it to attack that stack of bullshit paperwork on my desk.

"Here. This one's new." She hands me a red manila folder. "I just got the inquiry from Brant Miller. Definitely want to check this one out, boss. The file is mighty *interesting*." She smirks knowingly.

Chances are it's yet another old rich couple looking to retire here. Should've made this place a damn old fogies home.

I flip open the folder, and skim the contents "Did you read any of it?"

"Nope, not at all. That's your job. You pay yourself the big bucks for that, not me." Her lips quirk up as she fights a smile. "Tell me what you decide, so I can call to confirm or deny."

"You got it."

"Hey, Mae—Maeson, we've known each other how long and you still won't tell me why you're hiding an accent?" She raises a brow and waits for the response I won't give her.

"Don't have an accent. You're hearing things woman, now go back to work." I wave a hand and continue on the path to my office. With a long drawn out sigh, I push away files to make room on my desk for the one in my hand. The sole name listed on it entices me.

Might not be an elderly couple after all?

I flip it open, picking out the first sheet.

RUBY BENNETT (BENEVITI)
BORN - JANUARY 1, 1991
RESIDENT OF - MANHATTAN, NEW YORK.
INCOME - FAMILY TRUST

That's surprising. Why would a wee twenty-five-year-old relocate and uproot her life? Interesting…

I absorb the information on the page and my interest in this woman grows. Wealthy, young, probably a sexy city girl, and she's willing to shell out the cash for the penthouse?

Yes. Hell yes to that!

Between the many retired doctors, lawyers, and athletes, young anything is a rarity, let alone a young *woman*—now that's a fucking miracle! Questions bombard me. Why is she leaving a fast-paced city for one that is much less so? Who might she be moving for? A man perhaps?

Boy am I nosey.

Regardless, I have no way of finding out those details, with the privacy act and all.

Why do I care anyway? She going to pay a pretty penny for the place and that's all that matters.

Maybe she just needs a get-the-hell-away-from-reality move. *I'd know all about that—I'm an expert in that shit.*

Eh. Doesn't matter what her reasons are, either way, I've made my decision. I hit the intercom button on my desk phone. "Hey, Mo money." I chuckle to myself. "Bennett's file is a yes. Set it up." I release the button and wait for Molly.

"You got it, chief. Once it's done, I'll send you the signed finalized papers."

"Thanks. Now get back to work, slacker." I cut the connection before snickering to myself.

"Asshole." Her mutter carries across the hallway. "Thinks he's so fuckin' funny... Mo money? Like I haven't heard *that one* before. He's the damn slacker, *not me.*"

It never fails to surprise me at how fast a joke turns into something serious with Molly. Sometimes she gets too sensitive and turns into a not so nice woman—and that's putting it lightly. Not wanting to fuel the fire that's been lit under her ass, I don't respond.

Before I can move on to my next task of the day, I set the *'Ruby Bennett'* file aside. Don't want to lose it in this massive pile of crapola, I'll never find it again.

First things first, this desk needs to be cleaned off.

No time like the present, I suppose. Even my fucking assistant thinks I'm a lazy assed ole bum. I flip open the closest file, barely even needing to move my arm to reach it. A quick scan tells me it's garbage. Complete shit. No job, really? How do you afford the bills? Nope, not a fit for damn sure.

To the shredder pile.

There are now two separate stacks formed before me—the *'to be destroyed'* pile and the other one is *'accept applicant'* pile. One last step remains before the cleaning begins. Email Molly to advise her which candidates need rejection letters.

And now for the fun stuff... shredding the shit out of these pages.

I revel in the sound of those little blades destroying every last inch of this lousy excuse for paperwork. I grin maniacally, one down... only ten thousand or so to go. Once I get started, I can't stop. Flip. Scan. Shred. Flip.

Are you fucking kidding, you work for the president?

I call bull!

Creative idiot, are you?

Shred. Flip.

Save me from these moronic assholes!

Shred. On and on it goes. It's strangely addictive, watching the piles on my desk get smaller as the shredder bin fills.

My grin widens as I think about my surprise for Mo. Her thirtieth birthday is coming up in November. In five more long boring months, she's getting that promotion!

"Mae—" Molly pops into my office, her eyebrows flying upwards as she stares at my overflowing shredder. She scans my desk and the floor, smirking. There are shreds of paper literally everywhere. "Been busy have we? Finally working, are we? Hmm. I should take a picture, no one's going to believe you actually work."

Seriously? I make one damn joke and she's taking it to whole other level.

I sweep the bits of mangled folders off my pants, absolutely fucking sick of that damn condescending tone. I want to wipe that knowing expression off of her smug face. I've seen it before, and I loathe it. It drives me insane. All women who have a bone to pick or want to make a man feel like shit use it. Especially one woman in particular. She would always use that damn tone and had that same fucking look on her face.

My beast rises within, my heart pounds and my throat threatens to close up as I erupt. "Quit fucking calling me that! I'm a grown ass man, God damn it, not some fucking little boy! And of course, I work. What the fuck is that supposed to mean? I built this place from the ground up and if wasn't for me, you wouldn't have a job!" I thump my fist onto the desk and give the stacks of files a vicious shove. They scatter everywhere, but I don't give a flying fuck.

She takes a large step backward, and a flicker of fear flashes through her eyes before they turn sad. Her mouth sets into a grim line. "Fine, Mr. Alexander. We've received an email from the sellers about the property you want to buy. Mr. Maxwell said he's looking forward to closing as soon as possible and would like to schedule a meeting with you to discuss the final details."

Shit, now who's the sensitive one? It's just a nickname and Molly isn't... the one you loathe.

I clench my jaw as she retreats, and drop my head in shame. As soon as the man I used to be rises, she shuts down, making me feel like the bastard I really am. I focus on her feet, and take several deep breaths, sinking onto my chair. "Okay. Thanks. And, Mo," I whisper. "I'm—"

She holds up her hand. "Save it."

I dare lift my eyes to hers and open my mouth.

Molly throws me a warning look and shakes her head. She pivots, her brown hair swinging, but stops to shoot a glance over her shoulder, a smirk on her lips. "By the way? I held back a page from the Bennett file, but surprisingly, you didn't even notice. Maybe if you came to work sober more often you wouldn't miss the small details."

My brow creases as I rack my brain on what the absent page could be. Didn't I read through the entire file? "What page? I would've noticed something missing."

Molly laughs. "Oh, you're so clueless." Suddenly, she strides out of my office but returns with a sheet of paper in her hand and waves it in the air triumphantly. "This, my friend, is a copy of her license. Knowing you so well, I withheld it so you could accept or deny the application without using your second, brainless head. And guess what I did?"

"Well, since I'm so *brainless* and *clueless*? I have no idea. Why don't you fill me in, *my friend?*" I grin, playing along.

"Ha-ha. Old man, you're in for a hell of a ride. Once I saw her license picture, I was intrigued. I did a Google search and found a few more images. Would you believe Miss Ruby's nothing like the raggedy blonde thin mints you usually bag and tag? Oh yeah, she's far from that, this one's a real voluptuous, certified hottie with curves in all the right places and wild dark brown curls. I think my wish is about to come true, she could be a learning opportunity comin' your way, and *real soon* too." She snickers and sashays out of the room.

"Yeah, right! Like that'll ever happen! Blonde or Brunette, they're all the same, no one's going to teach me a damn thing!" I yell after her.

Her laugh echo's down the hallway, and it seems to be the only response the woman will give me.

Fuck! I should've checked the entire file!

I sigh and rub at my throbbing temples.

Why, oh why did I drink so damn much last night?

Sinking back in my oversized leather chair, I tip my head.

It will be okay, not all curly haired brunettes with real woman bodies are my weakness.

Picking up the piece of paper with the driver's license printed on it, I stare at the face looking back at me.

Ruby Bennett.

The mysterious, young, trust-funded woman, with features I normally steer clear of. This bit of information can be dangerous, but I'll deal with it later, won't I?

Push everything aside until you're forced to face it.

For now, though, I need to somehow manage to get through the rest of this day with my ridiculous hangover. I close my eyes and relax, but unbidden, a picture pops into my head.

Wild... brown... curls...

-3-

Ruby

MY PLANS ARE COMING TOGETHER. The townhouse has been sold, and the only thing left is the answer on the rental in Dallas. It's mid-June already and I'm getting anxious because if the application is denied I'm not sure where to go. When I saw the pictures I fell in love with the place. I didn't have any other options lined up in case my first pick didn't work out. Silly me, considering the anxiety over it had me checking my phone every two minutes for the past several weeks.

Today is the day, it has to be!

A few hours later, my phone rings.

"Hello?" My hands shake so hard, my phone slips from my fingers, but I catch it before it hits the floor.

"My name's Molly, I'm the assistant at Rose Garden Luxury Condos. You've been approved for move-in next month." A woman's sweet Southern voice drawls.

I jump up, waving my free arm in the air. "Thank you, I'm beyond ready! Would you mind emailing a copy of the finalized lease?"

"Of course!" I hear her typing. "Alrighty, it's done. All I need is for you to e-sign and you're good to go."

"I'll get it done as soon as we hang up. Is there anything else I need to do?"

"No, sweetie, all that's left is to meet on moving day to give you your keys."

"Perfect, I'll call you once I arrive." I hang up and immediately open my email.

* * *

LONG AT LAST, THE DAY arrives and I'm in Dallas. I spent the entire flight fidgeting in my seat and absently flipping through a magazine. Not a single word was absorbed, but I did notice that the man next to me spent most of the time shooting me dirty looks.

Too bad, so sad, buddy. You don't own me. No one does... anymore.

Traveling through the airport was a breeze and I easily find the well-dressed man holding the sign with *'Bennett'* written neatly across it. I greet him with a smile. "Hi! I'm Ruby Bennett."

"Please follow me. I parked your car right out front." He hands me the two duplicate sets of keys, which I take happily. "Here you go Ma'am, these are yours." He waves and heads toward the terminal, pausing to glance over his shoulder with a big smile. "Welcome to Dallas, young lady!"

I smile and wave back. "Thank you!"

My brand new black Honda Civic Coupe welcomes me. Sliding behind the wheel, the wonderful smell of new leather surrounds me. Tipping back my head and closing my eyes, I grip the steering wheel tightly, savoring the moment. *Freedom. A new start.* Virtually all the reminders of my past have been left behind.

Not wanting to stay in Manhattan any longer than needed, I'd arrived a day early and booked a hotel room near my new apartment for the night. This will give me a chance to explore the neighborhood before I meet with Molly from Rose Garden's tomorrow.

My phone rings, breaking my reverie. Speak of the devil, it's Molly.

"Hiya, Miss Bennett?" Her now familiar heavily accented voice is music to my ears.

"Hi, Molly! I just arrived in Dallas. What's up?"

"I wanted to schedule a time to meet. However, if you're here we could set you up today instead of tomorrow."

"There's no need to, I booked a hotel room nearby."

"Okay, if that's what you'd like to do, but if you change your mind you have my number."

"Thank you, but that's not necessary. I want to take a day, tour the area, and get acquainted with North Dallas."

"Good idea! It's beautiful here. There are so many different shopping centers, restaurants, and even a pretty neat hang out spot called Crossroads that's walking distance from the complex."

"Great! I'll have to check it out then! Thank you for the suggestions!"

"No problem. If you need anything, let me know. If not, I'll see you tomorrow morning."

"Sounds good. Bye, Molly!"

After hanging up, I set up my GPS and the British phone voice maps my route out for me. The drive is only thirty minutes, and it appears to be mostly highway. I was worried that it would be the opposite, with hidden country back roads filled with creepy tumbleweeds and such.

I'm already in love with this city. The people here seem friendly and helpful, and not as old school southern as I imagined.

As I drive, I relax and admire the scenery. The landscape is flat but filled with great architecture, tons of homes, complexes, and convenient shopping centers. There's an instantaneous sense of comfort being here. Dallas seems to have the perfect combination of city convenience and the cozy charm of country life. It's far less crowded than the streets of New York City, and it's refreshing.

Driving through Dallas is an adventure in itself. The highways take me skyward, looping and twisting like a roller coaster. I've never seen anything like it.

Approximately forty-five minutes later, I arrive at the massive hotel and I'm in awe of how beautiful and spacious it is. The ones back home were nice but crowded, space and people wise. My room here is twice the dimensions, with a full-size bedroom, bathroom, and living area, unlike the pint-sized offerings in the city. Businesses and homes can be spread out in Dallas as there's a lot more land to do so.

And I love it!

The clock on the nightstand beams six o'clock, the night is young. I have my life back, so what do I want to do first?

Take a nap, that's what!

My body concedes to my mind's demand and I lay down for a power snooze. Then I'll have the energy to take a drive around town, and even grab some dinner.

So much for me seizing the day.

"Hey, that's not true!" I berate myself aloud. "I'm single and free of any hold. I have all the time in the world to seize every damn day not just today! Get a grip girl!"

If someone was watching right now, they'd assume I'm crazy. But realistically, who doesn't give themselves a pep talk occasionally? Out loud or not—we all do it.

I wrap my arms around the crisp white hotel pillows that I have a hate/love relationship with. They're always so comfortable at first—then they flatten the hell out and kill your neck!

Closing my eyes, I hope for a dreamless sleep—I beg for it.

Give me a few hours with nothing but darkness, that's all I ask.

* * *

STRETCHING OUT ACROSS THE BED, a moan of pure relaxation

escapes me.

Best nap ever!

I peer at the clock—nine o'clock pm. I asked for blissful sleep and that's what I got. For three full hours, I was oblivious to the world around me. Three painless hours... three nightmare free hours.

Hanging my legs off the edge of the bed, not quite ready to get up, I sigh. Why can't all my days be this easy?

Because real life gets in the way.

Taking a deep breath, I hop off the mattress and discard my clothes.

As I shower, I muse about where I should go. I've spent so much time being told what to do that now I long to escape anything resembling confinement—which includes this hotel room.

It's past nine on a Sunday night, what's open at this hour?

The only thing I can come up with is the hotel lounge downstairs. I noticed a sign when I walked in—music and drinks till one in the morning—my kind of place. I'll never turn down that kind of stimulating combination.

Ready at last, I gaze in the mirror. When my eyes meet the reflection, I find a different woman. She appears confident and strong with her long, sleek pin straight hair.

She's not at odds with her identity at all.

Turning to the side, I admire how long my hair has grown in the last few months. It reaches the top curve of my butt, and as much as I love that, I also despise it because it takes twice as long to straighten.

Is that truly why I hate it?

No, it's not. This girl with shiny and smooth hair isn't who I am. She's masking her pain by projecting a fierce and uncaring woman who is unaffected by the cards life has dealt her. Yet, in its natural state, my curls fit how I feel inside—unsure, wild, free, and can no longer be tied down.

A woman with multiple sides to herself. A woman struggling to balance each one without losing who she truly is in the process.

Shaking my head, I dismiss my worries and throw on a pair of black tights, a sheer royal blue shirt which reaches the top of my thighs and simple black sandals.

The elevator ride to the bar is short and sweet and to my surprise, the lounge is bustling with life. As I wait for the waitress to bring my jack and coke, I admire the décor or lack thereof. The alternating blue and purple LED lights are the only things offsetting the stark white furnishings and walls. Then there are the people...

I'm not so sure I belong in a place this fancy.

The lounge is crowded with older well-dressed business men and women, yet here I am in tights and sandals looking like a bum. I'm tempted to slither out of here as some of them notice me and give me peculiar looks.

"Here you go." The waitress appears from behind me and I jump. "Oh sorry!" She smiles and sets down the drink.

Even she looks amazing in her tight black skirt and bright white button down shirt. I shouldn't have come, I don't fit in here. People probably think I'm a pathetic lonely girl drinking alone since everyone else has company by their side.

"That's okay. Thank you."

"Can I get you anything else?" Her smile widens in a nauseating—*she's trying too hard*—way.

"No, thank you." I plaster on an equally fake smile.

She disappears and I turn my attention to the beverage before me. This will be the first one I have since I was released from the hospital. Part of me wants to shove it away, knowing it won't help me in any way, the other part craves it and the power it holds. Alcohol has a way of providing the extra courage a person needs to keep on going, and it masks all your problems for a time. For some, that's not an option, but for others—like me— it's the best I can do at this moment.

My third glass is almost empty when I spot him. Looking up, directly at the man, who's but a few steps away from me, I lick my lips and smirk.

Well, hello sexy...

Tall, dark, and exuding that '*fuck me with no attachments*' vibe. His dark, slightly shaggy hair is pushed back in a messy yet sensual way. He's wearing an all-black suit, with his shirt buttoned up to the top. Everything about him is crispy clean, down to his shiny black shoes. My gaze zones in on his face, his features are rugged, raw, and strong. He's what I like to call a '*man's man*', a '*bad boy*', and one of those guys a woman rips her panties for at the drop of a dime.

Including me.

The man doesn't smile, smirk, grin, or move a damn muscle. But his eyes...

Shit!

They're eating me alive and gleam with hunger.

Okay, there is no way he's looking at me that way. Someone must be behind me.

Now I'm an even bigger fool. Not only do I not fit in here, but I thought one of the sexiest men I've ever seen was checking *me* out. I should know better since no one was ever starved for what I brought to the table.

Time to go.

When I stand, so does he. Our eyes meet again and I'm frozen in place. He moves forward and each step he takes brings him closer to my table. My lungs constrict.

He was looking at me!

One last footstep and we are face to face. I'm unable to speak or move being this close to such an overpowering essence.

Deep breath.

With him in my personal space, I'm instantly aroused.

Who wouldn't be?

He's hot and I'm lonely, which translates to—I'm in need of *that* kind of *company*.

The man smiles—if it can even be called one—it's more like a straight line going across his ferocious face. "Can I get you another drink?" His voice is so deep it's guttural.

No to the drink, although, I wouldn't mind a tall glass of you naked—I *don't* say. "Sure." I sit back down and gesture for him to join me.

He motions for the nauseatingly beautiful blonde and orders two more Jack's. As she struts away, purposely swaying her stick figure ass and hips, his eyes never leave my face.

Seriously? Barbie just strutted away and he doesn't even peek?

He must've had her and tossed her. That would be the only logical reason he's not interested. Men like him, which I've met a few—slept with—don't usually stick around for round two if the first one sucks.

That's why you always make the main event count.

Speaking of the main show, why is he wasting my time?

Get to the point, guy.

Up until our drinks arrive he simply watches me and I return the scrutiny, eye for an eye, stare for a stare. This inspection is ridiculous. I'll never see him again—might as well get the deed over with and say goodbye forever.

"Business trip or pleasure?" he says quietly, then raises the glass to his lips.

That's the best he has?

"Pleasure." Fact. "You?"

"Business." He licks his lips. "Which I hope to end with a side of pleasure?"

There it is. About time!

"Play your cards right." I wink and offer a sly, sexy grin. The whiskey is getting to me quicker and harder since it's not my usual vodka.

"I plan to." Still no smirk, smile, grin—nothing! He simply downs the remaining liquid in the glass and waits for me to do the same. He extends a hand toward me and helps me up, then wraps it around my waist. "Ready?"

"You betcha." My smile widens, and my insides churn in excitement.

This one's going to be vastly better than the others.

No matter what I've been through, there will always be a difference between sex and making love. A long time ago, I learned how to separate the two. One doesn't require emotion, and the other suffocates you with it. Until the right person comes along who won't abuse the latter, it will always remain as the former—just sex—for me.

Riding to the third floor, the man next to me stood stiff as a board and as emotionless as I felt inside. But now as he's tearing off my pants and underwear in this dark room, I'm alive again. Fire and ice blaze through me while I claw at him.

Half-naked, he throws me onto the bed and drops his own pants. I can't see a thing, it's too dark, and I want to see—

"Oh!" I moan.

Forget seeing—I feel it.

"I wanted you the moment I saw you." He grinds out between harsh thrusts and I wither beneath him.

He pounds his delicious body into mine and my mind decides this isn't the right time to process his words, dissect them, and argue against them.

Only drunk men want me. Ones too far gone to notice my 'thickness', my fucked-up self-esteem, and how much I'm hiding underneath.

I shut it down immediately. Now is not the time for self-loathing. The man said he wants me and that's what he's going to get—

The fierce and fearless side of me… only for the night.

* * *

THE COMPLEX IS ONLY A five-minute drive from the hotel and soon the sign for Rose Gardens comes into view.

The massive block of white stone buildings rise before me. It's a picturesque community consisting of five buildings surrounding a peaceful courtyard. The green expanse of lawn is dotted with benches and small flagstone patios with casual seating arrangements for the comfort of the residents.

I follow the signs and park in the first level garage assigned to building A. Before relaxing into the well-cushioned seat, I yawn widely, the desire for sleep pleading my name. I'd tossed and turned for hours after I left the guy's room. The combination of nerves over moving and my self-loathing over the one night stand brought on the vivid nightmares I despise.

As I'm stepping from the car, I realize I'm early and can't get into the building until Molly gives me the code. I send her a text telling her I've arrived.

While waiting for her reply, I gather my things and retrieve the large suitcase which contains very few of my belongings from the trunk.

Geez. My muscles kill.

My body is as sore as can be expected after—yes, I'll admit it—the best damn sex I've had. Too bad I'll never get another go around with that one.

Today is a new day, no need to reminisce about it any longer.

The weight of the baggage reminds me of how I couldn't even stomach the thought of ever setting foot in my old apartment again. My sweet neighbor had been kind enough to pack for me so I could avoid entering the source of my nightmares.

A shiver passes through me when I step into the elevator. Looking down at my phone, I nervously punch in the code Molly just sent me. With a shaky finger, I press the last number and suddenly there's movement.

Tenth floor, here I come.

* * *

THE DOORS SWISH OPEN REVEALING a spacious and very white entry way.

It official, I've arrived at my new home.

As my gaze sweeps across the expanse of the visible parts of the apartment, every kind of emotion imaginable floods over me. I'm unable to take more than one step inside... not yet. I want to bask in this happiness vibrating through my body. There's pride building inside me, knowing I've not broken down since I left the psych ward over a month ago.

It's far too soon to say I'm fully recovered, especially since

I'm taking anti-anxiety medication to manage daily living and as of last night, I'm drinking again. One step at a time is all I can ask of myself.

The elevator doors open behind me, and a slim smiling woman bustles out. She's nothing like I imagined. I fully anticipated a short voluptuous blond with poofy hair, not this elegant glamazon. She's several inches taller than me, with a tiny waist and long well-rounded legs that go on for miles. Molly sports a fabulous, long, pin-straight bob, and her glossy chestnut hair swings as she strides the few short steps toward me. When she moves aside, I notice we're not alone.

The man towering over her is even more surprising—and unexpected. I find myself gazing directly at his muscular chest, and my eyes travel upwards slowly as I inspect his body.

My mouth goes dry as I catch sight of glittering emerald eyes behind black-rimmed glasses. His brows are furrowed and he sweeps long fingers impatiently through his dark brown hair.

"Hi, Molly!" I shake her hand firmly while concentrating on not ogling the well-built man who seems to dominate the space.

"Hi, Ruby, great to meet ya!" Her vibrant blue-gray eyes sparkle.

I extend my hand cordially to the imposing Fabio impersonator. I eye him warily and tip my chin up, determined not to flinch. "And you are?" My heart pounds, but I manage to keep my voice level.

His touch creates an unexpected shock from my fingertips all the way down to my toes. I would like nothing more than to yank my hand from his strong, powerful grasp, but I force myself to stay calm.

"Maeson Alexander."

A momentary but extremely awkward silence falls. "Uh... um, okay then, well, nice to meet you." I force a smile and take a few steps back. I sneak a glance at Molly, and the corners of her mouth are twitching.

"Maeson is your new landlord." She clears her throat and shoots an enigmatic look at the mysterious Maeson. "Shall we do our walk through?"

"Sure, sounds like a plan. Give me the lay of the land." I exhale a burst of air and follow them.

We walk through the eat-in kitchen, and I admire the top of the line appliances. It opens to a light and airy living room, the wall of floor to ceiling windows seem endless, and allow the room to be flooded with natural light.

"Wow, amazing." The view is magnificent, and I stop to observe it. This also allows me a much-needed moment to compose myself. I take a deep breath before turning to face them again.

My new landlord has barely uttered, muttered, or grunted a damn thing.

How can a person make arrogance appear to be so sexy?

My eyes seem to have a mind of their own and peer over at the sight of him leaning against the expanse of gleaming granite countertops with his arms crossed against his chest. But of course, he doesn't notice because it seems his have glazed over from boredom.

Why is he even here?

"Just wait until you check out the master suite." Molly pats my arm and I almost jump out of my skin.

Maeson pushes himself off the counter, standing ramrod straight before stalking out of the kitchen. Molly's eyes widen and a frown flashes across her face. If I hadn't been looking directly at her I would've missed it entirely.

What a cocky asshole.

Brushing off his rudeness, I follow Molly into the master bedroom. It's enormous and has a huge walk-in closet, with a connected bathroom big enough to dance in. Even better it's completed by a large shower, and I can't wait to have my first soak in the tub that graces the room.

The only thing spoiling it is my grouchy new landlord. He has his back turned, staring out the window, hands in his pockets. The guy can't even stand to look at me.

I peek into the second bedroom which will be my office, and

the rest of the tour takes only a minute.

"That's all down here. Ready to go up top?" Molly asks.

"Yes, I've been dying to since I arrived!"

She shoots me a mischievous grin and peers over at Maeson the Grouch. "Coming, boss?"

We all proceed up the glass enclosed staircase next to the kitchen. I flip my long curls over my shoulder and turn my back on Maeson the moment we reach the top. My breath catches in my throat. It's worth every penny in rent to gain the view alone. I certainly made the right choice with this place.

"The pool is heated," Maeson speaks up, startling the shit out of me and I turn to face him.

His voice is extremely deep, tinged with an accent I can't identify. Definitely not a Southern drawl, but he's spoken so few words I can't pinpoint the origin.

Before I can say anything, he opens that kissable mouth. "In a few days, the patio furniture will be set up as you requested." Maeson continues barely looking at me.

Look this way and show me those green eyes.

What am I saying? I snap out of that thought immediately. "Thank you." I'm not quite sure how else to respond. I wipe my sweaty palms against my jeans.

Maeson's eyes travel to Molly, his head bobs ever so slightly, and his gaze sweeps over to the stairs.

I *know* that look. He wants to leave.

I stare right at him so he knows I saw the signal he gave her. His eyes meet mine and the heat of his gaze travels all over my body.

I clear my throat. "Everything is so beautiful, perfect in fact. Thank you so much for the tour, Molly." My chest tightens under his intense scrutiny.

This one's dangerous, he has a hot guy complex. Might want to stay away from him.

"We're so glad you like it! I hope you'll enjoy living here, it must be a big change from New York." Molly's eyes flit from me to Maeson, and her lips are twitching again.

"It sure is, but I think I'll like it."

"I'll make sure you do, sweetie." She pulls me into a long warm hug, which is unexpected.

I haven't been hugged in such a long time, it throws me off, and I back away slightly before I settle into the embrace. Unfortunately, my reaction probably gave Maeson and Molly, the impression the contact was unwanted. Yet, it's the exact opposite—it's been wanted for many, many years.

"I'll be in touch soon to make sure you're settling in alright." Molly motions toward Maeson. "You can contact him with any questions or concerns you might have." She raises an eyebrow and winks at him.

They must think I don't notice the silent communication.

Maeson crosses his muscular arms, his brow knitted into a frown, and he narrows his eyes at Molly.

Oh, I see. He thinks he's better than me, not worthy of being spoken to. Mr. High and Mighty, staring down his nose at me through those damn black rimmed glasses.

I roll my eyes in irritation, and stare up at him, waiting for him to speak the hell up.

His chin lifts and he clears his throat, his arms still crossed tightly across his chest. "Miss Bennett. I left my card on the counter in the kitchen, it has all my contact information. I hope everything is to your satisfaction." He pushes those ridiculous glasses up against his face and struts away without another word.

-4-

MAESON

DETAILS! I DON'T HAVE ENOUGH damn details on this woman! I'm so furious my hands twitch as I storm into the empty elevator. The heat rises, and the beast claws at me viciously, wanting out.

Each forsaken useless thing I do know didn't prepare me for her reaction. I had created this fantasy in my head that she was a young impressionable female who would easily fall at my feet, like women normally do.

Boy was that not the damn case.

My frustration rises. "Aye, fucking fantasies! That's all it was." I punch the metal wall and revel in the pain. "This is what happens when you let go and *desire more*. You fucking start to believe in fairy tales which don't bloody exist!"

Control yourself.

She's an overly fucking confident, patronizing, yet a drop dead sexy-as-fuck, grown ass woman.

But her eyes, oh God her eyes...

They told me a different story, deep amber orbs that drew me in, filled with hate, anger, sadness, confusion, and pain. Each crushing emotion came through loud and clear. Her behavior contradicted everything I saw in them, making a read on her nearly impossible.

Fuck! She's trouble! Double mother fucking trouble!

Molly couldn't have been more right and now that I've seen them in person, I admit I'm a sucker for those beautiful wild curls. I've said it before and I'll say it again, women like her are dangerous to men like me.

Must stay away from her.

I take off my glasses to rub the bridge of my nose and slump against the wall of the elevator as I watch the doors close. My eyes unwillingly droop shut and I let my mind wander.

I envision her face. Her plump pink lips are undeniably perfect, and her unshielded almond brown eyes gutted me every time I peered into them. Then there is her hair! Oh God, that hair. I want to drive my fingers through it and tug—

My eyes snap open at the ding and the swish of the elevator doors opening. I look around in a daze. Pulling myself upright, I drag my leaden feet toward the exit. My whole body feels heavy and sluggish, my mouth cottony and dry.

Man, I was a dick to her.

Just the thought of it brings the pang deep in my chest, and no matter how hard or often I work at it, it refuses to budge. I rub at that tender spot over my heart, and realize the whole *'being an asswipe'* is not out of character for me. Especially after my latest tirade at Molly.

I trudge across to my building, swearing under my breath.

Wait!

I'm not a complete dickhead. I did leave a welcome gift, which should suffice. It's not like she was any nicer to me, the pretentious princess *rolled* her eyes at *me*. Like a fucking spoiled two-year-old!

If it were only the two of us, I bet she would have spit on my shoes. She stared at me like I was this vile creature who rose out of the swamps, perhaps some freakish, disgusting ogre or the like.

Her reaction dictated mine. I had every intention of gracing her with the full extent of my charms, but if she chooses to act like a damn spoiled princess, fine by me. Won't waste my time, I can find plenty of *'thin mints'* to distract me.

What the fuck am I saying?

Thin mints are used simply to entertain.

Heehee. I slay myself! Enter… tain!

I roll my eyes at my own crass humor. This is no time for jokes. I remind myself that those vapid women are only to pass the time until the real deal shows up.

I stalk past the empty reception desk and stab at the elevator button to my floor. I'm in rough shape, my head's spinning, and my skinned knuckles burn. I grind my undamaged fist against my eyes, which are dry and gritty like someone's pelted me with sand.

I can hear Mo's voice taunting me, saying it's my own damn fault.

Yadda, yadda, yadda. Nag, nag, nag.

She can drill me all she wants; my drinking is not out of control. It's almost out of control. There's a *huge* difference.

Though, it is a dumb idea to show up half-assed and brutally hungover for a new move in. I'm becoming careless and it should matter more because I worked my butt off to build this fabulous empire after…

"Doesn't matter anymore asshole." I berate myself.

Ding!

Home at last. Thank fuck for that. I've had enough of this day and I can barely keep my eyes open. Sleep is overrated, but sometimes I too require it.

I discard my suit jacket, slinging it over a nearby chair, yank off my useless fucking torturous tie, and unbutton my shirt. I stand and stare at my torso in the mirror. The reminders are always with me.

Pivoting away, I can't bear to look at myself even a second longer. I set my phone on the nightstand and flop down on the massive king size bed. The moment I close my eyes I picture her... *Ruby*.

I tower over her. Gazing down at that perfect voluptuous body of hers, I image her thick thighs wrapped around my waist as I—

My dick is hard. My fucking dick is hard just thinking of her.

I don't fight it, I am a man after all. I glance out the windows and the setting sun's certainly creating a glaring reflection off my windows. No need to shut the shades. I could dance around buck naked and no one would see.

My hand involuntarily wanders downwards, and I let my hand linger between my legs. Imagining her full lips, I firmly cup my balls and sigh. My dick is so hard it hurts.

Is this what my life has become?

Rock hard dick while imagining that woman sucking my balls?

I've sunk to a new all-time low.

Immediately, I drop my hand, the moment extinguished. I sit up and lean against my headboard, my eyes drifting toward the windows. Across the way, tenants are moving throughout their condos, and my eyes focus on one in particular. She's pacing like she's pissed off.

Normally, I'm a gentleman and don't snoop, today I'm not extending such courtesies. Needing a closer look, I slide off the bed and take the few steps over to the window. She stops to stare out at the vibrantly lit city view, taking it all in. She tips her head down, clearly looking at a bottle in her hands.

My gift.

I can imagine her little eye roll now. Picturing the expression on her face brings a sinister grin to mine.

Not such an asshole am I, Princess?

I settle back in bed grinning like a mad fool.

Finally! A woman who might present me with a challenge.

I've been waiting for this a very long time. Should make my life interesting... might be time to kick the *'thin mints'* to the curb.

-5-

Ruby

THE ENCOUNTER WITH MR. STICK-Up-His-Ass-Alexander certainly put a damper on my mood. He stormed off like a petulant child. Poor Molly looked embarrassed at his attitude and left shortly after with a heartfelt apology.

Screw him and his attitude. If that's how he wants to act—fine by me, two can play that game.

I think my blood pressure has risen above normal level and my palms are clammy because of him. Spotting my purse on the couch, I grab my meds from inside it and take one right away.

Flustered, I yank open the fridge looking for a drink.

What am I thinking?

I've been here less than an hour, how could there be anything in it? This place is bare aside from the suitcase I dragged up from the car.

I grip the handle and my eyes open wide as I spot a bottle of champagne sitting on the top shelf. A wide grin spreads across my face as I snag it and swing the door shut. I must thank Molly for being so kind.

Making my way to the window which faces the gorgeous new view I get to see every day, I take notice there is an extra paper on the bottle.

Peeling off the attached note, my smile fades.

'*Miss Ruby Bennett, welcome to your new home. Please enjoy! Maeson Alexander*'

His gesture throws me off and it irritates me to no end.

Mr. Stuffy and Arrogant, gifts do nothing for me, so I'm not changing my opinion of you.

Letting the note flutter to the floor, I examine the label.

Armand de Brignac Brut Rose.

I stare at the bottle for a moment and trace the intricate pattern over the symbol. It appears to be a spade, like from a deck of cards, with a large A embossed in the middle.

Looks expensive.

Not being much a connoisseur, I shrug and peel off the foil.

Whatever, I'm thrilled to have something to drink.

The cork is a challenge, but after a short struggle, it pops open, fizzing, and bubbling up. I immediately tip it into my mouth... don't want to waste it, and it would be incredibly rude not to drink it.

The first swig goes down smoothly, and I smack my lips in satisfaction. Perhaps rather than standing right in front of the window in this depressingly unfurnished space, there's a much better place to celebrate my new-found freedom.

After one last long look out my living room window, I make my way up the staircase to survey my rooftop haven. Of course, I have no furniture to lounge on here either, but that's fine with me. I drop onto the edge of the pool and dip in my toes.

Damn him!

Not for a single second did I expect my landlord to be so incredibly arrogant, or annoyingly sexy-as-fuck. And now that I've *met* him... the gesture seems out of place.

Oh please, who am I kidding? I bet Molly went out and bought it, not high and mighty Maeson.

With another swallow, I let the delicious rich fruity flavors swirl in my mouth and gaze over the amazing view in front of me. Dismissing the nonsense going through my head, I focus on how grateful I am for what I have in this moment.

I've survived so much.

Watching the vivid orange and purple hues cover the sky as the sun starts to go down, Maeson invades my thoughts again, certain things nagging at me. Like how his body language and superiority ruffled my feathers from the moment I laid eyes on him.

Who cares? He's your landlord, you don't have to like him.

He was too close. That jackass purposely invaded my personal space, and he treated me like I was below him for not reacting to his maneuver.

Sorry… Not sorry. I'm not that desperate.

Despite initially following my gut instinct, this almost primal need—or a want perhaps—hounds me internally to tell him to get lost.

Being rich and good looking doesn't give him the right to act that way.

Doing as my doctor suggested, I take a deep breath and reflect. Closing my eyes, I visualize him and my heart instantly speeds up. His piercing and vivid green eyes reached deep into my very soul, seeing it all before I'd broken the connection. My gut twists at the memory and I lift the bottle to my lips, drinking deeply.

Acknowledging the effect this man has on me infuriates me to no end. Maeson is the only man who has ever made me uncomfortable in my own skin within a minute of meeting him. I'm disgusted with myself for having a reaction to him.

I know better.

While I was in the psych ward, I swore off men. Yet here I am, panting on the inside for the first good—scratch that—best-looking man who's ever crossed my path.

I'm not ready. Deep breath.

I need to learn how to handle my reactions properly. What I need is a better poker face, and to maybe spend less time constantly reigning myself in. I never let myself just *feel* since I'm always at war with my own mind. Inhaling deeply again, I try to calm my inner turmoil how I know best.

Bottle meet lips. Lips meet bottle, your new best friend.

Hey, doc! Great advice on taking a step back before reacting. How about zero to sixty after meeting my new landlord. 'Ruby,' he says, 'Stop and take a deep breath.'

What a cluster fuck of thoughts.

I have no idea how to stop. Well, except maybe breathing, that shit stopped the moment I saw Maeson. This time I take another extra-long swig, even knowing alcohol is not the best idea when you're taking medication.

Right now, I don't care... Annnnnnd that's the alcohol talking.

Letting my mind wander back to the encounter with him, I realize the handshake was firm, but his palm seemed clammy and he pulled away quickly. Maybe, I wasn't the only one caught off guard?

Did his lack of speech today mean he wasn't interested?

Which is fine by me—less complicated.

Business as usual for Mr. Alexander. Well except the note, and champagne he left in the fridge. Seems to be an extravagant gift for a landlord to leave his tenant.

I'm so confused.

I swish my feet through the warm water of the pool and chug more bubbly, then another mouthful for good measure. Warmth builds, and builds, coating my insides.

For an arrogant, overly confident man it was odd to see his impressive suit covering so much of that yummy olive skin beneath it.

I might not be ready for a relationship, but I'm sure as hell not blind.

Lost in my musing, I don't notice the sun has gone down, until I'm surrounded by darkness, with an empty bottle clutched in my hand. I look out and the city is lit up beautifully, making me certain it was the right choice moving here. Giddy with alcohol induced happiness, I laugh uncontrollably as I make the water splash all around me.

Peering down at the building next door, I see the lights go out in the main office. My eyes widen, and I bolt upright, almost falling into the pool.

Working late, Mr. Alexander?

Second try's the charm, and I push my swaying body to a standing position and manage to stagger down the stairs. I grab the card Maeson left me, typing his mobile number into my phone. My fingers fly across the keys surprisingly well considering I polished off an entire bottle of champagne. I click send. That does it, I told him off all right.

Wait... What... What did I just do?

I haven't felt this light headed in a long time. It's so freeing and yet so bad. Incredibly bad. Mixing medication and alcohol wasn't the finest choice—I know—but I desperately need to wind down. So much change over the course of a month is taking its toll on me.

I laugh as if I don't have a care in the world, and it quells the silence around me. My laughter fades as I realize; I'm sending stupid drunk texts, like he used to, simply to be spiteful.

No…

The room spins as my body collapses limply onto the floor. My vision is fuzzy around the edges and I stare blankly at the ceiling, allowing the dreaded memory to invade my mind.

* * *

HALF ASLEEP, I PEER AT my phone to check the time and the light of it blinds me. I look around and find myself alone. He should be home by now.

I sigh as the phone bleats and the message pops up.

INCOMING MESSAGE: Baby ur sweet cunt made my night. So sad I had to leave, the ball n chain waitin at home. Till next time XO

I shoot up from the bed, tears blurring my eyes as I reread the text. This wasn't meant for me, and he's out with another one tonight. I hit reply.

MESSAGE SENT: Really? You should stay there. Ball n chain doesn't need you.

Guaranteed he was too drunk or high to even realize his error. I lay back down and wait to see if he decides to come home, if he does should be soon based on the message.

Ten minutes later, I hear him stumbling around and slamming doors, making his way to our room. I tense up, he's most definitely gonzo.

"Bitch! Get your ass up!"

I squeeze my eyes shut, his roar piercing in the still room. I silently pray for him leave me alone and to knock out. My prayers unheard, he grabs me by my ponytail, dragging me out of bed. I tumble to the floor, curling into a ball, protecting my head and belly. His usual go-to spots.

"I said get the fuck up, you stupid whore!" The toe of his shoe connects with my knee.

I bite my lip hard so I don't cry out. It will only make it worse if I do. It feels like my hair is coming out at the roots as his hand wraps into it, and he forces me to stand. I cringe as his hand comes up.

This is gonna be bad. I flinch and cover my face. "I'm awake, babe. I'm sorry about the text, I was upset. Forgive me?" I should've known better. This is all my fault for taunting him, for back talking.

"Forgive you for being overbearin' and nosey? Never! Fuck you n your badgerin'. I come home 'cause you need me, 'cause I pity you since you were nothing but a pathetic woman begging for scraps when I met you and not the other way around. Did you assume I was hiding from you?" His hands encircle my wrists like iron vises.

The ink on the left one burns but I don't have the willpower to dig for that part of me right now. "No." I shake my head, keeping my eyes downcast. "No, I'm sorry."

"No. That's right bitch. I'm done being a little pussy. I do as I please,

when I please, dear. There's no need for your sarcastic response. Don't you dare question me! Ruby when will you learn! I own every part of you." He laughs maniacally like he's made the funniest inside joke.

"I'm learning, baby. I made a mistake."

"You know your place, so stay in it for fuck's sake. Take it or leave it, baby. Take it, and stop naggin' the fuck outta me, or leave it and see what happens then." His glare is deadly.

"Take it," I whisper, too afraid to find out what would happen if I said 'leave it.'

"Exactly, Ruby, you'll take me as I am! Maybe if you shut the fuck up once in a while those bruises will get a chance to heal. And quit showing them off, people are asking questions, there's makeup made for these things." As he shoves me away from him, my thighs hit the edge of the mattress and I slide into a heap on the floor.

I pull my knees up and nod. My hand lifts to my face, the shame rising. I know how it looks. The yellowish circle on my cheek, the purple, and black adorning my eye. I'm too frightened to speak, but I crawl up onto the bed and pat my hand on his side. A silent request to lay down.

He nods in agreement, and mutters, *"Suffocating bitch drive me crazy."*

I cover him with the blanket and curl up next to him. My body is frozen in place. If I stay still perhaps he will forget I'm here. Thankfully, within a few moments, he's snoring, and the tears stream down my face. I hide my sobs beneath his loud snorts, grunts, and heavy labored breathing.

* * *

I TOUCH MY FACE, THE memory of my past merges with the present and the pain of Ray's wrath strikes me all over again. Not being able to let go, my last thought before I fall asleep in that past and this present is...

Someone please, please, stop this never-ending pain.

-6-

MAESON

I ROLL OVER, PLUMPING UP my pillow. Darkness envelops me, and I couldn't have been asleep more than a couple of hours.

Damn, then why am I awake?

I should be comatose, but here I am wondering what in the fuck woke me up this time.

"Mae Mae."

Sitting bolt upright, I rub my hands over my face. Must be hearing things, dreaming. Can't get away from the sound of her voice, the damn woman is nagging me in my sleep too.

"Mae, pleeease." The voice is accompanied by a firm rap at my bedroom door.

"Mo?" Maybe I'm not dreaming. Dazed, I fumble with the tangled sheets, kicking at them to release my feet. "Fuck!" I grasp at my crotch as I knock morning wood with the bedside table. After tripping over my shoes, and stumbling into a chair, I make it to the door.

What is Mo doing here?

I yank open the door and freeze. My eyes snap open at the

sight of the woman barely able to stand on her own two feet before me. "Molly..."

She's a complete mess with tears streaming down her face, mascara smeared all down her cheeks, and her eyes are bloodshot and puffy. She cries harder, her body visibly shaking as if she's in a lot of pain.

My heart pounds as I scan her body for injuries, but my sleepy haze filled eyes find nothing major. "Molly? You ok? It's four in the morning!" Looking at her hurts my heart and I want to ask her what the hell she's gotten into this time, but I refrain.

"Yeess." She slurs, her head wobbling like a bobble head doll, snuffling and wiping at her nose. "Nooo." She shakes her head, her hand grasping at my arm as she pitches toward me. "I dunno." A half shrug accompanies her quivering lips and hiccupping sobs. "Didna know where to go."

I pull her gently against my bare chest. "It's fine, you're always welcome here, you know that. What's wrong?" I brush the hair from her face as she sobs harder. "Shhh, it's okay. Here, sit." I guide her to my bed.

"Mae?" She peers up at me with those sorrow-filled pools of blue. "Mae, I'm s-sad, an l-lonely, an afraid, an sooo drunk. I'm o-old. An old bag lady. N-n-need a c-c-cat. How you drink so much all the time? Hate it. Don't wanna be alone fer eva."

I sigh and snag a wad of tissues from the box, patting at her face. "You're not alone, woman. You've got me. You'll always have me." Sinking onto the chair near the bed, I take her hands in mine. "What else happened to make you so upset?"

"I'm turning inna a ho! Like one a the pathetic, scraggly thin mints." She bows her head in shame and covers her face with her hands. "Had a one night stand," Molly whispers, before bursting into a fresh round of tears.

I squeeze her hands gently. "Listen to me Mo. You're not a ho. So, you had a little fun. Nothing wrong with that. If you want to call someone a whore, it's me. One nighters are my thing." A disturbing thought hits me and my protective instinct roars. Dropping her hands, I jump to my feet and pull my sweats over top my underwear. "Did you come straight from his place? Did he kick you out? I'll fucking kill the bastard! Who is he?"

Noticing my near nakedness, she giggles. "'Bout time you covered your half chub, old man. Not that I'm impressed." She smiles tearfully and it eases the fear in my gut. "Don't kill 'em, best lay I eva had! I left, was embarrassed, who wanna be with a slut like me? Not his fault." More tears cascade down her face.

So, she's a bipolar drunk.

"Stop saying that shit!" I run a hand through my hair in frustration. I can't handle a woman's tears. "You're not a slut for wanting to sleep with a man on the first night. Though running out gives *him* the impression *you* don't want him. Not that you're a whore. You walked out on him. Give it a few days, see if he calls you. If he does then he's into you, if not... well then, you got some great sex out of it." I wipe a trailing tear from her cheek and bring out the ole money makers.

She rolls her eyes and points at my face. "Put those damn things away." A smile brightens her face as I force a frown to mine. "You're right. I'll let it be, it's my fault. Shoulda stayed." She looks down at her hand, fussing with a nail. "Can I stay here an sleep? I shouldn't be driving, tad bit spinny in this room." Molly blinks up at me with huge puppy eyes.

"Aye, stay."

She curls up and I drop a fluffy throw over her.

"Sleep it off." Turning toward the door with the intent to leave her be, but I stop midway. "By the way youngin'—fuck off with your old man comments." I salute her with my middle finger. "Don't think I didn't catch the dick insult, either, but... I've never had a complaint. Except from the few who moaned it was *too* big." I wink at her and smile deeply and purposefully. "Sleep tight buttercup!" I trudge out to the kitchen for my daily medicine.

Call the doctor, Mae Mae needs his coffee stat.

As the machine sputters and the smell of fresh brew wafts around me, I lean against the counter. I glide my fingertips up and down my right arm as I stare out at the view before me.

I miss you.

My phone chimes and I force the thought away. The workday is starting already, and it's not even five in the damn morning. I sigh as I notice I've missed a text too. From midnight. Who in the fuck would text me at midnight on a weekday? A glance at the screen tells me it's my new tenant.

INCOMING MESSAGE: Helloo Mr. stick up ur ass Alexander, it was a pleasure to MEET u n thanx for the campange. Went down soo smooth. Nighty night.

She must've drank the *entire* bottle of champagne I left her. At least I hope she's drunk cause otherwise, she's even worse than I thought. 'Mr. Stick-Up-Ur-Ass Alexander'? No sane and sober woman would ever send such a scatterbrained message.

By now I bet she's out like a light, but it's only polite to text her back. As I type up my response, I grab my hot and ready mojo.

MESSAGE SENT: Ms. Pretentious and Spoiled Bennett, I glad you liked my gift. Maybe even too much?

A wicked grin spreads across my face as I hit the send button. I wish I could see her expression when she reads it.

Let the games begin.

I barely set my phone down before it chimes again.

INCOMING MESSAGE: Mace the ace, listen up I'm not pretentious or spoiled! N yeah I enjoyed every damn drop! Not that it's any of ur business! Now I'm goin back 2 bed like normal peeps @ this hour. Who the fuck is up at 5 am anyway?

I snicker and wander back to the massive windows. I'm in luck, she's left on some lights, and I have a perfect line of sight, right into her living room. Unless my eyes deceive me, there's a body sprawled out on the floor. I chuckle as I think of her passed out on the hardwood all night.

Nice and cushy, perfect for her snooty Highness.

I inhale deeply and allow the glorious scent of Colombian espresso laced with a hint of hazelnut bombard all of my senses before taking a 'required to be able to function' sip. Setting the mug down to savor the abundance of flavor the coffee provides my taste buds, I use this time to send her a new message.

MESSAGE SENT: Yes, you are a spoiled little child. You sure act like it with all that money from mommy and daddy. Who's awake at this hour? People like me who have real jobs. By the way, how much you drink or don't is none of my concern, as you pointed out. I was only stating a fact.

Now I wait.

I start pacing impatiently, all the while glancing at my phone screen about ten times in a matter of what? A minute?

What? Nothing to say, Princess? Was it something I said? Ruffle your precious little feathers? Well, too bad, I don't give a fuck.

INCOMING MESSAGE: Don't act like you know me or care. It meant nothing, so move along.

That's the response she sends me? I almost chuck my phone but stop and send a fitting reply. How is it ninety-nine percent of women are attracted to me and fall at my feet begging for a night with me, yet this one wants nothing to do with me?

Karma.

I pivot and stalk down the hallway, slamming my fist against the wall. The angrier I get, the more emotion I feel, the more my internal beast claws at me, digging straight into my gut. I need to cool the fuck down and only a few things tame the beast.

Sex.

I highly doubt any of my *'thin mints'* are available or would appreciate my five in the morning booty call, and no fucking way am I getting it on with Mo. So, it's between an icy shower... or a hardcore long-ass run.

I yank a sweatshirt over my head and manage not to slam the door as I leave, taking care not to wake Sleeping Beauty. It's hard not to smirk as I realize I now have ammunition against Mo, as her drunken ass is now snoring up a storm on my bed. Somehow even that thought does nothing to sooth the beast inside.

Long-ass run it is.

-7-

Ruby

I PUT A HAND TO my aching, spinning head, and try to sit as the sun beams through the shades.

Damn! What day is it?

I must've passed out after drinking the whole damn bottle of champagne. Very classy, Ruby, second day here and you're drinking like a fish again.

What time is it?

My phone shows five-thirty in the morning and a missed text. Flopping back down, I close my eyes to stop the room from spinning round and round, and try to concentrate.

Who would text me at this god-awful hour?

With a heavy sigh, I attempt to bring the ridiculously bright screen closer, peering at it through my bleary eyes. It's from an unknown number.

INCOMING MESSAGE: Oh? What's changed, Miss Pretentious Ass Bennett? You weren't saying that... before.

Wait! What?

I frown in confusion.

Why would I get this ridiculous text?

Turning slightly to get into a more comfortable position, a small piece of what looks like white paper catches my attention.

Ok, that's odd.

I feel disembodied as my hand reaches out, and picks it up. Tilting my head, I stare at the card and try to make out what is written on it with my fuzzy, overloaded senses.

Maeson L. Alexander

It's his business card. The mobile number's a teeny bit familiar. My eyes widen in horror and I scroll hastily down to my sent messages.

No, ohhhh, no, no, NO!

A flush of embarrassment heats my face. I must be as red as a beet! How could I do such a thing? I've been sending texts back and forth with him which I don't recall doing, at all!

Well, this is exactly why they don't recommend guzzling a whole bottle of champagne on top of your meds, dumbass.

I close my eyes and take a deep breath, it's the only thing that will help me summon the courage I need to reread the messages.

Miss Pretentious Ass Bennett?

He's making fun of me, but doesn't even know me, or what I've been through!

I'm the furthest thing from pretentious!

Needing to set his ass straight, I hit send on my response with a deep sense of satisfaction.

MESSAGE SENT: Not every woman pants after Maeson the Great. Move along, Landlord.

What an asshole! There! That'll show him!

I put my phone down, intending to go back to sleep, but it buzzes impatiently less than a minute later.

INCOMING MESSAGE: If that's what you so desire... *Princess*. Ps: I bet that hardwood was nice and comfy all night long.

My mouth is dry and cottony, and my headache is even worse after reading Maeson's smart ass remarks. I peel my hungover body off the floor and drag myself to the kitchen sink.

The man makes me want to scream and beat the crap out of something. I'd give all the money back in a minute if I could have my parents by my side. But of course, he just assumed.

Such a prick.

I sip water out of my palms, and splash my face, washing the sleep from my eyes.

There is no way I will allow myself to lose my head, and make this worse by letting him get to me.

That was Ruby 1.0, and now I'm the new upgraded version Ruby 2.0. I know I have the tendency to panic and flip out immediately but that's only because I let my anxiety take control. That seems to be my downfall in all things, never taking a step back to rationalize. I always react first without considering the repercussions of my actions. But these are the things the new me is working on.

Ass wipe! He has absolutely no clue!

It hurts when people assume without knowing the facts.

Deep breath.

Little does he or anyone else know my nights are filled with sad dreams, vivid, terrifying nightmares, and I barely sleep. Until recently my circumstances have prevented me from having a busy, fulfilling life. My fondest wish is to one day be normal, be like everyone else.

Yeah right! Be normal?

I have every intent of changing that and my plan is brewing. My intention is to not spend the rest of my life living off my parents hard earned money. I want so much more. On rare nights, I have happy dreams, and in those, I envision what a normal day would be like for me.

But none of it was real, because I haven't the slightest clue of what normal is. Will I ever find out?

The question makes me long for another bottle, but since my cupboards are bare, I don't have the luxury. Maybe that's a good thing since it's barely the ass crack of dawn.

Stomping into the bathroom, I realize the fact I don't have a damn towel. At this point, I'm too pissed off to sleep, and the floor isn't the most comfortable place in any case. A shower would go a long way to making me feel human, less gross, and sweaty. Needing to find something to dry off with, I dig through my suitcase and the best I can come up with is a t-shirt. I groan and turn on the water, staring at my red-rimmed eyes in the mirror as it heats up.

Stupid, Ruby, so much for new and improved version.

I practically crawl into the shower and the hot water beats down on me until I'm as close to ready as I can be to face the day.

Deep breath.

Rummaging in my bag, I yank on a tight t-shirt and pull on a pair of leggings. The rage rises again as I think about Mr. Pompous Ass. If he knows so much about me, then he should know my parents passed when I was barely ten years old. And I spent eight years in a crappy foster home. All my energy in the past fifteen years has been focused on merely surviving.

I wrap my long, dark, curly hair into a messy bun. If the jackass had cared to ask, I would've told him college was my first real fresh start. And I blew it. I let Ray convince me to drop out after I'd only been there for two years. I'd lived as much life as I could, and been the happiest I'd been since I'd lost mom and dad, then threw it all away on a complete asshole. Now at twenty-five, I'm starting all over again for the third time.

So much for that.

My landlord has to be the most infuriating and egotistical man in the world. Even if he is dead sexy with his mysterious accent... a perfect specimen of manhood who makes my heart beat faster.

Stop Ruby, stop! Get that man out of your head! Deep breath!

Dr. Miles advised me in one of our many sessions to learn to relax. To stop feeling the need to control everyone and everything around me. *"Control doesn't stop a person from hurting you or make them good for you. Not everyone has to fit your criteria to be trustworthy. If you let go, and not be too harsh with those around you, things will go smoother. Ruby, as humans we make mistakes and must ask for forgiveness. The cycle either repeats, or it ends. But only if we've learned the lesson in that mistake."*

How can I do that when everyone in my life has controlled me in return? Now it's my chance to have a say in the what's and how's of my life. I'll constantly have to remind myself that feelings don't have to rocket from zero to one hundred in a mere second. My progress depends on taking things one step at a time and letting go of my latest devastation slowly. Which I plan to do with all of my might, starting now.

I open the windows in my bedroom and let the cool morning breeze stream in. It's barely six in the morning now, but I need to get out of here. Perhaps a nice long walk and some air are exactly what will help me relax.

Today's a new day, make the best of it.

Stepping out into the clear, fresh morning air, I inhale deeply and force my mind to settle down, clearing it of all my doubts and worries.

Deep breath. Deep breath. Hold on!

I stop dead in my tracks.

How the hell did he know I was on the floor?

-8-

MAESON

MY LUNGS CONSTRICT AS I pound the pavement at top speed. The sweat trickles down my body and my thighs burn, begging me to end the torture. I've been running for almost an hour and as long as she's still consuming my thoughts, stopping is not an option.

Coffee… I need more coffee.

It's about time a sane thought hit me, and I'm in luck because a small food truck always parks a mere few blocks away. All I need to do is make it there. My mind fights my body but I use every bit of energy I have left. Rounding the corner, I spot it and jog to the window.

I push my sweaty hair away from my face and fix my gaze on the pretty brown-eyed blonde in the truck. "Morning. Do you have espresso?"

Thin mint. With no wedding ring…

"Mornin' handsome." She smiles with a wink, showing off her impressive dimples. "We sure do. Anything in it?"

"No, just black. Make it a double." I don't return the wink

but I do return the dimples... tenfold.

She falters and her eyes widen. "Oh gosh... umm." Her cheeks turn scarlet. "Right, yes. Um... okay coming right up."

Hehe, I've still got it. Works every time.

I've always known the effect I have on women and I use it to my full advantage. It's not just an ego boost, that's how I can tell I'm still desirable at my age. Bachelor life has a million benefits in the twenty to thirty-five age range, after that it becomes mundane and a reminder of desirability is often needed.

"Here ya go Mister...?" She raises a thin brow.

I reach for the cup, being sure to brush my fingers against hers. "Maeson Alexander."

Her flush deepens, and her hand lingers, holding onto the cup. "Mr. Maeson Alexander." My name rolls off her tongue as she tests it out.

I've seen that too many times... or not. And will I never tire of it?

"Aye." I slip easily into my accent. Another guaranteed panty soaker.

"Ohh, umm... well, I'm here till about three if ya need a refill." She bites her lip and glances down as she sweeps her fingers away.

"Thanks." I take a sip. "Mmmm, good." My gaze travels over her and I grace her with another wide smile before sauntering away. I sense the thin mint's eyes on me, so I add a swagger to my walk.

Five am ego boost?... Check!

Caffeine boost?... Check!

I take my time enjoying the scenery as I head back to the complex. It's a rare treat, the last time I took a stroll around the neighborhood was when I bought the empty lot.

That was ten long years ago.

I approach Rose Gardens and truly *see* what I built. Blood, sweat, and tears, poured into the very foundation of each building.

Admire the fruits of my labor?... Check!

Ruby coming my way?... Check!

Wait. What?

Doing a double take, I manage to stumble over my own feet. *Smooth.*

I shoot a look around to make sure no one saw my ineptitude and locate a nearby bench. Sinking onto it, I shield my eyes with shades and pull my hat from my pocket. I doubt she'll recognize me, especially in this getup. My beanie covers my hair; sunglasses cover my peepers and my sweatshirt and sweats the rest.

Feeling confident in my incognito status, I relax and lean back. I savor my espresso and unabashedly watch her approach. At the sight of those messy curls piled on the top of her head, the beast claws to get out and be seen. That will not happen... yet. I don't even know her; how can I desire her so much already?

And of course, my eyes are drawn directly to her breasts as they bob up and down. My mouth waters, imagining her salty skin, wishing for a taste. Unexpectedly, a dirty picture forms in my mind when my gaze drifts down to admire those full, thick thighs. I long to have their lusciousness tightly wrapped around my waist.

She stops abruptly, massages her calves before she drops onto an adjacent bench. A wince flashes across her face and she stretches her legs out in front of her. I catch a glint from the screen of her phone.

Finally going to respond to me, Princess?

I turn my head as she glances up, the last thing I want to do is scare her. I'm not a fucking creep. Well, maybe a tiny bit of a stalker at times. Unconcerned with my presence she types rapidly, she must be writing me a book.

Such beauty.

She peeks up again, this time catching me and she waves. Her smile makes my heart stop. It's the most beautiful and radiant I've seen to date.

Are you fucking kidding me?

My heartbeat picks up and blood flows to my rising dick. A grin surfaces as I lift my hand briefly in return, and pretend to be busy with my own phone. Still, her gaze burns into me and I flick my eyes toward her a few times trying to determine what's catching her interest. I look down at my arm, then her face and start to panic.

Did she notice it? I need to get out of here.

Guess I'm not the only one with a caffeine addiction, I notice her eyes glaze over as I bring my coffee to my lips.

She didn't see a thing. It's the coffee she wants.

Of course! It's too early in the morning for prissy pants to be out and about. My covered eyes meet hers, she shakes her head as she pushes off the bench and straightens her extremely tight t-shirt. She doesn't look back to catch the pathetic man drooling over her sexy swaying ass.

Once she's out of sight, I begrudgingly stand and stretch out before heading back to my own.

* * *

THE RUN HELPED UNTIL I saw her. The icy shower I took ten minutes ago did shit, but the coffee woke me enough to get to work. Except I'm not actually working, because now that I'm sitting in my office, I can't find the motivation to do anything. I need company or my sour mood will kill the whole day.

I hit the intercom. "Mo, my office now."

She doesn't respond but I hear high heels clicking on the marble floor as she approaches.

"Boss?" She peeks in, her face a blank mask. No smile, no intrigued eyebrows, no emotion whatsoever.

"Come in. Sit." I wave her in and point to the chair in front of my desk. "How are you feeling?"

She takes a few steps and slumps into it. "Ok, I guess." Releasing a long breath, she continues. "You?" She looks defeated.

"Same." Trying to relax my body, I recline the chair and put my hands behind my head. I close my eyes because looking at Molly is depressing. "You want to talk?" Opening one eye, I peer over at her, the silence deepening.

"No." She focuses on her long, bright pink nails.

Why chicks do the whole 'stare at your nails' bit boggles my mind. "I'm not a woman, but I can help you. Or try to."

She's been through so much lately and still manages to come to work. I don't know the full extent of it, but she's a trooper. When I met her at my club all those years ago, she was living on the streets, bouncing between *friends'* houses. Now she owns a condominium in downtown Dallas and is about to become the Vice President of this complex. After so many years of doing it on my own, I can't wait to unload it all.

"I'm good Mae Mae. I need girl time but I have no girlfriends." Her full lips form a pout and a tear falls. "I'm lonely."

I let the name slide, it's starting to appeal to my senses. "Me too, honey. I'm almost as friendless as you. How about I take you out for lunch?"

She wipes away the lone tear sliding down her face and smiles sadly. "I have to decline, not in the going out mood."

I nod and we sit in silence for a somber moment.

She wants girl time? I have the perfect multi-beneficial suggestion.

My eyes remain steady and unblinking, not letting her wet face affect me. "What about the new tenant? She's young and new here, I doubt she has any friends in town."

Her brow arches. "What now? You want me to spy on Ruby Bennett for you?" She gives me a cheeky grin.

"I didn't say that, *woman*." I don't move a muscle as she inspects my deadpan face. "I *said* you should get to know her, and make friends. I don't need a spy for a person I'm not interested in."

"Lie, big boy and you know it." She laughs and wags a finger at me.

I drop my arms and lean forward to fidget with the papers on my desk. "This isn't about me. Now quit looking for something that's not there."

"Fine. I'll let it go for now, but don't lie to yourself for long.

You might lose exactly what you've been looking for."

Doing anything to keep from looking into her eyes, I open my laptop and pretend to write an email. "Not losing something if I don't want it." I shrug.

She coughs. "Bullshit." She coughs again.

Not a good idea, calling me on my bull woman.

"Don't you have somewhere to be? Work to be done?" I glance up and raise a brow at her.

She misses nothing.

"I do now, but let me say this. It's barely day one after meeting this girl and you're affected by her. If I can *see* the fire between you two, then you definitely *feel* it and it's about to get too hot for you to handle. So, man up or back the fuck out gracefully before someone gets hurt. She's a nice girl, too nice for the likes of your beast." She bounces up and flounces out of my office.

"Mo—"

She doesn't hear me and I refuse to call her back and admit she's right. Not in the mood to dwell, I slide over a stack of folders and begin my ritual of denying and shredding applications.

Two hours later the bin is overflowing with shreds, and my desk is empty. A lone application has been approved out of the hundreds I receive each week. I set it aside to stand and brush the stray papers off my clothes.

Stepping out of my office, I glance down at my watch, the approval will have to wait until after lunch. Mo is gone and I'm not doing it. I put a sticky note on it and drop it off in the *'Approved-Needs Call'* bin.

I lock the front entrance and head up to my floor. My stomach grumbles loudly as I walk into my kitchen. The fridge is full yet nothing is appealing and I slam it shut. On the countertop are a few ripened bananas, which will have to do. I take a bite as I stroll over to the windows.

Seems I spend a lot of time here lately.

I suspect Molly's going to take my advice since she left early.

She knows I'm right and should listen to me.

I'm always right.

A pang of jealousy hits me. The need to have someone I can laugh and be myself with builds each day.

I must change that, but how?

Call a few guys, maybe go out for drinks rather than moping around?

Solid idea. But not yet.

Hitting the home button on my phone shows I have no missed messages. My heart sinks and I rub a hand through my hair. There's a small part of me that was hoping Ruby would've responded, but *only* because I could continue enjoying our little game.

Phone in hand I pace back and forth, thinking of who to call when it rings.

"Hello?"

"It's me. Don't... don't hang up... please." A familiar voice comes through the line.

"You have one minute. Talk." I continue to pace, leaving tracks on the marble.

"I... I... miss you." She sighs heavily.

My skin crawls at the sound. "Don't! Your minute is up. Lose my number." I hang up immediately and clench my phone, ready to fling it across the room.

The nerve! The bitch has nerve!

The unexpected, and unwanted call has the beast rearing his ugly head. There's only one way to drown out his anguished howls. I yank open my liquor cabinet and grasp the first bottle I see. Bourbon. It'll do. I throw my head back and chug.

It burns down my throat, hitting my virtually empty stomach. My gut churns. It's so potent and excruciating, I dry heave and my breath hitches in my chest, spots appearing before my eyes. I lean my hands on the countertop, slowly breathing in and out, and the stars fade from my vision.

Bad idea.

But the beast is clawing, rising and it's not nearly satisfied. I stumble to the cabinet and survey it with bleary eyes. No, I shouldn't be doing this. I need Molly. She's one of the only people who understands and who I trust. The only one who can easily talk me down without using booze as a remedy to calm and soothe the man struggling to come out.

But she's abandoned me, gone off to cozy up to the *Princess*. Right now, she has no use or need for me. I take one last longing glance out the window and make my decision to do the next best thing.

Go find that thin mint coffee girl. I can picture her spreading wide for me already. A good fuck always tames the beast.

At least for a little while.

-9-

Ruby

COFFEE! I'M IN DESPERATE NEED of my coffee. It's been preying on my mind since I woke up. Especially after walking around the complex for what seemed like an eternity. Realistically, I know it was more like twenty excruciatingly long minutes, but my legs are more than tired, they're limp French fries. Not wanting to waste any more time rubbing my achy legs after the unaccustomed exercise, I throw on a pair of dark jean capris, a black t-shirt, tie up my hair in another messy curl filled bun, and head out into my new hometown.

Spotting a Dunkin Donuts, I zip into the drive-thru and order a large hot latte with sugar and of course, whipped cream.

My little slice of heaven on earth.

The first sip is glorious, the smooth espresso flavor igniting all of my taste buds. It's like I've never had it before!

Or more like you have a ridiculous hangover and need the caffeine more than ever.

During my crack of dawn walk this morning, I unsuccessfully

searched for one of those fabulous coffee trucks people talk about. Luckily, the extensive grounds of the complex are littered with benches, so I took a well-deserved break before tackling the walk back home, empty-handed and disappointed.

Even so, my time was productive. I managed to write my entire to-do list for today. It's a long one. I have no furniture, no bed, no anything to make my apartment a home.

Thankfully, spending time outside in the fresh and crisp morning air did, in fact, help relax me. It was oddly pleasant, sitting there in the sunshine, typing away into the notepad on my phone. One of the things I do best lately is organize the few things I can control. It's soothing and makes me feel like I have a small slice of personal power back.

No, the thing you did best was ogling that hot guy on the bench across from you.

I didn't ogle. It was more like I stared politely at his steaming cup of coffee that I could almost taste from a distance. My craving for caffeine intensified and I simply had pondered whether or not to ask him where he'd located the elusive vendor.

Not for a second was it a craving for that sexy enigmatic man.

The guy was simply delicious in those dark aviator sunglasses, so maybe I was checking him out a little bit.

Just a little!

Who in their right mind wouldn't enjoy a few look-sees when a gorgeous man shows you his heart stopping smile? Or maybe another peek or two when you catch a glimpse of the tattoos on his arm?

Oh, lord almighty! It took all the strength I had at six in the morning to tear my eyes from him.

My most secret fascination and weakness? Tattoos! I find them terribly sexy! They appealed to me, so on the night right before my eighteenth birthday, I snuck out of the foster home and got one for myself.

Seeing the tattoo on my wrist every day is what has kept me going for the last few years. It was the only one I found to represent me, the only one that represents who I am inside.

Forever it will be a constant reminder of my strength, and not once have I regretted getting it. Maybe it's time I get more, bite the bullet and go for it.

No one can scold me for marking my body voluntarily.

Taking the last sip from my cup, I realize I've wasted enough time dilly-dallying. My need for a shot of caffeine is satisfied, now I can get on with my errands. A Google search on my phone confirms there is a small family owned furniture shop nearby. In fact, it's less than a five-minute drive.

Ready to tackle my next adventure, I walk into the store, the sound of jingling bells on the door and the smell of old leather reminding me of old time movies I used to watch with my parents. I smile to myself as I browse the small and cozy place.

"Howdy, young lady! How can we help you?" A gray-haired, grandmotherly woman behind the counter greets me immediately in her charming, accented voice

"I'm looking to furnish my new home. I don't have any furniture what so ever, so I'm in need if a lot of help."

"That's not a problem, sweetie. I'll gladly assist you." She speaks in a warm loving tone that's foreign to my ears after all these years. "What would you like to look at first?"

I wonder if she has many grandchildren, she seems like she'd make the perfect grandma. Affection seeps from her, and my heart aches for the love of the grandmother I never knew as a child.

"Thank you, Ma'am!" I pull out my phone and show her my list.

* * *

AFTER ALMOST TWO HOURS I have everything picked out, and the bill to prove it. I don't feel bad, though. It feels good to support a locally owned family business. The owners are a sweet couple, they are the epitome of Southern hospitality.

There's one last thing I need to do—call Molly from the complex.

The phone rings twice and her cheery voice fills my ears.

"Hiya, Ruby! What can I do you for?"

"Well, this might be an odd request, but would you mind letting the furniture delivery guys into my place? They should be coming by in about an hour. I still have a few errands to run and might not make it back in time." I ramble on nervously, over explaining in hopes she agrees.

"Oh, sure! I'll be there and I'll text you when they're done."

"Thank you, you're so kind!" I sigh in relief.

My home won't be so empty for much longer.

"No problem at all. Glad to help!"

Wow, people are so kind here. Kinder than I expected.

We hang up and as I'm walking to my car, a pang surfaces in my stomach. It takes me a few moments to recognize it as yearning, a wish for a family, for friends, and after meeting Savi… for the grandparents I've never met.

* * *

ANOTHER HOUR AND A HALF and two more stops later, and my list is complete.

It takes several trips, but I manage to wrangle the many boxes and bags into my apartment, including the groceries I picked up at the local market. This is the first time, and I'm sure the only reason I'll regret picking the top floor. Good thing the chore is finished. Now that my hands are freed, I can admire how amazing my purchases look.

Practically hopping, I rush into the bedroom and jump on the new mattress.

Finally, a soft bed to sleep on.

A few more hops and skips, and I'm in the living room. I pounce on the brand spanking new sectional and sprawl out on the plush cushions.

Oh, how much I love it!

The entire thing is black suede, including the huge matching ottoman. Although something is missing. This space needs a touch of color to break up all the black.

My shopping bags!

I dig in, scattering my purchases across the floor. I spot the bright red pillows I'd bought specifically for the sectional. Scattering them randomly across it, I step back and admire the sexy black and red combination.

Amazing! It looks better than I expected!

With that done, I organize the rest of my purchases and being stocking the cabinets. Amid finding space in the cabinet for the plates, I receive a text from Molly.

INCOMING MESSAGE: Are ya home? Can I come up?

Perfect I can thank her in person now! Before I can respond, the elevator door dings signaling her arrival. "Coming!" I call out and drop everything to dash across the apartment. "Hey, Molly! What are you doing here?" A smile breaks out as I survey the bags in her hands.

"I took my break late so I could come by and see how ya like the new setup."

"Thank you, Hun! You saved me an extra trip by letting them in. The place looks fabulous, I truly love it! And because of you, day one of living here went down without a hitch!"

She smiles then looks down at her bags and back at me. "So, I know this is impulsive but I brought lunch. I hope you like Mexican!"

"Who doesn't like Mexican? I'm so in for this lunch!" It's as if she can read my mind and knows my favorites things. What a pleasant surprise, I haven't had an authentic Mexican meal in a long time.

She sets everything on the counter and gives me an unexpectedly warm hug. I return the embrace and regretfully pull away. "Thank you for doing this, it's nice to have company!"

"I thought you'd say that. Oh, and I brought beer to go with it." She pulls them out of a plastic bag and waves them in the air before she cracks the caps off two of the bottles, and offers one to me.

I take a long grateful drink. It's crisp and cold, exactly what I need after working so hard on my apartment. "Heineken, you're my kinda girl!" I laugh, it's such a fantastic feeling to laugh out loud, not having to worry about anyone or anything. I almost forgot what it feels like. "Oh! Where are my manners! Let me get us some plates."

"No way, doll, don't fuss with the extra stuff. We can sit on the floor and eat with our fingers! No need to ruin your new furniture! Tacos don't need utensils and our asses don't need fancy seating. We got this, now sit!" She pats the floor, gesturing for me to join her.

Dropping onto the floor beside her, I laugh again, the feeling is so freeing. This is the best I've felt in a long time. Dallas was a good choice; the people, for the most part, have been incredibly welcoming. "Alright, give me one of those bad boys!" I motion to the tacos in her lap.

While our mouths are too full to speak, I think about how different Molly is today compared to yesterday.

I swallow my last bite and break the silence. "Molly, don't take this the wrong way, but why did you *really* come over today? I wasn't expecting to hear from you for a while. I'm glad you did, but I'm curious."

She shrugs. "Oh well, when I'm with the boss"—She rolls her eyes— "I have to be all professional, ya know. Plus, I liked your vibe, your sauciness reminds me of *me* at your age." She pauses. "To sum it up, I wanted to get to know you. The furniture thing was my excuse. I could've easily called and checked in. Honestly? I don't have many friends, and figured since you're new in town you don't either so..."

"I get it, we're loners and loners recognize each other for what we are! Got to support the friendless community by lending a hand or... some tacos!" I giggle, and she joins me. It's infectious and soon we both have tears of laughter streaming down our faces.

We're making a mess, taco bits escaping and spreading across the shiny wood floor, but I don't care!

Screw the mess, I'm making a new friend!

"Yes, girl!"

"Well, I'm so happy you did. You're right I don't have any friends or family, so it's nice to have someone care to come by." I shove more taco into my mouth, chewing thoughtfully. "So. Exactly how old are you?" I arch my brow as I study her face.

"I'm an old lady compared to you. I saw on your application, you're twenty-five and I'm the dreaded three zero. Well in a few months I am." She makes a gagging sound.

I laugh. "Wow, woman, we're only five years apart, and thirty is not old! Please, when you're eighty I'd agree that you're ancient."

Molly's blue eyes widen. "Listen, I'm an old woman, with no husband or children! At my age, I should have those things. Instead, I'm all alone!" Sadness sweeps across her face.

I can relate, I fear being alone too. The loss of my parents, my time in foster care, and my doomed entanglements with men have left me empty.

"Look, I'll be the family you're missing and you can be mine. Guaranteed I can qualify as a problem husband and child all in one package." I laugh, attempting to make Molly smile again.

"Yes! I love that idea! Let's drink to that!" She grins and we tap our bottles. "Cheers to a new friendship!"

We both chug our beer, finishing them at the same time.

"Sooo. Since we're best friends now, and you probably don't have much time left, I need the scoop on someone who lives here."

Molly perks up, her eyes bright with interest. She seems ready for some bonding time, sharing good old fashioned gossip. I'm all for it, I've never had much chance for girl talk either.

"Oh, sure! I'm the source for all info on this place, being Maeson's assistant and all." She pauses and looks at me expectantly.

How do I phrase the question without being stalkerish?

"Spill already! I'm on the edge of this floor and getting older by the second!" She sounds exasperated.

No point in beating around the bush, I must know who I saw this morning.

"This morning there was a guy lounging on a bench in the courtyard. Total hottie! He was wearing a sweatshirt with sweats, a beanie and sunglasses, semi-longish dark hair. But what stood out for me was, he's got a tattoo and probably more by the looks of him. Didn't talk to the guy, but... do you who he could be?" My heart beats faster at the mention of my mystery man.

"Ruby, you've seen the kind of people who live in this place! Most of the tenants are old couples, not hot young guys." She looks away, then brushes at the crumbs on her pants. "No men with tattoos live in this building." She shrugs. "I'd know!"

"You're right. Well, keep a look out and put in a good word for me if you do see him." I giggle.

What am I thinking? Like I'm ready to handle a relationship right now?

"Of course, sweetie." She glances down at her expensive looking rose gold watch. "I have to go, but we can do dinner sometime soon to continue our girl time! Maybe tonight? I'll have to see how work goes, but I'll text you."

We both stand, brush off our clothes and I nod happily as I see her to the elevator.

I nod happily. "Sure, it's a plan! I'm not doing much."

"Well, you could always take a tour of the neighborhood. There are a few shops, that small pub I mentioned before, and a grocery store all within walking distance. It'll get you out of the house for a while if you get bored." Molly halts. "Speaking of things to do. We could go out for drinks Friday? Work won't be an issue for sure that night."

"Really? Hell yeah! Haven't done that in a while... would be nice. I could use a girls' night."

Especially since I've never had one.

The only *'night'* anything I ever had or did was with the random men I met in college. Girls typically stayed away from me. They would say I was weird and odd, but apparently, that was not the case in the eyes of the guys I came across.

"Me too, doll. We'll just have to finalize our plans, but I'll be in touch." She hugs me again and walks into the elevator.

I watch the doors close and sigh. This is my chance to be a *normal* twenty-five-year-old. My ex never allowed me to go out, Ray kept constant restrictions on me. That's the main reason I didn't have any friends.

Looking back now, I see how much control he'd had over me, which is my biggest regret. There's no longer a person who can stop me from having fun, and I won't let anyone make me regret anything, ever again.

Excitement bubbles within me at the thought of going out for drinks and dancing. Well, until I realize I don't have any clothes appropriate for a nightclub. I need to find something to wear right away.

Not even giving it a second thought, I grab my keys and I'm out the door in a split second.

* * *

THE CLOSEST MALL IS A ten-minute drive via the highway. With the help of my GPS, getting there's a breeze, but finding the perfect outfit is a different story altogether.

The first three stores were all duds. Now I'm in the fourth one—which is a plus size store—giving me a few more options for my curvaceous figure. I find several pairs of jeans and leggings which fit my size fourteen frame like a glove. Next are the tops, this section is usually tricky for me, but somehow, I manage to find a bunch of sexy tops women my age would wear. I don't particularly care for dresses or skirts, so I skip them altogether.

I'm passing by the shoe department when I notice them in the window. Red is my favorite color by far; it contrasts beautifully with my long dark hair and my olive skin tone. The pair of red flats I spotted would be perfect, they'll match one of my new outfits.

My goal accomplished, I'm ready to complete my purchase. I scan the store, thinking I can always come back some time later this week to fill my closet. This place has turned out to be a gold mine. I pay for my new items with a big thank you to the cashier and bounce happily to my car. Again, the sense of freedom strikes me sharply, and a rush of joy strikes me.

Fortunately, I didn't get stuck in the infamous Dallas rush-hour traffic I've heard about, and I make it home in ten minutes exactly. Just in time to put away all my goodies, and get ready for a night out in town with Molly—if she can go, otherwise it will be a night out...

Alone.

As much as the word scares me, I need to acknowledge that it also means I'll be able to get out of the house without asking permission, stay out late, shop as much as I want, and go to a damn bar without having to hide the alcohol from my breath. Tonight, I get to enjoy my own company.

It's been a long time since I've had this much freedom.

-10-

MAESON

I'M HOT. IT'S TOO FUCKING hot, it feels like I'm stuck to saran wrap. I bat at it with my free hand and attempt to move my other arm. But I can't. Something is weighing it down. I make another futile effort.

"Maes—" A female voice purrs in my ear.

I leap to my feet, almost toppling over. My head spins and I cling to the edge of a desk.

My desk? What the fuck? How and why the fuck am I here?

I stare at the surface, blinking rapidly to clear my vision. I gradually lift my head to confirm. Definitely my office, though something doesn't seem quite right. Dropping my head slowly, I realize I'm buck naked. In the middle of the room.

Shit! Where are my clothes?

"Maeson."

I almost forgot about the voice. A glance at the floor clears up the mystery. The thin mint coffee girl is on her back, as nude as I am. She blinks her big brown eyes several times as I take a deep breath and images surface.

Blondie's on top of my desk. Spread eagle, all wet, and moaning my name. I pound into her, pound till my legs shake. The room is spinning, but I don't stop. She yells out in pleasure, and I open my eyes. Her face. Her face isn't hers anymore...

"Mae-"

Another voice, a familiar one right behind me. I twist and face a frozen Molly. Her eyes are bulging and her mouth is hanging wide open.

Fuck. Not good.

"Molly..." I stagger as I snatch a folder from my desk to cover the goods.

"What did you do? This place reeks of liquor and sex!" She lowers her gaze to the floor and curls her lip at the woman lying there. "Who's the skank?"

The girl pipes up. "I'm—"

"Nobody. Mind yours, Mo. Out!" My haze filled eyes don't leave Molly's face.

Who does she think she is?

I never explain myself. I'm a fucking grown man.

"When this one..." Molly pauses and scowls at the naked woman, her brows lifting in disdain. "Leaves. I'm coming back. No buts about it. Minus your naked one, which better be fucking dressed by the time I return. No one wants to see... all of that." Mo waves a hand then pivots. She doesn't wait for a response, but storms off, heels clicking harshly against the tile floor.

"Um. Sorry about that..."

What's her fucking name?

"That's okay. I need to go anyway. This..." She motions between our two bare bodies. "Was great! If you want a repeat, call me. Here." She extends a small black card.

I take it from her long fingers and place it on my desk. "Thanks." My eyes travel down her body trying to find the reason for why I went after her. I'm unaffected, utterly unaffected.

Most men would give anything for a woman with a physique like hers. Well, except me, obviously. She's beautiful but is missing something. A lot of something. Like thick, full thighs, brown curls, voluptuous curves...

Eva Mendes's fabulous ass.

"Hey." She gently touches my arm, bringing my attention back to her and away from picturing Ruby's glorious round ass. "Looking for these?" She grins, holding my pants up, waving them, before tossing them onto the desk. Scooping up her dress, she wriggles into it, covering her nakedness.

"Thanks." I tug on my pants, not bothering to locate my underwear. "*So.* I can... uh... take you home."

Fucking awkward.

"Don't make this weird, sweet cheeks. I'll see myself out. You're in no shape to drive anywhere. I'm a big girl." Rising on her tiptoes, she kisses my cheek. "Like I always say, *'a fuck is a fuck is a fuck'.*" She laces her fingers with mine. "Keep in touch, big boy." Her eyebrows wiggle and her fingers travel south to cup the boys.

Watching her hips swaying seductively as she walks out of the room, I purposely stare at her ass as she goes, and feel nothing. Not an ounce of regret or attraction. She was a replacement fuck, an anger bang, and she knew it from the beginning. When I showed up, she called me out. 'Drunk and horny huh? What woman pissed you off?'.

What woman indeed, or should I say, women?

"You cover those old balls of yours yet, or what?" Molly's in the doorway shielding her eyes with her hands. "When you said you were picking something up for lunch, I didn't think you meant a 'mint'."

"Yeah, yeah." I pinch the bridge of my nose and squeeze my eyes shut as I try not to vomit. "Get in here and quit coverin' your eyes! You're giving me a damn complex!"

"Yadda, yadda." Her hand waves me off. "Let's skip the formalities and get to the real shit. Why on earth would you get wasted mid-day? Even worse, get loaded and bring one of your bimbos here for an office fuck?" Her hands are glued to her hips and her eyebrows rise in confusion.

"Sit and stop yapping." I sit on the desk facing Mo and rub my aching temples. "Why I drank is none of your business. Who an' where I fuck is *ouutt* of your question ranges. Got it?" Taking a deep breath, I give my stomach a chance to settle.

She crosses her arms over her small breasts and puffs up. "Oh, I got it. God forbid someone looks out for ya." She looks away and shakes her head, then regards me with shiny eyes.

"Mol—"

"Don't, Maeson. Forget it. I came here for a reason." Her eyes narrow and her lips twitch.

This is going to be good.

"Oh? What?" I cock my head to the side.

"Well. Ruby saw some super-hot guy on the property." She holds up a hand. "Her words not mine! So, this guy she saw has a tattoo or as she said, *'probably more by the looks of him'*. Know anything about it? She seems *verrry* interested." Her smirk turns into a sly grin.

Are you fucking kidding me?

"No. Don't have a bloody clue for fuck's sake!" I clench my fist and slam it on the wooden desk. Realizing I didn't feel that impact, I bring my hand up and inspect it. Being pumped with liquor has its advantages, well... until it wears off.

I'm going to regret it tomorrow.

"Hmmm... interesting. The guy was incognito mode—beanie and shades. Not many round here like that. Not many at all." Molly's brow quirks up.

I need to play it cool. "So? What is your point? Hook her up all you want, but leave me out of it." I shrug.

"Yeah, right. Talk to her. Stop running and fighting it. Open up for once."

I roll my eyes and look around for my shirt. Spotting it in the corner of the room, I wobble over and pick it up. "Anything else?" I clench my jaw and the muscles on my face painfully tighten.

Silence. I turn to find myself alone. Molly left without another word. She might be upset with me right now and that's fine. I can deal with her sour face for a few days over the alternative.

Open up... right... not happening... again.

There is no way I'm disclosing any information about myself to Ruby Bennett anytime soon. Instead, what I need to do is figure out a way to get Ruby to even speak to me. And since Mo has an in, I can possibly use her as an excuse.

With that thought in mind, I collapse in a stupor on the chair and pass the fuck out.

* * *

A FEW HOURS LATER MY annoying desk phone goes off, waking me with a start.

I clear my throat. "What?"

"Wake the fuck up, boss. It's four already, I need to go. I'd like to show Ruby around town and maybe even take her to Crossroads." Her high-pitched voice penetrates my sensitive senses.

I squeezed my eyes shut and rub the back of my neck. "The hell you will. We have things that need to get done."

Like I'm going to let her have more time with Ruby. It's my turn.

"No I don't, *you* do." Molly huffs.

"Then you're fired!" I bellow, my voice echoing down the hall.

I hear her tapping away on the keyboard and sigh heavily. "You always resort to that bull. What do you need?"

I lean toward the new stacks that came in the mail today and almost fall out of my seat. "Come... to... my... office." I barely get the words out as I steady myself. Even after a few hours of sleep, the room is still spinning and this headache pounds through my brain. "There's a folder waiting for you and some callbacks I need to be made *pronto*." I pull out a bottle of water from the mini-fridge under my desk and shake out two pills from the small bottle of Advil in the top drawer.

I feel like utter shit.

Reclining back into the chair, I lay my head against it and let out a harsh breath. Once Molly stops taking her sweet ass time to get here, I can give her plenty to keep her occupied for several hours.

Then I can make my move.

I sniff at my armpit and wave my hand. I'm rank and in desperate need of a shower. Can't make a move smelling like I ran for ten miles and then bathed in cheap perfume.

A grin spreads across my face.

Yes. After I scrub my skin raw.

Tonight, I'll face her and *not* as her landlord.

We'll be meeting again, Princess.

-11-

Ruby

SAVORING A QUIET MOMENT BEFORE I finish getting ready, I realize it's getting late and I have yet to hear from Molly. Picking up my phone, I check for missed calls or messages and sure enough, there's one from her.

INCOMING MESSAGE: Ur landlord's an ass, I gotta be here for longer than expected, can't do dinner tonight. He's all pissy for who knows what reason and now I'm paying for it! Bullshit! DEF going for drinks, start shopping for the perfect outfit! XOXO -Mo-

I hit reply right away.

MESSAGE SENT: I knew he was a sophisticated jackass from the moment I met him, woman! Give em grief damn it! No problem on dinner. I'll check out the places you suggested in town. See you Friday! -No Nickname-Ruby-

Well, it looks like it's going to be Me, Myself, and I tonight. How can the idea be so liberating and exciting, yet terrifying to me?

Because any glimmer of hope I've ever had has always been extinguished too quickly for it to ever fully develop or be enjoyed.

* * *

THIS COMPLEX IS LIKE A city all on its own. The brightly lit buildings stand tall and proud amongst a mass of vibrant red roses and seating areas surrounding them.

Such a vision to behold from this distance.

The cool evening breeze is utterly relaxing, quite the opposite of the midday sun which makes you sweat on impact. As I approach the semi-main road, I notice more cars passing by.

I must be getting close to the shops and local bar Molly mentioned.

In New York, the hustle and bustle was constant. People and cars were everywhere. Small shops and bodegas were scattered on practically every corner and here, in Dallas, that's not the case. You need to drive to get to a destination. There are a few options close enough to walk to, and not a five-minute walk but more like ten to twenty, which my poor legs are currently struggling with.

I wish I would've taken the damn car. A little exercise never killed anyone, so you'll survive!

Right, and with my luck, I'll be that special case who dies from walking of all things! But I manage and end up in front of a small building with a big blue sign on it.

Crossroads. How Ironic.

Besides the symbolic name of the place, the exterior looks insignificant. Then again, some of the hole-in-the-wall spots I frequented in The Village weren't any better on the outside and turned out to be gems.

My fingers twitch in anticipation of what I might find inside, so I quit stalling. It takes my eyes a minute to adjust to the dim lighting. The scents of alcohol and men's cologne invade my senses and I sigh. This is exactly the kind of place I was looking for—my very own hole-in-the-wall bar close to home.

The interior is bigger than it looked from outside. The left side has a bar that extends from the entrance towards the back and has stools alongside it. On the right side, there are black leather booths and black wooden tables with chairs that have intricate filigree engraved on them.

The bar area is full, not a single empty seat remains at the counter. Spotting an empty booth at the back of the pub, I wind through the crowd awaiting drinks and take a seat facing the entrance.

Weird, I know.

I've developed this ridiculous insecurity.

Paranoia.

I hate having my back toward a door, and remain hyper-vigilant of my surroundings. I can't help it, not being able to see a threat coming scares me.

What doesn't scare you?

Point made. I need to relax, and I have the perfect way to do so. Near the sign for the restroom, I spot a waitress leaning against the wall, talking to a patron, and I wave my hand in the air. She notices me, nods, and mouths *'coming'*.

Within seconds, she's making her way to me. As she approaches my mouth drops at the sight of her... *outfit*. The blue bra is barely covering her breasts, her blue skirt is so tiny I can almost see her goodies, and her tiny waist is bare.

Good God, look at that body!

Only in my dreams will I ever be thin to dress that way. But good for her on keeping up with such a beautiful body.

I wasn't dealt that hand, was I?

My metabolism quit on me once I turned fifteen. Ever since then all I have to do is breathe and it sticks to me, let alone eat. Accepting my *'fat'* gene is a process and I've even started appreciate what I do have instead of hating what I don't.

When life gives you rolls and cellulite, you embrace them, right?

Yeah, right up until the next beauty passes you by and the self-doubt sets in, continuing the nasty never-ending cycle.

"Hey, sweetie. What can I get ya?" The blonde beauty smiles brightly.

"Vodka, cranberry, and lime." With a grin, I add, "Double on the Grey Goose, please?"

"Sure, an extra strong Cape Cod coming right up!" She winks and struts away.

Once she's out of sight, I tune into my surroundings. There's music playing in the background, people dancing in the middle of the pub, and everyone seems to be having a great time. Watching people mingle so effortlessly is inspiring. I'm not shy by any means, but I also don't jump into a person's lap without them initiating it.

Crossroads.

How fitting. That's where I am in my life and I bet I'm not the only one in this bar. Even this place seems to be at odds with itself. The music and parts of the decor are new and up-to-date, but the furnishings and the design of the building are old school.

Why choose one or the other when you can meet in the middle and mix both, right?

I must say, I'm glad there's a place like this so close to home. It will be an outlet, somewhere to escape.

What am I still trying to escape from?

My own insecurities and fears, that's what! They won't disappear overnight.

"Here you go." The waitress's voice startles me. She sets down two tall frosty glasses which are filled to the brim and topped with a slice of lime.

My mouth waters, it looks so damn good! "Thanks, but I didn't order two!"

She laughs and bobs her head toward the bar. "That guy there told me to bring it. His gift to you."

I frown and scan the crowd, and not a single person stands out. "What guy?"

She points across the way and my eyes about pop out of my

damn head.

You've got to be kidding me!

"Tall, dark n' handsome over there. Jade colored eyes, dimples, and an accent of some sort. *That* guy." Her eyes freaking sparkle.

Like he's a fucking God or something.

"I don't want it. Return to sender," I growl.

"Nah, come on, sweetie. Be smart. When a sexy guy sends you a drink? You take it. No complaints. No expectations."

No such thing with a man like that.

My frown deepens and I grumble, "Fine. It stays. Please tell the bastard, *'No thanks'* for me?"

"Sure, it'll be my pleasure. I like you, you're a feisty one." Her smile expands. "Anyway, name's Sammie. I'll be over there if you need anything, flag me down."

This time, I smile at her. "Thanks, Sammie. I'm Ruby. I'll be here a while, so keep an eye out for that signal."

We both laugh and she turns, disappearing through the dancing patrons. Those same individuals are blocking my view of my asshole landlord. It's for the best anyway, because his too damn handsome face will only ruin my night.

My heart thunders in my chest, knowing he's here is enough to make me sweat. Images form in the corners of my mind— dirty ones—so much so, I'm already wet. They're pushing to be re-experienced, but I shove them back before they can take over.

I should've asked for a straight shot, not this prissy drink.

To obtain the same effect, I chug these, one right after the other. It'll have to do for now. Within a few minutes, both glasses are empty. The buzz I wanted sets in, and the alcohol hits my system... *hard.*

My entire body feels warm and cozy, even vibrating with excitement. Everything around me seems so much more alive. The music is louder, and I'm noticing the hot guys shooting curious glances toward me. Fixating on one in particular—a dark-haired man with piercing blue eyes—I smile deeply, hoping it'll express my *'hello there sexy'* thought.

Letting loose again, are we?

Heck yeah! Why not?

It's my turn to enjoy life.

The man grins eagerly and points to himself. I nod and shrug shyly like I've never done this before.

I've come out to play and that's exactly what I'm going to do.

Right before he reaches me, Sammie side steps him. "Need anything else, honey?" She picks up my empty glasses with an all-knowing grin.

"Yes, Grey Goose on the rocks with a twist. Keep them coming, Sammie." My voice sounds odd, lower, and huskier.

"Oh, Lord almighty! You're in it to win it tonight, aren't you?"

"Sure am!" Smiling, I hand her my credit card. "Open a tab, easier to keep track of."

"Okay!" She takes it then leans forward to whisper, "Tall, dark, and green eyes is way better looking than blue eyes behind me." She shrugs. "Just sayin'."

The girl is right, one hundred and ten percent, but that is one man who I will *not* get close to.

Not a chance.

"Noted, *honey*," I tease before she walks off.

With Sammie gone, Mr. Blue Eyes stands before me in all his glory. Up close and personal, he's not as good looking as I thought. The dim lighting fooled me, but he'll do. This is supposed to be fun, not a search for a husband, or happily ever after material.

"Hey!" I say cheerily and point to the empty space. "Please sit."

"Thanks." He extends his hand across the table. "I'm Dave." When he smiles, there's no sign of dimples, and I'm slightly disappointed.

Those are my ultimate weakness.

I lean in and clasp my hand in his. It's smooth, so very

smooth, maybe *too* smooth. There's something sexy about a man's rough hands caressing your body. Coarse and rugged fingers against smooth skin is such a turn-on. This guy's missing yet another quality I look for in a man, too bad. "Ruby. Nice to meet you."

"Can I get you a drink?"

"No need. I have one coming"—I look to the right and see Sam approaching with my shots— "Right about... now." On cue, she sets the glasses down. "Perfect timing, my friend."

She shakes a finger at me. "I sense this is going to be a Coyote Ugly kind of night for you." Sam laughs.

Dave's eyebrows shoot up and a big smile spreads across his face.

Oh, interested now, are we?

I give them a cheeky grin. "If you're lucky, it'll be even better than that."

Sam continues to laugh and pats my shoulder. "You've got about"—She peers down at her watch—"half an hour before I crank up the music. Once that happens, this place will turn into the best place you'll ever visit. Just be careful." She pretends to scold me in a motherly way.

My grin widens. "I *sure* will! And thanks to the company I have now—I'll be just dandy." Lie, but Dave or Sammie have no way of knowing that. The man sitting at my table isn't exactly my kind of *company*—I was referring to... someone else. Who, I don't seem to sense any longer.

Did he leave?

I look around briefly, and he's nowhere to be found. Maeson has disappeared. Part of me wants to sigh in relief. Without his I'm-better-than-thou attitude killing the mood, I'll be able to have fun, right? Wrong, because the other part—the sad and pathetic one—liked knowing he was near.

Why? I have no clue.

"He didn't leave," Sammie says randomly.

What is she reading my mind now?

Somehow, she knows exactly who I was searching for. Sam

doesn't wait for my response, though, she simply strolls away.

There wouldn't have been one anyway.

* * *

"YOU'RE SO CRAZY!" DAVE SHOUTS above the music as we dance.

"Only sometimes!" Laughing, I move in closer to him, right against his body. My hands trail up and down his chest a few times, then stop at his shoulders, using them for leverage. Leaning in, I nibble, nip, and kiss my way up from his neck to his mouth.

If he won't take charge, I certainly will.

We lock lips and I literally feel nothing. As drunk as I am right now, I should've felt *something*.

I'm always horny when I drink.

Has my ex ruined me forever? Damn asshole! Of course, he did! He's ruined everything else, why not my sex drive too? I need more to drink, that'll fix me.

You know that's not true. The other night you felt plenty.

My conscience rebukes me, but I ignore it. Slightly pulling away, I stand on my toes, tilting in closer so he can hear me. "Need another drink."

He nods and goes back to his friends.

No offer to buy it for me? Or join me? Wow, class act kind of guy, aren't you?

At the bar, I flag down the petite, dark-haired bartender and ask her for a Cap Cod. While she preps it, I peer toward the end of the bar and my eyes lock with Sammie's. She smiles deeply and nods her head to the left.

Following the movement, I spot *him*. Maeson's in a booth with three women surrounding him and as if he senses me staring, he gazes up at me with a huge smile.

Fire blazes through me—like hot lava—at the sight of his dimples. When Sammie mentioned he had them, I dismissed her words, but *seeing* them—

Shit. Shit. Shit.

Closing my eyes, I try to maintain control and take a deep breath.

In and out. Inhale and exhale.

Just like my mom taught me to do when I would have panic attacks. It's the same technique I've been using since then.

Slow and steady breaths.

It's not working, so I do the next best thing and shift my position. That way he's not in my line of vision at all.

"Here you go!" the bartender says with a smile. "He's got all the women going wild tonight. Seems to do it every time he comes around."

"*Not* this woman!" I roll my eyes and stalk away from the bar.

On my way to Dave and his buddies, I've downed half the glass. Once I reach them, I finish it and slam it down on the table. "Let's go." Grabbing his hand, we move toward the middle of the pack of dancers. I don't face him this time, instead, I keep my back to him hoping I'll sense some type of attraction to the man this way.

Our bodies won't synchronize, his movements are awkward, no rhythm at all, but he won't give up his incessant grinding. In this drunken state, my aggravation rises quicker than expected.

This is when you need a backup friend with you.

One who can help you escape a man you're not into at all. Since I don't have one of those, I'll make do with the only other option I have at hand.

Sammie wanted to see Coyote Ugly?

That's what I'm about to give her. She's in her usual spot at the back corner of the room, watching the clienteles, and making sure they all have drinks. "Who controls the playlist?"

She raises her eyebrow to the max and smirks. "I do. What should I change it to?" she says, seeming to already have contemplated what I'm planning.

"Ed Sheeran, Shape of You." My grin is so wide, my cheeks ache. I'm so far gone—too far gone—at this point to stop and sit my ass down like a good girl. The desire for *actual* fun is too strong this time around.

I gave it up once before, never happening again.

"You know these guys are hungry, right?"

"I do, but I don't give a shit. Let's have us a good time, huh? Life's too short!" I wait for Sammie to enter the back room before zeroing in on my next destination. Swaying and stumbling, I somehow accomplish maneuvering through the crowd and get close enough to the bar.

The woman behind it is grinning from ear to ear and gives me a thumbs up. My stomach fills with fluttering butterflies who are as excited as I am to be *freed*, to be *unleashed*, and to feel *alive* again.

The song starts on full blast. The bass thumps throughout the room, vibrating through me and pumps into my ears. My palms are clammy and heart beats rapidly as I grasp the edge of the shiny wooden slab.

I can do this! Tonight is all about having a good time. Nothing less and nothing more.

Before I climb up onto it, I spot an untouched shot with some sort of dark alcohol. Raising it to my lips, I throw my head back and the molten liquid harshly slides down my throat. I stuck in a deep breath as—*whatever the hell that was*—burns its way down to the pit of my stomach.

Don't lose focus!

I take another deep breath and the familiar warmth liquor provides gives me courage.

It's now or never. You're not that lost ten, or fifteen, or eighteen-year-old anymore.

"*Oh shit!*" I hear the people behind me say when I lift myself up onto the bar top.

Thick thighs or not, I've got this ladies and gentlemen.

Besides the mass of alcohol coursing through my veins, Mr. Sheeran's smooth and sexy voice heightens my senses, and I lose myself within the lyrics. My body moves of its own volition. My hips sway back and forth, round, and round, slow and steady with one purpose in mind.

Enjoying myself for once.

Lifting my arms, I seductively slide them up to my breast, then down to my hips. Stopping there, I slowly repeat the motion. The song is turning me on more than Mr. Dave, who's currently watching me intently, practically salivating. I smile, showing off my pearly whites and crook my finger in a come here motion. He doesn't move, he seems to be stuck in place.

Well, I might not have been into you, but I guess you sure are, huh? Okay, you stay there then.

People around the bar shout, whistle, and clap, rooting me on. I use their excitement as motivation to keep going. Shifting, I move down and grab Sam's hand, lifting her up beside me. "Shake that body, girl!"

With an immense grin, she follows my lead. She doesn't falter or miss a step, her movements are calculated, precise and sensual, exactly like a professional dancer.

Every man's wet dream. Flexible Sammie.

Next up, I find the adorable bartender hiding at the edge of the bar and help her up as well. "Coyote Ugly, Bitches!" I stomp on one of the glasses, spraying liquid, and shards all around us.

The other two women each grab one of those hoses behind the bar and start spraying the crowd with water. In a mass of shouts, they all go wild, everyone's in the party mood—move your damn body mode.

This is what all my college years should've been like.

Closing my eyes, I push the tears threatening to spill and destroy my night. Expertly, I put on a happy face and keep moving in tune with the beat. Lowering myself, I twist my hips all the way down and right back up with a snap.

Suddenly, my body tingles and each of the little hairs on my arms stand up. Without having to look, I recognize the sensation for what it is. I had it when I first met *him* and every time he's been around me since then. It only happens when my dreaded landlord fixates on me. Unable to resist, I cave and flit my gaze to the same spot he was in before. He's still surrounded by thin, ditzy, breakable women.

Our eyes meet—fiery green against molten brown. Refusing to look away and hide behind the fear he makes me feel, I welcome the intensity of his gaze. He thinks he can handle me?

Yeah, right. I'm too screwed up in the head.

But if Maeson's as stubborn as I'm assuming he is?

My insanity won't stop him.

Dismissing every scattered thought, I focus on the piercing emerald color of his eyes. Zoning everyone else out, I let the beat and lyrics of the song take full control of my mind. My movements increase in speed, dripping with sexual desire, engulfing me with what I'm always afraid to feel. Happiness...

Love your body. Someone... please... Love my body.

-12-

MAESON

OH, THE NERVE THIS DISTURBINGLY attractive woman has!

She sacked my act of kindness by sending Sam back with a *'No thank you'*.

Seriously? Attitude much? Trust fund must be getting to her head.

Too bad that sort of thing doesn't impress me in the slightest. I have plenty of my own money. So, thanks but no thanks to *you*, Princess. Only if she'd realize what's in her bank account does not make her sexier. Quite the opposite for a man like me.

What about the way she's moving those hips right now?

That's a whole other issue. Her body... well her—thick in all the right places—body makes Ruby absurdly erotic. Although, I do wish she had the personality to match the goods.

You don't need a personality for a good fuck, though.

True, but I had a decent sex sesh today and maybe it made me realize I want more than a run of the mill, good enough lay.

Don't get over your head there. That's not a possibility for you anymore. You gave up on that sort of thing remember?

I did, but times change when someone entices me enough to

budge on my own rules.

Not that I've found such a person yet.

I'm simply learning you can only hold on to the hurt for so long before it devours you whole, leaving nothing left behind.

I said, learning, not learned. Clearly, I'm not there quite yet.

"Baby, are you listening?" One of my usual females is wrapped around my neck like a damn noose.

"Yeah," I mumble, my eyes never leaving Ruby's.

"So, will you take me home with you tonight?" She purrs in my ear and my skin crawls at the sound.

"Nope. You know better, kitten. No one allowed in my house." Irritation with her stupid question rises, as does my voice.

"Humph!" Her pout is far from cute, but I keep that bit to myself.

Cindy or Mindy—whatever her name is—slides off my leg and sits near the next dumbass man on her list of '*fuckables*'.

Good riddance.

Ruby's eyes glide over me as this all takes place. There is no sign of any emotion or a reaction toward me and the thin mints surrounding me as I'd hoped for. She simply continues to dance her ass off on the bar alongside the other women.

How is she so unaffected by me?

This is a first and not a pleasant one for sure. Yet, somehow, she's into that loser, Dave? He's here almost every night trying to score with anything that walks. Tonight, it seems the fool's set his eyes on my hot new tenant, Ruby. Well, she's an adult and will eventually figure out his stupid game—the more a woman drinks, the harder this douche bag tries. He assumes drunk women are the easiest lay of them all.

Good luck with that man, this one's colder than ice.

Forget that sucker, I need to get back on track with my plan.

Seduce Ruby Bennett with my charming qualities.

Everything I've seen so far from Ruby should be a turn-off, instead, I'm intrigued, interested, and a bloody sucker for it. The way her body moves makes my blood boil and my dick hard.

Of course, now my mind does what it always does—fills with sexual imaginings. Images of—her bent over that wooden bar, her on this damn booth spread eagle, or even her buck-naked dancing for me—just like she seems to be doing right now, except for the bared skin factor.

Bloody hell! She's on fire with those dance moves!

Ed Sheeran, my friend, you must've made this song for me, read my damn mind, didn't you? Her physique is nothing like all these thin mints in here—thighs you can easily get lost in between, a small waist that curves deeply before it meets her hips, and large breasts to die for.

If only I could get close enough to touch that body and feel that soft tanned skin against mine. Stop!

I shake the vision away and return to admiring the women on the bar who are dancing like it's been choreographed. Seeing them side by side you notice the stark differences between each one. Sammie is blonde, tall, and super thin—too thin for even my tastes. Then you have sweet southern charm filled Bekka—also a blonde—is what Mo likes to call a *'classic thin mint'*.

Skinny mini and as ditzy as they come.

Lastly, there's the one I can't quit staring at. She is hands down the best of them all. Big up top, has a curvy waist, wide round hips, and an ass to worship.

Gods, it's like she was made to torture me!

Oh, and I how can I forget her long, wild, curly hair? The dark and tantalizing mass cascades down her back.

I need to quit bullshitting around and make a move.

Clutching the shot glass in my hand, I chug it and follow up with another before I stand. The lovely ladies in the booth all sigh as if they know where I'm headed and I look back at them with a smirk.

Sorry girls, this guy is on a mission.

Yes, the undertaking of enticing a girl who could care less about my existence, much less speak to me.

Hard to believe, I know. Must be losing my touch damn it.

I refuse to be discouraged, though. I'm not a sad and pathetic kind of man who gives up without a fight. What I am is the kind who adores challenges, which is exactly what Ruby is.

A damn sexual challenge.

When I reach the bar, I'm front and center and able to watch her without interruptions—even if it's for only a minute before the song ends. I lick my lips and purposely smile as deeply as possible, all to watch her reaction. My fail proof, '*get a girl in the sack*' grin gets them every time.

Ahhh… there it is.

If I wasn't observing her so intently, I would've missed it. Her coppery eyes flicker with the heat I expected to see, but what I don't anticipate is the most mischievous smile I've ever seen spreading across her face. The '*I'm wasted and you're asking for trouble*' kind. Exactly what I seem to be searching for tonight—*trouble*—that's named after a beautiful red jewel.

As the music moves on to the next track, she hops from the bar and brushes past me with a scowl on her face.

What happened to the sexy grin she was sporting a fucking second ago?

That does it! I gave no idea what the fuck her problem with me is, but it ends tonight.

I'm not a fucking child, nor will I be treated like one.

Pushing through the rows of swaying people, I find Ruby and *fucking Dave* in a dark corner by the men's bathroom.

Great…

I clear my throat, but it's useless, the music is too loud. Moving in closer, I tap on Dave's shoulder, and he turns to face me. "I need a minute with her."

His eyes widen at the sight of me, probably remembering the beating I gave him not too long ago. "Yeah. Gotta go anyway." He leans in and whispers. "If you're gonna try, I should tell you she's not givin' any up tonight. Waste of your time," he slurs and walks away.

Getting rid of him was easy. Now for the hard part.

Ruby eyes me suspiciously, and I smile, hoping to ease her

animosity. "*What?*" She frowns and crosses her arms across her chest. "What is it you could possibly want? You made it very clear you're an asshole. Just my damn luck, my landlord's a stiff dick and not in a good way."

Is she serious?

Like she should talk, she's not a ray of sunshine either. I'm not the only one who gave a bad first impression. I can't help but laugh at her audacity. "So, are you saying you want it in a good way? Cause I can make that happen... *again*, if you'd like." My smile deepens and I wink.

Maybe there's still a chance my sex charms will work on this odd female.

Her mouth sets into a grim line and she shakes her head. "That—you presumptuous prick—is not at all what I'd like. It was a mistake. Shouldn't have happened. You're my damn landlord! Never again. So be on your way." She waves her hand in a '*get out of my face*' motion.

Oh wow. Money has gotten to her pretty little head. Who does she think she's brushing off?

Hell if a woman is going to dismiss me! That is my job! Instead, I do the opposite of what she's asked and shift closer, as close as I can without our body's touching. "You say I'm stiff? How about you? Have you looked in the mirror lately? There are quite a few choice words I can use to describe your *pleasant* personality. Hmmm... let me think..." I tap my chin, pretending to struggle to conjure up a few descriptive words. "Oh, I know. Fancy, stuck up, spoiled trust fund brat, and too good for those below her. You want more, *princess*? I could go on all night long." My voice rises.

I'm being attacked by anger, sexual desire, and frustration all because of her. Each emotion swirls through me with such force, I'm unable to hold them back for much longer.

When she doesn't attempt to retort, I go on. "Never again is right, Ruby. You're the last woman I'd ever want to spend my nights with." I sneer right in her face.

How could she not want me again? All women do!

That sums up my problem with this whole situation—she's rebuffing me and it's not the other way around. Well, either she breaks or I do because that issue is going to be resolved tonight. I refuse to leave here without removing Ruby Bennett from my mind. Sex will certainly do that, one and done—better said, one more and done—it'll be all I require to flush her out of my system.

I should've never rented to her or been at that hotel.

When was the last time a woman caught my interest this quickly?

Never. Not even…

With the women I've slept with, it was a matter of learning to love the person, or it was purely a relationship of mutual convenience. That first sight—first love—bullshit wasn't for me and never will be. There's no such thing as once upon a time we met, fell in love, and lived bloody happily-ever-fucking-after. Then why am I so affected by this lass before me?

Simple, because she's hot and I'm a connoisseur of mind blowing sex and all things involving sexy women.

Something I said makes her snap and she shoves into me. Ruby's less than an inch away from my face, breathing heavily against my skin. She is so close it wouldn't take much movement for me to lean in and kiss her. The idea is appealing and might've been worth her wrath for trying if it wasn't for the deadly look on her face. I don't move a muscle. There's a fire sweltering in her eyes, the yellow and copper sparks flying around them tell me to stay the hell put.

"Don't. Ever. Call. Me. That. Again! You fucking entitled, overinflated, egotistical jerk! Who the *fuck* do you think you are? You don't know shit about me, aside from what my application told you. How can you judge me?" She's yelling so hard, red blotches creep up her neck and onto her cheeks. No one else seems to notice her flipping out on me, though, everyone's too drunk to care.

The same way she's been dismissing me all night, I'll do the same to her and disregard her question.

Mr. Entitled and whatever other ridiculous names she used to describe me, never explains himself and always needs to get his way.

Payback's a bitch, *Miss high-and-mighty.*

This time, when my internal beast knocks, I don't fight against it. I allow him to claw his way out of his cage, and let him loose on the damned woman.

Have at her.

I reach for her face, grasping it between my hands and she freezes, surprised by my reaction—*I guess*—but it doesn't stop me. My mouth crushes hers with such force from a hunger and a desire I haven't felt in a very long time.

Maybe even ever.

The moment our lips touch, shock courses through me and my heart pounds profusely.

It feels as good as it was the other night, maybe even better this time.

Her kiss nourishes and fills my malnutritioned veins with the sustenance they seem to be lacking.

How can this be possible?

It's not. The liquor in my system is providing false advertising and giving me the impression Ruby has more to offer than a great roll in the sack. She's too uptight to be '*bring home to mom*' material or anything more substantial than sex.

If that's the case, then why is my mouth still glued onto hers?

Because it *feels* too damn good. Her lips are like plush, lickable, and suckable pillows of cotton candy. How can my dick be hard as a rock, all from a kiss?

Although, it did get hard from mere images of her. He has a mind of his own, I suppose.

She's not pulling away or slapping me in the face like I predicted her doing, instead, she's clawing at my shirt, my face, chest, and anything else she can get her hands on. Wrapping my arms around her body, I guide us into the men's bathroom and lock the door behind me.

Guess I'm not the only one who's hungry...

The only difference for me is once I've let myself loose, I'm unable to rein the beast back in. He's too famished and my mind is too muddled at this point. Lacking any sense of control or common sense, I slam her against the wall. All my sexual aggression coming out at once, I tear part of her shirt open, exposing her glorious cleavage. At the sight of her smooth olive skin, I no longer contain myself from the need to caress them.

"Oh God!" Ruby moans.

The sounds of her pleasure push me over the edge and I continue my assault. Sucking on her neck, I make sure to leave a mark, then slowly I move back to her lips, nipping and biting the whole way up.

We're lost in each other, scrambling to touch, kiss, or grasp something—*anything*. She pulls at my shirt and I still her arms.

I want the focus on her, not me.

"Not so entitled am I now?" I growl into her ear.

"Even more so," She snarls back and bites down on my bottom lip.

Fuck! It's even hotter this time around. The aggression was missing.

My dick twitches for more and as if she felt it, she bites down again.

"Fuck yeah, *princess*!" As soon as I utter the words her onslaught abruptly stops, forcing me to open my eyes. Staring directly into hers, I notice something in them that wasn't there before.

Fear.

"I have to go." She fumbles with the lock while holding the torn pieces of her shirt together. After a second try, she dashes out of the bathroom, leaving me standing here like a fucking chump with a hard dick.

Goddamn it! What is wrong with her?

As brusquely as whatever this was started, it ended even quicker. Only to leave me hungrier than before.

I had but a tiny taste of her.

How is such a minuscule amount enough to feed my beast?

It's not. Need more.

There's no more... It's done. She's run off... She doesn't

want me.

She's one and done with me.

Which doesn't suit me at all! And what am I supposed to do with this horny, alcohol induced, adrenaline coursing through me?

Give chase, dumbass.

Bolting out of the bathroom, I do just that. She couldn't have gotten very far since she walked here.

Within seconds, I find her stumbling through the parking lot. "Wait!"

"No. Go away. *Please*," she begs.

"Why are you running away?" Catching up to Ruby in a few strides, I steady my pace to match hers.

"I'm not."

"Yes, you are. Am I *that* unappealing?" I tease, knowing that's impossible. I appeal to every gender.

She freezes and then faces me. "That's exactly the problem. I felt nothing when you kissed me or even when you touched me. So why waste my time?" With a roll of her eyes and a shrug, she proceeds to shove past me.

I grab her arm, twirling her back to me before she can escape. We're closer than before, face to face and nose to nose. Our bodies collide with such force we're panting. My body's hot for her all over again, heat rises, and emanates from my very being.

This woman is beauty in its harshest form.

We say nothing for a few minutes, merely stand in the middle of this full parking lot with our gazes fixed on each other. Questions, concerns, fears, and desires passing between the connection. The moment seems to never end until she opens her mouth to speak, but I cut her off with mine, in need of another taste.

I don't need. I want. I'll never need a woman or anything from a woman again.

Ruby pulls away swiftly with a shove to my chest. "How many times do I have to tell you? You're not my type. That night changes nothing! It meant nothing to me, so stick to your job and only be my landlord." She looks down at her feet and kicks an imaginary rock. "I gotta go."

Before she can stagger off, I clutch her hand once more. "One day that sophisticated attitude will be wiped off of you and all that'll be left is the scared girl cowering behind a wall she's built." I lift her chin so she can look directly at me to *see* what I'm saying, hoping it'll sink into her young mind. "I am not blind or stupid, Ruby, so don't play me for a fool. And when you grow up and are ready for an adult relationship, *Princess*, let me know. But if all you want are quick fucks? Then say so. Don't pretend. *Stop* pretending. You might be new here, but life works the same across the world. Grow a set and quit running. I don't need to know shit about you to see what's written all over your face."

Her bright amber eyes are bursting with questioning tears. "Wh—What... is?"

"Grief. Fear. Stubbornness. Pain. And most of all... anger."

"You're wrong, Maeson. So wrong in fact, you can't even notice when a woman is playing you." That mischievous smile reappears on her face. All signs of the woman I described is gone—vanished into thin air—leaving behind the sexy one who danced her drunk ass on a bar like she didn't have a care in the world.

Her words strike me like a knife slicing through my gut. "That's the game you want to play, *princess*? Game the fuck on. Have a nice night." I turn my back on her and this time it's my turn to leave her to standing there looking like the idiot.

"Don't call me that," she mutters.

I refuse to weaken and turn around. She's a big girl who had no problem in hurting me with words so, she should be able to handle mine.

She's drunk, has no car, is alone, will have to walk a good ten to twenty minutes back home by herself in the dark, and you're okay with leaving her?

Yes, damn it! Fuck, this had to be the instant my conscience decides to come out and play? "Ruby?" When I face her, she's standing in the same spot. She hasn't moved and inch.

Her body sways side to side. "You're still here? Go home already." She giggles then frowns.

Bi-polar much?

"Let me take you back to the complex." Pulling out my phone, I open the application for Uber and request a pickup. I might be drunk, but I'm not senseless. I know exactly how it will look to Ruby if I left her out here all by herself.

Cool, calm, assertive, and most important chivalrous Maeson is back and in business.

* * *

WHEN THE FIRST WEEK PASSED and I didn't hear from Ruby, I chalked it up to her feeling too ashamed to face me for a little while.

When a second week went by with no sign of her, I started to worry, but Molly assured me she was fine and swamped with *things* to do. So, that kept me in check for a while. Stopping me from making any moves in hopes that at some point—maybe sooner than later—she'd come around looking for another shot with me.

How pathetic I've become. Salivating like a starving dog, for what? Hopes of a few crumbs being tossed my way?

I can have the pick of any damn litter, literally, any and all, but somehow, I'm stuck on this random one?

Well, looks like my pathetic gene gets worse. It's officially been three whole fucking weeks since I last saw her and I'm going crazy. I'm even prepared to act on my plan b. I've given her a chance to come around and that was obviously worthless. Why I even have *another* plan boggles my mind. I'm working too hard for a measly cause.

A woman.

All because why? She presents a challenge and it's been a long time since I had one, that's why.

It's the only logical reason I can come up with.

Ruby's crowded the fuck out of my brain, I'm having a

difficult time thinking about anything else which doesn't involve her *highness*.

I'm royally fucked!

I try to convince myself I crave her so much because she's only given me a tiny slice when I wanted the whole damn pie.

Sex—it's always going to be about the sex and nothing more.

Picking up the receiver on my desk phone, I dial Molly's extension. "Hey, Mo." Not giving her a chance to respond, or even answer the phone properly, I continue. "Can you handle it on your own for the rest of the day? I have something I need to take care of." I keep my tone leveled and as monotone as possible, not wanting to give my intentions away. Molly has this freaky ability to read people, even by their damn voice through a phone.

"You got it, boss man. Date tonight?"

"Nope. Business."

"Liar. Well, *whoever* the lucky woman is, make it worth her time, *Mae Mae*." She teases.

Damn it, she knows!

I laugh, "I'll do my best, *Molly Ann Briggs*." Using her full name pisses her off and it's exactly why I do it, exactly like she uses my abhorrent nickname, *Mae Mae*.

Blah!

I shake my head and hang up the phone, all the while Molly's bitching in the background.

Serves her right for using the name I hate all the damn time!

Back to this business at hand. Three weeks is more than enough time and space for Ruby to grow a set, right?

Well, ready or not, I'm coming. It's time to face the facts, Ruby Bennett.

There's a pull between us I refuse to ignore, even though she might want to. I won't even entertain the idea of not getting what I desire. No matter how tense and superior she might be it doesn't deter me from...

Wanting her.

-13-

Ruby

THREE GLORIOUS CAREFREE—*PROBLEM FREE*—weeks have gone by and I feel renewed, refreshed, and reawakened. Almost a month of deciding what to do, when I want to do it, and how to has been such an eye opener for me. There was so much I missed out on and never knew how fun life is or can be.

When I decided to move here, I was terrified—scratch that, petrified—about not knowing anyone or being able to adjust to a whole new city that's nothing like Manhattan. They're polar opposites in fact, although, that hasn't been an issue for me so far. The people I've had the pleasure of meeting are pleasant and accepting individuals.

Most recently, I've made friends with another woman, Sammie. When I met her, I assumed she was my age or younger, but I was wrong. She's thirty-three years old and the actual owner of Crossroads—not an employed waitress as I initially believed. Her father passed away a few years ago, leaving everything to her, including the bar.

The day after I went a little crazy in her establishment, I felt so terrible and went back to help with clean up. Unfortunately, by the time my hungover brain could process the what's and who's it's from the night before, it was too late, everything was cleared out and spotless. So, I did what most hungover people do at two in the afternoon...

Drink some more and continue the damn party.

I ended up spending several hours with Sammie and the bartender, who I now know as Rebekka—Bekka for short. The bar didn't open till later, so it was the three of us drinking, laughing, and acting like three best friends who've known each other for years.

When I learned that Molly's known them for three years and hangs out there often, we invited her to join our private bash.

That day will forever remain with me. It was the first time I'd ever been that content and relaxed. No worries of being home on time, making dinner for an asshole, or simply pissing someone off for not doing something their way.

A day made for me and only me.

I've gone back a couple of times in the past few weeks for a drink or two, but nothing like the first night. It's become part of my schedule now. My down time at Crossroads keeps me going, keeps whatever sliver of hope I have left flourishing within my soul.

I know, I have yet to acknowledge the big bad elephant in the room, and I don't plan to just yet. I'm not ready.

That elephant tramples my mind day and night without my permission, but how does one stop that?

It's a subconscious thing, I guess.

I've developed too many different impressions of the man. Nothing written stone, though, no final decision has been made on my like or dislike of him. He's too complicated.

Is he sexy as hell? Yes!

Is he an upper-class asshole? Hell yes!

Is he kind? How would I know, he hasn't shown me any kindness!

It all comes down to him being more than the regular run of

the mill hot guy. He has this ridiculous ability to fry every nerve in my mind and body with one kiss.

ONE DAMN KISS!

Like that ever happens in real life?

Never.

I'm blaming it on the many problems racing through my head on a daily basis. The drinking habit which seems to be evolving, the night at the hotel, and then there's my inability to be alone for too long. The need to be surrounded be people sickens me. Why can't I be happy living my life all alone?

Maybe because ever since I was ten, I've technically been alone the entire time.

True contact with another human being is what I miss, what I crave, and what I need more than ever. My mother was the last person to provide that and everyone else couldn't give two shits about me.

Keep friends close... I didn't have any, so I couldn't.

Keep enemies closer... I had plenty, so I did and almost died.

I should've kept *every single* person that crossed my path at an arm's length, given that my foster home was absolute shit and my ex-boyfriend was a mess and a half. My one night stands meant nothing—including the one with a person who shall not be named. They were all an escape in passing.

But that's all behind me now.

Think positive. Deep Breath.

I do have those rare moments when looking forward to something better that sparks filled with bits of hope and promise appear. My landlord aside, everything has been going great. There is a real chance for me to make lasting friendships here.

Now, back to that elephant...

He is the kind of challenge I want to run far, far away from but don't know how. Maeson's too alluring for a ravenous woman like me. The desire to acquire all of the things I never had is too strong since I've found out what independence tastes like.

It tastes like him.

If that's the case, then why does he bring out an urge to get the hell away from him? Maybe because my mind flashes *'DANGER'* the instant I lay my eyes on him.

Danger my ass. I won't let him get close enough… again.

I already did. It's the only way to explain why what he said to me almost a month ago still bothers me.

Even though I was drunk off my ass that night, I remember every word—well until I passed out in the Uber. They stayed with me this whole time, running on a repeated cycle nightly before I fall asleep.

Am I that transparent?

* * *

TODAY HAS TURNED OUT TO be one of those putz around, do nothing but binge-watch Orange is the New Black, and stuff my face with potato chips. These are the small things people take for granted, where someone like me cherishes them.

When I motivate myself enough to get off the couch, it's already dark, and too late to go anywhere. Spotting a few unopened bags by the elevator, I finish unpacking them and begin a much needed, full-on cleanup of the apartment.

It ends up taking me almost two more hours to finish tidying up and settle into bed. I plump up my pillow and get perfectly comfortable when I hear the elevator ding. My eyes pop open and I lay frozen.

Who in the world is here? It's nine o'clock! And I haven't given anyone my extra key fob, either.

Tiptoeing from the bedroom to the living room, I pick up the closest thing to a weapon I can find. A roll of paper towels.

Great. I'm saving myself with freaking paper towels?

I pause at the end of the hallway and listen for movement. Heavy footsteps echo on the hardwood floors.

Shit, shit! Someone's in here! So much for fuckity, fuck security.

"I have a weapon!" I shriek and hold the so-called weapon in front of me.

More footsteps, bumps, and muffled cursing have me cowering against the wall. My heart thumps harshly inside my chest and it takes me a good minute to gather enough courage to take a step forward and peek out. There is no one visible within the darkness. "Who is here? Show yourself, I have a gun and I called 9-1-1!" I steady myself against the wall and listen.

No answer and all movements have stopped.

I'm going to die. This is the end.

My hands tremble and I hold my breath, trying to catch any sound that will give the creeper's location away. Nothing.

"Molly?" I hesitate. "Mo? Is that you messing with me?" Widening my stance and crouching, I'm in full attack mode, bracing my body against the expected assault. I can take it, I'm sure I've had worse beatings.

"No." A deep man's voice carries from the open living area off the kitchen.

I stiffen. "Who... are... you?"

"Maeson."

The voice and name calm me instantly and I harshly release the breath I've been holding. My legs shake as I amble further into the room and turn on a lamp.

I'm no longer scared... I'm nervous.

There he stands in a crisp black suit with his hands in his pockets, all glorious and confident. Fucker is so cocky, with his perfect damn hair neatly slicked back, and his smug face sporting a sly shit-eating grin.

"Shit! What the hell is wrong with you? Fucking psycho! You scared the shit out of me! I almost killed you!" The words spill out in a violent rush, my voice rising hysterically.

His eyes rake over my body. "Really? With what?" He focuses on what's in my hands and laughs. "Oh, I see, paper towels? Man, I'd better call next time, could've lost a body part." His grin widens into a full smile as he covers his man bits.

Dimples. All I want.... ummm... see are dimples and luscious kissable lips.

My mind turns into mush and I have to force myself to snap

out of it as my mouth waters. I shut down the visions flicking through my mind immediately. "Your sarcasm isn't welcome in my home, especially after you break in!"

Can it be breaking in if it's your landlord? Hell yeah, it is. No permission to enter has been given!

He's still zoned in on my body and I follow his searing gaze. My low cut, tight, short, and skimpy gray ribbed cotton jumper comes into view and I instantly try to cover up. It's so hot I picked the thinnest thing I own without being fully naked. Now I regret my choice of barely there pajamas.

He's too close, taking up too much space and I back up a few steps, hitting the edge of my couch. I'm blocked in, I can't escape him or that starved look.

"I did not break in. I have a keycard and know the security code. I'm more of an..." He pauses and smoothly continues. "uninvited guest." His eyebrow quirks up and he folds his arms across his massive chest.

I cross my own, remembering my overly exposed breasts. "Well, un-invite your ass out of here. I'm going to bed." I plop on the couch and tuck my knees up, wrapping my arms around them.

"Nice pjs." His eyes focus on my bared legs.

I shiver and shift from his unrelenting gaze. Pulling at the fabric, I attempt to cover more than half of an ass cheek, but it's impossible. "Thanks. Untraditional attire for one like you, I bet. That tie *must* be suffocating." I roll my eyes and put my legs down, feeling way too exposed.

He yanks his tie, loosening it. "Oh. It *is*." He glares at me as he rubs his neck.

"Right. So, why are you here? A call or text would've been nice." Considering how much rent I pay you'd think it would include privacy!

"I would say the same for you. Been waiting to hear from you after... Crossroads. Never did."

"Oh please! You insult me and you want a response to that? Well, here it is... fuck you!"

His brow lifts and a predatory glint appears in his eyes. One I recognize far too well. My breath catches as a sexy grin appears on his face. He moves a few steps closer, his hands casually stuffed in his pockets. The way his eyes rove over me from head to toe makes my mouth go dry.

"Anytime... princess." His voice is soft, dripping over me like warm honey.

I gulp, and look away. "Hardy-har-har, funny man. Not happening. Once was more than enough." Glancing at him, I raise my own brow. "Spill. Why are you here? Rents not due yet and last time I checked landlords don't do house calls to collect."

"Aye, I do... for certain beautiful tenants." His accent tinged words excite me.

Oddly, instead of being creeped out by his uninvited intrusion and clearly suggestive words, I'm intrigued and aroused. I shouldn't be surprised since I know exactly what he feels like, how his lips feel against my body, and how—

Stop!

I cross my arms and lean back, keeping my tone casual. "Smooth one, aren't you?" This conversation is going nowhere fast. He needs to go, and I need a drink. Or five.

Maeson shrugs. "I try. Is it working?" He takes in the space around us when I don't immediately respond. "Looks good in here. Lots of color. Not exactly what I was expecting."

"Like you, Mr. Alexander, know me well enough to expect anything? I hardly believe a one night stand and a background check informs you of my favorite colors or decor preferences."

"You're right. I apologize. I'm not judging and I'm sorry for scaring you by showing up unannounced. I just... wanted to speak to you privately and try to start over. Our first few run-ins didn't go... *well*." He hangs his head, gazing at his shoes.

So, he does have a conscience alongside that big fat ego.

His words relax me a smidgen and I lean into the cushions, forgetting all about my outfit. "Thank you for the apology, it's accepted. And no, none of this went as I planned either. My life has been uprooted and the last thing I expected was to unknowingly sleep with my landlord who also happens to be a sophisticated asshole. I was excited about the move until I met you."

Maeson sighs and his eyes meet mine, regret clouding them. "I never meant to make you feel that way and you haven't given me the slightest of chances either." He closes his eyes for a moment, inhales, and exhales, using the same technique I use to calm my overbearing nerves. His gaze is darker now, exactly like at the hotel. "You caught me off guard too, you know? I didn't expect to see you there that night, but when I did? I recognized you right away from your license picture and I couldn't help myself. There is something about you..." He trails off.

I'm not falling for any of those things he's saying, they mean nothing to me.

Words. Are. Useless.

"I didn't know I was supposed to give you any chances? We weren't supposed to see each other again. Then when you appeared on move-in day, you acted like you've never seen me before, like I wasn't even worth your fucking precious time. So, all I did was return the sentiments. Now here I am, not looking for anything, yet here *you* are, pushing yourself into my life. And for what reason? I haven't the slightest clue, other than we had sex *once*, mind you—a month ago." While I speak, I envision our half naked bodies slapping against each other, hear our moans of pleasure, and I shake my head. There must be a way to rid my brain of the memory. "Look, I respect you as my landlord, but anything more is not acceptable for me. I don't do emotions, so, I'll keep my space—as I have been doing—and you keep yours."

"First of all, *you* acted like I was a piece of shit on the bottom of your shoe. I was the one returning the sentiment, not the other way around. I knew I'd see you that day, was even hoping we could talk afterward, but you were the one pretending like we never met before. So, I assumed you didn't want to discuss it. All *I* did was follow your lead, so don't blame me for *your* misunderstanding." He frowns and his forehead creases, confusion is written all over his face. "How can you possibly *not* want me again? Was the sex not as good as you led me to believe?"

Of course it was, but I'm not going to admit that.

Shrugging, I feign boredom. "Mediocre at best. Don't look so shocked, you're no God. I've sure as hell had better, with even better-looking men. Regardless of what happened—*or didn't*—the next day, ultimately, you were a means to pass time. That is all, Maeson."

"Fuck. That. Shit." He growls and moves to sit next to me, but checks himself. "You're lying through your teeth. You wanted me so bad we didn't even get fully naked!"

I huff and throw my hands in the air. "Bullshit! You couldn't wait long enough to fuck me, let alone get undressed. So, Mr. Alexander, who wanted who more?" I raise an eyebrow and smirk, knowing it was him *not* me.

"Technicalities and different point of views here. Either way, we both wanted it to happen and it did. You're the one acting like it didn't and to go even further that you didn't enjoy it!"

"What does it matter anyway? It was a one-time thing, damn it! I won't let you wiggle your way into my life over a mediocre—*at best*—one night stand." I watch him for a moment before I speak again. He looks defeated, confused, and surprised by my words. And that's when comprehension strikes. "You can't handle that, can you? You don't understand how it's freaking possible for a woman like me not to desire more from you. Well listen up, *bucko*—I am not one of your fancy little whores you like to prance around with! This girl"—I point to myself— "doesn't need to hang around on a man's shoulder to make herself feel better. This girl knows, better than most, that men only make a woman's life worse. You, *my friend*, expected to find this young and innocent woman who believes in fairy tales? One who could easily be swept off her feet with your shiny armor and those run-of-the-mill charms of yours, but guess what? This girl isn't the one you were hoping for. That privileged life you assume I've lived? I didn't, so fuck off!" My fingers are trembling. Every emotion conceivable smolders through me.

That's enough!

This conversation is getting too deep and I'm in need of a drink now. I lift myself off the couch, bypassing Maeson on my way to the fridge. With a quick scan of the freezer, I spot what I'm searching for. A chilled bottle of Grey Goose.

Deep breath. Don't let him get to you.

I'm fighting so hard not to let myself relive what he made me feel that night, otherwise, I *will* fall victim to those dimples, and to everything else this man is offering. I'm not stupid, I can *see* how good looking he is. He's even great in bed—*better than great*—and he has the power to reel me in if I let him.

Which I won't!

"Am I bringing you to drink?" His forehead crinkles and a dimpled smile spreads across his face.

He needs to stop that shit, like right now.

Grabbing a tall glass from the cabinet and setting it on the counter, I pour the clear liquid in generously. "You sure are." I exchange one bottle for another.

"Apple juice? Really? And what's that?" He walks over to watch me with those sexy green eyes, which are full of interest.

He's changing the subject, fine by me. We don't have to speak on it anymore. His insecurities are his own, they may be clear as day, but I won't be the one to shove them in his face again— unless he pushes me to it. Having my own and not being able to face them is hard enough, let alone when someone points them out consistently.

Damn it, he makes me think too much!

Then there is the problem of ignoring the pull to be nearer to him when he's so close to me, nonetheless, I do my best and continue the task at hand. Adding a splash of juice into the drink, I nod at the bottle filled with red syrupy liquid. "It's Grenadine." I mix it in as well. "It's delicious so don't knock it till you try it." My tone comes out cocky and defensive, mimicking the same exact way I am feeling right now. Rounding the kitchen counter,

I hand the finished beverage to him. "Here, one sip is all you get, only to prove my point, and the rest is mine."

He takes a sip and peers into the glass swirling it around. "Not bad. Never been a girly drink guy but this"—Another sip—"Is very good."

Watching him swallow then seductively lick the rim of the glass, invites more unwanted visions… of him licking… me…

Clear your head. Clear. Clear. Delete. Memories. Delete.

"Okay, that's enough." Grabbing the tumbler from his hold, I practically inhale my concoction. The slight burn of it centers me enough to dismiss the crap in my head. "I call it the Ruby Apple." My confidence rises and I give him a cheeky grin. "It's my very own blend."

"Well, if I owned a bar, I'd add it to the menu."

"I don't think it's *that* good. But thanks." Pouring myself another, I take a large drink and find the liquid slides down my throat too easily this time. Either I'm too focused on Maeson or after so much use it no longer affects me.

"It *is* that good." He raises my empty glass, demonstrating his point.

I bow my head appreciatively. "Glad you like it. However, your subject change didn't go unnoticed—which is fine by me, no need to go any further—but why else did you come here unannounced, and so late for that matter?"

"I told you, to apologize and ask for another chance. Nothing more. If I could go back, I would've called or texted, but I didn't want you to deny me a visit." He removes his glasses and uses his sleeve to wipe at his brow. "Why the bloody hell don't you have the air-conditioning on?"

Hot, isn't it? Exactly why I'm almost naked.

"Let's get two things straight. First, I don't know how to use the damn thing, it's too fancy, and has too many buttons. Somehow, I made it stop working and now since you're here? Fix it!" I wag a finger at him, my frustration rising. "The second thing? I'm not a pretentious princess as you seem to like to call me. If you wanted to come by you should've asked and I would've welcomed a damn visit. What I don't welcome is my landlord being a creeper who breaks into my apartment. I need my home to be safe and now you've made it seem very unsafe!" I turn from him, scuffling to the windows, and let the view of this beautiful city calm me. I can barely breathe with him around. "Like I said, space... give it to me. And if you need something, say so."

Deep breath. Pretending to be fine with him around is harder than I thought.

"You're right. I'm sorry, it'll never happen again." His voice is barely a whisper, coming from right behind me. "And I'll fix it before I leave, even teach you how to use it properly. But, until then, I don't mind seeing your half naked sweaty body. You said if I need something to say so... well, I wouldn't mind..." He doesn't finish his sentence but I get the drift.

Not happening. This man must've lost his damn marbles. Comment ignored.

I don't move a muscle. He's so close, I can sense the heat radiating from his body. "How many times must I say it? Back off, it's hot enough already and you're crowding me."

Is it him crowding you that's the problem? Or you liking it too much?

I roll my eyes and curse my damn over active brain.

He doesn't say anything but he moves away. Self-assurance brims inside of me. Even though my ass is exposed before him, the self-doubt I normally have about my body vanished the moment he showed up here so, I let him get a good eye full before I face him. "Have you seen enough?"

His eyes bulge and he clears his throat. "Oh aye, I have."

The attraction to him is inevitable, he's sexy as hell and I can only deny it for so long. Nevertheless, I'm going to fight against it. He's dangerous to someone with an addictive personality and Maeson meets one of the three addictions I currently have— falling for the wrong kind of man.

With Ray, I fell fast and hard but broke even faster and harder. Who's to say that won't happen tenfold when a good-looking man crosses my path? Like the one before me, Maeson

L Alexander.

I wonder what the L stands for.

"Well, that's good, because it's the last look you'll ever get." I stroll past him toward the elevator. "Now it's time for you to go. My inclination to host the person who broke into my home has diminished, fine sir. I bid you a good night." I laugh inwardly as I motion toward the exit.

I bet that's how he and his stuffy rich friends talk all the time.

"What about your air-conditioning?"

"Tomorrow is a new day. Send someone else to take care of it." Wrapping my arms around my chest, I try to appear stern and ice-cold like he usually is.

He bends at the hip and smiles deeply. "I'll refrain from doing this again. Good night, Ruby lass."

The doors close and his last words linger in mind.

Lass? Who says Lass?

* * *

THE NEXT FEW DAYS FLEW by, each one more relaxing than the next. All I did was lounge by the pool, go shopping, hang out with my new girlfriends, and explored the massive grounds.

Today my procrastination ends along with my mini vacation of enjoying life again. The fun stuff has been put on hold for real-life objectives, such as the important phone calls that need to be made.

But first, I want to find out what Molly's doing and see if we can get together. I'm in need of some advice and she'd be more familiar with what I'm looking for and could point me in the right direction. I tap her name on my phone, it rings once and she picks up.

"Hey! You busy?"

"Nope, I'm off today. Had a couple of errands to run. Why? What's up?"

"Nothing much. Think you could come over and help me out with a few things?"

"Sure, I'll be there in an hour, *if* I don't get stuck in traffic." She laughs, knowing she will as the route from downtown Dallas to Allen is nothing but traffic.

"Sounds good. I'll be here."

A little over an hour later, Molly arrives with a bunch of bags in tow.

"What *is* all that?" My mouth drops at the sight.

Molly looks like she's going to collapse, there are four big bags filled to the brim on one arm and another four on the other. "A housewarming gift. A little late—I know—but you've been here what…" She looks up at the ceiling and puckers her lips, pondering the date. "Holy shit! Over a month and I'm just getting to this! What a bad friend!" Molly laughs and drops everything on the couch with a humph once she's freed from them.

My heart wants to explode in my chest.

No one's ever done that for me before.

She hardly knows me, yet was thoughtful enough to get me a gift. The surprise is probably written across my face, but I don't hide it, even though it might clue her in on how special this gesture is to me. "You didn't have to do that! Really Mo… I… have no words. Your friendship is more than enough!" I stride over to her and do what I normally would never do—pull her into a hug.

She embraces me, then swiftly pulls away, dashing to the bags with excitement. "Don't thank me yet, wait till you see the goodies!"

In the first three, there are all sorts of colorful pillows and in another one is a comforter set—sheets and all—that matches them.

"Wow! Look at all that pink, yellow, lavender, and green! I love the combo, so cheerful!" Picking up the bright fabric, I admire its beauty and how perfect it would look in my bedroom. "I love it, Mo! Thank you!" I move to hug her again and she stops me, holding out a hand.

"Wait! There is more!" She giggles, brimming with childlike

excitement.

If she loves giving gifts this much, what's she like when she receives them?

From the remaining shopping bags, she pulls out turquoise bathroom towels in all sorts of sizes and a few brown ones as an accent color. She even went as far as buying the matching shower curtain. Once all the items are displayed across the floor and the couch, I take them all in and am floored by how gracious Molly is.

"You... didn't have to do any of this. It must've cost you a fortune. Those sheets are pure Egyptian cotton!" Just thinking about how expensive these things are and how she spent it on me—a person she met only last month, causes me to choke up a little.

"It's nothing truly. I wanted you to have these things, every girl needs a touch of color in her bathroom and bedroom. Not that all this red and black isn't killing it, but... maybe a little less... dungeon sex room and a little more... PINK!" She explodes with laughter.

Molly's laugh is contagious and I join her. "I'm guessing that's *your* favorite color?"

"You know it!" She gathers up the bedroom items and points to the bathroom ones. "You like them?"

"Yes! Everything is beautiful! Thank you so much!" I help her gather the rest and motion for her to follow me. "Let's put them away and then we can sit and chat."

It takes us a few minutes, then we settle down on the sectional. Molly's leaning against the pillows, facing me with a huge smile on her face.

"What's on your mind, Smiles?" I tease.

"Oh, nothing, just glad you like your presents! I was worried you'd hate them." Her grin widens further.

"I couldn't hate any gift! If you'd have put thought and effort into a making me a simple 'Welcome to Town' card, I would've loved that as well. Price, color, and item aren't what matters, it's the person who cared enough to give the gift."

"True!" The smile lingers on her lips for a moment longer before she speaks again. "So, what did you need help with?"

"Oh, that! I almost forgot!" Leaning forward, I grab the notepad laying on the ottoman. "There are a few things I'm in need of. First, is a good lawyer. Searching online was useless. All of their websites claim how amazing their work is and narrowing it down was nearly impossible."

"Search no more my friend, I have one to recommend." She reaches for my notepad and pen. "He's a great guy. I've used his services a few times, so I can vouch for him." Molly jots down his name then looks up at me, squinting as if thinking hard. "Ugh. Left my phone in the car, I don't know his number by heart, but search his name online, he'll come up there."

"Okay, and if I have trouble, I'll call you." I smile and look down at her scribbles. "Axel Don—Donovan? Your chicken scratch is terrible!"

"I know and it's too late to fix now, but yes that's him!"

"Perfect, thanks! What about a hairdresser and a nail place? Any suggestions there? This is the bad thing about moving away, starting over might have its positives, except when it comes to these sorts of changes."

"Oh, I bet! I couldn't do it. Born and raised here, I'll probably die here because change isn't something I enjoy at all. Shit, even the idea of rearranging my furniture freaks me out!" She shivers, proving her point. "But, yeah, I know of a few great places for some spa treatments, hair, and nails. I'll add them to your list." As she's writing them down, her hand freezes mid-way. "Women's shelters?" she whispers.

Shit. I forgot to change the page to a blank one.

My whole body tenses up, how could I forget the list I had on there! "I'm going to volunteer. I want to give back to the community." I shrug, making it appear like it's not a big deal.

Molly's eyes widen in surprise. "Oh! Wow, that's a very good samaritan thing of you to do! For a second, I was worried you needed… help… that kind of help."

"Nope. Not for me, at all. I'm fine," I choose my words

carefully and wave it off.

"Well, good for you! That's a great thing to do, those women can use all the help they can get." She's smiling again and her voice is laced with something resembling pride.

"Yes, they can." I smile back and the muscles in my body relax.

Catastrophe averted.

Molly sits and stretches. "Alright, doll. I should get going. I have a few more things to do before I head home."

"Okay, thank you for the gifts and the suggestions! I'll text you later, let you know how that lawyer works out."

Once the elevator doors close behind Molly, I let out a harsh breath.

I was so close to having to explain more than I'm ready to at this point.

Opening my laptop, I search for the name Molly provided me—Axel Donovan. A few articles come up along with his website.

Many wins, few losses in court.

A plus.

Big time women rights supporter.

Big plus.

Family Law, specialty.

Perfect!

Tapping the number into my phone, I hit the little green button and hear the first ring. I hang up.

What am I going to say? He's going to ask me questions. He's going to want to know why.

And I'm going to tell him. I'm going to grow some balls and tell him everything, so he understands, so he can help me to best of his ability. Lawyers, like doctors, are bound by the law to keep their mouths shut.

It's all going to work out, right?

My subconscious is as unsure as I am, but I won't give up hope, not for one second.

It's not over until it's over.

* * *

YESTERDAY IT TOOK ME THREE tries until I let the phone ring long enough for someone to answer at the lawyer's office. And I'm glad I did. We had a very long conversation, and he seemed kind and caring. Not one ounce of judgment came through his voice while I spilled my life story—even when I broke down crying a few times. He didn't rush me so he could get off of the phone, instead, he urged me to keep going. It was odd to talk, and talk, and talk without thinking, letting everything out at once.

Poor guy had to listen to it all and he doesn't even know me!

This morning wasn't as overwhelming when I made calls to a few women's shelters in the area and found one nearby that I could offer volunteer work to. Now, everything I had on my most recent to do list is crossed out and my life is starting to fall into place.

Only one thing left, and I've been anxiously waiting for the time to arrive—the appointment with my lawyer. After hearing me out for about two hours, he agreed to meet me right away— literally the next day. Axel Donovan gave me the impression he understood from a personal point of view. Other people listen and agree with distance in their tone, but not him... He had empathy in his. Making him the perfect fit for the lawyer to assist me further in my endeavors.

At this point, I have about one hour to get ready and meet him outside in the courtyard. Choosing an outfit will most likely take me that entire time because the ridiculously warm weather doesn't allow for my usual jeans. I scour my closet for something to accommodate the damn heat, and I end up picking a pair of royal blue Bermuda shorts, a white V-neck t-shirt, and royal blue flip flops.

Good thing I got my toes done recently at that salon Molly suggested. They were a mess!

The walk through the courtyard is a short one and I spot the silver-haired man in a well-cut gray suit, carrying a briefcase.

Google is amazing at everything, even finding a picture of the man I spent maybe too much time speaking to and am currently approaching. "Hello, Mr. Donovan."

The handsome, older man stands and extends his hand. "Please call me Axel or Ax."

My lips quirk into a playful smile. "Axel, then." The man is a total fox, and my heart speeds up as I take him in.

So much for all lawyers being old and boring.

"Please sit, Ruby." He gestures to the stone bench. "We have much to discuss. Where would you like to start?" His eyes glide across my body before coming back to my face.

Our eyes meet briefly, and jolt from the connection shocks me entirely. I force myself to break the contact. My palms are damp, and not just because it's hot out here. Covertly I swipe them across my shorts. "Well... I have one main concern. The... uh... charities need to be set up as soon as possible." I try not to stare at him, keeping my gaze focused on the notepad in his hands.

Men here are different than the ones I've encountered in the past, the southern charm which accompanies them is unsettling. Even the way they smile at me and the hungry look in their eyes is more noticeable.

Especially the older ones like Axel have shown an unexpected interest in me. Could it simply be my imagination? Maeson's attention is unmistakable, his desire openly reflected in his eyes and in his actions. Axel's much subtler, and it doesn't bring the same raw emotion to the surface, but the undercurrent is there, and I'm unsure how to react.

I must be utterly desperate; he's too old for me and about to become my lawyer. Damn it, keep it professional!

"Alright. From our phone conversation and the documents you emailed me last night, I understand one will be a foundation for children in the foster care system?"

"Yes exactly. They need someone. Those homes are not always what they seem." I pull out my copy of the folder containing the outline of my plan so I can follow along and take notes.

"Very true. And the other is for women's shelters?"

"Right. We could categorize it all under abuse victims, but I would like them to be funded separately."

We spent the next twenty minutes or so discussing the plan in more detail, and Axel recorded the extra information. Our conversation somehow veered off to explaining my past to him and that is when his whole demeanor started to change.

"Alright. Now that I know more information." Axel looks down, skimming the contents of the paperwork and nods. "And this is your vision, we'll do it exactly how you'd like." He pauses, a small furrow appearing between his brows. "Are you really thinking about volunteering?"

"I am." Crossing my arms, I lift my chin and narrow my eyes. *Where's he going with this?*

"Don't go on the offensive, Ruby. I'm here to help you. I understand your reasoning for funding these programs, but personally? I wouldn't advise mentoring anyone quite yet."

"You don't—"

Axel's eye's shift, his attention abruptly diverts from me to something behind me. "Well, well. Maeson out and about this early in the day?" He rises and shakes the intruder's hand.

I turn to see who it could be.

Are you kidding me? They know each other?

"Donovan." Maeson's voice is stern and clipped. The warning is clear as day—shut the fuck up.

Axel winks at me. "Right, right. Not in front of a lady."

"Not in front of my *tenant*." Maeson crosses his arms, glowering at Axel. His face shifts and his furious eyes meet mine. "Ruby. Meeting with my lawyer? Are you pressing charges for the other night?"

"No. I had no idea he's your lawyer. I need one for... a personal matter."

"I see. Well, I'll let you continue." His angry gaze drifts back to the lawyer. "*Donovan.*" His brow raises and his green eyes blaze before he struts away.

Green eyes. Wait. He has no glasses on today.

Axel nods toward Maeson's retreating back. "He's an odd one. Don't let him frighten you." He shakes his head and brings his attention back to me. "Anyway... Please take my advice on the mentor thing, give yourself time. In the meantime, I'll set everything up and let you know when we have the green light."

"I'll think about it. Thank you for all your help. It's about time someone does something."

"You're right, this world needs more people like you, ones who are willing to help others. Just know I'm here for you anytime, I'm only a phone call away." He pats my knee before tucking away the notepad. "Remember, as the founder, you'll have to share your story. So, prepare, maybe meet with someone to get comfortable talking about it."

"Okay." I nod numbly.

Nothing and no one can prepare me for sharing what the men in my past have put me through.

Fumbling in my pocket for my sleek, black cigarette case, I give into my latest addiction and light up. My lungs expand as I inhale deeply and watch Axel catch up to Maeson. A tear slides down my face, the past invading my mind. Memories that could take over my reality. If I let them.

Deep breath, baby girl, you can do this.

-14-

MAESON

AXEL'S FOOTSTEPS ECHO IN THE courtyard as he trails behind me. "Alexander! Wait up!"

I don't stop, instead, I take longer strides, getting a sick satisfaction from his pursuit. Dumb jackass can catch up!

Mine!

My inner beast possessively roars and pounds its chest, even though she's not mine.

She can't stand me.

Perhaps, that's for the best as certain women are too damn dangerous. They wield an invisible power over men that you can't fight against or explain. Add intriguing to a natural beauty, like Ruby Bennett, and it's a straight up death sentence.

Proving the point of why showing up at Ruby's place was a terrible... absolutely fucking disastrous idea. Not only was the legality of what I did questionable at best, but the incessant visions of her in that unbelievably short adult onesie attacks my very core.

It's as if picturing her in those impossibly tight jeans wasn't enough for my already crowded brain, now I have to constantly fight the image of her perfect heart shaped ass peeking out at me too.

Fucking fabulous!

It's scary how she's beginning to consume my every thought, even though I barely know anything about her.

Must change that. But how?

"Hey, man, slow down! I'm in a damn suit. I can't run in this shit."

I can't help the evil grin that surfaces. Serves him right for hitting on a vulnerable young woman.

Run, fucker, run.

I'm not slowing down for his perverted old man ass.

She's too fucking young for you, Grandpa.

Now I'm glad I didn't ask the crafty ole silver fox to lunch today... obviously, he wouldn't have been available, being too busy cozying up to the woman driving my mind, body, and soul crazy.

Was I really in the mood for him today? Nope.

I'd seen him far too often as it was with my up and coming deal to purchase extra land. The goal is to build and expand my brand, which is why I can't avoid the fucker during business hours.

"Maeson!"

He sounds desperate, so even though I want to shout at him, the better part of me steadies my pace and lets him catch up.

"What's your deal, bro?" Axel reaches my side puffing slightly and wipes his sweaty brow.

I shrug. "No deal. Next time shut your trap about my nightly binges. It's no one's business, especially not hers."

"I didn't say anything, and since when do even you care?" Axel's eyes meet mine and he grins.

Smug asshole. I know that grin.

My lips seal shut, I refuse to dignify his question with an answer. Talking more than necessary gets people into trouble.

"Oh, I get it. You want to bag her!" He studies me with such intensity it's like he sees right through me. "Shit, you already did, didn't you? I had no idea, man. I wouldn't out you like that, and she isn't your type. How was I supposed to know?"

"Like you know my type." I stop in my tracks, glaring at him, recalling those dangerous words spilling from his lips only moments before.

He almost ruined my chances by making me look bad.

The bastard was on the verge of saying things she doesn't need to know.

I wanted to punch him in the face to shut him up, but instead, I resorted to a pointed stare. His deadpan expression had told me he read my thoughts loud and clear.

Chill. Or you'll say something stupid and regret it forever.

"We all do, man. Thin as rails and absolutely no fuckin' personality." He shakes his head and his lip curls in disgust.

"Well, tastes change, *bro*," I sneer the last word at him.

He shakes his head seeming to not believe a word I said. "Not once in eleven years have your tastes changed. And to go even further, I know more about her than you do, which I'm sure you tried to dig up on your own... *unsuccessfully*." Axel's eyebrows lift significantly. "The things I do know tell me she's not your kind of woman. Now that I've seen her, it confirms the fact, leaving no doubt in my mind."

"You're wrong, Ax. She's everything I purposely stay away from. All that hidden baggage? Those curls? That face? Those eyes? That amazing fucking body? Those are the reasons I stay away from women like her." I raise a hand in the air, stopping Axel before he can speak. "And don't play dumb and ask why. You know *why*." Ready to finish this conversation, I force my legs to start moving.

"I do, that's what confused me when I saw that special look in your eyes where you tell me to fuck off." Axel grabs my shoulder, bringing me to a halt. "Let's get something straight. My intentions to help Ruby are real, and not once did fucking her cross my mind. She's fragile, too fragile for the likes of you or me. For your sake? Relax. Tone the barbaric caveman, and the protective shit the hell down. You'll scare her away and it's bound to happen anyway. All she needs to do is find out how drunk you're getting nightly and how far gone you're becoming all over again. You're not letting the past go, man, and you need to." He shakes his head and sighs. "You're no different from her, you know. Both of you are running away instead of facing reality."

I chuckle humorlessly. "My all-knowing lawyer giving me advice, yet you're the one who recently got divorced! Keep it to yourself, Donovan. I'm not the lost young man you first met." With that, I stalk off toward my car.

I don't need anyone's fucking lecture.

Even though he might be right. Once upon a time, I was a better man, a good person. But I've been this sad excuse and shell of a man for almost nine years. Life changes you. Events take place, molding you into the person you've become over time. It's unavoidable and inevitable. You can rage, struggle, and try to escape your fate. But in the end? You learn, there is nothing you can do but accept it.

"No, you're worse." Axel's words echo my very own fears.

* * *

SLIDING INTO MY SEAT, I slam the car door, intent on getting some lunch. I've already spent half of this day accomplishing nothing.

Even my pathetic attempt at lunch was a failure.

Molly was busy at work, showing new prospective tenants the condominiums we offer. I'd been tempted to ask Ruby, but she'd have denied me with a big fat *'hell to the no'*. Not that I'd blame her for telling me to fuck off after my little stunt.

And that had left me... no one.

I'd known it was a fat chance my brother from another mother, Jax, who's also my business partner, would be available. Lately, it seems he's always too busy for anything other than work.

Even so, I'd sent the text, knowing what to expect as a response.

SENT MESSAGE: Lunch?

The message had quickly changed from delivered to read and the oh-so-familiar gray bubble filled with three dots popped up. For the split second before his reply came in, I had hoped he would say yes.

INCOMING MESSAGE: Hey man, sorry can't crazy busy. Next time, though.

Short, sweet, and to the damn point.
Typical and predictable, Jax.
So, since it seems to be my new usual, I had resigned to my solo lunch, just to be met with Axel and Ruby.
Great fucking times, Maeson.
Just dandy times ahead for me, I bet...

* * *

AFTER MY RUN IN WITH Ax, I spent the next two weeks keeping to myself. His and Ruby's points were made and they affected me more than I wanted to admit. He knows me too well and she sees right through me. She'd said so herself the day I showed up at her place.
Fucking great, they're conspiring against me.
Doing what I do best, I ignore their words and stay busy. I've managed to finalize the plans for my next housing project and the paperwork for Molly's new position is drawn up.
Three more months. November will be here, and I can unload this bitch of a job and move on to what I do best. Design, build, and execute.
I sigh as I think of Molly. She's been incredibly busy overseeing so much of the business already. We haven't held a conversation long enough to give me a chance to find out what

she's been up to. The one person I relied on has her own life now, and it's getting lonely. She doesn't mind splitting her time between work and Ruby, but for me, she's too busy.

'Sorry boss, hoes before bros' she'd said the other day.

As if on cue, the clicking of high heels on tile approach my office. It's like the damn woman has ESP and knew I was thinking about her. Pretending not to notice, I keep my head down and continue typing on my keyboard as she strolls in.

"Bossman, are ya busy?" She smiles as I raise my gaze to her.

I shake my head. "Never too busy for you. What's up?"

"Nothing much, just checkin' in. Ya got a minute?" Her smile fades.

"Yes, shut the door." I motion her in.

She flops down on the seat in front of my desk. "So, long time no talk, right?"

Nonchalantly, I give her a half shrug. "I'd say so."

"I'm sorry. Been... busy. Ya know, girl stuff." Her eyes flick to the windows then back to mine.

"Too busy for an old friend in need?"

"Huh? You're in need? Since when?" Her brows shoot up in confusion.

"Not in need per se, but I miss your company."

"Oh. I had no idea. You're usually so... *grumpy.* It's like pulling teeth tryin' to get ya to talk so I stopped... tryin'."

"I know. It's who I am." I rub at my chest, working at that nagging, fucking pang. "Enough about me, what's new? You okay?"

A grin spreads across her face, her eyes lighting up. "Nothing new, same old. I'm good. I'm... happy. I know ya worry about me, but I'm doing great."

Her smile is infectious and my own lips unexpectedly turn upwards. "Now that's great news! I can stop thinking the worst is happening. I understand you have friends now... lady friends, who get the whole *'girl talk'* nonsense. Nowadays you seem to have less time for this old guy." I point to myself.

"I knooowww! I'm sorry, Mae Mae." She jumps out of her seat

and tackles me. Her long arms embrace me, her warmth comforting.

I honestly cannot remember the last time I was hugged, and I furrow my brow in concentration. And I mean truly embraced by someone who cares. Women have their arms around me all the time, but they're usually digging their nails into my back as I fuck them. Not the same thing, and the idea of after sex snuggling makes my skin crawl.

"No problem, buttercup, you can make it up to me by having drinks with me tonight." I gently unwrap her hands from my body and look up at her, smiling deeply.

Her eyes flicker. "I can't, I'm sorry." She sighs. "Put away those dimples. You know they won't work on me." Despite her protest, she looks sad at my obvious and pathetic attempt to make her feel bad enough to relent and come with me for drinks. "I have plans already. Ugh! Boss, I'm sorry! How about tomorrow night?"

"No, that's okay. Don't worry. I'll go out alone, nothing new there." My chest tightens as I realize she's probably going to hang out with Ruby. Leaving me alone. Again.

Oh God, I'm turning into a pussy. Next thing, I'll be weeping into a tissue.

It's not like I don't have friends, I do. Axel's one of them and Jax who's more of a brother to me than a friend. But my relationship with Molly is different. I have more of a big brother protectiveness when it comes to her. I promised her father a few years ago to always keep her safe and there's no turning my back on that.

"You're going to Royale?" Her lips twitch.

Our eyes meet and I notice something brewing, the wheels are turning. "Yes. Why?" I narrow my eyes as suspicion creeps over me.

"Just askin'." She nonchalantly lifts the full box of approved tenant files from my desk. "Good talk, Mae Mae. Gotta get these done. Talk to ya later." Her steps falter. "Oh Mae, love the trimmed scruff you got going on and that new sexy haircut.

About time you got something from this century. The undercut is *very* becoming on you." She blows me an air kiss and continues out of the room.

What an oddball. But I love her like a little sister.

As she leaves, I self-consciously run a hand through my hair. I had it changed a while ago, and sadly it's taken this long for anyone to notice.

Sighing, I glance at my watch and realize it's already eight thirty. Time to get the hell out of here. I've spent enough of this day mired in self-pity. I rapidly finish the last email and shut down my computer.

Thank fuck, this horrible day is over, and I can go find me some pussy instead of being one.

Molly's voice and laughter carry down the hallway as I lock my office. On the phone, again. I hate myself for doing it, but I take a few steps closer and listen closely. I can make out a few words here and there, and hold my breath for a moment. Now I can hear the most important keywords.

My heart pounds and an odd twinge of loneliness hits me, which makes me feel like a total shit. I told her to make friends, and now I'm wallowing about it. But I also know who she's talking to, and that's somewhat better. A grin spreads across my face.

Princess. My sweet assed Princess.

-15-

Ruby

ANXIOUSLY, I PACE AROUND MY room, while staring at the letter agreeing to hire Axel as my lawyer.

Now that I've reread it a few times, all I need to do is sign it, and my dream of creating a Foundation to help women and children will come true. I'm not hesitating because I don't want this, it's because of the shock and reality sinking in.

Deep breath. It's time to make this happen.

With shaky fingers, I pick up the pen next to the papers and sign them. My name seems inadequate on this crisp white sheet, but the simple signature means so much to me. This is my chance to stand for something—to make a difference, no matter how small it might be.

It's done and there are no take backs in this game.

A sense of peace washes over my body as I set down the pen. There's only thing left unsettled is my poor mind. It knows what I'll have to reveal to so many people.

I'm not ready, am I? You have to be. But I'm not…

Before panic sets in, I'm saved by the bell... well ring. Molly's number lights up on my phone. "Hey, girl. What's up?"

"Just checking on when you'll be ready."

"Half an hour. Is that too long? Oh, and where are we going?"

"Not at all! I need to finish at work anyway. And we are going to Royale Nightclub in Uptown."

"Okay, sounds good."

"See you soon!" Molly's excited voice rises.

There's an overwhelming edginess about going out that I can't seem to get rid of. "Where's my damn purse?" I mumble to myself after hanging up. Finally locating it, I rustle through it in search of my medication. Even as I shake those pills into my hand and wash them down with water, I remind myself I'll be drinking. However, the need for relief subdues my rational thought.

If I was stronger, I'd resist the urge to use pharmaceuticals to manage the anxiety, and keep them only for emergencies—but I can't. I understand being on edge or scared because I'm doing something out of my comfort zone doesn't constitute an emergency, and mixing meds with alcohol is certainly not recommended. I've already learned my lesson on that front, but I'm willing to chance it anyway.

In the half hour I have before Molly arrives, I dress, do my makeup, and finish styling my hair. Taking one last look at myself in the mirror, I see the woman that's usually hiding behind that wall Maeson mentioned.

My dark brown hair is loose and in its natural state, cascading over my shoulders, and down my back in wild, unruly curls. My makeup is smoky brown shadows with black winged eyeliner, which I exaggerated to intensify the golden specks within my amber eyes. The final touch is an almost nude lip color, so not to overpower the rest of my face.

For tonight's outfit, I chose dark skinny jeans that hug and define every single voluptuous curve from hip to ankle. My beloved new red flats provide a pop of color, and a black low cut top, showing just the top of my full breasts in a very sensual and seductive way. I was never allowed to dress this way before, so I'm taking full advantage of my new-found freedom.

When did I become this sexy, mature woman?

The familiar chimes resound throughout the house announcing Mo's arrival, and I rush out of my room to greet her.

Molly's eyes about pop out of her head at the sight of my outfit. "Holy shit! You look hot! Look at that ass and those tits!"

"Thank you! You're not so bad yourself for an old lady!" I tease. "Go get ready!"

She playfully slaps my shoulder. "Tonight, age is of no concern to us! We're young, single women who are out for some fun, and drinks to start the weekend off right!" She grins from ear to ear. "Be right back." She disappears into the bathroom.

A few minutes later, Molly comes into my room checking me out hungrily as I'm looking in the mirror still in awe of the person staring back at me.

"Quit watching me like I'm the juiciest steak you've ever seen!" I laugh to hide how uncomfortable I am and how anxious it makes me. Being admired is yet another thing I'm not used to and I don't know how to accept.

How does one handle compliments, when the last honest one I was given was fifteen years ago?

Granted when someone stares at me it heightens my fear of them being able to see what has marred my soul.

Shattered it.

See the things hiding underneath the mask, and underneath these clothes.

Deep Breath, Ruby.

"Are you crazy?" Molly's animated voice snaps me back into reality. "How can I not? Ya look amazing, and ya don't even know it! I'm a woman who loves the sausage all the way, but sometimes when a cute pussy cat walks by, ya gotta admire it," she drawls.

Somehow, without realizing she's doing it, Molly has this way of easing my fears so effortlessly that I find myself laughing, all the worry gone.

Poof. Like a puff of smoke evaporating.

You can't take a person like her seriously because she's always making you laugh. She has this tendency to say the craziest things! Most people have a filter when speaking, but not Molly. Whatever is on her mind she spits out freely—consequences be damned. Which is exactly what makes Molly Briggs a shiny gem amongst a bunch of dull stones.

"Right, well... *Rico Suave*, I appreciate the admiration. Now let's get moving!" I shoo her toward the elevator, ready to get our night out started.

We are almost at the first floor and a random thought strikes me. "Hey, did you ever find any information on our mystery guy?"

"Oh shoot, nope. I got nothing." She looks away.

"That's weird. Oh, well, maybe he was visiting someone who lives here." I shrug. "Maybe I'll get lucky and see him again. All I need to do is wake up at the crack of dawn and go for a walk."

"Yeah, I guess so," she says quietly as the elevator doors slide open. "Why don't we forget about that guy and go have us a blast tonight? Maybe you'll find yourself another hot man there!" She laughs.

I smile back at her, but not for a second did I miss the abrupt change of subject or attitude on her part. "Yeah, you never know. You could be right!"

Maybe she does know him? Maybe she's into him and I overstepped?

Tonight's not the time to ask but soon I'll have to find out for sure, especially since I'd never want to trespass onto someone else's territory. Girl code and all.

-16-

MAESON

TRAFFIC WAS ODDLY LIGHT TODAY, I assume everyone is off having their family dinners or getting ready for their night out. Works for me because I've reached the club in record time. I'm half an hour early, which will give me plenty of time to set up my 'make Maeson look good' plan.

After snooping in on Molly's phone call, all the pieces of the puzzle came together. She'd planned it, the little sneak, and purposely made sure they'd come to the bar I own. I knew she was up to something, with those odd looks she'd given me in my office, and then the offhand comment about my nightclub.

One thing I'm unclear on is her intentions.

Does she want to expose my bad habit to Ruby? Or bring us together?

Which leaves me with a dilemma. The woman already thinks I'm a total ass, and I need to find a way to change her false impression.

So, how do I score major brownie points?

The office door's wide open, and as usual, my business partner's leaning back in his chair, intently watching the security monitor.

Silently standing in the doorway, I notice how much his age is showing. His hair has a lot more salt and far less pepper every time I see him. Not quite a silver fox like my lawyer Axel, but getting there.

"Jax. I need a favor."

His arms flail in the air and he almost falls out of the chair. "Fucker! You scared the shit out of me!" He swings around, all wide-eyed, with his brows raised in shock. "Damn near gave me heart failure." He pats his chest for effect. "What do you need, ole man?"

I laugh loudly. "You're the old man, not me. You're the one starting to scare easily like a wee lass."

Jax's lips thin, he's clearly not amused. "Yeah, you're so funny. Your dick's a wee lass. Now, what do you want? Some of us actually have work to do."

Well someone's not in the mood to joke around. Right to the point it is.

"I need to add a drink to the menu and make it our special tonight. If it's a hit? We make it permanent."

Abruptly he stands and scans the empty hallway. "Who are you trying to impress?"

What's he thinking? I have a groupie hanging out in the wings?

Fucker knows me too well. He's going to laugh his ass off if he ever finds out I did this for a woman. He'll be calling me a big ass pussy. "No one. It's good and should be a money maker, that's all." I cross my arms and eye him suspiciously. "Why are you so skittish tonight?"

"I'm not, man. Just don't want people overhearing us and stealing those money-making ideas." He snickers.

"Right. I'd call bullshit but I'm too busy tonight to call you out on it." I hand him the paper with the name of the drink, the ingredients, and approximate measurements.

"Ruby Apple, huh? Ruby... I've heard that name—"

"From who?" I get in his face immediately, leaning on the arms of his chair.

If Axel said anything? I'll kill him!

He shoves me away. "Chill man! I think I heard it from you."

"Again, bull."

"We're getting off topic here. Let's try out this drink of yours. You sure need one and our doors open in less than half an hour."

Shady fucker. Something's up, but I don't have the time to argue with him right now.

Once we're on the main floor of the club, I wave over one of the bartenders who's getting ready for his shift. "Isaac, we have a new special for the night. I need you to push it and keep track of sales."

Jax hands him the sheet with the recipe. "Make three for us now so we can all to test it."

He frowns at the paper, giving us a funny look "All right, you're the boss." In less than a minute he hands us two tall frosty glasses and keeps the third one for himself.

At first, they both stare at it like it's going to bite them.

Isaac is the first to speak. "I know you're in charge, but... apple juice? Really?" His lip curls as he eyes the glass warily.

"Yes. Apple juice." I nod. "Try it. *Then* judge."

Isaac nods, accepting the challenge, and we all raise the glasses to our lips at the same time, letting the flavors sink into our taste buds. My guesstimate on the mixture seems about right.

For watching her only do it once? Not bad.

"Damn!" Jax and Isaac say in unison.

"I told you fucks it's good. Maybe trust me next time?"

"Not bad at all Maes." Jax smiles and clinks his glass with mine. "To the latest member of our money maker club."

Oh, her money maker is all mine. Not ours.

Before I can stop myself, my smile widens at his words. "To the Ruby Apple."

"To the Ruby Apple is right, boss. I think you've got something great here." Isaac finishes off his drink. "I'll let everyone in the back know, and make sure we have enough in stock for it."

"Thanks. I'll let the creator knows it's a hit. I need this"—I point to my glass on the bar—"full at all times tonight. You know, to help promote our menu addition."

"You got it." Isaac nods knowingly, not fooled at all. "Jax? How about you?"

"No. One was enough for me. Someone needs to stay sober and keep this place running smoothly. I have an actual job to get to, since this tool"—His head gestures toward me—"plans on getting lit."

Isaac laughs. "Aaaaand on that note, I've got work to do too." With a smug look on his face, he flips a small towel over his shoulder and leaves us.

"You coming out of your office tonight to enjoy some fresh meat instead of pouting like a little lonely pup?" I raise my brow and smirk.

Jax shakes his head. "Nah, I'm good."

"You're a weird one. At your age, you should be pouncing on them. Maybe even get lucky and find *the one*, someone who will give you a couple of rug rats to run around that empty house of yours."

"At my age?" He stares down at his feet awkwardly, and mumbles, "Asshole. I'm not much older than you, and you haven't done much soulmate searching either. So, lay the fuck off." His voice is bitter, laced with anger.

Pain lances through me and I wince inwardly. "Feisty much? You're like a brother to me, I'm only teasing. You tell me to chill? How about you take some of your own advice." I spin, stalking out the door for some much-needed fresh air before I say something I'll regret.

Something's going on. He's acting like... like... me.

Standing outside this *fresh air* does nothing for me. Maybe because it's *not* fresh. It's stifling hot and makes me instantly sweat. I pull at my collar, knowing the perspiration dripping down my back is not only because it's the middle of summertime in Dallas. I'm all paranoid about my friends, and I'm actually nervous about seeing Ruby.

Me? A nervous wreck? Someone take a picture—this needs to go in the record books.

The parking lot is filling up and a line is forming at the door. Two cars stand out, my driver who's on call for the night, and the familiar blue Toyota Yaris pulling in.

Molly steps out first, she's wearing the tightest and shortest dress I've ever seen. Who's she trying to impress by baring so much of those never-ending legs? A boyfriend?

If that's the case then good for her. He'll die when he sees her.

Trailing behind her is Ruby, her big brown eyes are wide with what seems to be awe spread across her face.

I know the building is a sight to be seen. The exterior is surrounded by metallic windows which make it look like a massive mirror, and there are neon lights on the front of the building flashing the name of the club.

Royale.

The hesitation I witnessed evaporates as quickly as it appeared. Her chin lifts with confidence as she approaches the entrance, disappearing from my view.

But not before I got a good, long look. Those dark rimmed eyes give her an incredibly sexy and exotic, Amazonian appeal. Every single one of my senses drink in those amazing, womanly curves, clad in skin tight jeans, and her tantalizing cleavage. I can't help salivating while I watch her maneuver through the parking lot, or stop the dirty images that pop into my mind.

Goddamn it, she's a true beauty.

Just my luck I'd meet this one.

-17-

Ruby

WHENEVER I STEP FOOT INTO a nightclub, the first few minutes inside overpowers my senses. The atmosphere of places like this are jam-packed with over the top... *everything*. The music is so loud my entire body vibrates.

Weaving our way through the masses while everyone's in full dance mode is a pain in the ass, especially when no one ever moves over to let you through. It doesn't help that the flashing neon lights mess with my vision. At least I'm able to make out the couches lined against the walls and the huge, stainless steel, mirror-like bar that we're approaching.

Molly stops at the end of it, waving to get the attention of one of the bartenders. "What's the special tonight?" she shouts.

He leans over the counter, his face only inches away from us. "Ruby Apple. New drink."

What? This must be a mistake. Maybe I didn't hear him right.

"Hit us up..." The rest of what she says is lost in the loud pulsing music, except for the name Maeson at the end of her sentence.

My gut sinks. Something's not adding up.

The bartender simply nods and pours our drinks.

Molly drops a few dollars on the bar, snags the drinks, and leads me toward a section with two small couches and a table in the middle of the action.

She nonchalantly removes the large 'Reserved' sign. "Sit!" Molly yells in my ear and hands me the booze. "Drink up!"

I lean across our table and raise my glass. "What is this?"

I know exactly what the hell it is!

The mixture is blended beautifully, served in a tall glass with lots of ice.

Bastard! Exactly like I made it.

Her grin spreads into a saucy smile. "Your namesake it seems!" She pauses to quench her thirst. "The bartender said it's Grey Goose, apple juice, and grenadine. How good is this shit? Best drink ever. Don't chug it, he added extra vodka for us."

Little does she know this is my drink of choice, and chugging is far from an issue for me. I lean back and relax in my chair, annoyance pumping through me while I absorb the scene around us. Involuntarily, my head bobs to the music, and I let it take over. My foot taps in time to the beat, and I sway slightly in my seat.

Molly surprises me by grabbing my hand and tugs me toward the dance floor. I gulp down the glass in my hand and follow her.

We're both moving to the beat, my eyes close as the vibrations wash over me and my body moves freely. When I open them again, there's a tall man right behind Molly. I can't see his face through the darkness, but I do notice the protective way his arms wrap around her, and how his hands slowly slide over her hips, pulling her in closer to him. She glances over her shoulder, and a smile spreads across her lips as her body molds into his with ease.

Okay, hoochie mama. You go girl!

She gives me a thumbs up and nods at something behind me,

then there is a set of hands on my body. Turning my head slightly, I peek to see who it is.

The man behind me is blonde—too blonde for my tastes—but he's good looking so, I let him stay. This is my opportunity to enjoy the sensation of another body close to mine. The look on Molly's face says, *just enjoy myself* and enjoy I will.

I remember how Ray used to do the very same thing before he changed and before he turned into yet another man in my nightmares, no longer the prince of my dreams.

At first, we were happy together. It felt like he cared, and his mission was to heal my scars. During those glorious days, he loved dancing and showing me how therapeutic the rhythm of a song could be.

Once upon a time, I felt loved and treasured...

Closing my eyes, I envision him... Ray...

The music picks up speed and I can't tell if it's happening now, or if it's in the memory. Everything is blending together. Grinding, his body is grinding against mine, making me so aroused. My eyes drift closed again.

In this moment, I simply don't care if it's past or present...

* * *

HE'S BEHIND ME WITH HIS body tight against mine. "Just let your body relax baby, trust me. I won't hurt you again, that was a mistake. I promise you."

"Okay." I'm unsure if I can trust his promises anymore. I don't disagree with him, though, because we all make mistakes and learn from them, don't we?

He turns up the music and starts to sway, rubbing against me. Placing his hands on my hips, he guides me. Our bodies find a rhythm and I push into him, enjoying the rarity of his good mood.

"That's right, baby, there you go." He encourages me, his arms wrap around me, holding me tight against him as we move, showing me affection like he did when we first met.

Ray used to love teaching me how to build my confidence. He would find a million and one ways to make me smile, until more recently when that started to change. Now I only get to see that man when in his words— 'I'm a good girl'.

I guess I'm doing something right since lately, it seems nothing is good enough for him.

"Like that, baby girl, grind harder... harder, faster!" He rips my thong off, tearing the scrap of material apart in a flash and roughly enters me from behind, continuing the grind of our bodies.

We're both turned on by the sensual dance we're creating. I'm dizzy, my body is burning up, my legs are shaking, I'm going to come.

"Baby! Gonna come, ugh, baby. Yes, so good!" He throws his head back with a groan. "Melissaaaa!"

We both freeze. Our intimate moment is gone... this special moment... ruined.

This is the exact moment my trust in him is replaced with suspicion and doubts. "Ruby, asshole! It's Ruby. How could you?" I spit the words out in disgust, the tears streaming down my cheeks as I struggle out of his iron stiff grasp. I can't get away from the bastard fast enough. My heart is breaking all over again.

My knees give out and I drop onto our bed, curling up in a ball.

* * *

STILL FEELING HANDS ON MY body, my eyes snap open and I throw a panicked glance over my shoulder to reassure myself it's not Ray haunting me. Molly has a questioning look on her face, but I give her the most reassuring smile I can manage to let her know I'm all right.

My hips refuse to move again as I try to get back into the dance and the music. The energy I had has evaporated and all that's left in me is sadness and pain brought on by the memory that overtook my mind.

Deep breath.

Needing a moment of privacy, I search for the bathroom, spotting one in the back corner. "Ladies room!" I point for good measure, letting the guy behind me know I'm leaving. Tears build in my eyes as I hurry toward the bathroom, desperate to reach it before I lose control.

I bump into a hard body, mumbling an apology while keeping my head down to hide the tears rolling down my cheeks. Escaping into a stall, I slump onto the toilet, reminding myself that was the past! Tonight is about having fun, not reminiscing about the asshole who broke me in so many ways. My lungs expand as I struggle to inhale, but it's impossible with all my emotions collapsing over me.

Deep breath, Ruby! Deep breath!

He'd lied so well. He'd made me believe he wanted to help me recover and find who I was meant to be. The Ruby who I've concealed underneath, the one who'd never had a chance to grow up like normal girls.

I believed everything he promised like a damn fool!

When I tried to heal on my own and erase the memories of my tormentor, I'd ended up sleeping with one man after another. I'd lost myself even further, falling deeper into a darkness I wasn't sure how to escape. Each and every guy I slept with were the same—they all wanted to fuck me, but never to fix me. When things got too deep? Off they went.

Then along came Ray, a false knight in shining armor, who *did* want to 'fix' shattered Ruby. And fix he did… until I became exactly what he wanted me to be—that perfect, overly dependent, malleable girlfriend who always obeyed his every command.

After I'd met his standards, our life was perfection. I convinced myself I was happy, but even that was short-lived once he noticed my craving for independence.

Why did I have to want more?

Well, because it dawned on me that I was settling again—settling for any scrap of 'love' or 'kindness' someone showed me. Ray's façade had me fooled until I realized that he was the worst kind of settling. It was far worse, even compared to the guys who'd simply wanted a quickie. He didn't want to help me at all! Ray wanted to control me… every part of me.

Too much control… everyone's had too much control over me. When is enough, enough?

Once my sight cleared, I was no longer jaded by false realities. My desires grew for friends, spending nights out in the city, and having drinks at the pub, or anything else that would expand my horizons. I wanted to have real fun, to know what it's like to be around people you can hang out and laugh freely with all night long. Unfortunately, these epiphanies came too late… I was firmly trapped with no visible way to escape.

Take a deep breath, Ruby. It's over, you're free now.

After what seems like forever, I regain my composure, and exit the stall, peering around to ensure I'm alone. With a hasty inspection of myself in the mirror, I repair the damage to my tear ravaged face and take a few more deep breaths for good measure.

The door opens, and Molly barges through it looking stricken. "Are you ok?" She asks, her tone full of worry.

"Yes. Just needed a sec." I smile brightly, trying to show her I truly am fine.

"I don't believe you, but I won't push. Go sit. I'll grab us some fresh drinks."

"I like that idea." I pause. "Hey wait up, why did you say Mr. Alexander's name to the bartender earlier?"

"Oh, I use his open tab every time I come here. It's a perk of working for him, and he's part owner of this place." She smirks, seemingly amused at not having to pay a dime to be here.

That's how the bastard got the drink I made on the damn menu!

"Oh! He owns this place? Well then, I can pay for my own. I don't need his tab." I don't want Molly to think I'm a freeloader, and besides, why would I take any charity from that arrogant ass. I spent too long under the thumb of my ex, I'm not in any hurry to be indebted to another man!

"No way! Since the bastard gives me hell daily, this goes on his tab, and we are gonna build it up tonight." She laughs as we leave the bathroom.

Molly points to the bar and shoos me off toward our section.

I sit on the couch facing the packed dance floor, and take in the scene, scanning the room. My gaze stops dead when I spot him sitting alone at the bar. His eyes are blazing with fire as he stares directly at me.

Why is he staring at me like that?

My breath catches in my chest. It feels like I'm underwater, and I can't breathe all over again. Our gazes cross and I'm powerless. I simply cannot tear my eyes away from him. A jolt zaps through me like an electrical shock. My whole body tingles, right down to my toes.

Deep breath. Don't stop breathing.

I'm frozen in place. Pinned down under the intensity of those vibrant green eyes.

-18-

MAESON

FOUR, FIVE, SIX... TEN DRINKS LATER.

The infuriatingly oblivious woman finally noticed my presence at the bar. Yet, I couldn't take my eyes off her since I planted myself in this spot. I'd been trying to focus on her for what seemed like for-fucking-ever, but the crowd was too dense.

Her eyes have locked on mine, openly regarding me across the mass of people as if we're the only two people in the entire club.

Why am I going this far for someone? And why does it mean so much to me?

Woman come and go from my life. I change them like I change my underwear—*daily*. Yet, some-fucking-how she brings forth a craving, a need, and a longing for something... *more.*

What troubled me was that no matter what part of the club I'd be in, I'd find myself watching her. I practically had to force my eyes to stop staring at that gorgeous, curvaceous body. Without lifting a fucking finger, she has that kind of power over me. The damn woman is most definitely hazardous to my sanity.

She tantalizes me to no end! What. The. Fuck!

Surprisingly, she's the only woman I've met who's managed to entice me without even trying. Quite opposite, in fact, she's constantly rebuffing me.

Now she's noticed me, and the connection seems to last an eternity. My heart pounds at the sight of her, literally pounding like it's going to leap from my chest. Her searing gaze bores into me as if she's peering directly into my soul. Something stirs inside, something foreign, and familiar, but entirely unwanted, all at the same time.

Walk away, damn it.

I need to fucking quit playing with fire.

I'm not so sure I'm ready to handle it.

Primal animalistic desire roars within, the thought of walking away is driving my inner beast into a frenzy. She's made me powerless. I'm unable to resist her feminine wiles.

I'm powerless and immobilized as it attacks, the monster within struggling to escape. The alcohol coursing through my veins provides it strength, the fortitude it needs to rise to the surface. I force it back down, remembering my dad's advice.

'Son? Court a hen first. Find out who she truly is. If she's th' right one fur ye? Then, an' only then, open up to her.'

Not once have I taken my ole man's words to heart and look how well that turned out.

Settle down, beast. It's not time for you... yet.

Have patience dear friend, the time has come for step two of my plan... find Ruby's true self.

-19-

Ruby

MY ENTIRE BODY SIZZLES, CRACKLES, and pops as Maeson's hungry stare devours me from across the club. Everyone in the room instantly disappears and all I see is him. It reminds me of those classic fairytale movies I used to watch and once believed in as a kid.

I focus on him, letting these false unrealistic emotions take over. All too soon, the realist in me rears her head. My harsh memories are a constant reminder my life isn't like those mythical tales of one true love I wished to have one day.

Never has been and never will be.

Over time I've learned in the worst possible ways that lust is not love, and obsession isn't a type of devotion. It's destruction in its simplest form.

Should I disregard everything I went through, for the lust I currently feel? All for a man who's practically a stranger? Risk destroying the small pieces of myself that are left intact?

My judgment is clouded by my good old friend—vodka, and

my heart and mind are finally on the same page—they both scream the same thing...

Try again.

How can I when my childhood was filled with the worst of the worst experiences, and then my initiation into adulthood wasn't any better? I was once told, 'misery is continuously looking for its next victim. If you let that misery in, it will take you down... hard'.

Too late. Too damn late.

Only one man in my life has been good to me, and that was my Dad. He was the kindest soul you'd ever meet and treated me like a real-life princess.

The next two significant men in my life made it their mission to hurt me, to drill in the fact I'd never be anyone's princess again. Then Maeson decides to constantly use that one word I despise hearing.

He'll never understand the extent of the pain and damage it truly causes me.

No matter how insignificant the reminder might be, it still has the power to affect me. Tears blur my vision, causing Maeson's face to become fuzzy, but I refuse to look away.

How can one person make my emotions so wild?

One minute I'm hot and bothered and desperately want to rip off that tight shirt and kiss every inch of his amazing body. The next? I want to run as fast and far as I possibly can.

After I kill the bastard of course.

His smug face makes me want to wrap my fingers around his throat and throttle the life out of him.

Then there's the constant worry—*since I have such great judgment when it comes to men*—that Maeson might end up being another one of those endless guys I've slept with, only using me for sex. Even worse... he might be a Ray in disguise. I simply don't know how to deal with this whole hot one minute, cold the next scenario.

The entire experience is different than how it was with Ray. Certainly, there were times when I longed to run away, but I was too scared to act on the urge.

Scared he'd follow me and kill me.

Or even worse? I'd run so far, he'd never catch me, and my deepest fear would come to fruition—I'd end up utterly alone. So, I traded my abusive, crappy foster home for a bunch of one night stands, and then jumped right on into my relationship with Ray. In the end, all I did was swap one fucked up home for another.

Physical versus mental—it's hard to compare the two, but it's my fault. I was the fool who believed in all the bullshit promises of love, devotion, and protection. At least before Ray, I knew what to expect. Ray only started the physical toward the end and it was nowhere near as bad as in the foster home.

Bastard foster father was all about the physical pain—breakfast, lunch, and dinner.

Before the thought sinks in and ruins my night even further, I focus on the man across the way. Surprisingly, I'm grounded instantly.

"Ruby?" Molly's right beside me, but her voice seems to be coming from miles away.

"Yeah?" I barely register her presence as my mind is busy battling past versus present.

"Earth to Ruby!" She snaps her fingers in my face. "I got more drinks!" She frowns and looks around, searching for what's caught my attention.

I tear my gaze away, desperate to bring Molly's attention back to me so she doesn't notice it's not a *what*, but a *who*. "Oh, thanks. Sorry, in a daze."

"That's alright, love…"

I vaguely register Mo's still talking, but her words aren't connecting with my brain. Taking the fresh glass on the table in front of me, I slug back half the drink, in need of extra liquid courage.

"Whoa, tiger! I said DO NOT chug!" Her crystal clear blue eyes widen in shock.

"Hey!" Annoyance rises as she yanks the glass away from me

and sets it on the table. It's still within my reach, though, and as soon as she lets go, I snatch the drink and down the remainder in one long gulp.

"Slow down, Ruby! Ya tryin' to become a drunk whore like some of these women here?"

"NO! Why'd you say that?"

"Because, once these hit, you'll become the biggest ho anyone's ever met!" She laughs again, patting my arm. "Slow it down. I don't wanna to be peeling ya off the bathroom floor. vodka's a sneaky motherfucker!"

I'd clue her in on my love for alcohol, but that'll cause too many questions.

Nope. Not going there.

Instead, I play along. "Well, I don't care! These are amazing! I want more! Besides, you're who I'm here with, so I'll be your problem to deal with!" A giggle escapes me. This playful side I'm feeling is something new altogether.

Maybe my tolerance isn't the same when he doubles the shots in these?

"Deal! In the morning, I'll be caring for your ho ass with my special hangover cure!"

"Deal, Mo. Noowww lemme get toasted!" I flash my pearly whites.

She rolls her eyes. "Okay, lil' daredevil. Be back with more!" She heads to the bar with a bounce in her step, looking so carefree and happy.

Was I ever like that?

I shake my head, ridding myself of the new somber thoughts, and peer toward Maeson. Wait!

He's gone!

My heart sinks, and his fiery green eyes flash in my mind. The memory causes my face to flush, and my body temperature to rise. A shiver runs down my spine, forcing me to look up—directly into those exact green eyes I was envisioning.

I must be drunk off my ass, now I'm imagining shit. Why would he bother to come over here when I told him I needed space?

I catch a whiff of aftershave, and those incredible greens blink. It's not my imagination playing tricks at all. Right in front of me stands Maeson L. Alexander.

In the rock hard flesh.

The familiar heat emanates from his body as he leans in and whispers against my hair in the deep, sensual voice. "Miss Bennett. Have I offended your Highness? Was it too much to ask a *'hello'* of you once you spotted me?"

What?

His words are slurred, but the now very thick accent is extremely identifiable. It fully sinks in and I realize where he's from. "You're Scottish?"

He nods and smirks, exuding an awful amount of disgustingly sexy confidence. "Och aye, I am. How'd you guess?" With the accent, his voice is deep, profoundly deeper than normal. The combination of his unrelenting scrutiny and listening to him speak has me at a loss for words.

I lower my eyes and concentrate on the black buttons of his shirt. "Well, the hottest actor in the world, Gerard Butler, has the exact same accent."

"Ah, my fucking nemesis. Didn't take you long to figure it out." He abruptly extends his hand and lightly touches my hair, picking up a random curl and twirling it around his finger. "So, soft," he murmurs in my ear.

Don't let him affect you. Play it cool.

No matter how *cool* I try to be, I can't stop these damned goosebumps from rising all over my skin. My head spins from his proximity, and the alcohol flowing through my veins amplifies that sex appeal I'm trying so hard to ignore.

Deep breath.

I smile and gently suck on my bottom lip, watching him rise to his full height. When he returns the smile, flashing his amazing dimples, I almost pass the hell out.

Mother of God. What a desperate fool I am.

The spinning intensifies, and I close my eyes. I need to move, take my mind off it, or I'll be sick. Pushing out of my chair, I crook my finger, beckoning him down to my level. He bends toward me, and I lean into him, entirely forgetting all of my internal battles and uneasiness. "A piece of advice for ya, quit askin' *allll* the wrong questions n' quit being so stiff." I chuckle and grab his hand, wanting to drag him toward the dance floor.

But before I can pull him away, he nods curtly, all emotion gone from his face and takes the lead.

So much for taking my advice.

He needs a chill pill. Nope, he's so rigid, he could use at least a couple, like the ones I took earlier.

Midway, we bump into Molly who's loaded down with drinks. Her mouth drops open, and her eyes widen as she sees me holding Maeson's hand. Her mouth moves, but it's like a silent movie, I can't hear a word of it. The drink in her hand calls my name, though, I certainly hear when those Ruby Apples speak.

Snagging one from her, I down it without blinking then extend the empty glass back to Molly, which she takes. A small shake of her head and twitch of her eyes toward Maeson is her only reaction. I manage a saucy wink as Maeson yanks me away.

Unquestionably, I have no idea what I'm doing, or why I'm testing the boundaries of my stability. Maybe faking sanity to escape those four padded walls wasn't the best way to reenter society. Especially when I know I'm far from equipped to handle this barbaric man. I'm not prepared for any of this. But that's the beauty of alcohol and pills for you, they smooth out the edges and ease those silly rational thoughts!

Ruby's... Apples... takin over. Pain and tears?... Nope. I-don't-give-a-shit-fun? Hell yeah!

We cram ourselves into an unoccupied space on the overcrowded dance floor, and Maeson awkwardly stands before me.

Oh, Mr. Big, Bad and Sexy doesn't know how to dance?

I unabashedly move my body to the current upbeat rhythm. Sean Paul and Sia's voices flow through me, their song providing the much-needed escape from my troubled mind.

I can do this, just breathe.

My earlier mini-breakdown has better prepared me to handle any overbearing emotions that might arise from Maeson being so near.

Hasn't it? Deep breath.

I gyrate my body, turning so Maeson is directly behind me. His touch is hesitant and light, a lingering caress that ends all too soon. However, I enjoy the gentleness of his touch and boldly reach back to grasp his fingertips, bringing them forward to rest on my hips.

Since when am I ready to be this close to him again, to have his fingers on my body, and to feel his breath on my neck? You're drunk, dumbass. Who cares?

Internally, I shrug it off and focus on our bodies as they move seamlessly to the rhythm of the music. Surprisingly, we're in sync immediately, and I'm impressed to learn this man has more moves than I believed.

Can't tell when he's normally as rigid as a steel pole. And not in the way most women would prefer, either.

He pulls me in tighter against him, and I let my head fall back as that last drink hits with a vengeance. The closeness and intimacy between us are intoxicating, almost as much as the alcohol racing through my bloodstream.

Maeson's warm, strong hands squeeze my hips, and with a jolt, I realize he's hard against my ass. Heat floods through my body and between my legs.

His deep, sexy voice whispers into my ear softly, and I strain to make out the words. They're indecipherable, lost against the loud music. I only know his accent is unexpectedly even more prominent.

It sounded as if he said something like, "show me yourself."

Yeah, right! Wouldn't you like to see me naked again!

The liquor is messing with my mind, making me think too hard! I dismiss it altogether and focus on the heat our dance is creating.

I sigh aloud, letting my body melt into his.

It's been forever since a man has touched me like this, with any sort of feeling or tenderness. I've forgotten what it feels like to be loved. Fuck-face Ray stopped touching me with anything but force and disdain more than six months before he died. Toward the end, it never felt good or right with him. It felt dirty and shameful. He treated me like his whore. Taking, he was always taking, and never giving anything of himself.

Lately, every part of me—heart, body, and soul—seem to be craving the affection more and more. Deep Breath.

Additional memories twitch to rise to the surface, to invade my mind, but I push them down, refusing to let them tarnish this perfect feeling.

Dancing with that stranger earlier felt awkward and wrong, but with Maeson it feels strangely right. By the way Maeson moves against me, I can tell he's enjoying himself. I turn, and for some strange reason each time I focus on his face it immediately grounds me.

Maeson's dark green eyes are visibly blazing. The passion in them is evident, even to an unseeing person. With a tug, he pulls me closer, his large hands resting on my hips. Our noses touch and his breath is warm and sweet on my skin. "You're so beautiful," he grits out roughly.

"Was... that a compliment?" I couldn't tell, the harshness in his voice canceled out the word beautiful. I almost wonder if he's taunting me.

"Aye. Very much so, Princess." His accent fades, but the idea that he's teasing me remains.

The word *princess* makes me want to slug him, and ache grows in my chest. However, I don't react. I refuse to rise to the bait. I won't let that single word wreck the moment.

Maybe it's not meant it the way I'm assuming?

In my drunken state, I have the courage to reach my hand up to touch his face. He flinches and my fingers freeze, lingering against his cheek for only a moment before I let my hand drop. With a pained expression, he sighs and closes his eyes.

He doesn't like being touched either?

Normally, I'd enjoy making him squirm for a change, but not after what I just witnessed. That brief moment told me so many things about the well masked, Maeson.

He has a troubled past of his own.

"Thank you, Maeson," I speak very softly, forcing him to lean into me, placing his ear close to my lips. As he does so, I make sure to exhale lightly, and he shivers.

Clearly, I affect him too.

"My pleasure." The pain vanishes from his eyes and he shows me those panty soaking dimples.

Oh, lord almighty, give me strength!

My mind and body are on overload, and I slam into that invisible too-drunk-for-my-own-damn-good wall. The stupor provided by intoxication evaporates and the soporific effect engulfs me. I rest my head against his chest and close my eyes.

Inhaling deeply, I memorize everything about this moment, from the scent of his lightly spiced cologne, right down to the tang of cigarette smoke clinging to his hair. We hardly know each other, yet he's holding me as if I matter to him.

How many times did I wish on every star that one day someone would embrace me in such a way?

Too many. I might never get the chance at a real fairy tale life or relationship, so for me, this will be the closest I'll ever get, and I'm going to cherish it for the rest of my life.

"Let me take you home." The accent he had moments before, has disappeared.

Don't want to leave. He feels too good. But I can't tell him that.

Instead, I shake my head emphatically. "No! Came wi' Mo. We go home taaaagather." The words don't want to form, and I can barely slur them out.

"You're about to fall asleep in my arms. Not that I'm complaining, but you need to lay down properly."

I peer up at him, the sensual look in his eyes is gone and replaced by worry. "Okayyy, stuffy landlord, take me to Moo Moo. No friends left behind, ya hear?" I shake my finger in his face, failing to keep a straight expression as a giggle escapes.

He's clearly enjoying himself at my expense because those damn dimples appear again. I bet they've broken hearts all over this world.

Don't break mine. Please?

"Aye, Princess, no friends left behind." He holds me up by the arm and guides me back to Molly.

"I was gettin' worried ya'll ditched me!" She looks wracked with concern, but I don't miss the very visible flush on her face.

Not too worried, I bet. Someone's been keeping you busy, my friend.

"No. Ruby said no friends left behind, so I'll take you both home. Your car will be picked up in the morning and brought to Ruby's apartment." Maeson's in and out accent has evaporated as if never existed.

Am I imagining things? I know I'm drunk but something's off.

"Where your accent go?" I whisper in his ear.

"It's for your ears only. Tis' our secret lassie," he whispers back.

Is he ashamed of it?

I'll ponder that one later when my mind's less fuzzy. I nod my head in understanding and lay it back on his chest. My eyelids droop and my head's spinning. I regret chugging those drinks now, but they certainly gave me the courage I needed to even be near Maeson. My eyes drift close, ready for sleep. "Please don't hurt me. Everyone hurts me. Always alone..." The words escape easily and unconsciously.

"I won't, just let me in, Princess. Show me who you truly are."

But if I don't know who I am, how can I show you that?

The thought remains unspoken, lost in the abyss as I fall into oh-so-familiar darkness.

-20-

MAESON

RUBY'S WARM BODY IS SNUGGLED against mine, safely tucked into the backseat of my car. She passed out the moment we settled in and seems unaware her fingers are gliding up and down my chest. Her soft touch makes my skin tingle and itch simultaneously, but I don't still her hand. On rare occasions, like this one, I quite enjoy the feel of a woman's caress.

My vision blurs as I watch her, and pain lances my insides. The words she uttered before slipping into unconscious territory gutted me. They've been on replay since we left the club... '*Please don't hurt me. Everyone hurts me. Always alone...*'

What exactly has been done to her?

"Pssst." Molly peeks at us from the front seat, pulling me out of my thoughts. "She okay back there, boss?"

"Yes. She's fine. Passed out." I look up at Molly who has a devious grin plastered across her face. "What are you up to?"

"Nothing, Mae Mae!" She holds up her hand innocently. "Why would you ask that?"

I'm beyond drunk and my patience with her games is wearing

thin. "That smirk gives you away, you ass hat! Talk. Now."

"Ugh! You suck. You no fun!" She slurs and proceeds to give me her adorable pout. "Ya needed a shot sooo I gave it to ya!"

"What? I'm not a fucking child! I don't need help in the bloody hooking up department!" My voice rises a couple of notches causing Ruby to stir in my arms. Instinctively, I run my hand through her soft hair hoping to soothe her.

"Ssshhh! Asshole! You'll wake her up, and she'll kill ya for touchin' her!" She giggles and faces forward in her seat to speak to my driver. "Right, Stavros? Fuckin' idiot tryin' to ruin his chances." She pats him on the shoulder and continues to laugh.

Without saying a word, Stavros shakes his full head of black hair and smiles kindly at Molly.

His nonverbal response makes me smile. "Stavros, I made a good choice in you. You always pick my side."

Molly snorts. "He didn't pick sides, *dumbass*. The man hasn't said a word since we got in the car."

The clever, older Greek man speaks up. "Mr. Alexander, I could say many things, but I like my job."

"Oh? Like what?"

"You're drunk, sir. Not tonight. Tomorrow we talk."

"No tell me now, or you're fired." I keep my tone level, to not give away that it's a flat out lie. I'd never get rid of the old geezer, but I need him to tell me what's on his mind.

For his precious job? He'll talk.

"Don't threaten an old man with his life's work. You're better than that." He pauses as he turns onto another street. "But since you want to know so bad..." He smiles at me in the rearview mirror. "You're an asshole when it comes to women. I marry my wife forty years ago, and she's still my princess... my queen. Be the strong-armed man in business, not in love. What you Xenos say... 'more bees with honey'... make honey, yios." His stern, accented voice reminds me of my father's.

"English, Stavros!" I shake my head. The man refuses to stop using Greek words when he knows I have no clue what he's saying.

"Xenos, is you, Americans. Yios, is son. Expand your horizon, Maeson, learn a new language. That Google person or Miss Siri, use them."

"Oh right, Miss Siri." I mock. "Thank you for the lesson, sensei." I look down at sleeping Ruby and an unexpected guilt rise to the surface. "I'm not an asshole all the time."

Am I?

"Yes, you are. You're fake with them all. Why you hide your true nature and even your culture? Are you ashamed?" His questions are more like accusations.

"I don't hide." I peer at Molly, but thankfully, she's fast asleep. "And I'm not ashamed. Too much has happened, forcing me to be this way. I was young when I relocated, leaving everyone behind, including my childhood home. Fresh off the boat, it was hard." When it comes to my personal life the need to defend myself is always present and this time isn't any different.

"You tell me bout fresh off the boat? Do you *hear* my accent?" His retort crushes my pathetic reasoning, but he's not done yet. "If you don't hear it, go to the doctor, check those ears. People make fun all the time. You know what I say? Fuck you, fucking mother!"

I can't help but smile at his hysterics. "It's mother fucker, not fucking mother."

He lifts his hand from the steering wheel and shakes his fist at me. "Don't you correct me! You say you don't like when people say things to you, but you say it to me?"

More guilt slices through me. "You're right, I'm sorry." I close my eyes and lean my head back on the seat.

My world is starting to spin.

"It's okay, Amerikanos. Be yourself. Don't be ashamed of who you are. I know many of your kind, very nice people." He makes another turn and shakes his head. "You know, even now it's only us and still when you speak, it's forced English."

"I tried a little with Ruby, but I don't know how to stop." I twirl one of Ruby's silky curls around my finger. "And what if people don't understand me?"

"So, who gives a shit. People don't understand me all da time. I repeat or try to pronounce better. You don't have to turn into Scottish mountain man overnight, stop forcing proper words so much. Be natural." He rolls his R's expertly.

I nod my head in agreement and realize it's too dark for him to see it. "Maintaining appearances is getting increasingly difficult. Even my father rags on me about it, he's disappointed that I've become so Americanized."

Stavros pulls into the lot and parks the car, turning to face me. "God never gave me children, but if you were my son? I would be too. Be proud of where you come from. Let your polýtimo kósmima"—He looks down at the beauty in my arms— "open you up and release you from all the guilt and pain you carry."

I raise a brow. "My what? And what do you know of what I carry?"

"Your Ruby, your precious jewel, the Greek Goddess you hold in your arms."

My eyes drop to her face, and I notice it. The perfect olive skin and wild dark curls. She must have some Greek somewhere in her family tree.

Stavros speaks again, breaking into my thoughts. "And don't think I don't know." He wags a finger at me. "I'm old, but I'm no' blind. I figure you out long time ago. Now go." Waving a hand in the air, he motions for me to leave. "Put them to bed and remember what we talk about."

"I will." I shake his hand, then wake Molly and head inside.

* * *

WE'VE GONE UP THE ELEVATOR and into her apartment, but this sleeping jewel in my arms has yet to stir. I'd question her "alive" status if she wasn't lightly snoring in my ear.

"Fuck! Mae Mae, Ima regret all those drinks in the morning. How the hell ya do this so often?" Molly rubs her temples as she plops onto Ruby's king size bed.

"Practice." I'm not doing so well either, but I'd never let her know that. I lay Ruby next to Molly, and she moves, rolling over on her belly.

"Who, Mae Mae?" She mutters sleepily.

Molly and I freeze, but before either of us can answer, Ruby's fast asleep again.

"Should we undress her?" I take in her tight clothing, thinking she'll be more comfortable in pajamas.

"What? You fuckin' creep! No way!" Disgust drips from her and she shoos me away.

"Whoa! It's hot in here! That's why I said it! Relax!" I roll my eyes at her.

"Right, ole creep. Out... out ya go!" She points to the door.

"Fine. Night." With an about face, I stomp out of the apartment.

Fuck this shit!

Try to be nice and I get the boot. Drunk women are ridiculous!

* * *

IT'S FOUR IN THE MORNING, and I've been lying in my bed, unable to fall asleep for what seems like for-fucking-ever. Too many bloody things running through my head. Things like my conversation with Stavros and the intriguing question of Ruby's family history.

I've never been with a Greek woman. Could be interesting.

Though this world has changed, and there are so many more Non-American people in this country than Americans themselves. Maybe it is time I grow the fuck up, and quit trying so hard to hide my heritage.

Jax knows—for fucks sake, we practically grew up together—and gives me shit regularly, even Axel does too. Molly suspects but doesn't push. She knows better. Then there's Ruby who outed me instantly, thanks to Gerard-Fucking-Butler.

Damn the old Greek man for making me question the choices I've made. Who does he think he is? I'm a grown ass man!

Enough!

I pull at the sheet covering my naked body and slide out of bed. I'd go for a run or take a couple more shots, anything to help me pass the hell out, but I'm two sheets too far into the wind. Instead, I pace the open area of my room, back and forth, until my reflection in the floor length mirror against the wall stops me in my tracks. I push my hair back and peer at the man staring back at me.

I'm getting too old for this bullshit.

Fully bare, I inspect the physique I bust my ass to upkeep.

Muscles for days? Check!

Big dick? Double check!

Saying I'm hung like a horse wouldn't be a stretch, especially when it makes the many women who've gone for a ride scream in pleasure.

Conceited? You bet your ass I am! Rightfully so, might I add. Not only do I have it, but I know how to use it too.

Flexing my muscles, I watch as they ripple and bulge.

I must admit I don't look so bad.

Except during times like these, when I'm all alone and able to be honest with myself, I can sense my age creeping up and pulling me down. Physically, I'm a solid ten—easily—and I could pass for a young twenty-year-old stud. But mentally, I'm as exhausted as a sixty-year-old, overworked man.

Before me is a body which exposes the well-hidden story of my journey that a select few know about. The constant reminders are always with me.

Exactly the way I want it. Erase the pain with more pain.

With one last look, I drag my now very heavy body back to bed. A deep yawn escapes, bombarding me with the long-awaited sleep I'm in much need of. As I get comfortable and start to drift, my phone goes off.

What now?

I pick it up from the nightstand and peer at the message.

INCOMING MESSAGE: Please call me. I need you... I miss you.

Nope, not happening, not again, not today... not ever. I don't need to see the number to know exactly who it is. She's mighty persistent lately.

Like I give a flying fuck anymore. Ignore, ignore, ignore.

Not wasting another thought on her, I simply trash the message. For added measure I fling the phone across the room, hoping it will smash into a gazillion little pieces like that will eliminate her from my life—forever this time. She shattered everything that once was good... including my heart. I sigh, and push off the bed, trudging over to grab the device off of the floor.

No such luck.

Great, a measly crack down the screen. My anger rises a few more notches, the beast is upset all over again, but the need for sleep pushes hard against it and ultimately wins. My eyelids automatically shut, but one last thought slips through my mind before it all goes black.

The heartless bitch needs to stop... I'm still recovering from all the destruction she left in her wake.

-21-

Ruby

Lifting a hand to my pounding head, I grimace.

What time is it?

Based off the way I feel right now, I'd say it's too damn early!

Need more sleep!

My eyes are sealed shut by an unknown force.

I knew I'd pay for all those Ruby Apple's, but did I drink that much?

With this fuzziness in my hungover brain, I can't even begin to process the events of last night.

No more thinking until I get some caffeine in me.

I pat around, feeling for my phone. It's not next to me, so I stretch out further and touch someone's warm hand. "Shit! Who the hell?" The words tumble out of my mouth and I fly off the bed in complete shock and fear. Grabbing one of my biggest pillows, I smack it hard across the person beside me.

What have I done? Who's in this bed with me? Oh God, did I bring that way too blonde guy home?

"Whoa! Stop!" Molly's muffled, but familiar voice comes

from beneath the pillow. Her head is buried, and she's lying half-dressed across the bed.

"Holy shit! Molly, sorry! I didn't know it was you, I thought it was a guy in my bed! I panicked!"

"You freaked me out, woman!" She sits up, looking as rough as I feel. Her usually pin-straight hair is sticking out at all angles. "Need coffee, stat!"

My sentiments exactly. Without a jolt of caffeine, I'll be grouchy all day. Our killer hangovers can only be cured by a good strong coffee.

"I'll go make some, meet me on the roof." I drop the pillow onto the bed, no longer needing my latest weapon of choice. I probably look silly as hell, but it can't be any worse than the paper towels I used as a weapon last time.

Yeah, that'll show 'em, Ruby! Oh, well...

I shrug and drag myself into the kitchen, grabbing the Illy Italian espresso out of the cupboard. I brew the strongest pot of joe possible, add a touch of sugar and steamed milk, then top them off with fluffy foam.

Cafe con leche style.

Armed with the two steaming mugs, a few cookies, an ashtray, four Advil, and two huge glasses of water, we're more than ready to remedy our raging hangovers.

"I'm heading up, Mo!" I yell out toward the bedroom before heading up the stairs.

Being on this rooftop is so peaceful. It's the one and only place I have to escape it all. The native birds are chirping away with their beautiful morning songs and I smile as I watch them flying around without a care in the world.

I wish I could be like them. Fly little ones… be free for me too.

It's a gorgeous sunny day already. The rays are beaming the right amount of heat, perfect to spend it outside. Well, at least until the mid-afternoon sun engulfs us with its immense dry heat. Taking a peek over the edge of the glass banister, there are people walking their dogs, and lounging on the benches. The city spreads out for miles below, but you'd never know, it's so quiet.

"Mornin', girly." Molly groans and shades her eyes from the bright sun as she strolls over, and takes up residence on one of the lounge chairs.

I curl up across from her on the end of one of my outdoor couches. "Morning, honey bunches of oats! Sorry about the pillow attack." I grin ruefully.

She laughs and waves it off. "You got goodies for me?" She eyes the tray hopefully.

Nodding, I extend a hand with two of the Advil and an icy, cold glass of water. She downs them both with a smile. Her head must be pounding as hard as mine.

"Coffee's fresh and waiting for you," I say and hand her a steamy cup, which she sips gratefully and gives a huge sigh of relief.

Molly tactfully lights a cigarette while holding the mug. I smile and pick up my own case, which I'd added to the tray.

"So, how long you been smoking?"

"A few years? But I stopped for a while, then started again not too soon after I moved here. Long story." I look away, not wanting to see the concern on her face.

Ray controlled my habits long enough. Nobody controls me anymore, and since this is my body, I'll do what I please with it. I've let others have all the power for far too long, and I'm going to squeeze every moment of enjoyment out of my life.

Why am I rationalizing my choices?

"Well, of all the times we've hung out I never saw you do it, so I'm surprised. Hid it well, you sneak!"

"Not hiding. More like… Okay, hiding it is." I smirk and cover my face with the coffee mug.

"You shouldn't hide from me, or the girls. Honestly, we will never judge you! And just so you know, I looooove long stories if you're ever in the mood to tell one." Her eyes implore me to open up.

"I uh…" I want to tell her everything, but the words won't spill out.

"Spit it out, woman."

"I was constantly being controlled, stressed beyond my limit, always upset, and tired of being on someone else's leash, so I started smoking to help ease some of the anxiety. Then more recently, that leash snapped and now that I'm free? I smoke because I want to, because I enjoy it."

Or maybe because I can't handle life properly, and I'm addicted.

"Alright... based on those terrible and sad words, I know there's a huge story there." She cradles her cup and takes a sip, and then looks up at me with sadness in her big blue eyes. "I'm sorry, it sounds like your past was a rough one. No one should ever control another person, it's downright disgusting and inhumane!" Her lip curls in disgust. The look on Molly's face tells me she has much more to say on the subject, but she keeps it to herself.

She's right, but I never had enough strength to stop them.

I'm curious as to what exactly she's thinking, as I've inadvertently let out another clue to my past. Although, I do appreciate her not pushing too hard. Generally, it takes me a long time to truly trust anyone, but for some reason, Molly's different. I can't help but believe she's genuine, and my trust level is building rapidly. No matter how much I wished for one, I've never had a girlfriend to confide in, and now that I do? It feels unreal.

I nod slowly to confirm her suspicions. "There is and it was, Hun, but I'm not ready to talk about it. When I am, though, I'll come to you."

"Please do." She seems satisfied and doesn't push it further, instead, she lights another cigarette. "Know that I will never judge you!"

"Thank you. I needed to hear that. Also, I didn't hide my habit because I'm ashamed. It's just that too many people put you down for smoking, drinking, and whatever else you want to do. It's ridiculous. Especially when it's my life." Inhaling deeply, I let the nicotine take over and my body relaxes.

"Isn't that the damn truth. You know what? Fuck all them people, they don't know you."

"Yeah, you're right. I need to learn how to give fewer fucks. Otherwise, I'll go crazy and the looney bin will drag me right back." I instantly freeze, realizing what I said.

Molly watches me intently. Her expressionless face gives nothing away, but her eyes scream a thousand and one questions. She simply nods, continuing to sip her coffee and smoke.

I squirm in my seat. Frankly, I don't want to talk about it. A subject change is in order. "Why do you smoke?"

She shrugs and kindly moves past the awkward moment. "Because shit stresses me out and it's my five minutes away from life." She takes another drink of her coffee. "I know, bad for the lungs, right? But it's my body. My end will come someday whether I smoke or not."

"I get it. My parents died from cancer and neither ever smoked, drank, or did drugs." I haven't talked about any of this in years. Probably because no one ever cared to listen. I realize I'm opening up to Molly in a way I never have with anyone— aside from perhaps my doctor. However, that's not the same thing as having a true friend to confide in. With Mo things simply spill from my lips with such freeing fluidity, it's scary.

"What did you just say? You lost both your parents to the same disease?" Molly's jaw drops.

"Yes, within the same month," I say awkwardly.

"I can't even imagine that kind of loss. I'm so, so, so sorry! What happened?" Sadness and curiosity visibly cloud her eyes. "Wait. I mean, if you don't want to talk about it, you don't have to." She stubs her now finished cigarette and lights another right away.

"No, it's fine, I can tell you what happened. I'll start from the beginning, but I warn you, it's a long story. I don't want to bore you." I follow suit, needing the inhale and exhale breaks. It's been many years since I lost my parents, and I don't mind talking about it anymore. I know it helps to talk... sometimes.

"That's fine. Go ahead, I want to get to know you, honey." She adds an extra bit of southern drawl to 'honey'.

"Alright." I pause and clear my throat. "My mother was forty and a well-known lawyer in Manhattan, and my father was fifty and had a busy Therapy practice in Long Island. As if it was meant to be, they met at a cancer clinic, and fell in love immediately, regardless of the disease killing them. They both knew their lives wouldn't be long, but their journey to recovery would be. So, they decided to go through it together, putting up a fight as a unit."

Molly leans forward and braces her face against her arm.

I take a long deep breath. "Shortly after they met they got married. My mom had no family left and my dad had no family in America to attend the wedding, so a close friend was their sole witness. Then about six months later my mom found out she was pregnant, even after all the doctors had told her it wasn't even a possibility for them because of the all the chemo they went through." Tears are building in my eyes, and I dab at the corners. I try not to cry in front of anyone, my ex, and foster father used to taunt me mercilessly if I showed any weakness.

"You don't have to—"

I put my hand up, letting her know I'm all right and take another deep breath. "I was their miracle child, and they kept me against the advice of all her doctors. I was born early at seven months as a healthy child and they fought to live as long as they could to raise me. Both lived longer than anyone could've expected. I was ten when they passed, and the doctors said they lived so long because of me." I take another break as tears stream down my face and it becomes difficult to see. I blink a few times, drawing in as much strength as I can, and meet Molly's tear-filled gaze.

I can do this. I need to keep going.

"After I was born they saved every penny to build a trust fund, knowing they'd leave me behind. In that time, they also made a photo album of our lives together, which I still have and cherish." I shift on my chair and take a long drink of water to ease the burn in my throat.

Reliving the loss is harder than I imagined.

I'm babbling, but I can't seem to stop the words from spilling free all at once.

"Wow. I—" Molly starts, but a sudden sob cuts her off. "Please... keep... going."

I close my eyes, fighting off fresh tears and continue. "Well, my father passed away in his sleep one night, his body simply gave up. When my mother woke up and realized, she broke down. In her own way, she'd lost hope and surrendered after that. She refused to take her medicine or visiting her doctors. It took three weeks until she was gone as well. With my mother gone, I was all alone, and I was placed into foster care, which is a story for another day. But yeah, that's what happened to my parents." I wipe the tears from my face and try to smile.

"Oh, my gosh." Molly smiles sadly and comes over, wrapping me into a big hug.

I let her hold me and we both cry silently, allowing the emotions to wash over us.

"I am so sorry sweetheart, I couldn't imagine..."

I sigh into her shoulder and pull away to look at her. "Thank you, Mo. I'm alright with it now, it's been fifteen years. I cherish every moment I was given with them, and everything they sacrificed for me. I couldn't have asked for better parents."

She nods and wipes her tears away. "You're right. Your memories of them will always be with you. I can't believe it, here I thought you came from money, and that you had rich snobby parents. I guess the saying is right... shouldn't judge a book by its cover."

I bob my head in agreement. "Exactly. A lot of people think the same thing and have no clue. If they'd ask, I'd tell them what happened. I'm not a snob, nor were my folks. The money they saved for me was supposed to go to a mortgage and bills. They let our house go into foreclosure, just to give it all to me. How can I be a pretentious person when I know what they went through?" My stomach churns at the reminder.

Those days were so difficult, being thrown out of our house, and forced to move into a one bedroom apartment. The three of us slept in the same bed and some nights I'd be woken up by my dad's constant coughing. What I didn't tell Molly, is the morning my dad passed, I was sleeping next to him. Squeezing my eyes shut, I push the vision away.

Molly pats my leg, forcing me to focus on her, instead of the past. "You're right, Ruby, they did so much more than my own ever did for me. Being grateful and true to their memory is the right thing to do. I bet they're looking down at their beautiful daughter with so much pride." She rubs my shoulder and smiles.

"I hope so, Molly, I hope with all of my heart. I did the best I could, I still am." I squeeze her hand and point to her mug. "Drink up! It's getting cold. How about we talk about something less morbid? This is bringing us down."

"Good idea, and thank you for sharing." She hugs me once more. "Now let me think, what else am I curious about?" The corners of her lips quirk up. "Hmmm, well that's easy, why don't you tell me what the hell happened with you and Maeson?" Her eyes are bright with interest.

She's so easy to read, I knew it was only a matter of time before she started asking questions about last night.

I roll my eyes and laugh. "For me to even get into that I'm going to need another cig, maybe something even stronger!" I light up and inhale a long deep breath, sucking the smoke deep into my lungs.

Oh, yes! This is better than my pills. Instant satisfaction, instant relaxation of the mind, body, and soul.

I exhale and smirk. "I have no idea where I should start."

She giggles. "Start? At the beginning woman!" She's eager for every dirty detail. The evil grin doesn't leave my face as I take another drag, making her wave her hand in impatience. "Come on, don't leave me hanging!"

Do I tell her everything?

"From the beginning? You sure?"

Her head bobs up and down, excitement glittering in her eyes.

One of the first things I do remember clearly makes me blush.

"Well, you know how I arrived in Dallas a day early?"

"Yes, but what's that have to do with last night?"

"You want to know everything from the start, so I'm telling you." I grin.

Her lips turn down into a confused frown. "Okay..."

"Well, that night, I unknowingly met my future landlord—aka Maeson—and slept with him."

"WHAT!" Her eyes bulge and her mouth hangs wide open.

I laugh uncontrollably at the shocked on her face. "Yup, I did. He was supposed to be a simple raw, animalistic, anger bang. An all-inclusive one night stand, *not* my freaking landlord who I'd have to face again."

"He knew who you were, though, and still slept with you? I mean, of course, you didn't, but *he* did!"

"Yes, he admitted to recognizing me, and even said something about me being intriguing and what not." I roll my eyes. "I'm not mad about it, we were both consenting adults. He had his reason and I had mine for allowing it to happen. Now listen carefully, because I will only ever admit this to you and no one else—he's like a damn fantasy Sex God. Great in bed—I wanted raw—I sure as shit got it and then some. It was so easy to lose myself with him, nothing else mattered but our needs." A smile forces its way onto my face at the memory of our half naked, entangled bodies.

The entire time I'm speaking, Molly's eyes are still practically popping out of her head and I laugh. "Don't look so shocked, these things happen." I pretend it wasn't such a big deal.

"To who do these things happen? Not me! What were the chances you two were at the same place and met? Zero! Mother fucker planned this! What a pig!" She reaches for her phone and swipes her finger across the screen a few times, then looks up with an odd look on her face. "He didn't plan it."

"I never assumed he did. How was he supposed to know I arrived early?"

"Oh, trust me, somehow he finds a way to know everything. But, this time, I expected him to have screwed up—he didn't.

There was a scheduled meeting for the proposal to purchase more land that night at the hotel's conference room." She looks down at her cell and then back up at me. "Shit. That's a serious coincidence."

"I guess so. Doesn't make a difference to me, Molly, I told you—one nighter. Either way, I can't get involved with someone like him. I just got my freedom back."

Oops, didn't mean to say that!

Molly is starting to gain my trust a little too much, and I've spilled information again.

"Go back a second, did you say Sex God?" She puts a finger in her mouth and acts like she is gagging. "That man is no *God*, more comparable to the devil in a disgustingly expensive suit, damn it!" She looks at me with a teasing smile. "And, I didn't miss that slip-up, I'll get that story out of you soon enough." She wags her finger at me, like the old lady she says she is.

"Damn straight, you nailed it right on the head! Exactly why I don't want him, I bet he has a new woman in his bed every night. Not my kind of dream guy." I'm fully dedicated to avoiding assholes like my ex, and Maeson reeks with the douche bag vibe. I shouldn't have let the man get so close to me, but I know I won't be able to resist him for much longer.

"*You* didn't hear any of this from *me*, but he's a lonely man. I've never seen him truly *be* with any women. Fucking woman may be his specialty, but *being* with them is not." She shrugs and takes a sip of her coffee. "Not that I would praise him to his face about this, but he works his ass off. Unfortunately, he's going to ruin it all because he's back to binging at the club most nights." Her eyes become tear filled, but she regains her composure quickly and she smirks. "Being part-owner has its perks, right? Anyway, that's his life in a nutshell. I will tell you, though, he's usually a very kind and understanding man. Oh, and I'm not going to lie to you, I can't say for sure he goes home alone all the time. If there's one thing Mr. Alexander is—it's private." She rolls her eyes.

"See? Too many questions come to mind in regards to him.

Ones I'm not interested in asking." I seriously mean it—I don't want to get tangled up in his life or him in mine.

The thought of involvement does bring up a few concerns about last night. I'm missing a huge chunk of what was said between us, but how much? I know at some point I blacked out. Everything is so fuzzy, except for the emotions and sexual desire I felt for him.

Those are as clear as day.

"If you say so, but if I were you I'd give him a shot. You already got the *hard* part over with." She pretends to gag again and we both laugh. It takes us a good minute to calm down and she continues. "To me, it seemed as if you had a lot more going on than you're acting like. Before you passed out, you looked so horny, your eyes were smoldering. It was like you were visualization eating him for a midnight snack! There's no hiding that sort of attraction! You might tell yourself it was a one-time thing, but your body language and behavior tells me a whole other story." She points her finger my way again. I'm getting her *'I'm an old lady'* act.

I couldn't have been that obvious. "Mmmhmm. If you say so." I sound guilty, but it's difficult to hide how I feel. She did catch me with him. There's no fooling Molly, I guess.

Damn it, she's far too sharp!

"I knew it, you bitch! You want to screw his brains out and not just that one damn time, you little minx!" Her laugh is so loud and proud, with that, *'you go girl'* tone to it.

"Righteous bitch! Fine, since you've become my closest friend I'll give you my honest answer. Pay attention because I'll never repeat this again either. I'll even go as far to flat out deny it if anyone asks." I pause and crack a shy smile. "Yes, I'd want to *'screw his brains out'*, over and over and over again!" I cover my mouth, shocked at hearing the words out loud. Talking like that would've been sure to earn me some sort of... repercussions. Be it from my ex or my foster parents, it wouldn't have been tolerated. "I have a question for you, though, what's the accent I hear when he speaks?" I rack my brain for the answer, and it's at the tip of my tongue.

She gives me a clueless look. "You know I've heard it from time to time, but in the last five years, I've yet to figure it out. I'm not that great with accents, except for northerners. That's an easy one to spot. Do you know?"

Gerard Butler!

I laugh as the actor's face pops into my head. "I remember now! It's Gerard Butler! Girl, he's Scottish! I could've been dreaming, but I have a feeling that's what he is." Only bits of the conversation come to my mind but wish I remembered everything.

Damn me for drinking so much and damn the amnesia it produces the next day.

"Yes! I think you're right, he's used words like *'aye'* and *'yer'* before, confusing the shit out of me. I had suspicions, but every time I asked he pushed me away and shut down the conversation."

Molly seems to be on the same page, confirming what I thought I heard with my own ears. I seem to recall him talking to me in a very strong accent. "I think so too, but I was too wasted last night, so I can't confirm."

"No, but you can now." She holds up my phone, which I must've left it unlocked on the table. The screen clearly shows it's currently dialing Maeson Alexander's number.

-22-

MAESON

SHIELDING MY EYES FROM THE bright sunlight, I gratefully sip the extra-large coffee Jax had shoved into my hands as he pushed his way into my penthouse. It's the only thing that saved him from an ass whooping. Well, that and the pack of smokes he brought along for good measure. I have no idea what the fucking asshole was thinking, showing up at this ungodly hour.

Nine-thirty in the damn morning. Seriously?

After all, he knows I was at the club last night. I adjust my Ray-Ban Aviators, lighting a cigarette as I stare across the expanse between the buildings, hoping to see... *her*. "So, what do you want?"

"Nothing." Unlike his normal self, his voice is monotone and robotic. "I see you finished remodeling up here. Palm trees, new couches, and even a freaking... kitchen?" He wanders over to the newly installed, fully loaded kitchen, and idly inspects the grill. "Shit man, you said you weren't going over the top, but looks like you've managed to make this rooftop into a fucking paradise."

"I know, but somehow after the first upgrade, I couldn't stop. Ended up costing me a fucking fortune, but it's bad ass, right?" Admiring the gleaming stainless steel, I join him near my newest pride and joy.

"Looks good, man." Jax forces a smile to appear on his face, but I'm not fooled. The way his shoulders are slumped along with the sad, lost puppy dog eyes he has going on right now, I can tell he's making small talk for my sake.

"Thanks, the whole thing needed some sprucing up, since lately, it's the only place that gives me peace. Anyway..." I look directly at him and cross my arms tightly against my chest. "So, why are you here? Aside from cruelly waking my ass too damn early on a weekend?"

His hand drops to his side and he releases a long drawn out sigh. "I've got a lot on my mind and needed to get out of the house." When he speaks, the grittiness of his tone makes my head pound even harder.

"I see." I could bitch some more, but this man never comes around with personal shit. After a long pull from the coffee in my hand, I wave a hand impatiently. "Talk. What's going on? What problem needs fixing?"

Jax walks over to the sectional on the right side of the roof and lies back into the cushions. "Always the *fixer,* aren't you? Fix everything and everyone else's crap but your own."

Refusing to be antagonized and affected by his grumpy mood, I don't respond and give him my best 'don't fuck with me' glare.

Getting the gist, he lets out a harsh breath. "Women. Women are the problem." His brow creases as if in pain.

"Tell me about it. They're enough to drive you up the wall. But, like the saying goes, we can't live with em' and can't live without em'." I shrug.

Story of my life. My whole damn existence seems to be about women.

"That's my current issue. You ever met a woman who draws you instantly and you can't do shit about it?" He groans.

"Unfortunately, yes, I have." As I'm about to continue, my

cell phone rings. "Speak of the devil." Toward Jax, I hold up a finger. "One sec." I hit the green button and bring the phone to my ear.

"Hey, boss!" Molly's southern drawl feels like a drill boring into my overly sensitive brain.

I scowl and narrow my eyes, wondering why she's calling on Ruby's phone. Disappointment rolls over me, I would've loved to hear her voice instead. "Molly." My voice is laced with the annoyance I feel. "How bad are the hangovers?" I rub my neck, easing the pain of my own.

"Not too bad! How's yours?" Her perky and disgustingly cheerful voice carries down the line.

How can she be so happy at this godforsaken hour? It irritates the living shit out of me!

"That's surprising. Unlike you young bucks, I know how to handle my liquor, so I'm good." The bald-faced lie slips out smoothly. "How can I be of assistance on this fine morning?"

"Oh, nothing boss, Ruby wan—"

"Ruby doesn't want a thing!" The woman haunting my every thought pipes up and my heart beats faster.

What's happening to me? Why is she making me react this way?

Frowning, I motion at Jax to give me another minute. The last thing I want to do is say something embarrassing in front of him. I certainly don't want Jax to know how much this woman has affected me in such a short time.

I can't even admit that fact to myself yet.

Turning my back, I lower my voice. "*Princess*. Am I on speaker?" I can visualize Molly's evil grin and that mischievous look in her eyes as she listens in on the call.

She pauses for a beat and I hear her shuffling around. "No, not anymore. Maeson, I'm so sorry Molly called, but I wasn't looking to speak to you."

I sigh deeply. "Did you miss me, Princess?" I whisper, with my homeland accent flowing fluidly, *just for her.*

If she can accept me, maybe others will?

"Nope, not at all. Why do you keep doing that? Is it a secret?"

Her questions flood out in a long string.

"Oh, the pretty little high and mighty princess won't admit she misses me? Why is that? Is the precious shy doll you pretend to be coming out to play?" I stroll to the edge of the roof and spot them. Molly's lounging and Ruby's pacing back and forth, her long, wild curls trailing down her back. "And, no, it's not a secret. Maybe you're just special. Have I chosen the wrong person to share a part of myself with?"

Maybe I'm affecting her too?

"I'm no doll, nor do I pretend to be anything other than who I am. I have some self-respect. I simply don't have the need to fall at a man's feet to prove I'm worthy, you ass hat! And stop fucking calling me *that*."

"Why should I? It's what you are, *darling*." I use the next best term, knowing it irks her to no end. Why, though, I don't understand or care. I enjoy listening to her aggravation. Before she can bitch me out further, I continue. "And no one said to fall at a man's feet, but you have to show him you're interested so things can get *interesting*." For effect, I drop my voice an octave lower in hopes of making her shiver with the same desire that's coursing through my veins.

"Nice talking to you, Maeson. I'll tell Molly she can have Monday off. Have a great day!"

There's complete silence on the other end.

Freaking woman hung up on me!

I glare at my phone, cursing the crack running down the screen. Sure, the stupid thing still works, but even looking at my phone and being reminded of my stupidity bothers me. Having Ruby dismiss me too? Well, I can barely contain my annoyance at the woman.

I stare at it for a minute longer, then shove it in my pocket and face Jax who's still on the couch. "My apologies brother, where were we?"

He shakes his head. "No big. We were on the subject of devil women, who torture us." He smirks slightly.

"Oh right. Whose noose is on your neck? Never heard you

talk about anyone in particular." I raise a curious brow. "Keeping secrets, are we?"

He huffs and waves his middle finger. "Like you don't have any? Please save the lecture, *brother*." He rolls his eyes. "Anyways, I... met someone a while ago and things... well, things are getting... *real*... fast and it's problematic for us to... stay together." He's having trouble getting the words out, like he's hiding something or in pain.

I hope it's the latter and not the former. I'll kill him.

I'm not one to beat around the bush, so I go for it. "Do you love her, whoever this *her* is?" I know this man and everything he's been through. Love will make or break him, sex with one nighters won't.

"I think I do." He hangs his head as if the shame is overwhelming him.

This must be serious.

"Fuck man, no good. How could you let that happen?" I feel for him. We both know what happens when that nasty little word—love is involved.

"It just did. Certainly, I didn't ask for it." Abruptly, he stands, stomping over to the edge of the roof, and stares out at the city before us.

As I follow him, I do a swift look-see toward the two women across the way. They embrace each other, then Molly waves goodbye. I almost walk into Jax, bringing my mind back to his problems. "Your thoughts kill you, don't they? Take a deep breath, man. You can handle it, just do the opposite of what you usually do. Remember what I taught you?"

"Yeah, *'be a dick and don't wear my big ass heart on my sleeve'*." He clenches his teeth and balls his fists. "After all these years, it should be second nature, but it's not! Damn it!"

I put an arm around his shoulder pulling him in. "Hey man, don't stress. You are you, not an asshole like me. Do I know her?" I watch Molly disappear from sight and unwrap my arm from Jax to pull out my phone.

"No—" Jax halts, watching me.

"Sorry man. Give me a sec, business calls."

I send Molly a text.

MESSAGE SENT: By the way, you don't have the day off. Still with Ruby?

When I look up at Jax his eyebrows are raised in annoyance. *Shit. Pissing an already irritated Jax is a bad idea.*

I smile innocently, hoping it looks apologetic enough. "I said sorry! Now, what were you saying?"

He shrugs. "Nothing. I know you're busy."

"No man, not busy. Keep talking, I'm listening in between work stuff." I slap his shoulder. "Loosen up man."

"You're right, I need to relax. So, what should I do?"

"Look you went down once before, and hard. Can you handle it again?"

"I'm not sure. But I think she's the one Mae—Maeson."

For a second I freeze but immediately dismiss the thought fighting to intrude. "Molly's been around us too long, huh? Now you're using that fuckin' name too?" I laugh, brushing it off.

He chuckles and shrugs. "I guess so. I have no idea why I said that shit." Releasing his grip on the glass paneled railing, he turns and lays back down on the couch.

With one last fleeting look at Ruby, who's pacing the expanse of her very own rooftop paradise, I follow Jax and drop onto my own spot. "No big. I'll excuse you since you're distraught over your *feelings*." I pretend to retch and then laugh.

Jax doesn't find it funny, instead, he frowns. "Laugh all you want, man, but don't act like you've never been in my place before. And you never know when you'll be in that spot again, so watch how hard you laugh this time around. I didn't get kicks out of your heartbreak days, but next time, I'll get to laugh at you for your *feelings*."

Internally I cringe but externally, I chuckle to play it off. He knows too well how hard that time in my life was, and that's precisely why I shouldn't make light of his situation. "Yeah, right—" My phone vibrates in my hand.

INCOMING MESSAGE: I sure do have off. Wouldn't want me to leave Ruby stranded when she needs my help would ya? BTW— don't ask stupid questions. You know I am not with her. Ciao, Boss Man.

Fucking woman. This one will drive me crazy before I hit my next milestone age.

I hit reply and shake my head.

MESSAGE SENT: Fine you have off. Only cause I'm an amazing man, spread the word. And how would I know? I'm inside. Ciao, Pain in My Ass.

"You okay?" Jax's voice pulls my attention back to him.

"Yes, sorry." I shake my phone in the air. "Work." As I'm doing that, it lights up again.

"*Sure*, work... looks like"—He leans in closer and squints— "Molly's the business you have?"

I can't pretend like her name's not flashing across the broken screen, so I tell him a half-truth. "She wants off Monday, for who knows what reason. And of course, being the great boss I am, I'll approve the vacation day."

I sneakily check Molly's message, almost missing what Jax says, but I catch the end of it. "Great boss, my ass."

INCOMING MESSAGE: Lie. I saw you out there.

I don't grace her with an answer but not because I've been caught in a lie. I need to pay attention to the only brother I know and help him somehow. Not mess around texting Mo.

"Hey, dickhead!" Before I toss my phone on the couch, I type up another message, this time to Ruby.

MESSAGE SENT: Don't ever end a conversation until it's over by both parties Miss Pretentious Ass Bennett. Have a pleasant day on that rooftop.

I hit send and continue. "I'm a fabulous boss!"

"If you say so."

"I do. Anyway, back to you. What can I do to help?" Another vibration hits my thigh, without picking up the phone, I swipe and read her reply.

INCOMING MESSAGE: When the conversation is a bore fest, I END IT, asshole!

Feisty little one, isn't she? Or Bipolar. Yet I still want—

Jax's voice cuts into my thoughts. "Nothing right now. I need to sort shit out in my head first. We're good, right? No matter what goes down? Brothers, right?" He can barely look at me and stares down at his shoes.

"Of course, Jax. What's your deal? Why's guilt eating at you like this?"

"No guilt." He recovers out of the awkward daze. "I wanted to make sure is all. We might not be blood, but you're all I got now that Da is gone."

This time I'm the one to look away. The loss of his father was a big hit on us both. He was my mentor and a father in place of the one who's so far away. "I know and I'm here for you, you bloody sap. Come here." I pull him into a man hug.

He's a teddy bear in a huge man's body, and a fucking softy for a man who used to be Military.

During our 'moment', my damn phone goes off yet again. I don't bother with it, but Jax picks it up. "Dude, it's Ruby." He shoves the phone against my chest. "No feelings huh?" His lips spread into a wicked grin. "Och, Ruby, lass… you make me feel so good. Aye, you bloody sexy woman, come hither."

I roll my eyes and salute him with my middle finger before turning away to answer the call. As I put the phone to my ear, I hear Jax's loud chuckles.

I'm never going to get away from his nagging now.

"Yes?" For some reason, I'm the shy one all of the sudden. She's managed to bring forth an emotion that after so many years was lost to me.

"Hey." Ruby's silvery voice makes my heart thunder in my chest.

What. The. Fuck.

"Hello, Miss Bennett." I try to sound aloof, not giving a thing away.

"Have I upset his, Royal Highness?"

"No, I have a... client with me." Unexpectedly, an urge hits me. An impulse to ask her out, like a damn pubescent teenager, but I don't even give it a second thought. "Can I take you out for coffee sometime?" I ask as casually as possible to not give away the nervous edge to my voice. My gut tells me this is the right thing to do. The right way to start over and earn some points in the *'he's a good man'* department.

Start slow.

"No, Maeson," she says flatly.

Hmm, didn't expect that.

"Why the bloody hell not?"

"Space, landlord. I asked for space."

"Haven't you had enough? I thought last night... changed things."

"You thought wrong, Maeson." Her voice has a slight shake to it.

She's lying—pretending to put up a fight. Challenging me yet again, lass?

Time to change the route this conversation is taking. "You look beautiful up there." I lower my voice to a hushed whisper so Jax won't hear.

With a slight turn of my head, I check to make sure he doesn't sneak up from behind. But he's gone. Oh, well, less for him to snoop in on. I face her building again and watch as she freezes, then spins, looking around as if to spot me. A smile creeps across my face.

Gotcha, Princess.

"Th... thank you."

"Next week? Saturday night... *princess?*" This time when I use the word, I make sure my voice drips with desire and not the usual mocking tone she's used to.

"Why should I go out with you next week, or ever? You've insulted me at every turn and you haven't a clue about me. You say I run and hide behind a mask, but you're no different, at all. So, again, please explain to me how a *'date'* is supposed to happen between us?" She doesn't appear to notice my use of the term.

Quickly, I think of a valid response. One less Maeson like, not filled with sexual content, and one that's real and true. "Maybe, this is me asking for a chance to prove I'm worth your time? Or maybe, I feel bad about the assumptions I've made about you."

"Oh, you better feel bad! When you assumed, you made an ass out of you, and only you!" Anger rises in her tone and I realize I've struck a chord. "So, let me get this straight, you're asking for an opportunity to prove you're not the asshole I know you are?"

"Yes, Ruby, that's exactly what I'm requesting."

Can I be an asshole from time to time?

Yes.

Have I been one to her?

Yes.

Well, folks, there it is—I've admitted I'm not always as amazing as you all believe. I actually have faults, downfalls, and imperfections—can you believe it?

I know, I can't!

Ruby sighs loudly. "Fine. Next Saturday." Then she cuts the connection.

Without sparing the damned device another glance, I tuck it

into my pocket and sigh just like she did.

Am I about to go on a real fucking date?

Now I feel like a dumbass schoolboy with this stupid smile plastered across my face.

Haven't dated a woman in years, and I'm going to start now?

This woman is bloody distressing. Worst of all, Molly is going to gloat for days. I can already visualize her smug ass grin as she rubs it in. But there is no other way. Ruby is like a skittish foal, and I need to take it slow and easy, so I don't spook her.

That leaves me at a crossroad, pursue her because she'll be worth it? Or screw it all to hell and continue the normal kiss them, fuck them, and ditch them routine? I don't have to replay that thought aloud to hear how ridiculous it sounds and how simple the decision should be.

So, I have no better choice but to...

Go on a real date.

-23-

Ruby

WHY DID I AGREE TO *go out with him?*

Mason's behavior is truly confusing and it messes with my emotions. One minute he's a charming sex god, straight out of a romance novel, tenderly asking me if I've missed him. The next? He's that devil of a man Molly told me about. Poking his sharp horns into my side, he purposely tries to piss me off by calling me out on shit I have no desire to face. What's even more aggravating is, he's formed a biased opinion of me without getting to know me and it's causing us to clash—*bad.*

Well, if that isn't the pot calling the kettle black. I really haven't tried to get to know him or give him a chance either, have I?

So, it's not just him, but I can't help it. I've learned it's best to push people away before they shove you off the cliff.

Right now, all I want to do is run away again. Run far, far, away. Not from pain, but fear, because I'm utterly terrified of getting into any sort of relationship that involves *emotions.* Especially if there is even the remotest possibility it could end up badly, like the one with my ex.

Yes, I'm afraid. So, what's new?

What if I give my heart up too easily? Maeson's an easy man to fall fast and hard for, and Molly even said as much. What will happen to me when he loses his interest?

It's bound to happen, there are so many women out there who are far more exciting than me.

Well, that's when I'll tumble even harder, this time breaking more than my heart and a few bones on the way down.

How many things can I break till there's nothing left of me? When will my need to fight to live, to love, and to start over, end?

After a while it's exhausting, being left, abused, and taken for granted by those you love.

It was much easier having one night stands with men I was only slightly attracted to, zero emotions involved.

Eventually, my need will no longer be a necessity, it'll fade, becoming the beginning to the epic finale of me giving up entirely. A complete evisceration of the Ruby my parents raised and fought to live for.

Only time will tell. Honestly, I'm not sure I can hold on for much longer. I can't go through it all over again.

My stomach plummets as his words hit me hard. 'Saturday night, Princess?' Hearing his deep, hushed voice over the phone gave me instant goosebumps.

Will he become the beginning to an end I won't come back from? A new man, along with a renewed need to fight, that's completed with the same old disastrous ending? Will it be as deadly as the last time?

I stare distractedly at the stunning view spread in front of me, clearing my head of all the negativity and fears creeping into it. The memories crowd in, and for a moment I'm overcome with doubts. Ray's harsh face flashes through my mind.

Deep breath!

No! I can do this! I won't let the last words he said to me come to reality. My heart pounds profusely. Our life together incessantly haunts me, and I can't seem to get away from it. But the guilt he vowed I'd have for leaving him has never surfaced.

Am I a monster as he so wanted me to believe? A terrible person because he took the action he did?

He warned me not to push, and I did anyway. I got the courage to start packing, but before I could get away, he broke me. And I'm still picking up the shattered pieces.

His last words vibrate through me. *'If you leave me, my little Ruby, I will kill myself. I will make sure you will never forget me. That you will never forget us. You will carry the guilt with you, knowing you brought me to this.'*

The guilt I carry in my heart is for many things, but... trying to get away from my abuser will never be one of them. I shove the memory away, out of my mind, even if it's for a short amount of time. They always find a way to come back and haunt me.

Deep breath.

Stretching out on a lounger beside the pool, I close my eyes, needing to feel the soothing caress of the sun's hot rays on my skin. Slowly, I relax and continue to inhale deeply, as the next memory tries to surface.

After opening up to Molly and finding myself all alone like this, I can't help but replay parts of my past that have forever changed me. Right now, in this moment, the last conversation I had with my mom before she passed away pushes to be re-lived. This one I allow to take over. The bitter-sweet memory is as clear to me today as it was when it happened fifteen years ago.

* * *

AS I'M ABOUT TO FALL *asleep, my mother comes into our bedroom for our bedtime routine. Lots of snuggles and butterfly kisses. Usually, we talk about school and how much I hate homework, but tonight I have something else I want to talk about.* "Mommy? Where's Daddy?"

"He went to heaven, sweetheart." She twirls my curls around her fingers.

"Will you leave me and go there too?" I have so many questions, and I don't have much time to ask them. She's slipping away and all that's

left is a shadow of the mother I love so much. She's so thin and pale that I worry about her vanishing entirely.

"Yes, love, one day. Remember how I've always told you we're both very sick?"

"Yes, but I prayed you'd both get better."

"I know, my sweet daughter. Though, sometimes even with prayer, we lose loved ones along the way. God needs angels to protect you from above." Tears form in her eyes even as she smiles.

She has the most beautiful smile I've ever seen, and my heart swells with love. "But I want my two angels here, not up there. Who will take care of me when you leave?" Tears track hotly down my cheeks.

I'm so scared of being left all alone. My dad left me, how can I bear losing mom too?

"Good people will take care of you, baby. Daddy and I have everything taken care of for you, I promise." Still smiling, she tucks a strand of her thinning gray hair behind her ear.

"I trust you, but if you and Daddy watch me from above, will you always protect me?" I worry about this every day. Sometimes I even wake up in the middle of the night, the darkness pressing in on me as I clutch the only thing I will have left of my parents, a photo album they made together for me. They gave it to me not long ago, right before daddy died, and I need the security it brings, something to hold onto.

Her soft hands reach out and brush the salty tears from my cheeks. "Yes, agapi mou, yes, every day we will protect you." She pulls me into her arms, holding me tightly.

"Dad used to call me that. What does it mean?"

"It's Greek for my love. You were and always will be our love, our miracle."

"He told me when I get older I should learn his language and not forget where I come from. Where did you come from, Mommy?"

"Well, I'm Italian, but I was adopted by an American couple as a baby, so I never knew my birth parents or the language. Then Grammy and Gramps passed right after you were born, so you never had a chance to meet them."

"What about Dad's family? Can I meet them? Could I go there and not to strangers? Please?"

"*His family lives far away, in Greece, and I've never met them. Maybe one day when you get older you can find them. I've gathered things for you in case you ever wish to. Nikolas said he has a big family there, but we were so busy with… life… we never had a chance to take you for a visit.*"

"*Does that mean I have Grammys there?*"

"*Yes, I believe you do and aunts, uncles, and cousins.*"

"*Can they take me?*"

"*No honey, they can't. They don't know about you.*"

"*Why not?*"

"*Well, your dad didn't have a very good relationship with his parents, so when he left it hurt them.*"

"*Oh. So, they got mad and didn't talk to him anymore?*"

"*Exactly. I'm sorry baby, so sorry. I wish things were different.*"

I shrug. "*That's okay. I love you and when you see him? Tell Daddy I miss him every single day.*"

"*Of course, I will. I love you too, more than anything in the world. You're the reason we fought to live, Ruby. Please don't forget that.*" Her tears wet my hair.

I snuggle in closer, knowing one day soon she'll be gone too. "*I know.*" I squeeze as tight as I can, never wanting to let go of her. "*Can you please tell God to leave you with me? I still need you.*"

"*Ruby, I beg him every single minute of the day.*" Her arms wrap around me, tightening in return.

"*Me too.*" I have so much more to say, and I've already prayed many times for a miracle. I did the same for my dad, and it didn't work, nothing can save my mother from the cancer eating away at her.

"*Close your eyes, Ruby, it's time for you to sleep, I'm here. I'll always be here, baby.*" Her voice shakes, and I don't believe her.

Dad said he'd always be there, and he left. She will too, and I'm not ready!

"*Please don't leave me all alone!*" Panic sets in and my body shakes as fear rises at the idea. I can barely breathe and I begin to choke.

She quickly helps me up and caresses my back. "*Oh love, take a deep breath. Remember how I taught you? Breathe in. Deeply. Yes, like that. Okay, now exhale, let it all out. One more time, in and out.*" Once I *visibly relax and my eyelids become heavy, she tucks me back under the blankets and continues to speak. Her soft voice soothes my pained soul. "Never will I leave you all alone, baby. I'm always with you, right here." She places her hand over my heart.*

"Really? Forever, and ever, and ever? You're my agapi mous, like I'm yours, right?"

"Forever my precious gem, my Ruby, our agapi. I love you," she whispers in my ear.

I feel better knowing my heart will always be full of love for them and theirs for me. "I love you too, mommy." I smile and am finally able to drift off to sleep.

* * *

SALTY TEARS STING MY EYES as the memory washes over me and grips my soul. Even after all these years, I feel the pain of losing my parents acutely every single day.

Unfortunately, my sweet, loving mother died peacefully in her sleep that very night. Unlike my father who gave up and wished for the pain to end, my mother fought long and hard, terrified to leave me behind, but her poor body couldn't hold on any longer. That morning was the second hardest day of my short life. I called her name over and over, shaking her in the futile hope she'd wake up. With tears streaming down my face, I called nine-one-one as she'd instructed.

She knew one day soon she'd be gone, so she'd told me what to do when it happened. I barely recollect those next few hours, the apartment swarmed with strangers, and all I could do was curl up in a corner with my album and cried.

I remember staring out the car window as we pulled away from my home for the last time, with only a small bag of my most precious possessions the lady from social services helped me pack. That day forged the path my life would travel on, forever altering my life. Even thinking about it still has the power to bring me to my knees. Three times I've been slammed down to the ground and twice I've managed to pick myself up.

This third time can't be as hard, can it? Or has too much happened?

I sit up, brushing the wetness from my cheeks, and attempt to gain my composure.

On the bright side, I've made a great friend in Molly, and even in Sammie and Bekka from Crossroads.

And what else is bright for you right now?

Well... there is the possibility of a da—

Maybe I shouldn't get ahead of myself and call this thing with Maeson a *date*, but I think I have one to look forward to.

As much as I pretended to not care, or agreed to go to appease him, I know deep inside, I'm the only person standing in my way right now. All I'm doing is holding myself back from living and pursuing the things Maeson makes me feel. It's time I march forward, push through the fear and anxiety the man brings forth in me, and do the unthinkable—give him a chance.

Deep breath, Ruby, deep breath.

In a flash, Maeson's striking face appears in my vision. The thought of seeing him again makes my stomach twist and turn. Amongst the distress invading my insides, there's a tinge of fluttering butterflies in there, filling me with something foreign... could it be *hope*?

* * *

Saturday has taken forever to arrive and now that it's here, I'm starting to freak out. All I've managed to do this morning is make buttered toast and of course, there's no such thing as breakfast without—coffee.

I ended up spending the remainder of the week visiting a few local shelters and provided them with a few boxes worth of supplies and frozen foods. It was such painful sight to see all those battered women.

After finishing up with the last one yesterday, I couldn't bear the thought of going out with the girls. I wasn't in the right mood to go anywhere or be around anyone, especially not for some Friday midnight partying. But that didn't stop me. While the rest of the crew was drinking, so was I, binging on half a bottle of vodka—all alone.

Vegging out in my own misery.

Recalling or being reminded of my past affects me in the worst of ways. Each time I do, I find myself resorting to the quickest and most effective habits allowing me to escape it.

Naked, I flop onto the couch and let out a puff of air. My eyes glaze over as I search for the inspiration I desperately need to prepare for tonight. It will be a few more hours until he's to pick me up, but I absolutely need to occupy myself, or I'll go nuts.

Oh! I know just the thing!

Do what women do best. Try on a million outfits. That'll most definitely take me a few hours.

And then some.

I reach out across the ottoman and turn on my iPod that's laying there. Loud music fills every room in the house and the beat of the current song gets my blood flowing.

At last, a nice reminder of the good times of my life.

In my first year of college, I met many people from all over the world and their music stuck with me. Of them all, my favorites were Albanian, Turkish, Romanian, Bulgarian, Arabic, Indian, and of course, the Greek music my father used to play when I was little. The one playing right now is called *'Bow Down'*, its Albanian and the smooth upbeat rhythm seems familiar like I've heard it before and not only on my playlist. I rub my temples, trying to place it.

At the club.

I was so out of it that I never realized some of the lyrics weren't in English. Why would Maeson have such a playlist? Quite surprising, few people go out of their comfort zone when it comes to music. It's usually the same old Rock, Hip Hop, Rap, and Radio hits that are repeated all damn day long.

I'll have to ask him about it when I see him later tonight.

Oh, that reminds me! I need to drill him on why he put my drink on the menu without my permission.

He probably thinks I didn't even notice!

The melody changes, my cue to get the hell up and motivated. Begrudgingly, I lift my body and trudge to the bedroom.

After another solid fifteen minutes of dancing around my bedroom, I explore every outfit option in my closet and eventually work on perfecting my hair. After several attempts at hairstyles, I choose the safest option—leave it loose—letting it cascade in curls down my back. It's a little more wild than usual, but I must say, I like it this way.

When I was younger, I used to beg my mom to cut it all off, and now as an adult, I've embraced it. The curls remind me of my father's, even though his hair was usually short.

Taking a break from fussing with my appearance, I savor a few minutes to myself and enjoy another cup of coffee.

I raise the steaming mug in the air. "Here's to my first date in over three years, and to not giving up quite yet."

* * *

FIFTEEN MINUTES AND COUNTING!

Glancing nervously at the clock for what seems like the hundredth time, I struggle to grasp that the final countdown to his arrival has begun. Maeson will be here soon, like too soon.

What if this goes terribly wrong? What if it's like when we first 'officially' met and we hate each other? I must admit, initial impressions aside, that stiff and arrogant man has grown on me.

My hands shake uncontrollably as I pick up the small bottle and rattle it, listening to the pills inside. Trying to breathe, I use the technique my mom taught me when I used to have my panic attacks. It doesn't work. I need the medicine, I need to take them, it's the only way.

Right? I'm too weak still.

No! I refuse to take them! I need to try and live my life normally without them. Everyone has a form of anxiety but keeps on going, and so will I.

Will I, though? Can I?

The familiar internal battle between my heart and my common sense begins. Against my better judgment, my feeble mind wins and I take one tablet before I put the finishing touches on my makeup.

He should be here in five minutes! Yup, need the pills, I'm not strong enough.

I take one last look at my reflection and I'm immensely satisfied with what I see in the mirror, no need for any more changes. My red V-neck tee-shirt with a black undershirt peeking through, cropped dark washed boyfriend jeans, and black Keds are casual but still dressy enough for a date. I left the wildness of my hair alone, and my eye makeup is a vintage black eyeliner paired with Mac—Ruby Woo—hands down the perfect red lipstick. Of course, the name similarity didn't escape me either.

My appearance is put together without looking like I'm trying too hard. I don't want him to think I feel the need to impress him.

At eight o'clock sharp, my phone buzzes.

INCOMING MESSAGE: I'm here

MESSAGE SENT: Coming down

Well, here goes nothing!

I grab my purse, and moments later I step through the glass doors.

In front of my building is a sleek and shiny black car. Luckily, I have a secret love affair with cars, so I know it's a beautiful, brand spanking new Dodge Charger. The dark tinted windows initially make me anxious, and as I approach it worsens. The driver's side door opens and Maeson appears. Like a true gentleman, he comes around to open my door, waiting until I settle into the front seat.

He bows his head. "Ruby, you look... beautiful."

Now he's done it, with those few words, the butterflies have been freed, running wild with hope, and nervousness in my belly. I attempt to settle them down by looking away from his devastating dimpled smile.

Seriously? You know better.

Yeah… Of course, I do.

There's no need for me to get overly excited over meaningless words. It's actions that are more telling and worth that much energy.

-24-

MAESON

EVEN AS IT LEFT MY mouth, I knew the word was too simple—
beautiful. It's nowhere near strong enough to describe her, but it's
the only one I could come up with in the moment. It's like that
sappy shit where a woman's so gorgeous you're at a loss for
words.

*Stumbling and tongue-tied like a complete fool? Yes, that's me right
now.*

"Thank you. Not so bad yourself." Ruby's red lips move as if
in slow motion.

My eyes are glued to them, fixated, and all I can manage is a
smile before I close the passenger door.

Inwardly, I smirk.

Not bad at all is right on the money.

I made sure to choose the best of the best for tonight. I'm
impressively decked out in Armani. In black, *of course*, all the
way down to the tips of my highly-polished shoes.

What else would I wear?

"Ready for the best coffee you'll ever have?" Settling into the driver's seat, I fasten my seatbelt.

She follows suit and her amber eyes shyly meet mine. "Yes, for sure! Where are we going?"

What a sexy little minx. Shy one minute, feisty the next, and then back to the timid mouse.

"My favorite coffee shop downtown called Aroma Espresso Bar. It's nothing like the chains we are accustomed to, and it uses the freshest coffee beans from all over the world." I hold back a smile as I watch her eyes widen.

It's gratifying that I can impress her. Most women are so jaded and worldly, but there is something incredibly refreshing about Ruby.

"Well, that sounds... delicious!" She must notice my focus is solely on those red lips because she turns her head, staring straight ahead. Her voice changes to a whisper. "I've never been to a fancy cafe before." Sadness drips from her tone.

There's so much I don't know about this woman.

I'm instantly gutted by her admission, and awkwardly extend my arm, tenderly touching her fingers to provide some sort of comfort. "Then this will be a nice treat for both of us. It's my secret getaway. I'm sharing it with you, but you can't tell a soul about it." I smile deeply and meet her eyes with a wink.

Heat flickers in her gaze, but before I can interpret the meaning behind the look, she breaks our connection, and carefully removes my hand before turning away to face the window.

We drive in silence for several moments, until I hear her take a few long, slow, deep breaths then releases the last one in a rush.

Calming mechanism? Guess I'm not the only one who needs one.

"I won't say a word." She barely manages. "We all need a place to escape to occasionally. I... um... I get it, Maeson." She shrugs and leans her head against the glass.

There's tension in the air, and I'm unsure of what to say, but somehow, I need to find a way to diminish the hopelessness from Ruby's entire demeanor. "Thank you... Princess." I give her a sideways glance, obviously knowing how the term affects her, but I hope it'll make her smile.

Yet she has no idea why I use it and how much it truly means. If only she did... Only once before has it slipped from my lips, then never again... until now... until her.

Her head snaps in my direction and she glares at me with a death stare any grown man would fear. "Why? Oh, why do you insist on calling me that?" She huffs and crosses her arms over her well-endowed chest.

Of course, I noticed. What red-blooded guy wouldn't?

"Because that's what you are."

She throws her arms in the air and growls. "I am not the spoiled little princess you seem to think I am! How many times must I tell you? There's far more to me than meets the eye, you know!"

She thinks I don't realize that?

I do, that's why I'm putting forth so much fucking effort into this.

Am I not trying hard enough for her to notice?

Apparently not! Damn it! For the life of me, I can't fucking figure this woman out. Or maybe the problem is me and the fact I've never had to work this hard before. "I know, Ruby. I'm only teasing. Don't take everything to heart. Why does a silly nickname bother you so much?"

The way her body stiffens shows me that I've hit a touchy subject.

"I didn't always hate the name, but certain people made it so I despise the sound of it. That's why! Hearing it said with such sarcasm hurts. It literally pains me and brings back too many bad memories. Can you understand *that*, Maeson? Or are you too dense?"

If I hadn't been peeking over at her the entire time she spoke, her tone alone would tell me she's thoroughly irritated now.

"Of course, I understand that, but how was I supposed to know? Most women enjoy cute pet names. Who knew you'd be the oddball of them all. Damn, for a young woman you're very tense and sensitive," I say matter-of-factly.

"You'd be too, living in my shoes, Maeson. At least I'm trying to change. What's your excuse?"

"I could say the same, only difference is I've had more years to become this uptight." I chuckle. I'm not afraid to admit who I've become or ashamed of it either.

I be who I be, simple as that.

"Good. Then we have some sort of understanding of each other. Let's call it the fresh start you wanted. We've established we each have our own stories that made us... who we are today. No judgments, no questions."

"Agreed." I sneak another glance at her. "Well, minus the questions part, I might have a few."

She shoots me another killer glare. "Not tonight you don't." Then her brow furrows as she nibbles on her bottom lip. She doesn't peer my way again, she's back to focusing on the road ahead. "So. Uh. How many years *do* you have on me?"

I can sense her eyes burning holes through me.

It's about time she asked. Surprised she hasn't till now.

Guess curiosity isn't killing this pretty little pussy cat. Although, most women do have a hard time nailing the exact number down. It must be the combination of my stellar looks and heritage making it too tough to figure out. They always say the same thing, *'You're definitely older than me, but by how much? I just don't know?'*

"Enough of them," I grumble.

"Please! Tell me. How old *are* you?" She rotates her body, demurely crossing her legs.

I continue to look straight ahead, using my peripheral vision to avoid an accident. "No, lassie, you won't like me anymore if I tell you." Unexpectedly, I'm engulfed by sadness and fear, and I let the hold I have on my accent go, allowing it to sneak through.

Where did that come from? I've never given two shits about my age!

"I promise your age will make no difference to me. Weeelll... if you're not over fifty, that is." Her tone is light and teasing.

From the corner of my eye, I see the cheeky grin on those

tantalizing lips, and I give in to her pleading. "Fine, you win. I'm thirty-seven years young." I'm attacked by feelings of inadequacy and a touch of self-consciousness. This must be the first time I've ever been taken over with such weakness for a woman.

Bloody hell, and for one I barely know anything about at that.

"WHAT?" Her loud voice startles me, and I almost jump out of my skin. "No way! You don't look a day over thirty!"

Smart woman, she knows how to stroke my precious ego.

"Thank you, Ruby, I appreciate that. You know how to make an old man feel good about himself." I laugh appreciatively and pat her thigh.

Not in a creeper way, more like… I reached out and it's all I could touch without crashing the car.

Oddly, the contact makes her flinch, and even though she regains her composure, it doesn't go unnoticed. "You're not an old man, and I'm twenty-five, not a spring chicken anymore myself!" She lets out a soft giggle.

That right there makes the now very familiar pang reappear full force in my chest. Surprisingly, I burst out laughing. "You can be so adorable when you're trying so hard to be serious." A sobering desire bombards me. "I noticed that the first day I met you." Without me even trying, there's a huskiness to my words which wasn't there before.

Random thoughts pierce my skull, rushing and gushing in all at once, and I panic internally.

She's changing me.

Run.

She's affecting me.

Run faster.

But the beast roars against my fears, giving me the courage I need *not* to turn this car around. Instead, I keep to the intended path and reduce my speed as the familiar sign appears. We exit the North central expressway and take the ramp on the right.

"Well, I am serious. Every morning when I get out of bed, I hear the cracking sounds my bones make. Anyway, I have another question for you. What is your middle name? I know it starts with L."

"Hmm. How about you guess."

"Leroy?"

"*Oooookay*, obviously *not* Leroy! Stop guessing, that's a terrible name." I cringe at the thought. "It's Lachlan."

"Ohhh. That's unique and not even close to Leroy at all!" An adorable giggle escapes her. "I like it. What about your parents' names?"

"Inquisitive one, aren't you?"

"I always am. You just don't know me well enough. So, spill."

"Fine, since you insist. My da's name is Taveon Lachlan Alexander and my ma, Freya Catriona Alexander."

"Wow, such beautiful names! Don't hear them too often."

"Nope." I don't elaborate. My parents are not up for discussion quite yet.

I think this time she notices the change in my demeanor and moves on to another subject. "Alright, so back to what you said before. What else did you notice about me when we first met?" She quits ogling and the heat of it leaves me instantly.

I take my eyes off the road. No matter the consequences, I need to see her reaction. "I noticed how beautiful you are, how hidden you keep your heart, how sexy your attitude can be, how broken you are inside, and how badly I wanted to fuck a woman I just met." My voice drops and my accent grows thick with those last words.

Realizing I could've just ruined my chances with her, my heart about stops. Panic sets in and I want to say more to explain myself but nothing comes out. Either way, she should know why I took her to bed that night and what I truly felt that day, no holds barred.

Since when do I over explain? Since never.

So, bottoms up and here's to me trying... yet again. Even though I could quite possibly fuck this whole thing up.

-25-

Ruby

His startling response leaves me stunned. I didn't expect those words to come so freely from his mouth.

I thought he would've at least beat around the bush a while longer.

There's a long, awkward silence between us, while I scramble to gather my thoughts and find enough courage to meet Maeson's eyes. My mouth waters at the idea of being sexual with him again, but my damaged heart quivers in fear.

This time more emotion would be involved. More than I'm ready for.

Maeson's not one of those random guys you meet who you know nothing about or care to, and you simply want to sleep with as an escape for the night.

Boy, do I know that fact now.

He's the kind of man that pulls you in the moment his green eyes meet yours. He's the kind of man who drips with primal desire and a primal instinct to devour whatever is left of a woman's soul. And if I let this dangerous man close enough?

Guaranteed he'll do the same to me. He's already started.

Ray always used vulgar language to hurt me, to make me feel like shit, and keep me under his control. *'I want to fuck you.'* Ray would say and I'd never had a choice in the matter.

Rubbing my temples, I attempt to clear my mind of my ex and concentrate on the man next to me. Maeson almost made this common vulgarity sound like a compliment, and it's sexy in a weird sort of way. I'm not quite sure what to say in return, and I'm at odds with myself.

Do I play along and show him the hungry woman I am inside? Or do I steer clear of her, keeping my mouth shut and make him squirm?

Maeson looks so confident and powerful that I can't help but stare at him, memorizing everything about him, all the while trying to decide what makes him tick.

As if sensing my eyes on him, he glances my way, giving me one of those grins, his killer dimples appearing. It seems he knows how his smartass comment affected me, and he's enjoying it!

"Don't look so smug, old man." I'm trying to stay serious and let him know he can't get away with talking to me like that. However, those dimples suck me in. The corners of my mouth twitch as I unsuccessfully resist the urge to smile back at him.

"Old man? So, the old jokes are going to start now?" That damn cocky grin on his face widens.

I narrow my eyes to show I'm annoyed, feeling the need to keep some control here. "Yes! Now that I know you're twelve years my senior, I have rights to old man jokes."

"Oh! Right, lassie, tease me all you want! Payback's a bitch." He laughs evilly, but in a joking kind of way.

At least I think so.

I can't help but laugh too. "I *can* take it, Grandpa."

"We shall see. Until then, why don't we go back to the fact you never responded to my observations of you? I might be old, but my memory is intact." He's so busy looking at me, he jerks the car to the right, swerving to avoid an oncoming car.

I clutch at my seat. "Stare at the road, *Lachlan*, not me!" I say using his middle name. It's very sexy, almost as sexy as his first name.

He chuckles, unfazed by our near-death experience. "Again, changing subjects, trying to distract me by using my middle name?"

"Yes, for now. How long till we get there?" I release my death grip of the seat cushion, relaxing slightly since he's back to focusing on the road—like he should've been this entire time!

"Why? Are you in a rush to get this over with?"

"No, just looking forward to having some fresh coffee with decent company." I take a stab at being as smooth as he is with words and let the banter flow easily back and forth between us. This is something altogether new for me.

This isn't so hard. I've got this!

"Lass, we should be arriving in a minute. But you can't fool me, you're only in it for the coffee, not the company." His accent is coming through loud and clear tonight.

He's right about the coffee, but I won't admit it.

"No!" Instantly defensive, I cross my arms over my chest and pout. "You're wrong, you seem like a nice enough man. *When* you *want* to be."

"I'm always nice. Anything more requires a friendship, which I typically avoid."

What an odd thing to say.

"You don't want friends?" This is truly confusing, he sounds so serious about staying away from friendships, whereas I crave them.

"Friendships are things I enter into very carefully. People tend to give you false hope and end up letting you down too many times to count. I have many acquaintances, but *very* few close friends. All it takes is one bad experience to learn an important lesson about trusting people." He pulls into an empty spot, turning off the engine, but neither of us moves to get out.

The validity of his words affects me and the need to speak up rises. "Now, that's a truth I've learned the hard way."

"Then, that's another thing we have in common, Ruby." He gives a little nod before he opens his door and comes around to my side of the car.

Few men are chivalrous these days, and I appreciate the gesture as he holds out his hand to assist me from the car. "Thank you."

"My pleasure. Ready?" His hand is so warm and reassuring as he leads me into the espresso bar.

The cafe is small and dim, lit by a few flickering candles.

Oh, how much I love the smell of fresh coffee!

The different chocolatey, nutty, and spicy scents immediately take over my senses. They're so powerful, yet they have such a calming effect on me.

Maeson picks a spot in the back corner, where we can watch the baristas make the specialty beverages. "Is this okay?" he asks as we take our seats.

"Yes, perfect." I'm immediately enamored with this place.

Before we can look at the menu our server comes over to greet us. "Howdy! Name's Helen, I'll be serving ya'll two tonight. Do you guys know what you'd like?"

"We need a minute, please," Maeson responds.

"Alrighty, take your time." She smiles and walks off, stopping to chat here and there on her way to the front counter.

Reading this long list of options on the menu is giving me a headache. Setting the confusing thing down, I peer up at Maeson. "Do you have any suggestions?"

"Aye, the macchiato or the cappuccino are the best here."

"I'll try the cappuccino…" I notice an extra flavor selection available, and add, "with a dash of hazelnut."

"Great choice. Nice extra touch, it enhances the whole experience." Maeson calls over our waitress and places our order.

"Why do you drive a Dodge? You seem more like a Lamborghini or Maserati kind of guy?" The random question pops into my head, and of course, I ask it since it's been nagging at me for a while. He's so successful, but his car is quite modest in comparison.

He frowns, looking quite offended by my inquiry. "Is my

vehicle not good enough for you, *Princess?*"

That word... again.

My skin crawls. No matter how he says it, and no matter the tone he uses, it still bothers me. The way he used it this time tells me he's insulted by the comment on his car, but it wasn't my intention. It's a nice car, just not what I expected.

I look down at the wooden table, focusing on the different shades of brown that remind me of the color of my eyes and use this moment to calm myself before speaking. I can barely say words, but grit them out as best as I can. "Please. Don't. Use. That. Term." My voice is hushed and tinged with irritation.

Why can't I be like other girls and enjoy being called one of the sweetest things a man can say to a woman?

He hangs his head. "I'm sorry. I—" Those piercing green eyes meet mine again. "I don't mean it the way you think. I'm not mocking you, quite opposite in fact. Well maybe at first, but not anymore. I promise you that. But if you prefer I don't use it, I won't." He no longer appears affronted and the angry tone has evaporated, replaced by a softer gentler one.

I shake my head and push my hair back as a few curls stick to my lipstick. "I don't know what to say. I should enjoy hearing it, but right now? I can't. Maybe knowing you're not being an asshole about it will help?"

"I can accept that. There's a nickname that's been used for me and believe me I wasn't a fan at first. But now it's growing on me and until it does the same for you? I'll respect your request and only think it, not verbalize it." He smiles deeply. Somehow, he finds a damn loophole.

I nod appreciatively and smile back. There's something new I'm noticing about Maeson tonight. It's the more I talk to him... the more he reveals himself. Not only is there that hot and cold factor, but there's a hard outer shell to him that protects a surprisingly soft inner section, which only shines through when he *allows* it.

Permitting one's true nature to show at will takes a lot of control. I know that for a fact from my own experiences.

After a moment of awkward silence, his deep voice breaks my internal inspection of him. "So, back to my car. You don't approve?"

"Sure, I do! You're a wealthy businessman, so it threw me off. I assumed your possessions would show off your funds." I give a small shrug.

"Not everyone needs to prove they are wealthy, Ruby. I live modestly for the most part. I work hard for the money I make, and I know what it's like to have none. For that reason, I refuse to blow any of it on bullshit fancy cars."

I bob my head in agreement. "I understand you, yet at times, I find myself spending money mindlessly since my funds are no longer controlled by... others." I smile at him, hoping to lighten the mood, and hide my slip-up. A stupid opening to questions about my past I don't want to answer.

"But, like you said, *'at times'*, not always, and that's the point." He gives me a cheeky grin, seeming oblivious to my omission. "Shopping and such makes sense, but spending tens of thousands on cars doesn't. My Dodge does the job and that's all I need."

"You're right, I'm sorry for passing judgment. And honestly... I must confess, before I chose my current car, I almost bought the gaudiest one I could find—simply because it was something I was never allowed to get, even though it's my money." I freeze as the wrong words leave my mouth. Yet again, I'm confessing parts of me to someone way too freely.

His green eyes flicker and deepen with anger, but he doesn't acknowledge or question my slip up. "Ruby, you don't have to feel bad about it, everyone makes assumptions—including myself—as you've said a time or two. Never regret the things you do, it's your right to own whatever you want. As you said it's your money. Make a choice and stand by it." His forehead creases and his mouth is set in a grim line.

Maeson's words fill me with determination and bravery.

"Don't worry your pretty face, I'll do as I please. No one changes me or my wants that easily—anymore." I wink and straighten, trying to develop a backbone.

I have many upcoming changes in the next few months. I'm driven to grow up and become that strong woman who is lurking deep inside.

Ruby Bennett is a conundrum, even I don't truly know who she is.

Over the years, it feels like I've split into three separate, but distinct parts. I desperately need these vastly unique pieces to become whole.

But it's never that straightforward, is it?

First, I have my outer shell—poor, confused Ruby who's blossoming from a frightened little girl into a mature woman. She must find her way, and learn to live alone and be independent. She's had no one to lean on all these lonely years. Who else can she count on, other than herself?

No one, that's who!

Next, comes broken and beaten Ruby, the damaged child who never had a chance to grow up and leave that horrific foster home. She longs to escape the nightmares, but that's not so easy, either.

Finally, hiding behind these other two, is the center, the inner and deepest part, the Ruby who is biding her time until she can break free. She's waiting for that perfect moment to come forth and shine, proving her strength to all those who doubted her, knocked her down, and forced her into submission at their hands.

But will that time ever arrive? I want to cry for her, tell her not to give up and to be patient. That day will come! Won't it?

Maeson was mistaken when he said there's a girl within me cowering behind a wall. In reality, she's the one who is seen more often than not. The fragment that is in hiding is that woman who's not afraid to stand tall on her own and voice her opinions.

The challenge is to change who people see. I'm determined they not judge me as the spoiled rich princess. Rather, I want them to see a woman. One who has repeatedly lost everything, but who has picked herself up each and every time, becoming stronger and more focused with each round she's had to fight.

Maeson reaches out, lightly touching my hand, and pulls my attention back to him. "I'm not worrying, I can tell you're headstrong. I can also see you haven't always been that way." His Scottish brogue comes through again.

"No, I haven't," I say somberly, knowing I certainly never displayed any perseverance or tenacity when faced with my abusive ex.

"And it's about bloody time you tap into who you want to be! No one can hold you back except for yourself. Lass, at your young age, you have plenty of years to evolve, but it will only happen if you free yourself once in a while."

"I guess so... Wait! Why does your accent only come through at random times?"

"Because when my emotions are on overdrive I stop concentrating on covering it up." He stares at me blankly.

"Why would you want to cover it up?"

Before he can answer, our cappuccinos arrive. Taking a generous sip, I sigh in pleasure. It's amazing, the rich, nutty flavor with a smidge of caramel drizzled on top literally makes me moan out loud.

"Woah, moan like that again and you're going to make me cum in my pants, Princess." He shows me those deep dimples, but then immediately frowns, noticing his slip up.

I brush it off because his crudeness has me blushing like a virgin bride. "Oh, shut it! Don't start with your wanna-be-sexy-potty-mouth again. It won't work on me. Now, answer my question!"

He turns serious, emotions flooding his eyes. "Fine. To prove my intentions are pure, I will answer and clue you in on who I am." He takes a deep breath and releases it harshly. "At eighteen, I moved here from Scotland, and obviously, I had a rough accent. No one would hire me because they told me my English was shit. Said they couldn't understand me. So, I practiced, and eventually, I perfected the art of speaking without the accent. That's precisely when my life started to turn around.

But sometimes, when my emotions are high it comes out." He pauses and thinks about something before he continues. "It'll never be the same again, and my father gives me hell about it. He's always saying I've forgotten where I came from, but I haven't! Scotland will always be in my heart and soul." His voice rises as if wanting to prove it to me and defend his choices.

"I get it. This world can be harsh. My dad had an accent and he had hard times as well, but I was too young to understand why back then. He even went as far to change his last name from his original Greek name of, Beneviti to Bennett, so it appeared more American. For the record, though, I think accents are incredibly sexy." I look up at him, and his deep green eyes are filled with specks of yellow, which can only mean two things—desire or admiration.

Knowing him, probably the latter.

"Och lassie, ah will gab tae ye wi' mah accent aw nicht lang 'en."

"Wha—" I almost spit out my coffee. It took me off guard how deep his voice became in his native tongue. The words are so foreign, yet, I understood a few of them. Talk about sex on a stick, if he keeps talking like that *I'll* be the one cuming in *my* pants, damn it! "Wow!"

He's never used the full-on dialect before, usually when he speaks only certain words are accented. Like when he says you it always sounds like he's saying ye or your sounds like yer. This part of him hits me by surprise, I had no idea he was hiding that much of himself.

Guess, I'm not the only one, am I?

Maeson's dimples take over the show again, his eyes dark with hunger. "You like it that much, Prin—" He cuts himself off and shakes his head. "Sorry."

Is it that hard not to use one word?

But I find instead of panicking or getting upset, the exact opposite is happening. "It's fine. Just promise me to never use it against me, or put me down. Especially since you know how much it pains me. Or maybe even find another one to use?"

Or maybe the better idea is, I focus on the good times, like when my dad used to call me his princess, and place less emphasis on the bad memories associated with it.

"If that's what you'd prefer, but I do enjoy using it. The way it has a negative effect on you, it's quite the opposite for me. So, know it's not meant in a rude way, at all. But you're the boss, so you choose." He leans back in the chair and folds his muscular arms across his chest.

I shrug slightly, mimicking his relaxed state. "I... think that it's fine then." For some unknown reason, a nervous feeling flutters in the pit of my stomach.

The thought of him being a sweet, kind man who uses tender names with a woman contradicts every single opinion I've formed of him. He's the exact kind of man that makes me anxious, one who's a full-on alpha male with a side of well-hidden tenderness.

From the moment I met him, I knew he was dangerous, and now I can confirm my presumption. Maeson is most definitely no good for me, my rationality, and my recovery.

In the distance, I hear Maeson's voice.

His hand is waving before my face. "Earth to Ruby! Hello? You with me?"

Just how deep in thought was I?

So damn out of it, I tuned everything else out, including the good-looking man before me?

How embarrassing!

I blink a few times trying to remember what we were talking about, but nothing comes to mind. "Yes. I'm sorry. What did you say?"

"I was asking the same question from before. Do you honestly like my accent?"

"Oh! Very much so. But I didn't catch everything you said. What I did understand is, lassie, gab which means talk, accent, and that's it."

He nods and gives me that sexy smile. "I said, I'd talk to you with my accent all night long."

"Oh please, yes. I'd love that!"

I don't know what's happening here but I'm beginning to let go, wanting to get to know this side of Maeson better. He has a sense of humor, we can laugh together, and I can be with him in a way I've never been with a man before.

"One day lassie, one day," he says quietly. "How about you tell me about yourself?"

"Well, I'm assuming you ran a background check on me before I moved in, so you probably know some things already. Have you read any articles?"

Google may have been my best friend when looking to move, however, it's also my worst enemy. There is a lot of information on me there. It's hard to remain private when anyone can type in your name and find out your whole life story.

"Aye, I ran the regular stuff but nothing deep. It's not a normal process when renting out a condominium. Your life story doesn't pay the bill, your job does—well, in your case the trust fund does."

"You didn't look anything up? Not even my parents?"

"No, it's not my place. If there's one thing I respect its privacy."

I give him a pointed stare. "Yes, you know how to respect privacy sooo well." I chuckle and he joins me. "How about this? Since you respected some of my privacy, and you've yielded some information about yourself, I'll do the same." I keep my gaze focused on my coffee, I hate to see the pity in people's eyes when I tell them. "I was ten when I lost my parents. They both passed away from cancer within a month of each other."

His eyes widen in disbelief. "Are you kidding me? That's harsh. I'm so sorry for your loss, Ruby. I can empathize with the feeling of a parent lost. My mother passed after I came to America. It's terrible to think of both around the same time. Takes a strong person to get through it, even more so at that young age."

"Thank you, and I'm sorry for yours as well." There's an unexpected kinship with him, and perhaps we do have more things in common than I anticipated.

Perhaps I've misjudged him?

"What happened after that? Were you put into the foster system or did you have a family to take you in?"

"I was in foster care until I turned eighteen. They weren't the kindest people, and they used me for the money. There were days of not being fed or allowed to take a shower, and I spent many of nights crying myself to sleep. It's a time I prefer not to think about or relive." That part of my life is harder to talk about than the loss of my parents and my ex-relationship combined.

"Och, I'm truly sorry, Ruby. We can leave that alone for now. What happened after that?"

"Well, afterward I went to college for a short time but dropped out after I met my ex-boyfriend. That is a story for another day, as well."

Though he seems to have a nice side, I'm not even close to being ready to bare my soul to this man. He already knows more about me than I wish he knew, and it makes me vulnerable.

"I understand, we can side bar that one also, to be continued some other time then." He looks down at our empty mugs. "Another?"

"No, I've had enough, thank you. This was the best I ever had."

"It was my pleasure. We could do this again, if you'd like?" He stands to leave.

This has become my new favorite place, and I will be back for sure. "I think... I would like that."

"Great! This can be our secret hideaway. Now, I'd like to spend some alone time with you. I want to know more about you, if you'll allow it." He's so close behind me that sweet warm breath hits my neck, making me shiver involuntarily and his accented voice whispers directly into my ear. "Are you cold?"

"No!"

"Then, why shiver? You alright, Lass?"

"Like you said to me earlier, do any more of that breathing down my neck, and I'll be the one cumming in my pants." I leave him standing there in shock, as I rush out the door. He's only moments behind me, flying out of the cafe as I laugh and toss teasing words over my shoulder. "See, Maeson, baby, you're not the only badass in town. Now, pick up your tongue and let's get out of here." Not sparing him another glance, I rush to the car.

Of course, Maeson tackles me before I can even reach it. His muscular arms hold my body tight, while his heavy breathing hits my neck, the combination makes me break out in goosebumps. "You sure like to pretend to be a badass, lassie, but you run away before you have to act on it."

"Let go of me old man. I do not run, I walk away fashionably fast!" I tease him lightly but the truth is, I ran because I simply don't know what to do! I panicked, the fear of history repeating itself overwhelming me.

I cover my fear with humor, but mentally I can't forget what's happened to me in my short lifetime. Especially the eight years I spent living in that horrible foster home, or the four years of abuse at the hands of my ex. After a year of bliss with that bastard, he changed and found a way to gain total control over all aspects of our relationship.

I never had to be flirty, naughty, or sexy with him, he didn't tolerate that sort of behavior. I'd had no adult guidance by that point, and I had no idea of what constituted a healthy relationship with a man. I simply didn't know any better. It wasn't until this last stay at the hospital that I learned his true nature. He formed an unhealthy obsession with me, but it was not out of love, it was all about power!

Dr. Miles encouraged me to be open with my next partner, to tell him what I've been through with both my ex and the foster home. It's the only way any man would be able to understand my episodes or give any future relationship a chance of surviving. He told me a good man would be nonjudgmental and could love me as I am, and not expect to change me. He would try to help me and we'd support one another.

"Fashionably fast my ass, Ruby. You fly like a bat out of hell and never look back." Maeson leans in close to me, his voice is low and soft. "I see who you are underneath all that padding you like to hide behind. I *see* you, *Princess.*" Tenderness drips from his tone.

The words pull me out of my incessant pondering, and I desperately need to lighten my dark internal mood. "I *see* you too, *Gramps.*" Wiggling out of his hold, I dash for the car, laughing the whole way.

"Gramps? Oh, I'll show you!" Maeson's not far behind, his laugh deep and resonant.

This moment is so light and playful, and I can't even recollect the last time I was ever being chased for fun.

It's wonderful!

The sensation of true happiness, freedom from worry, and being able to laugh freely with a man is a new experience in my life.

Maeson catches up easily as we reach the car completely out of breath. We get curious stares from the people around us as our laughter rings out.

"You're pretty fast for an almost forty-year-old man, I'm impressed!

"You're pretty slow for a young pup, but I'm not judging!"

He's so close to me, a wide smile on his face, and before I can stop myself, I do something impulsive. I stand on my tiptoes and lightly kiss one of those beautiful dimples. He freezes momentarily under my lingering lips and I reach up, placing my palm against his cheek, and kiss him again.

His breathing changes, gets heavier, and the dimples disappear, his face serious as I peer into his eyes. They're burning deep green with fire and passion, exactly like at the nightclub.

I'm caught in his gaze. Instantly, I'm wet and burning with arousal, and I can't look away. My lips quiver in anxiety—just like every single time he's this near to me, his face only inches away and our bodies almost touching.

He bends his head toward mine in the most intimate way. I

can feel his warm breath as his lips inch closer to mine.

He's teasing me! I want more! I need more!

"Hey, man, you gonna move your car or what? I need the spot!" The mood is ruined, this random stranger has killed the moment!

Are you kidding me?

Disappointment floods through me as Maeson jerks back. He looks around as if in a daze, not quite knowing where the voice came from.

I sigh deeply and hang my head as my cheeks flood red.

"Fuck! Och, aye, I will move it noo hauld your horses!" His voice rises, anger vibrating from him.

I lay my palm against his hard chest to try and calm him. Slowly I replay his rough words and this time I understand all of his Scottish brogue. Though *'hold your horses'* is something I've not heard in a long time, I can't hold back my laughter. It's such a silly old saying.

Maeson frowns at me in annoyance. "Whit you're laughin' at?"

"You said hold your horses! Such an old man thing to say." I smirk at him.

He visibly calms and the coarseness to his words dissipates. "Of course, you'd find that amusing!" The persistent man waiting for the parking spot honks his horn and Maeson flips him off. "Go find yourself another one, asshole." He waves the guy off, then brings his attention back to me. "Hurry that sweet ass into the car, that man lacks patience, and I'm in no mood to beat the puny kid to a pulp."

That man lacks patience? This coming from the guy who just told me to hurry my ass and flipped a stranger off?

I roll my eyes but comply, and Maeson pulls out of the spot moments later. There's dead silence between us as he drives out of the parking lot. Maeson's expression is hidden from me, but I can sense the frustration radiating from him.

We're back on the highway before I find the courage to speak. "Hey, Maeson, talk to me. Is there something wrong?"

"Aye, my damn balls ache!"

"Oh, how about some music then? It might sooth them." When I'm nervous, I tend to make jokes, and I desperately need to break the tension.

"Th' only hin' 'at can sooth them is—"

"Nope! Don't you dare finish that sentence, you dirty old man!" I can see him from the corner of my eye, and he has a devilish grin on his face as he glances my way.

"Music it is, lassie." He reaches out and hits a couple of buttons.

I immediately recognize the song as *Five Finger Death Punch— Wrong Side of Heaven*. I'm not necessarily a rock chick, but this song makes my soul ache, and I've played it a few hundred times on full blast. "Turn it up, please?"

"You like rock?"

"No, but I do like this song, and a few others by them, a lot!"

Maeson smiles and turns the volume all the way up. The beat takes over and we both relax in our seats, the tension seeping away. This song has a way of extracting emotions you didn't know you had.

I sing along and feel every single word, every part of the lyrics in my depths.

Maeson watches me, then puts his hand on my leg. I don't pull away, the heat of it is a small comfort I seem to need. The song picks up and tears fall down my face as I remember all the times I've stood alone, begging for help, praying for an answer, no longer knowing who I'd become.

Deep down I know my parents heard and protected me from death the many times I laid on the floor bleeding from all the beatings I took. Physically and mentally, I was broken over and over, but somehow, I kept going.

As the song ends, so do my tears, and I brush them away.

This is supposed to be a happy night. I need to get it together. Deep breath.

"It's alright, beautiful," Maeson whispers.

"It will be." My voice is barely a whisper in return, and

somehow, I know it will get better one day.

I'm here, I've survived this much already!

As if the stereo knew what we needed the next song on is *Sam Hunt—Take Your Time*. "What a random collection you have. I noticed that at your nightclub the other night." I almost add how I also noted the damn drink idea he stole from me, but I know it's not so important anymore and let it go.

"Oh right." There's a brief moment of silence and then he continues. "Well, music is meant to be enjoyed as a whole, not picked by genre. I have a love for all kinds of music, you'd be surprised by what you find on that thing or in my club. And yes, I own a club and yes, I pawned that drink from you. I'm sorry but it's very good, so I guess I'm not *that* sorry."

It's as if he read my mind and before I can say anything, he turns the volume up a couple of notches and starts to sing along.

His voice is unexpected, deep, and husky, and so beautiful it almost brings me to tears. He's sneaking glances at me out of the corner of his eye as he sings at the top of his lungs.

I smile at the gusto of his words, and just can't help myself, I reach out and squeeze his leg, leaving my hand there. The lyrics are so justified as if they are meant for me personally. It feels like we're the only two people in the universe, and he's singing directly to me, only for me. My heart flutters and I struggle to breathe.

He doesn't appear notice and continues the serenade. Suddenly, at the end of a verse, he stops singing and turns down the music. "Was the sex that bad? As mediocre as you said?"

"Seriously, that's on your mind right now?" I almost laughed at his question, but I'm too surprised by it.

"Well, yes. It's been bugging me since you said it." He shrugs, acting like it's not a big deal, yet his words tell a different story. "Usually, I don't have any complaints, and I surely wasn't expecting one from you. If a man has one thing that he lives for it's his ego and you, lass, have hurt its feelings." His deep grin makes my heart flutter and I almost spill the beans on how great it truly was.

"Sorry, Maeson, I'm unable to stroke your precious self-worth, I stand by my answer."

"I see." His lips turn down into a frown and he's silent for a moment. "You know what that means then?"

"What?"

"That next time, I'll have to up the ante and do a better job. And believe me, when I say better, I mean it. Miss Bennett, prepare to regret ever calling what we had that one night... *mediocre*." As the word slips from his mouth, he shakes his head in disgust.

"Assuming there will be a next time, Mr. Alexander?" I raise an eyebrow and keep my expression as deadpan as possible.

"Oh, I'm sure there will be. No assumptions here, princess."

"Confidence, you have too much of it. And next time—if there ever will be—I'll show *you* a thing or two about mind-blowing sex."

"Aye, Ruby, I'll hold you to that. I'm not the kind of man who is afraid of a strong woman, go ahead teach me all you want—I will praise you, not run away from you or put you down for it."

For some unknown reason, his words continue to shock me. Most men would prefer a woman to be the complete opposite and surely not urging her to be better than them. I have no words, there is no response I can give him to that statement. It's everything I ever wanted to hear from a man.

Let me find strength, be that which is the meaning of strength, and use it to the fullest potential.

"Embrace the woman you are deep inside. I have the impression you've caged her up for a very long time and for what reason I don't know, nor will I push to know." He waits for me to say something and when I don't he continues. "Can we see where this goes, stop fighting against me, and whatever this could be?" He motions a finger between our bodies. "No holds barred?" He seems so nonchalant as he speaks.

"I don't—" Stopping short, I give myself a moment to think before I say anything further.

My heart says no. Full stop. Capital N, capital O. I can't take the chance, I might get hurt again, whether be it physically or mentally. My mind is flashing DANGER!

The other parts of me argue back, urging me to take the risk. My gut says go for it! Find happiness! Nothing ventured, nothing gained.

Screw it, I just need to take the plunge, right?

"Yes." The single word signals my acceptance; it slips out of my mouth without another thought or a second guess.

Maeson nods and smiles widely, turning up the next song as he hits the accelerator, obviously pleased with my answer.

"I hope, I don't regret this," I mutter under my breath.

"You won't, Princess." His deep voice resonates over the loud music.

The old fucker has the hearing of a hawk!

I smile to myself and not because of his abnormal hearing. A realization strikes, that this time when he called me *'Princess'*, I didn't flinch, panic, or cringe. Instead, hope starts to flourish, next to all those little butterflies fluttering around in my belly.

-26-

MAESON

I WANT TO ADD *'I promise'*, to let her know I'd never hurt her, or make her regret putting herself out there for me, but those words are sacred.

Making a promise I'm not sure I can keep is a bad idea. Besides, there are no guarantees she won't regret giving me a chance at some point. All I can do is take small steps for both our sakes.

Once, I was promised many things too, and in return, all I got was the shaft. Promises are far too easy to break.

Not. Happening. Again.

I rack my brain, trying to think of something to say to break the silence that's fallen over us. I don't want this night to end so soon, yet I'm overwhelmed with the need to get away.

I've said too many things that involve my true feelings. She's not the only person who can get hurt.

After discovering a few interesting, yet, very sad things about this mysterious woman, the pull between us grows ever stronger. My gut tells me to haul ass. I've stopped listening to whatever my mind is telling me hours ago.

Go with the gut, it never gets you into trouble. Your heart and mind will fuck you the hell up if you let it.

She was supposed to be a fun challenge to get into bed... nothing more... then what the FUCK am I doing right now?

This feels right, though.

Heart meet blender... Blender meet your next dumbass victim.

"When can I... uh... take you out again?" I mumble.

Ruby's eyes glitter in surprise at my pathetic and insecure question. Her luscious mouth opens to respond, but she snaps it shut. One beat. Two beats. Then her lips part slightly. "For like another... coffee date?" Her slightly raspy voice is suddenly husky and my eyes fly to her lips again.

I smile, her hesitation at calling it *date* is truly adorable. "Yes. A coffee date, Ruby. Coffee and nothing more..." I trail off as images of her half naked underneath me pound into my head. The desire to pull the fucking car over to devour her, to stare into her stunning almond eyes, and suck on those plump red lips becomes unbearable. But, somehow, I manage to resist and continue to drive, my attention dangerously split between her and the road.

"I think I can handle being around you again, but I'll have to check my calendar to see when I can pencil you in." Her beautiful giggle attacks my very core, the sound is addicting.

Between sneaking a few more peeks at her gorgeous face and trying not to burst out laughing, I manage to answer her without crashing the car. "Why thank you, Miss-Oh-So-Generous. Then I'll leave it up to you to call me."

She sucks on her bottom lip. "Okay."

My dick twitches at the sight. For the sake of our sanity, I'm taking it slow, exactly what we need right now. Though, after that kiss, I'd have gone further with her, much further, but thanks to that fuck face guy needing the parking space, we didn't.

Ah! My fucking balls ache. Take a deep breath, asshole.

I turn into the complex and stop in front of Ruby's building. "Here we are."

This is always the part that sucks after a first date.

"Here we are." She avoids my eyes, and instead, fiddles with her fingers. "I had a great time, Maeson. Thank you."

The shy girl is back.

She wasn't this way after our one night stand, was she? Then again, with that it's easier to walk away from, it doesn't involve much talking or emotion.

Tonight, was different—for *both* of us. I mentally clamp down on the emotions wanting to escape way too early.

I reach out and touch her face. Her skin is soft and I don't want to pull away. "As did I." My fingers glide to her chin and slowly raise it so she meets my gaze. The distress behind her sad baby browns ignites the beast in me, which is both a protector and a fighter.

Something flashes across her face, and instantly I know she's seen too much. My hand burns from the intensity of our connection and I drop it. Avoiding her perplexed gaze, I hop out of the car to open her door and help her out. My fingers shake slightly as I lace them with Ruby's and walk her to the entrance.

Only one other has made my fingers shake like this and she will never be forgotten... for good reason.

The signs are everywhere, the emotions are as clear as day, yet, instinctively I still want to shove them all away. It's all fun and games until it comes to matters of the heart, but unlike Jax, I refuse to fall easily, or hard, or fast. Letting myself *feel* is one of the only times I lose all of my well-mastered self-control.

Slow. I can do this... slowly. But first I need another kiss.

I lean in and linger, my mouth barely touching hers, then lightly lick and nip on her bottom lip. Unexpectedly she moans loudly and my beast roars, reminding me to pull away before I go too far. "Good night, Ruby. Coffee, right?"

Sighing heavily, she nods her head. "Ye-yes c-coffee." She pauses, putting a stop to her adorable stuttering. After a few deep breaths, she regains her strength, turning into a different woman, and reaches up, gliding a sensual caress across my jaw. "Good... night..." The huskiness of her voice gives me chills and desire ripples through me. But she's not done with me yet, she licks her lips and continues. "Maeson... Lachlan... Alexander." Her cursed fingers stop short as she stands her on tiptoes and kisses me.

Ruby saying my full given name floors me, cuts me off at the knees, and I give into her plush *'Angelina Jolie'* lips. She's already pulling away after what seems like a mere second flashes by, and I want to beg her to come back.

Beg?

No fucking way!

Just a little?

Refusing to give in, I stay quiet, and watch her with a sad smile as she disappears through the entrance of her building.

Go after her. No! Go the hell home, you stupid pussy, before she takes the rest of what you have left of yourself and your dignity.

Now that Ruby's gone from sight, my mind clears, and the cloud over my eyes lifts.

She had the same exact effect on me almost two months ago, at Crossroads.

The invisible hold on my body eventually disappears and somehow, I manage to drag my legs up to my own place. Leaving the lights off, I find my way through to my bedroom by memory.

How can I be this dazed by a young woman? What's she going to do to me if I get too close? She's bringing forward too many memories.

With that last thought, I pass the fuck out. Pure exhaustion taking over, darkening my surroundings, and matching the blackness which is brewing inside.

* * *

IT'S ALWAYS THIS DAMN DAY of the week I hate the most and it always finds a way to make each one worse than the one before it.

The infamous, most dreaded, fucking Monday.

This desk is yet again stacked with papers and I haven't touched any of them because of *her*. Ruby's sexy smile is my ultimate weakness. I'm recognizing that the fucking woman has powers, like voodoo and shit.

My thoughts are jumbled and my body is tense and I'm on constant alert, waiting for her to show up. I heard Molly making plans for them to have lunch, so I know she'll be here soon. And what do I do instead of getting the hell out of this office to avoid her? The dumb ass that I am remains glued to my seat, anxiously waiting to see her beautiful smile again.

My broken phone vibrates in my pant pocket, shifting my attention momentarily, and I see Ax's name across the cracks. "Yes?"

"Can we do lunch? I need to run something by you." His tone is stern, telling me this involves business.

"Sure. When?"

"Now?"

"Give me ten minutes. In the mood for Fuzzy's Tacos in Deep Ellum?"

"Sure, I could go for some brisket quesadillas. Meet you there."

We hang up, and I lift my laptop screen and click on the Skype messaging app, to message Molly.

ME: Going to lunch in a few. Fuzzy's. Want anything?
MOLLY: Nope, got plans. Thnx anyways. Enjoy!

With that, I grab my keys and wallet and stride out of my office.

"Hey, boss! Look who's here!" Molly calls out.

As I approach the front desk I see the familiar brown curls and my heart starts to pound. "Hello, ladies. Lunching in today?" I deepen my dimples, hoping she'll smile back.

Score. There it is, the heart-stopping, million-dollar smile.

"Yes, we are," Ruby's cheeks flush a shade darker and she fidgets in her seat.

I bow my head slightly. "Well, I won't hold you up. Have fun." When I reach the doors, Ruby's disappointed voice echo's down the hall as she says something to Molly. No matter how hard I try to fight it off, the corners of my lips rise.

* * *

I ARRIVE AT OUR LUNCH spot before Axel, so I order the food right away, and pick a bench outside so we can talk privately. We always order the same thing every time we come here, brisket quesadillas with Latin fried potatoes. I douse mine with their hot sauce and take a bite as Axel seats himself across from me.

"Hey man," I mumble through a mouthful.

"Hey. Thanks for ordering." He douses his food with extra salt before he even tries any of it.

I grimace. "That's a heart attack waiting to happen."

"I know, right? But I need my salt, shits too bland for my tastes."

"What isn't bland for you? You put that crap on everything." I finish my first piece before Axel even starts on his.

"Eh, after all these years you're surprised?" He smiles and scarfs down his over-salted food.

"I shouldn't be." I take a sip of my soda. "So, what's so pressing?"

"I'm meeting with Ruby in the next few days, and I wanted to run something by you."

"Okay shoot."

"Well, you know that low budget apartment complex you signed off on recently? I wanted to combine forces and join your passion with hers. That is if you're both on board."

"Keep talking, I'm intrigued."

The chance at spending more time with Ruby? Hell fucking yes!

"Your plan is to provide low-cost housing for those in need, families and such, so is hers—but with a different angle. Now I'm close to breaking the rules here by telling you this, but I think it's a great idea. She wants to offer housing for foster children and abuse victims, and she certainly has the funds, but not the experience you have in managing apartments."

How close to the reality of her past are these ventures? Is this her idea of absolution?

"Hmm, that's deep, man. I had no idea she was so devoted to people in need, but most especially in that area of assistance. The idea is solid, though. We could build two, maybe three complexes and each one could be used for a separate cause. Full-time staff and security would be a necessity twenty-four-seven for the children and women especially. Draft up your proposal and show it to Ruby, if she's into it then we can finesse the details."

"Seriously? You'd do it?"

I put a hand over my heart, feigning shock. "You think so little of me? I'm offended asshole! I do have a heart you know."

"Sure, you do, but this is huge, Maeson. It'll take up most of your free time and energy. You sure about this?" He raises a thick brow.

"Yes, I'm positive. Do it and keep me posted on her response. Until then I won't say a thing."

"I will. We could do some amazing things for this area and help a lot of people. I wouldn't mind investing in the project myself. You know my history with abuse, my mom could've used a place like this before her scumbag boyfriend killed her." He closes his eyes and lets out a ragged breath. "So yes, I want to help out."

"I know, Ax, I know." I shake my head remorsefully, the sadness seeping from him surrounds us like a thick morning fog. "You're more than welcome on my end. The more hands-on-deck the better."

"This got morbid quick, I'm sorry. You got smokes on ya? I need one."

With a nod, I pull out the pack and his shaky fingers wrap

around it to pull a cigarette out.

"Thanks." He lights it and inhales, holding the smoke in before exhaling.

"No problem. We've all got things... to deal with." I light my own smoke. "So, what's going on with you? Still single?"

Axel shrugs. "Yeah..."

"That's surprising. Never seen you solo for this long."

"I know. Shocked me too. I have the lyrics, man, but no one has offered to sing the song."

I smirk at his peculiar words. "Your day will come, Ax. Just wait."

"I'd like to hope so. Until then I'll bide my time by doing what I do best. Wine them and dine them." He laughs and stubs out his cigarette. "What happened to that?" Ax points to my bashed in phone.

"Unfortunately, that was the end result of the *thing* I'm dealing with." I shrug. "Can you contact... *her* and tell *her* to quit calling and messaging me? I've given her enough. More than enough."

He nods, knowing exactly *who* I'm speaking of. "You got it, man. Same info?"

"Yup." Thinking about that woman makes me sick to my stomach, even vocalizing it makes it one hundred times worse. My fist clenches and unclenches, too much has transpired, and forgiveness will never happen.

Over my dead body.

"I'll put an end to it today."

I nod gratefully and we simultaneously stub out our cigarettes, both of us ready to leave. The somber memories invading our minds are becoming too much to bear publicly. I stand and shake Axel's hand before we go our separate ways.

My sudden mood change guides me to the nearest bar, and I forget all about the work sitting on my desk waiting to be completed.

Fuck work! Right now, I need to get drunk and try to forget the forsaken demons haunting me at every turn.

-27-

Ruby

MY HEAD SPINS, MY PALMS are sweaty, and my heart is racing. Every one of my senses are on overload, all because I briefly saw my landlord in his drop dead sexy navy-blue business suit.

Bastard had me all out of sorts!

A single thought was on repeat as I watched him stride over to us. When he spoke to me the words barely registered since internally I was like...

Maeson. Maeson Alexander. Maeson Lachlan Alexander. Maeson, sexy Maeson.

How anyone manages any response with him around, only God knows. I was mostly fine Saturday night, but after yet another breathtaking, knee buckling kiss, I felt things between us change even further. Our connection shifted into a new territory.

I raise a finger and run it across my lips, the reminder of our mouths locked while our bodies rubbed against each other hits me with an adrenaline filled rush, and my heart pounds even harder.

This annoyingly attractive man makes me feel again, and I'm afraid of what it means for what's left of my rationality.

A fear rises in my heart and mind knowing realistically Maeson could very easily have me spinning out of control. I push the thought away.

After all, how much trouble could one man be?

If I base everything on my past, then I'll never move forward.

I never did stand a chance at disliking him for long, did I? Or was I simply hoping to be turned off by him so I wouldn't get hurt?

Putting those questions aside to process on a later date, I focus on the conversation I unintentionally zoned out of with Molly.

I tap her on the shoulder. "Where did he go?"

"He's having lunch with someone, I guess." She pulls her hair up in a messy bun, then gives me a side glance. "Why you interested? Wanted him to stick around? Hmmm... does someone have that crush I called you out on before?" Molly laughs.

"No, you ass, I asked out of curiosity, *not* infatuation." I avoid Molly's gaze and focus on a crumpled paper on her desk, unable to face her with my lie.

"Right, you can't even look at me. I'll let it go, for now, lady, but it's written all over your face." She gives me a light shove and smiles. "So, what did you do last weekend? Never heard from ya."

Shit. I've some explaining to do now.

"I. Uh. Went on a date."

"What?" Molly jumps out of her seat, her eyes wide with shock. "With who? You keepin' secrets woman?"

"No way! It just happened and I didn't get a chance to call you!"

"Hmm. Fine, you're forgiven. So, who was it with?"

"Maeson."

"I knew it! I fucking knew it!" Molly's arms shoot up into the air. "Didn't take you guys long, did it?" The shock leaves her face and is replaced by a perfectly arch eyebrow rising in question. "Spill! How was it?"

"Honestly, it was nice. He's not entirely what I expected him to be. I saw a different side of him at the club and then the other night he showed me more of that part. Which… scares me."

"I know he can be a moody fuck face at times, but why are you afraid?"

I shrug. "It's a long story and we don't have enough time in the day for all of that."

"Sure, we do. Boss is gone for a while which means we won't be interrupted. Our crispy chicken salads are already here, so we don't have to go out. We can even use Maeson's office for privacy." She stands but doesn't move. It's as if she doesn't want to rush me into deciding. Instead, she kindly waits for a beat or two then asks, "What'd ya say?"

"Okay. Maybe it's time I talk about it all." Even though my mind is ready, my legs aren't, they're stuck in place and won't take the first step. Molly turns, watching me as I struggle to get up. Her sad smile does the trick and I reluctantly stand and follow her.

As we enter the big room, my hands start to shake. I'm so nervous I don't even notice the decor. My eyes lock on the messy dark wood desk and the two seats before it. Choosing one of them, I take my place. "Please don't repeat this conversation to anyone."

Molly sits, turning her chair toward me. "Certainly not, sweetheart. I can tell this is difficult, and you haven't even started." She tries to set down out salads and drinks but is blocked by the massive piles of paper and laughs. "Maeson's a mess and a half!"

"I see that." A small nervous giggle escapes me.

She hands me the food. "Here." With a few maneuvers, she has half of the space cleared off for us. "Let's eat and talk."

I nod and my stomach clenches. "Have no idea where to start, so much has happened." I set the once appealing salad on the desk.

"From the beginning?"

"Too much to start from there. Maybe what brought me here?"

"Sure. Whatever you want, doll." She gives me a sad smile.

"My memories are all jumbled so I might be all over the place. I haven't talked to anyone about this but my doctors, so please bear with me." I shake my head trying to sort out my thoughts.

My mind constantly replays the things my heart can never delete, no matter how hard I try to rid myself of them.

"I understand. Go ahead, tell me. I won't say a word, let it all out." This time she reaches over and squeezes my hand.

"Well, you may or may not know from looking me up online, but before I moved here, I was in a very bad relationship. His name was Ray. Asshole Ray." I look down at my hand and pick at a hangnail. "He was abusive, and I barely escaped." I give a small shrug, and peek up at Molly.

"Oh, sweetheart, I know this is hard to talk about, you sure you're okay with it?" She extends her hand and holds mine, giving it a squeeze.

"Yes, I think I am." My voice shakes slightly.

Molly scoots closer to me, then nods, silently encouraging me to continue.

Unable to look into Molly's blue eyes any longer, I stare straight ahead at the desk. An unbidden memory of our last encounter rises and a shiver runs down my spine.

His touch lingered on my skin, and I could tell my face was bruising. 'Ruby, baby, please forgive me. You wouldn't stop nagging me.' His eyes are full of an apology he didn't mean.

"No matter how many times he laid his hands on me, I'd always forgive him. I had no choice but to forgive him." I take a deep breath, the memory now hammering into me full force. "He hated being questioned on anything he did. I know he cheated on me, numerous times. I even made the mistake of asking him if he loved one of them, and the repercussions weren't worth it. Though, I still believe he did love her, in his own way."

I will never forget how his head snapped in my direction, his face displaying the deadliest glare I've ever seen on a person. 'Love her?' He grabbed my arm, his fingers digging into my flesh like claws. Shaking me, he leaned in close, his breath hot and heavy on my face. 'Love is for fucking fools! I fell in love with you and look at where that got me! I can't stand you, yet my heart can't fathom the idea of you not being mine.' His dark, icy stare burned into me, but that wasn't anything new.

Tears well up in my eyes. "When he would hit me, it would always leave these horrible bruises. They'd take weeks to heal."

I was able to pull away that time, wrenching my arm from his ever-tightening grip, the familiar purple spots already forming, and imprints of his fingers. I knew I shouldn't have fed the fire, but I couldn't help it.

A shudder passes through me as the past wraps its dirty claws around my heart and consumes my every thought. My lungs constrict, and it feels like I'm suffocating.

I take a deep breath, inhaling as deeply as I can, but there isn't enough air in this room. When my chest feels like it's going to explode, I exhale with such force that words begin to tumble from my lips. "He didn't love me, he wanted to fix me. No! He wanted to own me! When we first met, he was all I needed. Then Ray became possessive and started using me. All I ever desired was to be loved, but the asshole could never open his eyes wide enough to see that. Never had a problem hitting me, pushing me around and using my body at his beck and call." I close my eyes, trying to keep more tears from falling, in order to finish this.

I can barely breathe, my lungs want to collapse and give up, but I force myself to continue. "He would go out and be with who knows how many women, yet I wasn't allowed to make a single friend. I told him I wanted us to end, the toxic relationship between us needed to be terminated. But of course, I didn't have a choice in the matter!" I shake my head in disbelief, my voice rose the same way it did five months ago. The disgust is obvious in my tone even this time around.

I'm hysterical as the renewed hurt and pain courses through my body, the tears I could no longer contain streamed down my cheeks. Choking on my tears, I whispered, 'we're done. I cannot do this anymore.'

After a few moments, I'm able to compose myself, gathering the courage to look up at Molly. She must think I'm crazy, but she's crying and her fists are clenched, exactly like mine.

I'm not alone anymore, am I? Some else knows now.

"Keep going, love. You can do it. Let it out so you'll be able to let it go." Molly's sweet southern voice soothes me.

"Okay." I brush at my never-ending tears and go on. "His response was typical. *'End us... never... one of us will have to die in order for us to be done. That is your only way out.'* How nice, quite a gentleman, right?" I laugh bitterly.

His whisper told me I was in for trouble. He grabbed me again and shook me as if he couldn't believe I would say such a thing. Surprised I could ever want it to be over.

"For good measure, he slammed me against the wall so hard when I tried to breathe, so much pain shot through me, Molly, so much." Fresh tears burn my cheeks as they cascade down my face and Molly hands me a tissue. "But he wasn't done." I shake my head. "Nope, not done. I'll never forget the way his face changed in that instant. That's when I got petrified, the way he spoke seemed all wrong. I mean it wasn't something altogether new, but this time, it was very off. I tried so hard to escape, but I couldn't. I knew what was about to happen, I was afraid... so afraid." I stop and take a sip of the water next to me.

His voice turned into a growl as he spoke. 'You drive me insane. Insane enough to want to hurt you over and over, and love it each time. I love... and hate you so much. I can't breathe with you around. You suffocate me in so many ways.'

"Holy shit." Molly's voice barely registers.

"Almost done. You sure you want me to keep going? I—"

"Yes, you need this. Take a deep breath."

I do. In and out.

Deep, deep breath.

"Okay good. Now breathe, deeply in and out, till you're ready again."

It takes me a few minutes, but I manage to continue. "You

made me this way, he would say. The drugs, alcohol, losing himself in women, and hurting me, was all my fault. Always my fault. I don't remember what it was, but one day something had caused me to draw courage. I was no longer afraid. I was ready to die, ready to accept my fate at the hands of this man. Nothing in this world was worth living for anymore. My last attempt to find a place in this world where I fit, vanished like a cloud of smoke, destroyed along with my spirit, because of him!" I slam my small fist against the hard wood and pain shoots through me. I welcome it.

Scooting further back into the chair, I lay my head against it. "My parents had been gone for what seemed like an eternity, and I thought I had no one else to give myself to, just him. But after everything he did, I didn't have any heart left to give to him or anyone else." Instinctively, I rub a hand over my chest, where the emptiness lies.

He did this. He emptied me out.

"Oh yes, you do! You have so much to give, but you need time to heal." Her blue eyes shine with tears, and sadness pours from them.

"How can I? He beat my heart, soul, and spirit over and over. He broke them, smashing them like incredibly fragile glass. He didn't give a fuck!" I bring my knees up to my chest and wrap my arms around them. My body is visibly trembling with anger and hurt. My sole solace is he's gone—forever.

"You're right. You need more than time. You need to find yourself again. There is so much you're holding on to and dealing with a huge amount of pain." Her lip curls as if thinking about it sickens her.

"I'm trying to find who I am without him, or the constant control, but it's harder than I thought." I close my eyes, fighting the new tears emerging. "He was my breaking point, I lost everything including my mind." My head's pounding from the onslaught of the past and I gently rub at my temples.

"What do you mean you lost your mind?"

"Mentally, he finished me off. I was done, a shell of a human.

His last words, they did me in."

"Can I ask what he said?"

I nod. "He said, *'If you leave me, my little Ruby, I will kill myself. I will make sure you will never forget me… you will never forget us. You will carry the guilt with you, knowing you brought me to this.'* That was his last and final warning, before"—I stop, unable to complete the sentence—"Never going to forget watching him back away from me, shaking his head and mumbling, stumbling out of the room. I thought I'd won and found my freedom."

"Did you? What happened after he left?" Mo's voice is shakier than my own.

"Well, I was so shocked about everything that had happened and hadn't happened that the only thing I could manage at the time was curl up into a ball and let it all sink in. I felt pain everywhere; on my face, on my arms, and my sides, I couldn't have moved if I tried, I was just grateful and relieved I was still alive." I release the tight hold on my legs and let them drop to the ground, no longer needing the support. "I knew this time it was over. I'd no longer have to hear his name. I no longer had to see his face. No longer be hurt by his words and touch. I thought he'd given in and broke up with me." I sniffle. "Later, though, I found out how utterly wrong I was." I finish speaking and take notice of the complete silence in the room.

I look up at Molly and her mouth is wide open, her eyes are filled with unshed tears and she's gaping directly behind me.

Something's wrong.

Slowly, very slowly, I turn and freeze.

Maeson's standing in the doorway, with his arms tightly across his chest, breathing heavily… almost heaving. His eyes blaze with anger and his face is a scary shade of red.

I don't want to ask but I do anyway. "How long have you been standing there?"

With two long strides, he right next to me. "Long. Enough. Molly. Go." He grinds out and points to the door.

Molly bristles. "No. She needs me, not you. You need to go and I don't care if this is your office." Her voice is stern and demanding.

He looks at us, and for a moment it seems as if he wants to pick her up and force her out the door. "Fine. Ruby when you're done with her please don't go. We need to talk."

I wipe at my face, smearing mascara across my arm. "Not a chance. I don't need a pity party. Look, I'm good. I'll leave, you guys have work to do." I launch from my seat. My legs are shaky and even so, I manage to gracefully walk to the door, but before I can escape, Maeson wraps his long thick fingers around my arm.

"Please don't." His words are slightly slurred and a strong smell of liquor wafts from his mouth.

I force all my emotions to evaporate the way I've taught myself to do. "Let. GO!"

Our eyes are fixed on each other, his flicker and then he releases me. I don't look back or stop to hear Molly's last words.

* * *

AS SOON AS I'M OUT of the building, I bolt and don't stop running until my legs can't take the pressure anymore. My thighs are on fire and my lungs can't seem to collect enough air. I have no idea where I am or care to know. My chest constricts and shame overcomes me. It's one thing to talk to my girlfriend about my nasty past, it's another to have the man I secretly desire knowing I'm pathetic.

Where are my pills or a drink when I need them?

I survey the area to ensure I'm still alone and flop down in the grass. Closing my eyes, I concentrate on my breathing technique, taking many deep inhales to try and relax.

This didn't go as I expected at all. He probably thinks I'm incredibly weak and lame.

Even with my eyes squeezed shut tears streak my face. "Why did you do this to me? Why did *all* of you have to make me this way?" I shout at the top of my lungs but of course, they don't answer me. Ray's dead and my foster father... well, he's gone too.

I've been so stupid. I trusted too easily, but I didn't know any better. I still don't, do I?

"Who hurt you, Ruby?" The smooth familiar voice caresses my ear.

I refuse to open my eyes, it's a dream. He's not here.

He wouldn't follow me. He doesn't care enough. He barely knows me.

Hot fingers touch my belly and I flinch. "Princess." It's a question and statement all in one.

"Why. Are. You. Here?" This isn't a dream, he's here, and my heart starts to beat faster. Somehow, he has that effect on me and I'm not sure I like it.

"You need me." He makes it seem so simple.

"I don't need anyone anymore."

The heat of his touch leaves my body and for a moment I'm so cold, but then he envelopes me with it using his entire body. Strong muscled arms wrap around me, simply holding me, hugging me like I've never been held before by a man. Instinctively I want to fight him off, but it feels exquisite simply being held with such tenderness. I don't move a muscle or say anything.

With a comfortable silence between us, we stay in this position for what seems like hours. *'Hold me like this forever.'* I want to say, but I refuse to succumb and become that broken girl I was in the hospital only a few months prior.

Maeson shifts his body without releasing me. "Maybe it's *me* who needs *you*?" he whispers in my ear.

Nope.

I don't want to hear any of this. He's lying. No one needs me, they never have. Ultimately, I've always been the needy child, the needy foster teen, and the needy girlfriend. Now I'm all alone and vulnerable, at my lowest, and Maeson sees that.

He's using me, he must be!

"Lies. Don't feed them to me, I'm not hungry." My voice is flat, far from affected by his bullshit fancy feast words.

"I know you're not, your salad's untouched on my desk." He chuckles softly. "I'm not talking out of my ass here, I mean it, Ruby. Things shifted for me that night we slept together, then even more so after each kiss we've shared. You're... *different.*" He lifts slightly, putting weight on his elbow, and looks down at me.

"Oh, I'm different all right. I'm fucked up in the head. A basket case. You should run. Run far the hell away, or I'll ruin you like I ruined my ex." I can't bear the pity in Maeson's green eyes so I close mine. "He put a bullet through his brain because of me. I drove him to it. He told me so." Tears begin to slide down my face, and I let them.

Maeson's expression doesn't change, there is no shock to my revelation, not even an ounce of judgment. Instead, he moves closer and gently wipes a tear away with his finger. "I don't believe that. It wasn't your fault. From what I heard you telling Molly, he's the nut bag that pulled the trigger, not you."

"*Technicalities.* I pushed him and he had no choice, by default that's the same as me killing him."

"Therefore, you're going to carry that kind of guilt for the rest of your life?" His brow creases and his lips thin into a straight line.

"I don't have any guilt, whatsoever. I'm stating facts Maeson, plain and simple facts. There is no remorse, I'm glad I stood up for myself and told him to leave. Regardless if my choice ended up being his breaking point. And then—which probably was his intention the entire time—he took his final action, our ultimate goodbye. *That's* what broke me." I open my eyes and meet Maeson's grave expression.

"Then what makes you think *you'll* damage *me?*" His finger slides under my chin and brings it upwards, closer to him and his alcohol-infused breath.

"It's what I do. I need too much, want too much, which ends up driving people nuts. Shit, I drove myself mad, so crazy in fact I spent some time in the psych ward. What's that tell ya? I'll tell you what... stay the fuck away from me."

"Been there too you know. I'm already damaged goods, can't mess me up when someone's beat you to it, Princess." He leans in sealing my lips shut with his own.

I try to fight it by refusing to open up for him, but his tongue pushes, and my body softens into his. Two fucked up people making out in the grass. We must be a sight, but who cares, right?

I sure as hell don't.

Without a second thought or a deep breath, I give in, needing this moment, again needing, always needing.

-28-

MAESON

OH, GOD DAMN! I'VE MOVED too quickly.

What if she runs? Ohhhh… those delectable lips.

I didn't follow her with this in mind, but it feels so right.

Why am I pretending? I very well know I'm enjoying the feel of her regardless of my initial intentions.

But she needs someone by her side right now, and I want that someone to be me, not Mo. From all I've learned about her, and my own past, I can relate, and I have this desperate need to be there for her.

She's affecting me more than I'd like to admit!

"On your back," she murmurs and shocks me with a shove at my shoulders.

Keep your heid, damn it!

Staying calm in this state of mind is more difficult than it seems, though. My fists clench and unclench as I try to sustain some sort of control. The sensuality laced in her voice attacks my very core, waking the man I keep hidden deep within.

Down beast. Stay the fuck down.

"No." I manage between her assaults on my mouth. Fight or flight wants to take over, but her blazing amber eyes meet mine, advising me to shut the hell up. I'm afraid if I resist she'll be off and running again. So, I concede, rolling onto my back in the plush green grass, and wait for her to make her move.

Ruby pretends to be an innocent dove, but she's already shown me there's a passionate hot blooded woman in there too. I've seen glimpses of her in my bed at the hotel, and I'd bet it wouldn't take much for the underlying hungry lioness buried deep inside her to show itself full force.

The thought barely crosses my mind before she strikes with ferocity, her mouth covering mine, and I stop breathing.

Ahhh, there it is, the primal animal, coming to the surface.

Ruby's lips are the fuel to the fire igniting between us. She's all over me, and instead of freaking out and putting a stop to this madness—I'm loving every second of her onslaught and egging her on. She's on top of me with those impenetrable thighs, holding me down like iron bars as her hips grind on my hard dick, which is painfully straining against my dress pants.

My heart beats at top speed, and excitement courses through me like never before. Giving into a woman is so refreshing. She'd demanded control, and I simply gave. By no means have I allowed such a thing before, but somehow, she made it seem so easy and natural to comply.

Abso-fucking-lutely freeing.

"Fuck!" I groan as my dick throbs and twitches under her.

"Hmmm." She purrs, then licks my bottom lip, sucking it into her mouth. "Ditto." She begins to tug at my shirt, almost ripping it right off of my body.

Oh, there's a lioness in there for sure.

I lay my hand on hers, stilling her movements. "Not. Here." I hiss and groan as words I never thought I'd ever say leave my mouth.

I must be an idiot, why would I stop? Oh, right... need to take it slow.

As if my words snap her out of a daze, she stiffens. "Oh god!

I'm sorry. No idea why—" Flustered, Ruby covers her face and her body trembles.

I kneel and wrap my fingers around her slim ones. "Hey, it's okay. Trust me, lass, I didn't mind one bit." I smirk.

She frowns. "I bet." Moving out of my reach, she frantically brushes at the dirt and grass staining her pants. "I have to go. I'm sorry, not sure what came over me." Not giving me a chance to speak, she leaps to her feet and in the blink of an eye, she's gone.

This time I don't follow, understanding she needs some space. My little runner needs time, and if I give chase, she'll lose her shit.

Little does she know… I've got all the time in the world.

I've already waited this long for a woman to spark my interest again. I can be patient… for now.

* * *

I HAVEN'T MOVED A MUSCLE since Ruby took off, especially once I realized where we ended up. Shifting my eyes from the hidden pathway on my right, I focus on the vast apartment complex before me. From this distance, it looks incredible. Each white stone building towers skyward with aesthetically pleasing, crisp, clean lines. An architect's dream.

Exactly what I envisioned.

It's rare that I'm alone like this, and have time to truly appreciate what I've accomplished along with the second chance I've been given after everything.

Why did Ruby have to pick the one spot I try so hard to avoid?

It brings back bad memories, ones that tear my soul apart. I'm at their mercy and I follow the urgent need to see where they lead. I navigate the stone pathway, dodging the prickly branches sticking out all around me.

These ten acres of land were my first investment. As soon as I spotted the rare and lush two acres filled will trees and shrubbery included in the parcel, I made an immediate offer. At that time, everything in my life was up in the air and the only thing that made sense was this small paradise. I reserved it specifically for the precious gem I built with my own two hands.

How many years did it take? Three or four?

Every minute of my spare time was spent on these two acres of land, sweating profusely in the hot as fuck Texas heat. The young and hopeful man I used to be thought it would be a great idea to build a home and develop the apartment complex at the same time.

Some said it was irresponsible and risky, but I was determined and stubborn—like a true Scotsman. There was no way in hell I'd give up.

I'd fought too hard to assimilate here in Texas. After all the obstacles and struggles of saving money and getting loans from my dad and Jax's dad, I couldn't even think about going back to Scotland. Returning home with my tail between my legs like a whipped and beaten puppy to hear my father say *'Ah tauld ye sae'?*

Not a fucking option!

Clearing through the hedges, the house comes into full view and I'm immobilized.

When was the last time I came back here?

I run the math in my head and realize it's been three full years. At one point in my life, this was my pride and joy, everything I worked for with the hope I would one day raise my family here. It wasn't long after I finished building it when that dream life vanished before my eyes.

God damn! I shouldn't have chased after Ruby. I feel too much pain here.

I look up and sigh. Small palm trees and beautiful red rose bushes that I handpicked surround the small brick cottage. The big red door stands out like a sore thumb, but it's how I've always envisioned it. This is and will always be the only home I ever have that's surrounded and decorated with vibrant color. The only one that's truly ever felt like a real home... until...

Not going there.

I take a deep breath and with a huff, I move a few steps closer, then a few more, and I'm at the door. There's no need to knock or announce my presence, I always have the key with me. I fiddle with it before opening the door wide and cautiously take my first step, the last thing I want to do is terrify Stavros's wife, Maria.

He'll kill me. Never mess with a Greek man's spouse or family, you're asking for bad joojoo.

"Hello?" I call out. No answer, but I smell something sweet wafting in the air as I walk down the short hallway. Everything is exactly how I left it, the lavender floral paintings adorn the wall to my left on the right is the empty dining area. I never did get the chance to buy a proper table.

No need when there's no one to sit at it with you.

Further down is the open space kitchen and living room, both fully furnished and decorated. The kitchen is a happy space with a bright yellow accent wall with random red polka dots on it.

We did this one together. I remember. I'll always remember.

The sweet scent is heavy in the air and I search for the source since no one is answering me. It doesn't take me long to spot the Baklava drizzled with chocolate cooling on the countertop.

My favorite. Maria's been busy!

"Maria!" I'm greeted by silence and I feel panic setting in.

She's getting older and is all alone while Stavros is working. The last thing I want is something to happen to the sweet woman.

"Maria!" I try louder this time and still no answer.

"Boy, quiet down! You'll wake the dead!" She rounds the corner and wags a finger at me.

I smile deeply and rush toward her. With my mother gone, she's the closest thing I have to maternal love. "Maria! You scared me, I thought something happened to you! When I called, you didn't answer."

She pulls me into a great big hug and squeezes as hard as she can. "Can't an old lady go to the bathroom in peace? Don't you worry bout me, I'm very, very strong." Her accent is as thick as her husband's. "Come." She pulls at my arm, guiding me to the baked goods. "Eat. Look at you, so skinny. You need a Greek woman in your life, she will feed you good!" She smiles sweetly and hands me a large helping of the warm dessert.

With great pleasure, I accept it from her, taking a small bite, savoring the honey nut flavor mixed with milk chocolate. "Thank you, Maria. It's delicious, as always. And no woman for me yet, no one wants me." I shrug and smile at her disapproving look.

"Oh, you're a bad man. You lie to me? Woman all over the world desire you, but you don't want them as a wife. The one for you is somewhere. I know for sure but find her soon. I want to marry you off already!" She shoves another piece at me. "Eat! All that muscle, too much, you need a little fat on those bones."

I shovel this one in to appease her, gulping it down without even tasting it. Now satisfied, she begins to shuffle around the kitchen, pulling things out of the fridge and setting them on the counter. I can't help but smile as I watch her hustle and bustle. Even though I haven't stopped by in a few years, my appearance today doesn't faze her, she accepts my presence and begins cooking as if this is a normal occurrence.

She looks back at me. "Oh, those dimples! How much I missed them. You don't visit me anymore... I clean and make sure it's ready for you to come back every day, but you never come." Her smile is sad and her eyes glisten.

"I know." I look down at my shoes, shame filling me. "I'm not ready. I... I was close by today and I wanted to try and see... if it's easier now." I don't dare face her, I know exactly what I'll see.

It's hard enough being here, let alone seeing Maria cry.

Her small warm hands rub my arms before she wraps them around me. Another one of those pang in the chest hugs that I seem to need more than ever lately. I stand there unmoving for a moment, and then the urge to hug her back hits me. She places her head on my chest and begins to weep. A familiar pain is triggered in that exact area and I want to rub it or drink it away, but neither is an option right now.

"I love you, boy. God bring you to me for a reason, that's why I never questioned your bad behavior all these years. I know it's hard, but is it easier now that you're here? Maybe you come more?" She lets out another sob.

I slam my eyes shut, my emotions are going haywire, and it's becoming too much to handle. But for Maria, I'll keep it together. "I love you too." I pull away so I can see that wrinkled face I care for so much. "It's a little easier. Not much, but I'll try to visit. I miss you too, you know? I tell Stavros to tell you all the time."

"It's not the same! You tell me yourself, you hear me?" There she goes with that wagging finger again.

"Yeah, yeah. I hear ya. I'll visit." Agreeing with Maria is the only way to appease this feisty little Greek woman.

I thought she'd be pacified by my answer, but she continues. "I respected your wishes for far too long, boy. Seeing you once a month for dinner at *your* apartment is *not* enough. I can make you real food here. Not that take-out caca you buy from the restaurants. Or if it's too hard for you to come here, Stavros and me can move back to our old apartment, then will you visit us?" She raises a brow and a small smile graces her lips, knowing I would never go for the idea of them leaving this house. She keeps this place alive and has made it a home for her and her husband.

At least someone was able to.

"That will not happen, Maria. You will both stay here. Please understand it soothes my soul knowing you're taking care of the house in a way I couldn't after—" I slam my mouth shut, unable to finish the sentence and allow the words to spill freely. I refuse to reopen a wound I've barely been able to stitch up.

Maria lets out a small cry. "Maes—"

Don't want to hear it. I can't hear it. I'm not ready to.

I hold up a hand, cutting her off. I need to end this conversation or I won't be coming back here anytime soon. There are already too many memories surrounding me and talking about it will only make them real all over again. "Maria, I promise if you stay, I will visit more often. And you know when I make a promise, I never break them."

"You really promise?" Her eyes widen in surprise and her lips quirk up, but she seems to fight a full-on smile from appearing.

Probably because she doesn't want to have hope and then I let her down, like the asshole in me usually does. Now I went and did it and made a promise to someone I love—don't fucking let her down!

I nod and do the only thing that will quit her nagging. Picking up three pieces of the Baklava, I wave them in her face before shoving one in my mouth. "So good!"

"I know! I make the best! Now sit, and I'll make you dinner. Stavros working late tonight, so just us two." She turns away from me and starts chopping up who knows what. "Oh, and Maeson, next time you visit, don't come drunk."

I'm floored. I forgot I drank today, especially after hearing Ruby's story and chasing after her. But of course, Maria smells, hears and knows it all. Nothing, and I mean absolutely nothing escapes her.

-29-

Ruby

FROM THE SECOND I STOMPED into the foyer of my apartment, I've been pacing from the elevator doors to the couch. Back and forth, for the last thirty minutes. I tug at my hair, needing to feel pain, something other than humiliation.

I knew I wasn't ready, not ready at all!

How many times have I stared at his lips wanting them against mine again? How many times had I wondered if each time our mouths touched it would bring forth the same excitement I felt the first time?

Too many damn times!

I desired it and now that I've found out, it's all I want to do when I'm with him. His kiss is intoxicating, precisely like the man himself.

Making out with him on the grass was unlike the other times. It was deeper, more meaningful, and it created an unexpected yearning like it was essential to our existence.

So vital, I didn't want to stop once I got started.

I just answered one of my own concerns—yes, the man excites me every damn time so effortlessly it's disgusting. Whenever Maeson is near, my body catches fire, my brain goes haywire, and I crave more of him than I should.

Everything escalated so fast, and in that instant, it didn't matter to me that we were in a semi-public area behind the complex. The need to control was too strong, I'd simply let go and tapped into the suppressed part of me that I'd never been allowed to explore with Ray or any other man.

For Maeson the hungry woman deep inside flooded from me with such ease. She wasn't afraid to take exactly what she wanted.

She wanted out and I let her…

For once, all that mattered was me, and how I felt. I reveled in it, the sheer excitement of telling a man—demanding a man to do what I wanted for a change. Having him comply was absolutely exhilarating.

But why was it so easy with him and not the others?

Had his words from our coffee date given me courage and added an extra shot of bravery? They replay in my mind— *'I'm not the kind of man who is afraid of a strong woman. Go ahead, teach me all you want. I will praise you not run away from you or put you down for it.'* I truly grasp how much him saying that meant. I even *feel* the amount of power such a simple statement held for me.

Until I pushed for more, I didn't know exactly what it was I desired, and once I did? Oh, I wanted so much more of him.

He had to speak up, didn't he? The bastard killed the whole vibe. I needed it, and he took it away!

He's a man and that entire species wants sex, it's a known fact. Since when do they stop a woman from devouring them?

Oh, wait! Let me guess.

Mr. Alexander found himself a conscience?

Bullshit!

Like he has principles? Or maybe…

Maybe he doesn't want me in that way again?

Now that's just stupid talk. I could be a cardboard box and

he'd want to fuck it. Maybe it's because he doesn't want to have sex in a public area, and I'm overreacting. I'm as clueless as ever as to what to think anymore or what to want.

I'm at a complete loss.

Memories hound me, needs hound me, wants hound me, and stupid idealistic thoughts hound me. It's never ending.

I need peace in this brain. I should occupy myself. Do something productive.

I know Axel's in the process of getting my charities set up, but I haven't heard a thing on the housing idea.

No time better than the present.

My phone's exactly where I flung it the moment the doors slid open—on the plush area rug in the living room face down. I scoop it up, finding Axel Donovan's name in my recent call list.

After two rings, he answers breathlessly. "Hello, Ruby."

"Hi, Axel. Am I interrupting… *something*?"

"*No!* Not at all! Sorry, I was working out. Gimme a sec." There's some shuffling in the background. "I'm back. So, what's up?"

Not wanting to waste any of the man's time, I get the point right away. "You have any news on the project we discussed last week?" I hold my breath.

Please give me good news.

Axel clears his throat. "Oh yes! I was going to call you, but you've beaten me to it. I have an idea, although, I'm not sure how you'll feel about it."

"Go ahead. I'd like to hear it." I stop moving, afraid of what he's going to say.

"First, I'd like to join your venture and contribute. Second, I think we should bring someone in on this for their experience in housing." He rushes out each word.

"Oh. Hmmm." I process his words for a second, knowing he's probably right. I don't know the first thing about running an apartment complex. "I'm guessing you have someone in particular on your mind?"

There's silence on Axel's end, and as I'm about to cut in, he drops a bomb on me. "Maeson Alexander would be my top choice."

My mouth drops open. "Wha—? No! NO! Pick someone else!"

"I can do that if you want, but he's a great choice, given that he's built an empire practically on his own. I believe he's the right person for this job. Between the three of us, we can make this work, Ruby."

He's has a point.

"I'll have to think on it. I'd like to see what he has to offer for myself. I hardly know anything about his *empire*."

Besides, I'm betting Maeson wouldn't want anything to do with such a thing.

I shake my head dismissively, not even entertaining the idea of Maeson wanting to *help* fix people's lives. After all, from what I was told, he's a ruthless businessman through and through.

Something else Axel said comes mind, and I change the subject before he can respond. "Why would *you* want in any way?"

Axel sighs deeply. "Well, Ruby, for me it's a personal reason. I'd like to help make a difference, and what you have planned will give me that opportunity."

"I understand and any help would be greatly appreciated. We could make a great team, especially when it's a personal mission for us both. But are you sure about Maeson?"

How many layers of surprise could there be in one man?

"Yes. He'd go in as well. I know, for a fact, he wants to build another complex. His experience is vast and it would save us from hiring an outsider." Axel's deep voice is full of confidence, which eases my worry. "I trust Maeson beyond measure. He wouldn't screw us."

"I see." Needing to still the negative thoughts cruising through my mind, I grab a cloth and occupy myself with wiping off the dust gathering on my bookshelf.

"Doing it alone will take longer to get off the ground. We can join forces—a three-person partnership." He pauses, and I hear ice tinkle into a glass. "It's your idea, Ruby. I don't want to take that away from you, but I also want to give this the absolute best chance of succeeding. To do that, you need expertise and a strong team on your side."

"Did you talk to him about this already? You seem pretty confident."

"Yes, I did. I wanted to make sure he was interested before bringing it to you. All my facts needed to be straight so I could have a proper proposal written up. One that's fair to us all, but most of all, fair to you."

I almost roll my eyes but there's truth in his words. Can't show up to your job unprepared. "Well, I'm not a fan of you going to him before me since this is something I wanted done, but I get it. Explain to me what you guys had in mind?"

"We can build two, maybe three structures. Each one designated for a specific cause. All with top notch security installed, as well as an officer at the front desk twenty-four-seven. This will be a very secure and safe environment for everyone involved. What do you think?"

My hand stills and I smile. "That sounds fantastic! Better than what I'd envisioned, to be honest. Looks like I'm not going be too upset with you and old man wrinkle for scheming behind my back. But if we do this, we discuss everything together. Not you two deciding, then cluing me in at your leisure. Got it?"

Axel's deep laugh penetrates my ears. "Of course! I apologize. This is your baby, so you're the boss in all aspects. Nothing will be done without your approval. If you're good with it, I'd be glad to email you everything once I have it all together."

"Alright, send it to me. Now I'll have to have a new lawyer look it over." I sigh. The idea of searching for another one is not something I'm looking forward to. It's hard to know who you can trust nowadays.

"Oh, don't worry, I didn't write up the contract. A friend I went to law school with, Nathan McConnell is drawing it up. Nate can represent us in every aspect of the business proposal and I'll make sure to tell his ass not to fuck up this deal or he's fired!" Axel laughs. "All kidding aside, he's top notch. You can even call him directly if you have any questions on the contract."

"You thought of everything, haven't you? Thanks, Axel, you saved me some time on that end, and if you trust him then I'm good with it. Just set up a meeting for us all to meet and finalize everything."

"You got it. Take it easy."

We hang up and my fingers tremble as I set the phone down on the coffee table.

My dream is so close to becoming reality.

This is my chance to help people. Give that assistance and caring attention no one gave me when I so desperately needed it. A few more weeks and I'll have a contract before me to seal the deal, to seal my dreams, and my hopes of a better future.

Closing my eyes, I let the hot tears cascade down my face.

* * *

TWO WEEKS TO THE DAY, the documents Axel promised me have arrived. I'll forever remember the date. September twelfth will be engraved in my brain until the end of my days. I spent a few hours a day refreshing my inbox until it arrived.

Trying to contain my excitement, I slowly bring the cursor over Nate McConnell's name and hover there for a minute. My stomach does a little flip as I spot the attachment titled Bennett.Alexander.Donovan.

MCCONNELL, RICHARDS, & BRAYDON LLC

The form looks so official and fear envelops me.
What if we fail?
I scroll to the bottom and see my new lawyer's signature.

NATHAN MCCONNELL, J.D., ATTORNEY AT LAW

Oh, shit, this is happening.

Deep breath.

The contract is twenty-one pages long. Hot diggity damn. I'm going to need the biggest mug of coffee I can find in order to tackle this. Before I dig in, though, there's a call I should make. It's time I face him, after running away like deer in head lights fourteen days ago.

* * *

ACTING EXACTLY LIKE AN IMMATURE child, I do the precise opposite and avoid that dreaded phone call. Instead, I choose to go to In-n-out burger for dinner, which is the best option since it's the furthest place to grab something to eat from my apartment. Made my dinner decision pretty easy.

Well, that and their amazing milkshakes.

After a burger, fries, and a Coke, I can say I'm full and ready to tackle the massive, life-altering contract. But first, the time has come, unfortunately, that conversation needs to be had.

I power up my computer and start the printing process while my phone rings and rings, impatiently waiting for him to answer.

Voicemail.

"Answer your phone," I mutter, as I try again and then once more. Voicemail each time.

Screw it. I was going to apologize, but not anymore.

Two copies—forty-two long drawn out pages—are now face up on my desk, still warm from the printer, but I need a coffee. Stat. I tap my fingernails on the counter, craving that first sip, watching as it seems to take forever to brew.

I should try to call him again.

My conscience is ridiculous, I swear.

Can't let it go, can I?

I plunk the steamy mug onto my desk, eyeing the waiting contract, then sigh. Closing my eyes, I attempt to clear my mind. My obsessive compulsiveness begs for order before I tackle all these pages filled with shit I'm sure I won't even understand.

Once each sheet is marked with categories and stapled in groups, I'm able to read each subject and give it my full attention. I sit there highlighting, crossing out, and marking those pages until my eyes blur.

When I look up, I notice it's pitch dark outside. I didn't even take a bathroom break. I was glued to this chair for what?

Holy shit! Three hours!

Curious if Maeson called me back after all this time, I check my phone. Five missed calls, three from Maeson and two from Molly, as well as two text messages, both from Maeson, which I don't read. I try to fight the smile that widens across my face, but it doesn't work.

Bastard! Stop making me feel so much.

I hit the redial button and the familiar butterflies flutter in my belly.

Deep breath. Remember you hold the power now, you're not the same person you used to be.

Ring. Ring. Rin— "Ruby? What's wrong? Are you alright? Where are you?" The deeply panicked voice sounds through the line.

"Hey, ole man. I'm just dandy. Why do you sound so crazy?" I play it cool even though when I called him earlier, my insides churned as I hoped and wished he'd answer. When he hadn't I was sad, hurt and disappointed.

"You ran off on me two weeks ago, all upset, and I haven't heard from you that whole time. Then you call me a gazillion times out of the blue and left no message. What am I supposed to think? Especially after what I know about you now."

"Oh." I clear my dried-up throat and heat flushes my cheeks. I'm used to my up and down, all over the place emotions, but I should've known other people wouldn't be. "You're right, I'm sorry. I was overwhelmed, needed time to clear my head. You know?"

"Sure, I do. So, why did you call?"

"I uh. Well, I spoke to Axel and I have the contract you two talked about. Which by the way, you did without me. Not cool."

Maeson chuckles on the other end. "I—"

I interject before he gives me some bullshit excuse. "Doesn't matter now. Look, I was calling because I'd like the two of us to discuss it. Maybe you won't mind helping me with the legal jargon?"

See I do try. This is me extending an olive branch.

His previous chuckle turns into a laugh. A deep sexy as hell one for that matter. "Sure. When?"

"Now?" I say quietly and inhale audibly.

Please say yes.

Silence. More silence. "You sure?" His tone is so soft; I barely hear him.

"Yes." It rushes out of me, without a second thought.

"Okay. *Princess?*"

"Yeah?" I shiver. The term still affects me, but in a very different and much more pleasurable way now.

"Please stop running away from me." With that small proclamation, the line goes dead.

I stare down at the blank screen sadly and my heart starts to ache. He will never know or even begin to understand how much I wish I could be someone else, someone stronger, someone without so many fucked up problems.

The desire to one day be that girl everyone likes, the one men desire, the one that's loved by all is so strong I can taste it.

How can I find that unscarred woman I used to be when she's lost and been beaten to the ground too many times to count?

So, how can I stop running, when it's all I've done since I was ten?

The answer I would've given him is...

I simply don't know how.

-30-

MAESON

I HOP INTO A COLD ass shower before I go see Ruby. Anything to keep my way too active dick on ice, at least for this evening.

Holy shit!

The freezing water sprays down my body and my muscles cramp up, not used to such an extreme temperature. In less than five minutes, I can't take it anymore, and I haul myself out, shivering from head to toe. I look down and roll my eyes.

Tame yourself tonight… or else. We don't need her going MIA again because of you.

Not wanting to waste any more time berating, Maeson Jr, I wrap a towel around my waist and head into the bedroom. Dark blue jeans, a fitted red tee-shirt, and of course the most comfortable shoes I own, my Venice pitch black suede and leather TCGs, are laid out on the bed. I dress with care, and after fixing my belt, I take a glance in the mirror and notice my hair is a mess. The sides are shaved close, and the top part is longer and shaggy in an *'I don't try to look hot, but I do'* kind of way, so it's fine. Could use some gel, but fuck it, it goes well with the scruff I've been sporting on my face.

Quit procrastinating and go see her already. Stop being a damn pussy! I know, damn it. I know.

Key card and phone in hand, I'm out of the penthouse in a

flash.

* * *

THIS TIME I'M DOING IT the right way and I let Ruby buzz me in. The long ass elevator ride approaches the tenth floor and I fuss with my shirt, tugging, and pulling at it for no reason at all.

When was the last time I broke out into a cold sweat over seeing a girl?

Knowing me? Probably never. But somehow, this one has me all sorts of fucked up.

The doors sound once it reaches the top floor and out of a nervous habit, I push my glasses up onto the bridge of my nose. They open wide and Ruby stands before me... naked.

Ha! Yeah right!

I shake my head, clearing it of the wicked images, and stride into the apartment. "Ruby."

It's been fourteen long dreadful days of not seeing or speaking to her—something I never thought I would experience over a woman—yet, here I am over the moon, and nervous as hell standing before her.

There's an awkward silence between us before she answers. "Maeson." She steps toward me but hesitates. With a small smile, she waves me in. "Come in." She spins and is off toward the living room, dropping onto the couch beside a large stack of papers.

Was she coming in for a hug? Or maybe a kiss? You wish, buddy.

"So, are you on board with me joining the 'do good' project?" I don't mean to make light of the subject, but this awkwardness between us is messing with my common sense.

Her head snaps in my direction and she glares at me. "I'm

aboard until you say bullshit like that about something so important to me." She rises a closed fist in the air toward my direction. "I'll knock you out if you do it again. Got it?"

She's so cute when trying to be serious.

Smirking, I give her a thumbs up. "Got it, *Sweetie pie*." I lay back into the couch across from her and set my ankle on the knee of my other leg.

Her lips twitch but she doesn't fully smile. "Okay, *Snookums*. Start reading." She tosses a pile of papers on the cushion beside me. "While you do that, can I get you a drink?"

"Wow!" I reel back, feigning shock. "This much hospitality from you is something I'm unaccustomed with. I'm not sure how to handle it!" I chuckle.

Ruby narrows her eyes and places her hands on her hips. "*Well*, when someone's not breaking into my home this is usually how I treat them. But, you wouldn't know that, would you? No, because you're clueless when it comes to respecting boundaries." She tosses her hair back and spins, slowly strolling over to the kitchen. Purposely rolling and undulating her hips, teasing me, and showing off her ass...ets.

Goddamn...

"You're right. I've learned my lesson. Won't happen again." Tearing my eyes from her back side, I admire her long, dark curly locks, wishing I could wrap my fingers around them.

She peers back, shooting me a saucy glare. "Better not. Next time I'll be less inclined to let you stay."

With a smirk, I bow my head. "Noted."

Ruby stops short, opens the fridge, and bends over to peer inside, giving me an eyeful of that mouthwatering ass. "So, what do you want to drink?"

My brain short circuits and I imagine taking her from behind. "Ah... do you..." I struggle to form the words as my brain is currently occupied with more interesting *things*. "have any soda?" If I don't get it together, she'll notice my indecent gawking, which will probably piss her off enough to kick me out. It's already obvious something isn't right with me. My voice sounds strangled even to my own ears.

Luckily, she seems oblivious as she pops her head out of the fridge and holds up a can. "Ginger Ale?"

I nod. She grabs two and hands me one. "Thank you." I take a sip, then set it down to peek through the documents on my lap.

"Where should we start?" Ruby holds up her own copy.

"First, let's discuss what you have in mind. The logistics can be torn apart in our meeting with" —I look down, spotting the name of the new lawyer— "Nate McConnell. Therefore, tell me what it is exactly you want to accomplish?"

She shuffles through the papers and nods. "You're right, this can wait for the official meeting, especially since Axel should have an input." Setting the pile beside her, she stands again. "I'm going to need something stronger than a Ginger Ale for this. How about you?"

I slice my head to the left, in a downward motion—declining her offer. Anything other than soda will put a kibosh on the small amount of willpower I have left to keep my distance from her. Also, my second head doesn't need any more alcoholic encouragement that it's had already.

I need to keep my wits about me tonight since one of us needs to stay somewhat sober.

Besides, she probably needs it more than I do anyway, it's visible what she's about to tell me is going to take a toll on her.

"Is that a yes or a no? I'm not well versed in those sexy, *'I'm talking to you, but not with my words'*, head motions you seem to enjoy using."

"Maybe one day you will be—*well versed*." I laugh and Ruby rolls her eyes. "It's a no, but you go ahead."

"Not any day soon, I won't. Anyway, I'll make extra in case you change your mind." Ruby's behind the kitchen counter pulling out a few familiar bottles, along with a large glass pitcher, and a highball tumbler. Right away I know what she's mixing, the drink she introduced to me not long ago. The now famous Ruby Apple.

For that, I might have to change my mind and have a taste.

"Do you mind if I smoke inside? I usually go up top, but I'm not in the mood right now." She sits on the very furry area rug next to the couch with a drink in one hand and an ashtray in the other. The sleek cigarette case is already on the ottoman and she places the other two items next to it.

"Sure, go for it, this is your place. Do what you want and I'll even join you." I pull out my own pack from my jeans pocket, shaking it. Noticing her hesitation, I light mine first.

She twirls the case between her fingers for a moment before she gives in. "True, I pay a fortune for this place." She waves her hand around the space. "I could light up occasionally, not like my landlord would know." She giggles and smoke puffs out of her mouth.

Her laugh is contagious and I can't help but join her. "I won't tell him. Your secret's safe with me!" I shove the papers off of my lap and settle on the rug in front of her.

"You better not or—"

"You'll knock me out, I know." My smile deepens and I motion a finger across my neck. "Finish him!"

She laughs and pats my leg. "Exactly, Mortal Combat style. Now be a good boy and we'll get along just fine."

"Oh, then I'll definitely stay on your good side." I bob my head happily. "And to keep it that way, why don't you start by telling me the what's, how's and why's of our upcoming partnership?"

"Right." Her smile fades. "Back to business." Bringing the cigarette to her plush lips, she inhales deeply, seeming to hold her breath before releasing the smoke from her lungs. "Well, you already know my past relationship was... terrible. So, that's why I want to provide a safe-haven for abuse victims. They need to know there's someone out there who will go above and beyond to help them, same goes with foster children. This is the part you don't know much about, so I'll try and explain." She looks toward the massive windows and sighs. "When Mom and Dad died, I was put in foster care. They were told it was a great home and I'd be loved by this sweet middle-aged couple.

Unfortunately, my parents were very misinformed, so I don't blame them. But I do fault this fucking loophole filled system."

Oh, shit. I don't like where this is going.

My gut clenches and anger starts to rise. "Did they—"

As if reading my mind, she cuts me off. "Yes. They were bad people. No love for the children placed in their home, *at all*. And lucky for them, my folks had a fund to be used for my care. Did they use it? Yes, but not for me." She meets my eyes dead on and mutters. "Fucking assholes, if my foster father wasn't killed in jail, I'd find him myself and finish him off." She downs her drink and abruptly stands. "Need a real drink now?" She raises an eyebrow.

"Yes." I manage around the knot building in my throat.

I don't even know what he did to her or their other kids, but I'd kill him for her if he weren't already dead.

Children are precious gifts and should be cherished, not demolished, and treated like garbage. Most people don't appreciate the love of a child until it's too late, and some people have no clue what it means to be a real parent. One who loves unconditionally and would give everything up for them, including their very own life. Which—

"You want ice?" Ruby cuts into my thoughts.

"Please." My mouth is suddenly dry and I gratefully accept the glass when she hands it to me. "Thanks."

"Yup. So, that's a shortened version of why I want to make this happen. I need a foster home where children can receive proper care and a good education. I'm not sure if Axel told you, but I also set up charities. And if that's not enough, I'll spend every last dime my parents busted their asses for to help make a difference in this world."

I scoot closer to her and take her slender hands into mine, caressing the soft skin. Her eyes shine with tears she's threatening to shed. "I'll be there for you every step of the way. Between the three of us, we can make this happen exactly the way you envision it. I have experience in the building and management field. Axel in the legal field, and you, well, you my princess, have the most experience of us all in the 'reasons for these charities' field." I bend my head and kiss the tops of her hands. "If nothing else, Ruby, I'm here for you, even if it's only to talk." I stare directly into her beautiful eyes, making sure she *sees* the honesty in mine.

Her bottom lip quivers and a tear slides down her cheek. "Th..."—Ruby stops and takes a long ragged breath—"Thank you, but... you say that now and once things change you're a goner. I've learned the hard way that it's easier to prepare for the unexpected if I only depend on myself." Her golden eyes are filled with sadness, the normal burning spark in them has vanished, and the way she's fidgeting as if she's uncomfortable in her own skin tells me she's lying. Her mannerism begs for me to stick around and...

Tells me not to disappoint her.

Inching closer to her face, I wipe away the lone tear. "You can't live your life in fear, or always expecting the other shoe to drop. Bad things happen to us all, but it's how you choose to handle it. At the end of the day, that'll be what helps us heal and grow. We're adults who can or at least should be able to separate business from pleasure, so when I say I'll be there for you on all ends of our *'relationship'*, I mean it." Looking at her somber face, the urge to make everything better blasts me, and I find myself wanting to change this whole world for her.

Here I go making promises, when I know, somehow, I'll fuck it all up in the end.

Not only do I want to try, but she makes me feel like this time I can keep this kind of promise.

She blinks a few times and huffs. "You don't even know me well enough to make such a serious commitment! How can I trust a man I've known for what... almost three months? There's no way I can let go so simply, all based on your word." Her eyes close and another tear drops. "Things don't work that way in real life. What kind of fancy romance page are you on, Mr.?"

"The same damn page as you, *Sweetheart*, I just read it differently than you did." I shake my head side to side, noticing she's not getting what I am trying to say and before she begins to speak, I continue. "Don't misunderstand me. All I ask is you try, and I'll do the same. We're going to be attached at the hip for a long time to come with this project, might as well make it work between us. We can be partners and only that, nothing more unless you want to try to be friends as well."

Ruby's lip curls. "Friends? Seriously? That's what you want after sleeping with me, then kissing me every chance you get?"

I shift, relieving some of the weight on my left leg to the right one. "First off, you kissed me back. Second, my dear, I'm taking it slow for you. If it were up to me, I'd say I want—you to be— *more*. But I'd be crazy to expect that from you."

"Oh." She pulls her long curly hair to the side, exposing her tan neck.

I could kiss that bare spot... I could make her feel better.

Before I can lean into her to try, she grabs my glasses and tosses them on the table. "What's that for?" I rub at the bridge of my nose.

She shrugs and smiles shyly. "I like you better without them."

"But I can't see!" I laugh.

She sticks two fingers in the air. "How many fingers do I have up?"

"Three."

"Bullshit on a stick! You can see just fine. Or maybe you are that old! Your vision is shit cause you're an ole bag o' bones!" Her hysterical laugh echoes throughout the apartment.

"What!" I tackle her to the ground, tickling her until happy tears run out of those gorgeous amber eyes.

"Okay! Okay! I give in! No more tickles!" She holds her belly as she laughs and tries to push me away.

"Am I OLD?" I attack with more tickling.

"Yes!" She shouts.

"You little shit! More tickles it is!"

We roll around for a few more minutes and at this point, I'm laughing as hard as she is. It seems like an eternity since the last time I laughed this hard, that eternity being almost six painful years ago.

Ruby wraps her voluptuous thighs around me and tries to overpower me but of course, she fails. "Maeson... okay... okay... you're... not... old!" she says in between her giggles.

Since she's given in, I stop my assault and help her sit up. "Good. Next time you say I'm old, I won't stop!" As Ruby attempts to compose herself, I sip on my almost forgotten drink and admire her beauty, memorizing the striking features of her face.

The spark that was missing in her eyes is now blazing, brighter than I've seen so far. It's as if she's coming back to life, just from having a little fun.

"Hmmm. Well seeing as this was the most I've laughed since I was a kid, I might need a repeat experience." Her smile suddenly turns into a frown. "Thank you. I needed that."

"Honestly? I did too."

She nods. "Feels good, doesn't it?"

I grin. The thought of hearing her laugh wholeheartedly again is very appealing. "I would say so."

That smile I'm starting to fall for reappears. "Me too." She puts a cigarette between her lips and lights it, then takes one from my pack and slides it between mine.

The flame flickers as it touches the end of it and smoke billows around us. "Ruby? Can I be honest with you?

She exhales and a haze of smoke forms between us. "Mmhmm."

Deep breath fucker, it's time to man up.

"Look, I need to make something clear. I've said this already but, I'd like to be with you, in more than just a professional or friendly fashion." I lean over and tap the cigarette against the ashtray. "On our first *date*, I wanted to ask, but it was too soon, and even now, nothing since then has changed—you still run away and won't open up to me. So, I was thinking... if it's something you'd like, maybe we can pick up on the coffee date idea?"

God, I sound so lame.

She blinks a few times as if in shock. "I don't mean to... be this way... it's the only way I know how to be any more"—She pauses for a second, then her head bobs up and down— "but... I'd like to do that."

"We can start slow, going at whatever pace you're comfortable with. I'll let you take the lead, Princess mine." I stand and put out my smoke, then extend my arm to her.

I shouldn't linger too long or that 'take it slow' shit will be ruined.

She lets me pull her to her feet, but doesn't let go of my hand. "Okay, I can handle that."

Instinct begs for me to kiss her, instead, I gently pull her to me and hug her. At first, she is stiff against me, but in no time, she relaxes and we stand there holding one another.

My mind wanders and I envision her sprawled out on her couch stark-naked, moaning as I suck on her nipple, and simultaneously caress between her legs...

Shit! Too much!

"I should go." Abruptly, I pull away from her, needing to maintain some sort of distance before I do something she's not ready for.

"Right." She smiles sadly and guides me to the elevator doors.

I step in, hit the first level button, and as the doors close, she giggles. "See ya later, Old Man!"

Damn her! Her ass is mine next time I see her!

Behind closed doors, I throw my head back and laugh all the way down to the first floor.

Oh, this woman has me by the balls.

-31-

Ruby

I THOUGHT THE TEXAS HEAT was bad during the summer? Well, it's almost October, and it isn't any better.

No more good, old fall weather after a few hot months to look forward to anymore.

I knew lying out on the rooftop was a bad idea, sweat is freaking dripping from my body!

I'm drenched!

Once I reach the last step into the apartment, cool air hits my skin and I shiver in pleasure.

Oh! What a relief!

With a sigh, I strip off my clothes and kick them aside to be picked up later.

Shower needed stat!

After taking a nice cold one, I reset the central air to sixty-five and rush to get ready for another date—as promised—with Maeson.

I still can't believe how impossible it is to sit out on the roof.

My skin glistened within seconds, and it was even difficult to breathe! Molly told me it's not usually *this* bad this time of the year, but the heat is something I'll adapt to in time.

I'm not so sure about that!

Luckily, I live alone and can spend most of my time in the thinnest clothes I own or wandering around naked. The weather here is a drastic change from my hometown of Manhattan. Major adjustment curve, but I've managed all right for four months now.

Wow! That much time has passed?

I've barely felt the days fly by with everything going on. Although it seems like yesterday, a few weeks have passed since we met with our new lawyer, Nathan McConnell, and signed all of the contracts. Oh! How nervous I was that day, but thankfully, Maeson and Axel were by my side the entire time, explaining every detail I misunderstood.

My old self—the one who spent too many years with a bullshit excuse for a boyfriend—would've cowered in fear at so much change and the overload of information.

Tonight is yet another first, and I must say, I'm super excited. We're going to a restaurant called Hutchins BBQ in McKinney. Maeson says they have the best brisket around, but as I've never had it to begin with, I won't be a good judge.

Twenty minutes later he picks me up and we make our way to the restaurant.

We're driving along, accompanied by a comfortable silence, and unexpectedly my stomach growls loudly. There's no chance I can pretend that didn't just happen, so I do what I do best— pester the driver. "How long will it take to get there? I'm starving and my tummy is pissed!" I rub my belly and laugh.

Maeson looks over at me lazily, as if he was deep in thought and I interrupted. "Without traffic about thirty minutes, but it's worth the drive. I promise you and your stomach are going to love it." His tone is serious, but he smiles and extends his arm, comfortably laying his hand on my lap.

I want to ask what's wrong, but why ruin the night if it's

possibly something bad? So instead, I pretend not to notice. "If we don't like it then you're fired from picking the places we eat!"

We both laugh, knowing I wouldn't be able to choose any since my knowledge of the local eateries is limited at best.

"I can say with confidence, you, Princess, will not fire me, *ever*." He grins evilly without taking his eyes from the road.

Taking a moment to unabashedly admire the man next to me, it's hard to believe how much I despised him at first. I admit I was too quick to judge.

Self-preservation with a tablespoon full of fear maybe?

With time, I've loosened up a *smidgen* around him and he's been *selectively* showing me other parts of himself. At times, Maeson's so warm, then suddenly, the aloofness returns. It's like he's as conflicted with what is building between us, as I am. However, despite his multiple personalities, we've managed to enjoy more than a few coffee and dinner dates.

We're so different, yet we blend seamlessly. Our discussions go from deadly serious to laughing till we cry. That's something I've always dreamed of having in a relationship—the give and taking, the equality of it all.

Keep up the safety wall girly. Don't get too hopeful. Things can change very quickly and destroy what's left of you all over again.

I force myself to push away the negativity. Not everything needs to be so gloom filled. My focus should be on the good fortune I do have right now.

Like seeing Maeson's sexy smile almost every day.

I peer at him a moment longer, and he seems much more relaxed. Looks like I made the right choice by taking his mind off of whatever was bothering him. A teasing Maeson is easier to be around than the serious and pompous man I know he can be. "Don't let that confidence get to your head, Mr. Alexander." I squeeze his hand with all my might, and his deeply dimpled smile makes an appearance.

Instantly, I forget what I was thinking about and what we were even talking about. He's easily turned me into a flustered mess!

Damn him!

Within the next hour, we're at our table, and downing everything on our plates like little piggies.

"This is the first time I've had an entire meal and I couldn't say a word between bites! Thanks, Maeson, this was amazing. Easily, the best food I've had in a long time." I lick my lips, savoring the lingering sauce.

He reaches across and pats my hand. His touch is electric. "You're welcome, Ruby. When it's that good, conversation is not necessary. This means we'll have to come back soon."

"I'd love to!"

"Anytime. You just let me know. I'd like to show you more of Dallas as well."

"Sounds like a plan to me! I'm all yours, handsome." I wink and smile playfully.

There I go, being brave again.

After paying for our meal, Maeson places his large, warm hand on the small of my back guiding me out to the car, and my whole body tingles.

We've been spending a good amount of time together lately, and every time we do, I yearn and almost plead for more. No matter how hard I try, I can't deny the chemistry. With all our heated make-out sessions, the urge to turn them into something more is harder to resist than I anticipated. I don't know about him, but for me, the attraction is building to an almost overwhelming point.

At times, it's even hard to remember why I'm holding back.

Maeson assists me into his car, then slides into the driver's seat easily, glancing over. "Where to, Princess?" There's an invitation in his deep, low voice, and his green eyes are filled with those suggestive little golden flecks.

Which, recently they are there more often than not.

He rests his hand on my knee and the familiar heated pressure of it makes me inhale sharply. I knew the moment would arise at some point, and no time better than the present. I clear my throat nervously. "Your place?"

Maeson's lips spread into a huge grin and he nods. Clearly agreeing with the idea, he pulls out onto the main road.

Deep breath, Ruby. It's time.

I already know what he feels like, moves like, and tastes like. Nothing's changed.

Except your feelings have.

Dismissing that nonsense, I focus on the road ahead. As Maeson drives along, things start to look familiar. "I thought we were going to your place?"

"Aye! We are, don't you worry." He has a devilish grin on his face.

I'm confused, this looks like the road to my apartment?

"So, where is it?"

"Right across from your building, tenth floor." He smirks and wiggles his brows.

My mouth falls open.

That's how the bastard knew what I would be doing when I first moved in!

* * *

MAESON OPENS THE DOOR, USHERING me into his condo. Right away, I notice it has a similar layout as mine, except he has stairs leading to a second floor.

Bum gets a whole extra floor. Guess that's the perks of owning the penthouse.

"Please make yourself comfortable while I change out of this suit. I should've dressed down, but suits have been instilled in me for too many years."

"Go ahead. I'll be right here waiting. Oh, and by the way, I think you look sexy in suits." I nibble on my bottom lip.

Here is yet another thing this man is changing about me— I'm more playful and at ease around him. Maybe I never knew and that's who I am?

The person I've never had the chance to be?

"Thank you, Ruby. Good to know." He backtracks from the

steps as if he's changed his mind. "Maybe I shouldn't change?"

"No please, get comfortable. I bet you're sexy in anything you wear." I laugh and shoo him away.

With him gone, I can take some time to scout out his man cave. Everything is either crisp white or deep black, his belongings are all neatly ordered. His home makes me want to scatter the pillows around and move every painting out of its perfect position.

In this aspect, we couldn't be more different if we tried. I'm the complete opposite, my life and belongings are in complete disarray. I love color. My couches might be black, but they are decorated with bright red pillows. Even my plates are every color of the rainbow. Then Molly decided to add to my colorful scheme as well, thinking I don't have enough color in my life!

I don't own a single black and white painting, mine are all infused with color. It's as if I have color surrounding me at every turn in my home. I wonder if my obsession with brightness in my decor is a way of offsetting the darkness clouding my mind, and the deeply embedded scars.

Inside I'm colorless and empty like I might completely disappear.

"Ruby?" Maeson reappears, startling me from my reverie.

I'm frozen in place, staring at the painting on the wall. "Yes?" I turn at the sound of his voice and my eyes widen.

"Ye ok?" He frowns, his sexy accent popping up again. It makes its appearance so randomly, I can't keep up.

It's a sexy surprise when it does reappear, though.

And WHAT THE HELL am I looking at right now?

My eyes are probably popping out of my head. "Oh! Yes. I'm alright. You have a beautiful home, very crispy clean!"

Focus, Ruby. Who is this man?

"Thank you! It has to look professional as this isn't just my home, but where I hold most of my business meetings as well." His tone is very matter of fact as if I should know that already.

"I see." I cannot take my eyes away from him, he looks so damn good in those clothes.

Clothes I've seen before.

The outfit is what gives him away immediately, but I continue to stare and process.

"*What*? Why are you staring at me like that?" He turns in a complete circle.

More tricks up your sleeve, Mr. Alexander?

You've fooled me long enough.

"You, it's you! You... were on the bench that morning!"

"Bench?" A confused look settles on his face. "I have no idea what you're talking about."

He can deny all he wants, but he's not conning me.

The only thing missing is the aviators, he's even wearing a beanie.

"When I first moved in, I saw this guy in the courtyard. He wore exactly the same outfit! I never pictured you wearing anything so laid back, but... that on your head."—I point at his beanie— "Gave you away."

He touches the beanie and hangs his head. Knowing he's caught, he slumps onto the couch. "Yes. It was me." He may be looking down, but he can't hide the smirk creeping across his face.

"I knew it! That's why you were mad at Molly for asking you about the guy I saw. God forbid people see you in sweats from time to time." I can't help but roll my eyes at him.

I think this man likes to purposely find ways to irritate me to no end!

"That's not why." He doesn't elaborate.

I try to reason what else it could be, inspecting him once more before it hits me. "You have a freaking tattoo!"

That's the reason I didn't think it could be Maeson out there. He doesn't have the 'I have a thing for tattoos' vibe.

"Aye, lass." Again, he doesn't elaborate, he self-consciously pulls at the sleeve of his sweatshirt and has yet to look up.

"Well, no need to hide from me, I won't ruin your perfect reputation with your employees or business people. I know how to keep a secret—I don't give out information that's not mine to give."

He peeks up at me and nods. "Thank you, this world's a very

judgmental one and I'd like to keep parts of myself private. One day I'll explain the what's and why's of how I've become the man I am today. I'd also like the same from you, the deeper stuff, in time. But for now, let's continue to build this..." He waves a hand in the space between us.

"Alright, that's good enough for me." I know how hard it is to divulge parts of myself and I'd never force a person to do that. "Since my unidentified man mystery is solved, what should we do for the rest of the night?" As the words come out, the realization hits me. We're all alone in his private space. Butterflies flutter away in my stomach, and I feel a little nauseous.

"Well, I have a few things in mind but I doubt you're ready for such events." He gazes at me, those amazing eyes burning with fire, giving me an idea of how naughty those things are. "*Again.*"

"Oh? You sure about that?" I seductively raise my newly threaded eyebrow.

I'm not even drunk and I'm testing the waters?

Daring myself to push the limits, I wander slowly toward him. Running my fingers through my long dark locks, I wet my lips with the tip of my tongue and let a smile tug at the corners of my mouth. "What are those *things* you have in mind?"

I'm not sure who this teasing is affecting more? Him, or me? Probably me.

"You want to know, or see?" He puts his hands on my hips, pulling my body between his bent legs. He rubs up and down gently, skimming over my body.

"Just know," I whisper.

This closeness intoxicates me as he trails his fingers up and down my thighs. Goosebumps appear all over my body as he squeezes the flesh gently, then runs his hands back up to my hips. A gentle push from Maeson guides me backward and he rises to his feet.

"Where are—" My words are cut off by his lips covering mine, his tongue invades my mouth as his hands travel across my body. I can't think. My brain stops working and my heart pounds. Before I can stop myself, I unzip his sweatshirt and let my fingers wander up to push off his beanie. I pull back, desperately needing air.

Deep breath. This is different. You want this man.

Maeson stands before me, no hat, no sweatshirt, just black baggy sweats, and a tight black t-shirt which shows off every single one of the muscles underneath. He's sex on a stick. A nice long damn stick which shows no matter how baggy his pants are.

Damn… damn… damn!

I stare down at the floor—*I don't think I can do this*—he's breathtakingly perfect and I'm a mental case in recovery.

"I can help you with your recovery, if you let me."

Crap, did I say mental case out loud?

"No, I—" The unspoken words stick in my throat as something attracts my attention.

He doesn't have *one* tattoo—his arms are freaking covered with them. I can only partially see what is exposed from under his shirt, and the tiniest bit on his neck.

Holy mother of God!

My initial opinion of him was utterly wrong! He doesn't wear those suits buttoned up to the top covering every inch of his body because he's an old, stuffy, stick up his ass businessman at all. He does it because he's covered in tattoos!

There might not be much color in his home or outfit choices, but there's plenty on his body. He has ink all over his arms and who knows where else. This man might be more like me than he lets on.

No wonder he didn't get naked and kept the lights off that night we had sex! He was hiding his tattoos!

I silently stare at Maeson while searching to find the right words My shock must be evident in the expression on my face. His arms are fully decorated, covered from where they emerge from under his tight t-shirt right down to his wrists. The detail is astounding, and I'm having trouble making them all out.

Slowly my eyes adjust, and I concentrate on his right arm. A vibrant red rose stands out amongst the rest. It starts at his elbow and the stem appears to be black writing, which I can't read due to the position of his arm. It's eye-catching. The entire rose appears to be three-dimensional, the effect is amazing, and I need to know what's written there.

Not saying a word, I gently take hold of his arm, turning it so I can clearly see. The words are in script, giving the impression of a long-stemmed rose, which ends at his wrist.

It's a quote and it says *'New beginnings are often disguised as painful endings'*.

Truer words have never been said, and I feel the pain deep inside. The death of my ex became my new beginning after a very painful ending. However, I've been here before. I dared to hope for happiness, but it always ended badly, with sadness and pain.

The pain will stop, and there will be a hole. Always there will be that hole. One which can never be filled, but I must carry on. What a fool am I, forever hoping but always living in fear of the bitter end.

Maybe one day I'll learn.

I realize how awkward this must be for him under my scrutinizing stare, so I manage a few words. "Maeson, your arms!" Gently I place my hands on them and look deeply into his eyes trying to show him what I *feel* with my own.

"Aye, lass, my arms" He returns the stare, that intense green gaze blank and unseeing, dejected.

"They are—"

"I ken, don't say it! I ken you don't like them! I assume it's not your style." His accent thickens and a shiver runs down my spine.

"They're utterly beautiful!"

Maeson slams his eyes shut and shakes his.

"I mean it, Maeson!"

"That cannot be so!"

How is it possible that he doesn't believe anyone could love his body art?

He always seems so confident, but here and there his insecurities peek through.

They must mean a whole lot to him.

"But it is. What I see is beautiful art on your skin. I'd love to see more." I look away, suddenly shy, wondering if I've said too much or I'm pushing too hard.

The heat of Maeson's body wraps around me as he moves in closer. "Aye, you may. But this will remain between us, the state of my body is no one's business." His voice is stern and laced with what appears to be worry.

"I won't say a word." I take his request very seriously and match his tone, so he knows I mean what I say. Without thinking, I lightly trace the rose with my finger.

His hand is warm as he gently grabs mine and our gazes meet. "Come with me."

He leads me up the stairs and down the hall silently, my gut clenches with uneasiness. My legs start to shake as we near the doorway, and I pause, not quite ready to step inside. His king-sized bed dominates the room, and matches the rest of his decor, with black pillows and linens.

He points to the edge of his bed. "Please sit." It's a statement, but a question at the same time. His voice is soft; all the edginess has dissipated.

My legs are shaking so badly I can barely stand, and I all but rush to sit down.

"Are you"—Maeson voice cracks—"sure you want to see?"

The confidence I expected from him is not there at all, which takes me by complete surprise. Most men can't wait to take off their clothes!

"Aye," I tease, using his native tongue.

He takes a small step back and slowly peels off his shirt. I watch in fascination as they all appear. His body is a multitude of colors, like a well-utilized canvas. Zeroing in on the bright red script covering his pec, I run a fingertip along the writing, *'Never Settle'*. So much truth lies between those two simple words.

I wish I never did.

Not wanting to dwell on something I can no longer control, I move on, taking in the rest of him. His right arm is a full sleeve of red roses, entwined with black and gray leaves. I trail my fingers over top and down to his forearm, which bears the long-stemmed rose I examined earlier. I turn to his other arm. This one is an intricate Celtic design, knots upon knots swirling in exquisite detail, all in shades of dark black and gray with random traces of red, green, and blue. I can only imagine how many hours it took to finish such a beautiful piece of work!

My eyes fall to his abdominal muscles, and his six pack is fully visible. There's not one single tattoo, not even a speck of ink covering the glorious muscles. I touch his abs, my fingers gliding up and down each perfectly formed square. "You missed a spot."

"No, I didn't. When I find something worthy of filling it, I'll do so. Each piece has been placed with purpose."

I've definitely hit a sensitive spot there. He seems very serious when it comes to his body art, so I simply smile and nod.

Moving on with my tour of this specimen named Maeson, I let my gaze travel lower and notice something else. He's rock hard underneath those sweatpants and his breathing has gotten heavier. He's apparently enjoying this intimate inspection of his body.

Being so close to him ignites the hot and bothered feeling between my legs and causes it to creep up my entire body. "Is... there more?" I can't keep the shakiness out of my voice as the flush hits my face.

He smells so divine and his tattooed physique is truly incredible.

Best I've ever seen.

"Aye, Princess, much, much more." He turns around ever so slowly.

I gasp at the sight. "Oh, my god, you have... wings."

They look just like an angel in heaven!

The detail is glorious and utterly breathtaking, covering almost his entire back. They start at the top of his shoulders and reach down below the waistband of his pants. My eyes fixate on them and notice between the two wings is a name in deep black script. In addition to the name, right underneath it is a saying, *'For Those I Love I Will Sacrifice'*.

Quite interesting. Nothing like a woman's name other than your own on a man's back.

My hands instinctively reach out, touching and lingering on the name. She must've been very important to him, and more than anything, I want to know why.

As I trace the tattoos, he shivers beneath my touch. "Och lass, quit your teasin'." Maeson's accent is at its thickest now and of course, sexy as hell. His back is so warm, smooth, and alive underneath my hands.

"I'm not teasing, I needed a closer look."

"You're mighty close, I can feel your breath on my back."

"Who is she?" I whisper.

Immediately he tenses up, his muscles forming knots under my hand now. "That, Princess, is of no concern to you!"

I know certain things are hard to talk about from my own experience, and this is evidently a touchy subject for Maeson. That's another thing I must let go of… for now.

"Fine. I won't push you, Maeson." I let a short silence sit between us before I dare speak again. "Why do you have so many? Do you have an addiction to getting them?"

"No addiction, I simply see my body as a personal journal, an outlet for my story and the tattoos basically tell it. They're my way of expression. The daily reminders of the memories I never want to forget." He pauses and I'm tempted to force him to face me, but before I can make my move he begins to speak again. "A form of self-torture, I know, but for some reason, it makes it easier to bear. At least it makes me feel *something,* which is better than the constant numbness and the lack of true emotion— unless it's one extreme or another. Guess that's what happens when you shut parts of yourself down, isn't it?"

He has yet to turn around. Is he worried he'll see disgust on my face?

I wish he would look me because he would see the complete

opposite. He'd see the understanding in my eyes. "I get it. No judgments on this end. And that makes sense to me. I've always wanted to get some myself, and probably for the same reasoning, but never had the courage." I know I just lied, but it had to be done, otherwise he'd want an explanation I don't want to give quite yet.

Silence. Then more silence. If we weren't standing, I'd think he's asleep.

Time to move to a different subject? Or maybe ask—

My face begins to heat up. "Do you... have any more tattoos I can see?" I exhale heavily on his back and he tenses up again.

Maeson clears his throat. "I do have a few more, lassie, but they all lie below these keks. You still want to see?" His voice is hoarse and thick with his Scottish brogue.

Keks? Below these—

I flush.

Pants, he means pants!

"I... do... yes." My anxiety is now at a ten, but I still impulsively push forward.

At last, he turns to face me. His eyes blaze with passion and his heart stopping dimples are out full force. My knees buckle, he's mere inches from me, and my breathing becomes heavier.

I've never wanted a man this way or this badly before.

His long thick fingers grab the top of his sweats and ease them down slowly, excruciatingly so. The top of his black Calvin Klein underwear appears, and my breath catches in my throat. I can now see the tops of his thighs, and those lovely tight Calvin's outline his entire hard package.

The one I felt deep inside, moving hard and fast...

The air I've been holding rushes out, and I'm dizzy, my chest constricts, and my head spins. I can't move, my body is frozen in this spot as I watch this man drop his pants to the floor. I drag in a deep breath and stare at the tattoos scattered down his thick muscular legs.

Striding around his body, he stands utterly still as I take a tour of his back side. The Scottish flag on his calf stands out immediately, it looks as if it's underneath his torn skin, yet another three-dimensional effect that looks unbelievably real, the blue and white vibrant against his tan.

With nothing else to see on this end, I slowly move to the front side, admiring every inch of this man on the way.

There's writing on his right thigh, it's another inscribed saying: *"Today, I realized my life is at the mercy of my own hands and no one else's. Today, I decided I'll no longer apologize for being who I am. Today, I stopped blaming others for my mistakes. Today, I've failed you. Today is the day my life continues and yours doesn't. Today, tomorrow, and for eternity, I will love you."*

"Beautiful! Who wrote that?"

"I did." The stern 'don't ask' tone to his voice surprises me, but given what the inscription says, I respect his non-verbal request.

Maybe it's for his mother? The loss of a parent takes a great toll on a child, no matter how old they are.

With a nod, I take a step back to look at him fully from head to toe. My heart pounds in my chest, and I'm at a total loss for words. He's magnificent, not at all the man I thought he was.

His story of pain, sadness, heartbreak, and passion are drawn all over his body. It hurts looking at him, at the pieces designed to tell his story, but in the same token, it helps knowing I'm not alone in the pain I feel.

As he stands there vulnerable and bared to me, words are no longer necessary. I close the space between us, heart pounding, hands clammy, and legs shaking, I stretch upward on my tippy toes and lean my face into his. For a moment, I let my lips linger, not quite touching his luscious lips.

Mentally I convince myself I won't pass out.

Deep breath.

I use the tip of my tongue to caress his full bottom lip.

Maeson exhales, a puff of air strokes my skin, before he takes my tongue into his mouth, sucking lightly. Then he pulls back slightly. "Och lassie, you will brin' me to my knees."

Wordlessly in my own mind, I have the same line of thinking

until a familiar sense of dread takes over my body.

Maeson could be my new beginning, but what if he becomes my next painful ending?

Deep breath, deep breath, deep breath…

The panic overtakes my body as the realization hits me. This man could be the one to bring me to my knees not the other way around.

I need to walk away. I'm not ready!

I pull away from Maeson. "I need a sec. Where's your bathroom?"

He frowns and his brow creases with worry, but he points to a partially opened door. "Right thru there, same place as yours. Are you alright?"

Those green eyes are so full of concern and confusion that I abruptly break our contact, unable to handle seeing it any longer. "Yes, fine. Need to freshen up, you know, lady stuff." I walk away before he can say anything else.

Grabbing my purse from his couch, I hurry back through the room and into the bathroom. Normally I'd snoop around and check out this private area, but I can't seem to catch my breath. Pulling back the cuff that's usually covering my wrist, I lock on to my very own piece of ink, hoping it will give me the strength I am in very much need of.

Deep breath.

Nothing. No change at all. This means the job is left up to the reinforcements I'm always carrying. Opening my purse, I grab the anxiety meds, take two for good measure, not just one like directed. I need an immediate effect, and one won't cut it.

What's the worst that could happen?

I sit on the toilet, breathing in and out slowly. I need to learn how to handle this and not stay trapped with these fears for the rest of my life.

But how? How is one cured of this kind of anxiety?

After a few minutes of me berating myself, I there is a knock at the door. My freak out session ends abruptly, bringing me back to reality.

Can I do this? Can I face this man and truly be with him? Be with him the way a woman is supposed to be?

-32-

MAESON

She's seen it all. My body and parts of my soul bared to her. The tattoos I tried so hard to hide from her, she in fact *loves*.

Yet she still ran away again.

Not very far this time, just the bathroom, but it's running regardless. My heart sinks.

I thought we were making progress.

There's the familiar jingle of a bottle full of pills as I wait by the door for an answer to my knock. "You okay, lass?"

More rustling. "Yeah! Just dandy, Maeson. Be right out!"

I'm not moving from this doorway until she comes out of there and I see for myself that she's all right.

The door opens abruptly and she steps out, head down and walks right smack into me. "Woah! Damn, champ!" She shoves at my chest with all her might, but I don't move an inch. "Do you have to take up so much space?"

I give her my sexy 'melt your panties off' smile in hopes of calming her. "Only yours."

"Well, back up, big boy! I need breathing room!" She waves

me off and attempts to push past, but I block her with my body.

I smirk evilly. "Aye, lassie, you'll get that tomorrow. Tonight, I'm staying in your space." As I loom above her, all of the concern I felt before is gone, replaced by desire that's coursing through me like hot liquid lava.

She visibly shivers and my need for her increases. I want to be with this woman, I need to relive the touch of her soft hands on my body.

There must be a way of doing this without scaring her off... every time.

Taking me off guard, she grabs my hand, and a cocky smile spreads across her face.

What a sudden change, my little lioness. Are you coming out to play? Shall I signal my very own monster to join us?

If she continues this cat and mouse, high and low, take me or leave me game, he just might come out. That starved, well-hidden part of me doesn't need to be told twice.

Not yet. Not quite yet. Hold still. Let her take charge.

Inhaling deeply, she leads me closer to the bed. "Let's see what you got, ole man. Take *that* all off." Her eyes demanding the removal of the shirt I had put back on.

Oh, yes. She's definitely... grown a ball or two.

Whatever she did in the bathroom changed her, giving her the kind of courage only strong drugs provide. The thought sobers me up, and I lose all sexual desire. "No, Ruby."

"Why?"

"What was wrong before?" I'm not going to urge her for a detailed explanation, but shit, she could at least give me an idea. Right now, I'm entertaining the worst fucking kind of scenario.

"Nothing, just got nervous is all," she says nonchalantly.

"Lies," I huff and fold my arms across my chest.

"Truth."

Stubborn little one, aren't you? I can be just as stubborn.

"Bloody lies, I heard pills coming out of a bottle! Truth. Or this ends right here—right now." Anger vibrates from my insides. I despise lies, and I can tell she's hiding something.

"Truth. They're for my headache." She rubs her temples as if to prove her point.

"Aye, they were for something and not a bloody fucking headache. I ask one thing of you, Ruby, don't lie to me."

"Noted. Same goes for you, but they're for my headache. Now *please*, drop it."

I nod in agreement, temporarily appeased, but not entirely satisfied. I know she's still keeping something to herself, but for now, I'll let it go.

How many things can I let slide, until I've had enough?

I did once before. In the past, I'd tell myself not to push on a subject, not to force her to tell me things, and not to beg because it wouldn't work. All it would do is push her further away from me. And that outcome was unfavorable, to say the least.

Briefly, I close my eyes and try to bring my focus back to Ruby.

When I open them, she points at my shirt again. "Off with it."

This woman makes me feel too hot and too cold at the same time. And she says she's fucked up in the head? Mine isn't any better.

Prime example, the moment she utters something sexy like *'take it off'*, my desire returns full force. "As you wish, Princess, let the games begin." I smile deeply and purposely take off the shirt and my boxer brief's excruciatingly slow, knowing it will torture her.

I know the artwork is exposed again, in sections my story, the one few know, is revealed. But of course, plainly looking at them doesn't explain a single detail, which is exactly why each piece is chosen with the utmost care.

At last, I stand before her naked. "Better?" I hold my breath.

How many prissy women were turned off by my body?

Thankfully I stopped caring and lost count years back but now I find myself worried about it all over again. With Ruby, it's different somehow and for some unknown reason to me it matters what she thinks.

"Aye, much, Prince Alexander, so fucking much better." Her eyes widen, surprising us both with her vulgarity.

An unexpected laugh burst from me. "Trying to be a badass again?"

"A little. Can I touch you?" The words breathlessly rush out.

I nod. "Go ahead." My entire body hardens and stiffens, getting more so every second as she puts a palm on my chest.

Ruby's warm fingertip traces the writing on my pectoral muscle, before moving to the other, which bears the many Celtic knots traveling down my arm. She leans forward, placing a kiss on the knot on my chest. Over my heart—which is currently beating erratically for... her.

I glance down, yellow-copper flecks are overpowering the dark brown ring around her eyes. You can almost hear the wicked thoughts churning behind them. I smirk. "Your turn, *Princess Ruby*. I would like to see you bared to me, as I am to you." My voice is thickly laced with arousal.

She doesn't move nor stops me as I peel her shirt up and over her head. The combination of a cold as fuck air conditioned bedroom and naked skin has Ruby shivering. As my hands glide down her arms, trying to bring the warmth back, I notice the wide black strap covering her wrist isn't a bracelet like I originally thought. It's a thin piece of worthless, stretchy material.

Has she been hurting herself?

I start sliding it off but when Ruby tenses up, I pause, and ask, "What are you hiding?"

Her intense gaze meets mine, for a moment we don't move, and if I wasn't looking directly at her I would've missed the slight nod, her permission for me to continue, to behold something she normally hides from others.

Pulling the cloth all the way down, I reveal the modernized Celtic symbol for strength. It's smooth, flush against her skin filled in with the darkest black ink *I've* ever seen.

Even darker than my own.

There is such beauty to this simple three-knot design, that it speaks for itself. The dense thick lines visibly show the power of a person's deepest and most inner strength. There is a pull to it and I can't seem to stop staring at it.

For such a young woman to bear this kind of symbol tells me there is *a lot* more to her than she lets on.

"It's beautiful. Celtic, right?"

She blinks a few times. "Yes." She doesn't explain her reasoning for the tattoo, just like I can't—won't.

Fully understanding the need for privacy, I nod and tear my gaze from her wrist, slowly raising them to meet her gorgeous face. That's when I notice the redness flushing her cheeks.

Oh, right. Where was I?

Her half-naked body comes into view and before she can change her mind, I drop her pants to the floor.

Standing before me in her underwear and bra, she hastily tries to cover herself and that's when I notice… *them.*

What the fuck is on her beautiful olive tanned skin?

"Ruby." The pity brewing inside me comes through loud and clear in my tone.

She keeps her eyes on the floor refusing to meet my eyes. "Don't. Ask."

Damn this give and take part of relationships.

I have no choice but respect her request, same as she did with me earlier. But, I don't give up entirely, because I need to know. "Tell me one thing."

"What?" She continues to avoid looking up at me.

"Did you mark yourself?"

You know she didn't, just LOOK at them. Bloody hell!

"No." Her sad, glistening eyes meet mine and a single tear trails down her cheek.

Hearing that single word tells me exactly what I feared. I long to pound my trembling fist into the wall as an image of this precious woman being so brutally harmed flashes before my eyes. My stomach twists and turns as bile rises to my throat. "Oh, baby." Taking a breath, I lock her against me, holding her quivering body tightly. Gently, I raise her face to mine and brush the lone tear away with my thumb. Wordlessly, I lean down and kiss her.

I can't get enough. I need to protect her.

The ever-present beast in me claws and roars in horror. Fighting off the instinct to demand answers, I guide us to the bed and lay her down. She closes her eyes as if unable to witness the anguish written all over my face. Without looking at me, she squirms as if *feeling* the inspection happening. I touch them and she withers beneath my fingers.

Surprisingly, she doesn't stop me, as if she knows this is something we both seem to need. I caress the deepest and harshest mark, hundreds of questions screaming in my mind.

How could someone bring themselves to do this to another person? Why would they? And how the bloody fuck does one survive this kind of trauma?

She draws in an anguished breath, as if in true pain. The single touch isn't only a reminder of the pain, but she still feels it.

How could she not?

I couldn't imagine in my worst nightmares of something like this happening to me let alone a young girl!

"How?" I don't resist the urge to ask.

Do I want to hear the words when I know what she's going to say?

Yes, I need—must know for sure.

More tears slide down Ruby's grief-stricken face. Her bottom lip trembles, and her voice cracks as she struggles to say the horrendous words. "Whip. A… A… Whip."

Even though I suspected that would be her answer, a harsh gasp escapes me. I clench my jaw so tightly, it feels like my teeth will crack. The anguish I feel on her behalf practically tears me apart.

What sick fuck did this?

My anger is rising within. "Who?" I don't hold back on asking this question either, better to hear it out loud.

She frowns deeply. "Foster father—missed my back—la… lashing around to my belly. I was… only fif—teen." Tears cascade from her sad amber eyes, leaving a trail of black mascara all the way down her face, and onto my bed. "I told you... he was a... bad man." She can barely speak, each word she tries to verbalize appears to be a chore for her.

"Fucking bastard!" I explode and slam my fist into the mattress, even though I know violence isn't going to change her past.

She jerks and shrinks back further into the bed, fear flashing in her gaze.

Realizing my mistake, I bow my head. "Sorry. I'm so sorry. I let my anger get the best of me. I'd never hurt you like that. Please forgive me?" I look down at her, waiting for a response, or some sort of sign that tells me I didn't fuck this up by scaring her away permanently with my barbaric show of stupidity.

After all, I should know better than to do shit like that, especially after parts of her past have been revealed to me.

She slices her head to the right, imitating me.

The corner of my lip twitches and I slowly reach out, my fingers gently stroking her face. "Bloody hell, lass, I wish I could change your past. Fuck, better yet, I wish that man was never born. That way he wouldn't have ever had a chance to harm any children."

Her face turns to stone, her eyes even appear a few shades darker than before, and she practically sneers, "Couldn't agree more, Maeson. Couldn't fucking agree more."

Did she just turn off her emotions?

The way she changes from one minute to the next is freakily familiar to me. It's *exactly* how I coped. It's the only way to deal with those moments in life which are beyond our comprehension or your mind ends up splitting in two, keeping only the good and easy things to the forefront, and the other crap in the backroom for storage marked—Never Open.

He's lucky he's dead already.

How wrong was I about her? I've misjudged her so badly, but how was I supposed to know? Not once did she appear to be a fragile, abused woman. She carries herself with confidence and pride, sometimes there is a shy side of her which comes out too, but there haven't been any signs of the Ruby who is before me now. There are no words that can express what I feel for this woman, but actions can.

Actions always speak louder than words any day.

I kiss the harsh red and purple lines tenderly, and gently brush my lips over the worst scar on her belly. There is no hesitation or a sense of disgust when I look at her heavily scarred body, to me she's even more beautiful than before.

Not stopping, I caress and kiss each mark, in turn, showing her, making it known how truly beautiful, wanted and needed she is.

No wonder she picked such a tattoo, it represents her completely.

The knots of strength entwined across her wrist must be the reminder of everything that's been done to her and everything she has survived.

I must tread carefully.

"You're sure you want to do this, Ruby? We can stop now… I don't want to overwhelm you."

Her lip quivers. "Don't stop, I want this."

The moment she finishes her answer, I don't hesitate. I remove her bra, then slide her underwear slowly down her lusciously smooth legs.

She's exposed to my view, her beauty unmarred by the savagery but multiplied tenfold.

There you are, my princess. My heart and soul ache for you. But I can't tell you that, can I? You'll run away faster than Forest Gump.

Like my tattoos, these are her story. I wipe the tears falling down her sweet face.

I find myself unable to breathe, overwhelmed, and in need of a deep fucking breath or I'm about to go ape shit.

In the middle of my exhale, she changes direction and grabs my face, kissing me harshly.

Exactly the signal I needed. You're just getting started and not leaving me yet, are you?

I kneel between her legs, locking her lips on mine again.

Unlike our first time, my touch is gentle as I caress her body. Starting at her breasts, lingering before moving my hand lower and lower, finding the place I ache to touch. "Wet." I use circular motions with expertise. Not rough nor gentle either, it's just right.

"Condom." Ruby manages while trembling under my hand. "I want you, Maeson, please."

She isn't going to get an argument on that request from me.

I grab one from the nightstand, rip it open, and roll it down over my rock-hard dick. Positioning myself between her legs, focusing on her stunning face and those magical eyes. I see the yearning burning in them and ease into her, we both moan at this initial contact.

Oh, fuck, fuck, fuck, fuckkk! I'm going to cum before we even start!

It's been over a month since I last had sex, which is why I'm so overcome with pleasure.

I know, lame ass excuse, but every man needs one to explain away the minute man problems we have from time to time.

If I were to be honest, I'd say I'm unable to contain all the sad, happy, mad, and angry emotions swirling inside me. When there's too much happening at once, I panic. I guess that's exactly what happens for Ruby. After all, were not so different from each other, are we?

Momentarily, I stop and focus on gently kissing her marred skin before starting to move again. I fill her completely. Sex has never felt like this before, this damn good. Our moans of pleasure fill the air.

"Oh, Ruby," I whisper against her supple body, and the sadness lifts from my heart.

Will I be able to protect her against feeling any more pain... even if it might be against me?

But being with her feels so perfect, and so right.

Maybe I can help her forget her horrid past and she does the same with mine?

My body tenses as the pressure builds, and every single thought other than the right here and now is pushed to the back of my mind. With each movement, my need for her heightens.

I'm so close, but not before her. Ladies are always first!

Right when I wasn't sure how much longer I can hold off, Ruby's muscles clench around me and she orgasms, crying out with abandon. She lets it all out in this moment and I never want it to end. It's been so long since I've felt so much pleasure during sex, or could completely let go.

It's a fucking miracle.

I move faster, my own body starts to tremble. "So, damn beautiful!"

"Yes! Oh, God! Yes!" She encourages me.

It feels so fucking good, it's never been like this, ever.

I can't help myself, I want to see the passion in her eyes. "Look at me."

At the sound of my voice, she moans and meets my gaze. The copper sparks in those amber eyes make them so utterly vibrant, it takes my breath away. "Faster." Moan. "Harder." Moan.

I give her exactly what she asks for, and in the process, lose myself in her. Nothing else matters in this moment, not the past, not the scares, not even the pain within us.

My legs start to shake, and the pressure to release is overwhelming all my senses. The familiar tingle at the base of my spine surfaces, forcing me to let go. "Ruubbyy!" My shout combines with her name, as I finish with one last tremor and I kiss her lightly.

With a deep sigh of satisfaction, Ruby closes her eyes and smiles.

My emotions are at an extreme high, my heart's pounding heavily in my chest and I can feel Ruby's thumping in time as I sink down onto her. Even though I've never needed this before, I find myself not wanting this closeness between us to end.

But it has to, doesn't it?

With one last tender kiss, I roll off and close my own eyes. We lay in a comfortable silence, both lost in our own thoughts.

"That was…" Ruby breaks the silence.

"Exactly what we needed." I complete her sentence.

"Aye!" She giggles. The fun, happy and carefree Ruby, I've come to like—more than expected—is back to play.

"Your accent is quite natural, Ruby. Do you have any Scottish in you?

"No, though, different languages and accents fascinate me, always have. I'm Italian, from my mom's side and as you know, Greek from my dad's. But as you can see I took after the Greek side, ass and all."

I burst out laughing.

"What's so funny?"

"The expression 'ass and all', didn't expect that. But you do have a bonnie ass, Ruby."

"Thank you! It's my pride and joy, I love to feed it daily. Maintaining it is easy."

I turn on my side, facing her and use my arm to hold my head up. "Well, I'm glad for that, your body is beautiful. Your curves are something men drool over." My smile deepens at the thought of how much *I* drool over her body.

She reaches out and touches the dimple on my cheek and lingers there. "What kind of men do you know? I've never met a man who enjoys thickness in a girl." She raises a perfectly arched eyebrow.

"I know one man and that's me. No one else matters at this point." I frown as a jealous ache surfaces.

"That's very nice of you to say. At least now I know there's one man in this world." She sits up in the bed and dangles her legs over the end.

"Where are you going?" My eyes focus on that glorious ass and then higher on the numerous unforgiving raised lines across her back. They make me want to dig up the bastard's grave and show him what it feels like to be whipped against his will.

She peeks back toward me and smiles sadly. "Home. I need some sleep."

I don't want this to be awkward. I've rarely had sex and then asked a woman to stay, but I want to this time. "You want to leave?"

"Well, yes. I don't want to be an imposition and I usually…" She hesitates, tucking her bottom lip between her teeth. "Don't stay over."

Seems I need to simplify this for her. "If you were an imposition, and I didn't want you to stay we wouldn't be in my home, we'd be at a hotel."

She twists her body and her eyes meet mine as if searching for something. "Oh, I *know*, been there done that, but what I'm saying is… *I* don't stay over." Her eyelids close and she inhales deeply then exhales before continuing. "We aren't serious or anything, this was—just sex—and now it's time I go."

I incline my head, comprehension sinking in. "I understand you need to trust me first. What if I spend the night on the couch? You can also shower in peace. I won't get in your way."

Small lines crease in her forehead. "Yes, to the shower, but no to sleeping over. Maybe one day, just not right now."

Does she not do the 'sleep with a guy and stay over' scenario? *Fascinating. Most women prefer—fuck that—beg to stay over after sex.*

But those women weren't hurt over and over by the men in their lives like Ruby was, were they?

I shrug nonchalantly, yet inside I want to plead with her to spend the night in my bed. "I'll respect your wish, and I won't try to change your mind."

With a small nod, she hops off the mattress and slips on my t-shirt. As she picks up her scattered clothing, her stomach growls loudly.

I don't try to stop the laugh that explodes from my mouth or the huge grin on my face. "Are you hungry?"

"I didn't think so, but I guess my stomach has a mind of its own." She lifts a shoulder in a half-shrug and rolls her eyes.

"I'll whip something up for us. Got to maintain that ass, right?" I wink. "Go shower, there are fresh towels in the bathroom closet." I pause at the doorway and wait to make sure she's all right before heading to the kitchen.

Within a minute, I hear the shower turn on, but little does

she know I also heard the pill bottle shaking again before walking away.

* * *

RUBY GLIDES DOWN THE STAIRCASE with one of my t-shirts wrapped around her head and instead of laughing at the sight of her, it takes every bit of strength I have to contain my anger and not flip out.

"Another headache, lass?" I lean against the wall, my arms tightly across my chest.

"Fuck! Old man!" She grips the metal railing to hold herself up. "What! Are you spying on me?"

"Old man, she says! I'll show you old man! You keep popping pills, you'll be old before me, *Princess*." I all but sneer the word and push off of the wall, stalking to the stove. I know my tone will hurt her—which is not my intention—it's simply to get the fucking point across.

Why is she taking pills? Does she have an addiction because of her past? Those are the questions that have been beating through my skull the whole time she was showering.

How can I not be pissed off and worried, when I went through it myself!

I dismiss my inner conversation and uncover the pan before me, focusing on not burning the damn food.

Smells good. Maria taught me well.

The tantalizing aroma of onions and mushrooms sautéing wafts throughout the space and I hear her stomach growl again.

"Maeson?" she whispers my name her tone is sad and hesitant.

I look up from my task at the stove and stop shaking the frying pan. "Yes?"

"You asked for honesty, so you should know... I don't have headaches—well, I do get them from time to time—but what I'm trying to tell you is, the pills are a prescription for anxiety medication." Her eyes water and she looks away.

"Thank you, Ruby, I appreciate your honesty. I never judge, I just prefer to know what's going on. However, I figured you're on drugs of some kind. Glad you're not on the illegal stuff." A weight I didn't know was there is lifted off my chest.

Thank those above, not sure I could deal with that kind of situation again.

"Only the prescribed kind. It's been a rough few years for me and these help." Her puppy eyes are now filled with tears and her lip quivers slightly.

I lean across the island and take hold of her small hand, giving it a squeeze. "I understand, I really do." I point to a stool. "Please sit. Dinner's ready. Hope you're hungry." As if on cue, her stomach rumbles, and loudly. "Well, now I know you most definitely are, baby girl."

She giggles. "That's affirmative, Mr. Alexander."

-33-

Ruby

THE ALARM ON MY PHONE blares, scaring the shit out of me, and I fly off the bed. It takes a minute to orient myself, having forgotten where I'd fallen asleep.

Maeson's tangled in the sheets beside me, sleeping deeply, not even giving so much as a twitch. Good thing I didn't believe him when he said he's up bright and early every day, or depend on him to wake me for the meeting I have this morning.

The man is passed out! What a liar!

Regardless, part of me is glad I ended up giving in and slept over. Oddly enough, his presence comforted me, and for the first time in a long time, I slept through the night without a nightmare waking me every few minutes.

How can I learn to trust him if I don't take a leap occasionally, right?

Spending the night with him was truly amazing, but I have no time to reminisce. "Shit! Shit! Shit! I'm going to be late!"

"Hmmm?" Maeson mumbles and turns on his other side, without looking my way.

"Maeson, I gotta go to the women's shelter. Call you later. Kisses, *Old Man.*" I smile to myself and gather my belongings before dashing across the way to my building.

Those age jokes will never get *'old'* or overused, especially when they get a rise out of Maeson. Even in his passed-out state, I know he heard me from his grouchy muttering.

* * *

IN LESS THAN AN HOUR, I've taken a nice hot shower, put on the only skirt I own, fixed my hair into a tight bun, and my mask of makeup is in place. But the dressed-up woman looking back at me in the mirror is not *me* and I hate what I see.

Why pretend to be something you're not?

In need of another outfit which truly represents who I am, I beeline it for my room. This time it's light blue washed jeans, a navy tee, and black Keds. I'm not going to this shelter to impress anyone and even if I was? I wouldn't be fake about it. I want to assist in bettering a person, not give fashion advice.

Another look in the mirror shows me the real girl behind the story she'll share to help others like her. Between my foster father and ex-boyfriend, they left behind the most painful tale a body could tell.

Deep breath. I can and will do this.

* * *

THE DOMESTIC ABUSE WOMEN'S SHELTER doesn't look special or intriguing, and there's no sign or other evidence it's even a shelter. Perfect for being discreet and not standing out.

An older woman answers my knock on the door. "Yes?"

"Hello, ma'am, I'm Ruby Bennett. Your new volunteer."

"Oh, Ruby! There you are! Welcome! I've been waiting to meet you! I'm Connie!" She opens the door wide, ushering me to come in. "Thank you for the generous donation, dear. Your lawyer told me what you'll be doing soon and it's surely going to help so many people."

"I certainly hope it does. It's been a dream of mine for quite a while."

"Well, dear, I for one am glad there are more people out there willing to do something to help." She pats my shoulder.

We walk through a short hallway and into what seems to be the main area of the shelter. The entire floor is an open space concept with desks scattered around and people behind them busy at work. Connie guides me past them and once we reach the last one, which is empty, she calls out, "Ladies this is Ruby. She's the new volunteer we've been waiting for! Please welcome her to the family!"

"Hello, Ruby!" I receive kind smiles and the welcome from several friendly voices.

"I'm so happy to be here. Thank you for having me!" I say to the ladies, then face Connie. "Do all of these ladies live and work here?"

"No. Only a handful of us do and I'm one of them. You could say I'm the mother hen. And the others? They come and go." Connie gives me a warm smile. "Now, let's get you settled in."

Connie seems like the kind of foster mother I begged for during all those lonely nights of crying myself to sleep.

I begged, but my cries were never heard, were they? Instead…

The foster mother I was assigned to never once appeared after my beatings to clean the blood streaming down different parts of my body. Talk about a cold heartless woman, she never paid much mind to me. I think she was glad he was taking out his sexual aggression and preferences on me and not her.

Those two were the perfect couple made in deepest foulest parts of hell.

"You can use this desk today and the red folder contains the information on the young woman you've been paired with." Connie's sweet voice snaps me out of my upsetting thoughts.

"Thank you! When can I meet her?"

"She's here now. If you're ready, I'll bring her over."

Taking a seat, I open the folder and skim the details of the document. The name on the paper catches my attention, Aria Mikaels. It's beautiful and unique. "I sure am! By the way, is there a set schedule?"

"No, you can figure that out together. I'll get her."

With a nod in response, Connie walks away. My anxiety kicks on high speed. The two pills I took before I left don't seem to be working at all.

Might be time for a higher dose?

A few minutes later, Connie returns with a waif-like young woman following closely behind her. The girl can't be more than eighteen years old and appears terribly fragile. Her long, unkempt, stringy blonde hair falls past her shoulders, and her crystal blue eyes appear enormous in her thin, drawn face. Looking at her breaks my heart. I've looked in the mirror and seen myself the same way many times, and know exactly what it took to make me look that way.

Deep breath.

"Ruby, this is our young Aria."

I smile, wanting to be approachable and relatable, the poor girl has clearly been through hell. "Hi, Aria. It's a pleasure to meet you!"

Aria can barely meet my eyes. She looks like a frightened doe, her bloodshot eyes wide and wary.

Connie squeezes Aria's hand and smiles sadly. "Aria, I have to go, but if you need me you know where my desk is. And Ruby, my number is in your folder if you ever need anything." She steps in closer to me and pulls me into a hug. "Thank you for joining our team."

I nod, taken aback by the affection. "You're welcome, Connie. I hope to make a difference like all these ladies have been doing for years." I smile and wave as she backs away.

Aria fidgets awkwardly by my desk, and I want to put her at ease. It looks as if she might bolt from the room at any moment.

"Is there somewhere we can go and talk? I'd like to get to know each other."

"Yeah, um... my room's upstairs, or we can... um... go

outside?"

I've seen this kind of edginess before, *intimately.* "Whatever you prefer is fine with me."

Letting her choose should make her more comfortable. I want to give her some power and control as I doubt she has much of either at home.

"Outside." Aria leads me onto the empty back porch. Her fingers tremble as she lights a cigarette, and she runs a scrawny hand through her dirty hair. "Want one?"

I nod, accepting the offered cigarette from her as I left mine in the car. "So, tell me about yourself Aria. What brought you here?" I light up and release a puff of smoke.

"Well, uh, I'm nineteen, ex-foster kid. I come here when I've got no place to go." Short and sweet. Her voice soft and sad as she sums up her life story in a broken, two-second sentence.

I highly doubt that's her whole story, but I know it will take time to unravel it all. She reminds me of myself so much it's scary. "Ex-foster kid here too. I know what you mean."

"Did you... come to a... place like this too?" Her voice trembles with each word.

"No, I wish. I went to hell instead."

"Yeah, I make a pit stop there every week."

"What was the final broken straw that brought you here?"

"Being beat to a pulp by my boyfriend. The cops brought me here. Had no choice."

"Been there too, but they brought me back home. Ex had pull with the police force in my old town. You're lucky you have an out."

"Not an out. I go back because we *need* each other." Her tone changes, turning vehement as if attempting to prove their *need* to me. "This place is my time out when I need to heal a few bones or clear out a bruise."

I freeze. I have no words. I begged for an escape every single day. BEGGED to be released from my personal inferno, and she goes back willingly? How do you help someone who won't leave?

But who am I to judge?

I didn't leave either, he left me. Permanently. "Does he know where you go?" I panic, thinking he could come here and harm the other women.

"He's usually cracked the fuck out, has no idea. He just expects me to come back weekly or it's worse for me. How did you get out?"

"He killed himself." I don't want to open that can of worms, but saying it aloud pushes the memory to the front of my vision. Talking about it again won't be good for my sanity. I rub my temples, trying to fight it off.

"Damn! I wish that'd happen to Dave. Maybe he'll OD? Then, I'll be free." Aria sighs and closes her eyes as if praying for that kind of miracle.

"Sometimes you wait a lifetime for freedom and it never comes. You have to take it by the balls yourself, Aria. Shit, I'm not much older and I've been through it like you, but I'm fighting to find my way every day."

"I want to, but I miss him after a day or two, and I go back." Tears fall down her face as she lights another cigarette, and hands me one.

I felt the same way every time my ex left me. So many nights I cried wanting him back. It never mattered how much he hurt me or how many women he slept with. It never does when you're blinded by their well-practiced charms and bogus apologies. "I remember those days." I pause, trying to find a way to change the subject and bring the focus of the conversation back to Aria. "Do you do drugs like he does?" When I speak there's a calmness to my voice I don't feel inside.

"Not always." She looks down at the ground, avoiding me. "Few hits of weed here and there. Not too much of the hard stuff. I don't want to end up looking like all them out there." She waves around to the streets surrounding us. I can tell she's struggling or lying, but she sure looks like she does a lot of the *hard stuff.*

"I see. Never touched the stuff myself." I can't help but feel guilty at my white lie. Never touched is one thing, but I have considered hardcore drugs a few times in the last few months.

It's become extremely difficult to fight the thoughts of using something stronger. I long to rid myself of the constant pain swirling around in my mind.

For a few minutes, we both seem to lose ourselves in our own thoughts. The overwhelming need to break away from the silence and the memories churning and pushing around my brain surfaces. I stub out my cigarette. "What kind of schedule works for you? I'm available any day and time."

She shrugs, and I notice her shoulders are trembling. "Can we do this day by day? Who knows? Maybe I won't be around long. At nineteen, I've had more broken ribs than most football players." Tears stream down her cheeks. "Such a great fucking life, ya know?"

Oh, I know all right.

I understand her oh-so-completely. My heart aches for this poor girl, whose only a few years younger than me. With our kind of pain, words are never enough. So, I say nothing and impulsively pull her into a long deep hug, holding tight for as long as I dare. There's not much I can give her, but what I can give her is the one thing few have provided me since I was ten.

A simple piece of warmth and human kindness.

We both take a deep breath. I take an extra, finding that I need it badly. My emotions are on overload. This conversation has brought back many things I've refused to think about until now.

I need to leave—must get out of here. "Day by day it is, Aria."

* * *

LEAVING THE SHELTER AFTER MEETING Aria has me all out of sorts. My mind is re-living so many things at once, I can't catch my breath.

Walking to my car, I rummage in my purse for the Xanax. I

take three, and with nothing on hand to drink, they go down hard. I can barely unlock my car door with my hands trembling so badly, and my body shakes uncontrollably as I drive. Cranking up the stereo and play it on full blast, I try to relax.

Leaning further back in my seat, I let the song— '*Elastic Heart*' by Sia, wash over me. It's a favorite of mine when I'm in an unsettling mood. The words penetrate my ears and it becomes extremely difficult for me to safely drive.

My vision blurs as the tears stream down my face. A memory I've been avoiding viciously tries to force its way out. I can't hold on much longer, the weight of it is crushing me and I'm more than relieved when I arrive home.

I tap my fingers impatiently as the elevator ascends to my floor, and fly out the moment it opens, dropping everything in a heap on the floor.

Opening the top cabinet, I automatically grab a glass and the Grey Goose Vodka that beckons me. I don't bother with the glass, it would take far too long, I need the liquid straight up. The pain of the burn as it slides all the way down my throat doesn't faze me one bit.

The damn memory claws at me, desperately trying to escape, and my anger rises. I'm unable to push it back down into the cage where it belongs!

Stop. Please. Stop.

I grasp the unused glass on the counter and unthinking, I hurl it across the room. Screaming, I watch it shatter into tiny fragments against the mantle.

Deep breath my ass! I need something far stronger than a deep breath!

The vision pushes forward.

Deep breath. Shit, this isn't working!

My nerves refuse to be calmed and the memories stubbornly refuse to be expelled. No matter how hard I try, *that* day keeps flooding back.

His limp bloody body is laying there.

At this point, the best and only way to deal with this kind of situation is alcohol. I take a swig and then another, tears blur my eyesight, threatening to run free. Everything around me starts to spin and no matter how hard I try, I can't catch my breath.

Deep breath, Ruby, deep breath.

My calming techniques are not working, at all, and I collapse onto the couch, hyperventilating, losing the battle to keep control. I close my eyes as the tears spill freely. The vision hits full force—I give up—I have no strength to continue the fight.

* * *

I LAY FROZEN IN FEAR, dreading the moment he comes back to bed after our argument. Instead, I hear him moving, slamming things around in the living room. It took every ounce of courage to tell him I wanted him out and gone!

Of course, this conversation went nowhere and exploded in my face. Suddenly he punches a wall and screams in anger and pain, making me flinch. "Fucking bitch! You'll see, I've had enough! Where the fuck is it?"

What is he looking for? I'm about to call out to him when I hear a loud crack. Loud… like fireworks? What would he be doing with fireworks? I shake my head dismissing the ridiculous thought. No, it was loud like… like a… like a gunshot! I jump off the bed and rush out of the room toward where the sound originated, and immediately wish I hadn't. I'm immobilized, horrified, frozen in place.

His body is slumped over the edge of the couch. There's blood everywhere. In shock, my hand shoots up to my mouth.

Instantly, I vomit all over the floor, my stomach heaving until nothing remains. The smell of copper is overwhelming my senses. My entire body shakes profusely. I try to move forward but my body won't cooperate.

His face… Oh my God! Half of his face is gone! He shot himself in the head! Why would he do that? Why?

The blood sprayed everywhere. On the couch, across the floor, up the walls, everywhere!

When I'm able to move again, I race out of the room to grab my phone.

"9-1-1 what is your emergency?"

The moment I attempt to move my legs stiffen. Forcing them, it takes so much effort just to trudge into the room, all the while hoping and praying that I'm having a bad dream.

Nope, not a dream, it's a living fucking nightmare!

My vision gets fuzzy and my head is spinning. "Help! Someone, please help me! My boyfriend shot him…" I never finished my sentence, the floor rushes up at me.

* * *

THE MEMORY DISAPPEARS AS SWIFTLY as it hit, the smell of blood lingering in my nose. I bolt from the couch to the bathroom and throw up. The bile keeps rising, it feels as if there is no end. "Fuck!" I rest my head on the toilet bowl with no strength left to get up.

Through the haze in my mind, I realize my ringtone's been going off repeatedly. My head shoots up. I'm not expecting anyone, nor do I want to see anyone, so, there's no need to answer it. I lay unmoving, whoever it is will leave a message.

Unfortunately, the ringing doesn't stop. Ignoring them, whoever it may be, is clearly not working. They're mighty persistent.

I stand and grip the rim of the porcelain sink, steadying my hands. "I can do this. Move on. Start over. One. Last. Time." I whisper to myself before I drag my feet to the kitchen.

-34-

MAESON

I THOUGHT AT SOME POINT Ruby's old man jokes were going to get annoying and frustrating. On the contrary, I find myself still smiling like a bloody fool hours after she's left my bed.

Be it anyone else, I'd have flipped the fuck out by now, but with her, it's different, playful like. This sort of teasing is new for me, something out of the ordinary with any woman I've been with.

Not like you've given any woman a real chance or enough time to try.

I did once before, years ago, and got burned. That painful time in my life taught me a valuable lesson in exposing every part of myself to someone. Wholeheartedly trusting a person is a big no-no. That woman was the one who ruined me for all others, who changed me, and who fucked me up in the head. She fooled me with professional quality acting and when it was all said and done, I was the one left to fix the broken pieces left in her wake. I'd never suffered so much at the hand of another.

Thanks, Bitch.

When a human being is as heartless as her, then they deserve the title. Even her name fits her perfectly, Ashlie.

Ash lies through her teeth. Ash lied with many men. Ash lie to make it all better... for herself.

Every year she finds a way to contact me, no matter how many times I've changed my number, email, or blocked her from them. This time I've involved Axel because enough is enough. It's been six years, and I haven't been able to get rid of her on my own.

If she somehow manages to find me again, and I see her face to face, I'm not sure how I'll react to her presence. Last time wasn't so pretty. She tends to bring out the devil in me. All because of her, I tapped into the beast inside me, another part of me I constantly fight to control.

I noticed the more I'm around Ruby, the more he wants out, but I know better and clamp him down. On the few occasions he's come out to play, she's run away from me. Obviously, she can't handle that man, let alone the one she sees before her.

Not yet, but she'll learn to.

A person can only hide their true nature for so long, and that includes me. I used to be a kind young man who respected everyone around him. Then Ashlie stormed into my life and fucked it all to hell, especially at the end of our relationship. Though I can't say it was always bad or nothing good came from it, there were those moments.

Rare, but they were there.

"Douche!" Jax's voice sounds from the first floor.

Fuck, I forgot he was coming over!

I've been so busy with work, I lost track of time, which is unusual for me. Speaking of time, I have yet to hear back from Ruby. I texted her earlier checking to see how things went, but I'm guessing she's still there since there's been no response yet.

Shouldn't she have been done by now?

Seizing my phone from the nightstand, I call her. No answer.

Okay, another text it is.

Resigning to be patient—something I am not—I'll have to wait for Ruby to call me.

And worry like a bloody fool.

Tossing the towel wrapped around my waist, I pull on the sweats laying on the floor from last night and run downstairs.

No need to keep Jax the grouch waiting any longer than he already has been.

Jax is sitting on a stool and leaning against the island with a frown on his face.

Just as I expected.

I hold my hands up in the air. "Hey, man. Sorry, I forgot about you. Coffee?" I smirk and start the machine.

"Sure, thanks. What the hell was more important than remembering I was coming by? Jerking off?" There's a grim look plastered on his face.

"Nah. I got laid, no jerking necessary, asshole. I said I was sorry. Why are you so moody?" I pour the hot liquid into two mugs and pass one to Jax.

He accepts it and takes a long sip, then grins. "Lucky us! Maybe you won't be such a dick all the time since your actual dick is being satisfied."

"Yeah, yeah. So, what's your deal, being all grumpy so early in the day?"

"I'm not. Just got a lot on my mind lately." He shrugs.

"You want to talk about it? You know I'm a fabulous listener." I laugh and round the corner of the island, dropping onto the stool next to him.

"Sure you are, as long as Ruby isn't around. That's the only time you can focus. I see things quickly changed between you two."

"Unexpected for me, I know. I can't explain it and you know how I get when someone finds a way inside this black heart." I pat my left pec. "I'm all in or nothing."

"Oh, I know. That's why I'm surprised and worried at the same time. She has a lot more baggage than you're used to handling or even stand for."

"You're not the only one shocked by how intrigued she has me. Ruby makes me want to help her, yet so far, she's the one helping me crawl out of the darkness surrounding me. Do you remember how bad it got for me after Ashlie?" I clutch my mug, swirling the espresso around and around. Anything to avoid showing Jax the anger rising within from the memory.

"How could I forget? My dad freaked when he saw the mess you became, the shell of the man you used to be. It was worse than any of us expected, but considering the circumstances, your actions were justified in my book." He reaches out and pats my shoulder.

His brotherly affection calms me, slightly. "Once you all found out, I couldn't handle it. Everything that happened was all her fucking fault. These tattoos all over my body, the scars on my—" My fingers tremble and the mug shakes in my hand.

Jax lays his hand over mine and takes it from me. "Hey, don't go there, man. It's in the past. Why don't we talk about something else?"

"Yes. You're right. Let's go back to you and your drama." I walk over to the sink and rinse out the cup.

"I have none. And even if I did, I'm not ready to talk about it."

"Well, that's fucking bullshit, Bro. Talk to me." I need to get the old shit out of my mind and at this point, the only thing that'll help is a smoke. Grabbing the pack laying before me, I pull one out and light it. I'd offer Jax one, but he won't touch the stuff.

"I told you before. I met someone, it's complicated as fuck, and somehow, I've fallen in love with her. Which means one thing for me—I'm in too deep and it's going to cause a lot of trouble." He waves the smoke hovering around him and coughs. "Damn man, seriously? Blow that shit somewhere else."

I step back and turn sideways so it's not right in his face. "Sorry." I inhale deeply and ponder the edge to Jax's voice before I say something stupid. "I'm used to you falling for chicks all the time, so nothing new there except your tone of voice.

What's so different this time, and what kind of trouble can a woman cause?"

He's off lately, like way off.

"I wish I could tell you, but right now isn't the time. Like you hid how you feel about Ruby from me until like what? A few days ago? I need to do the same with my girl. No hurt feel bads right?"

"No hurt feel bads?" I laugh at his term. "I get it, but can you tell me anything about her?" This time, I release the smoke in his direction on purpose.

Maybe it'll piss him off enough to talk.

He blows the smoke away without a complaint and grins. "She's gorgeous."

"That's obvious for fuck's sake. You wouldn't be this shady about her if she wasn't. Anything else you can say?"

He smirks impishly. "Nope."

"Fine, then go home." Even though I'm not bothered by his tight-lipped responses, I maintain my serious expression, pretending to be annoyed.

It doesn't fool my brother from another mother, instead, he laughs. "No way, we have shit to do. So—stop being a pussy and get dressed. The gym is calling our names." He points to the stairs leading to my bedroom. "Go."

* * *

THREE HOURS, HUNDREDS OF PUSHUPS, and a bunch of other shit later, I'm pacing from the foyer to the living room like a madman. Ruby should've seen my calls and messages after her volunteering session, but it's already dark out, and still nothing from her. Maybe somethings wrong? Or the chick she met is a complete psychopath and kidnapped her?

Okay, that's enough 'Criminal Minds' for me.

I try Molly's number next—right to voicemail. Looks like the women in my life are too busy to pick up their damn phones, that mind you, are usually stuck to their hips.

Just walk over and see for yourself. She's probably fine, and I'm panicking like a worried mother hen for no reason.

Wow, my life has gone to shit in no time, all because those wild brown curls lured me in. I send another text, this time practically begging for her to call me back and let me know she's all right.

Still, no answer.

Okay, one more call.

Nothing. No ring at all, straight to leave a message.

She turned off her phone!

Last night we ended up talking about her going to the shelter before she's even ready and of course, I lost the argument. '*You have no idea what I can handle*' is what she told me. I might not know exactly, but I've been there. It's called running away from your own problems and trying to solve others instead.

Oh, you're not getting away that easy, Princess. You've been on the run long enough.

Try facing your shit head on. Now that's a real-life challenge.

-35-

Ruby

WHY WON'T MY PAST DISAPPEAR?

I wish I could block it out or wipe it from my mind entirely and be free of what once was, *forever*. All I need and want is to be alone with this drink in my hand without my memories haunting me.

Wallowing in your misery again? Yes, damn it!

"Release the feckin' elevator, Ruby! NOW!"

Oddly his familiar deep voice calms my racing heart.

I forgot I asked Molly to have the key access changed for my floor. I'm tired of people sneaking up on me.

Without a word, I hit the button to open the doors and he stands before me, sexy as ever with his messy hair, tight black V-neck t-shirt, and fitted dark blue jeans. His tattoos peek out from the top of his shirt, and his arms are beautifully exposed. His beautiful green eyes are wild and bright with an unreadable emotion.

We stare at each other with such intensity, my heart speeds

up, and I can't help but drool at the sight of him.

Even in this manic panic state, Maeson is gorgeous. Extremely edible for breakfast, lunch, and dinner.

Once I've had an appreciative look at him, my annoyance at his interruption sets in. "What's *your* problem?"

"My problem? What's yours? I've been trying to call you, and you refuse to answer. I got worried for fuck's sake. I *knew* you shouldn't have gone to that place yet!"

His accent is so thick, I've hardly understood a single word. Mentally processing the few words that stand out, I get the gist.

"I'm fine. Why are you here?" I cross my arms and look down at his fancy sneakers, avoiding his scrutinizing glare.

"You're no fine, lass! I told you already, I'm here because I was worried! Are you kidding me?" He reaches for my face.

I turn away abruptly and stalk back into the kitchen. Grabbing the vodka, I take a swig, but as I'm about to take another, he snatches it from my hand. "Quite worryin' and give that back!" I reach for it, but he holds it high over his head. Bastard has a good foot and then some on me!

Like I'm going to make that high jump to get the damn thing when he's six and a half feet tall? Hell no!

"Of course, I worry. I care about you, woman! You're not getting shit back! Now *talk*!" His accent appears then disappears again as he visibly tries to calm down.

"You *care* about me? Caring is such a weak, petty, little excuse for an emotion! You're such a pussy! What kind of man says he *cares* about a woman?" I sneer at the word, *'care'*. I can't stand hearing it, especially from a vibrant, strong man like Maeson. Such an oxymoron. "Weeks ago, you said you wanted to *fuck* me, yet all you have done is make *love* to me... I don't want *love*, asshole!" I curl my lip and shake my head in exasperation.

One minute he's a tall broody man covered in tattoos who looks like he can devour me for a snack. The next he's gone all soft and tender, whispering sweet nothings in my ear.

I don't want a sweet man, damn it!

I can't handle it, never had that kind of man, and don't want one either! Why doesn't he take charge, be a fucking *real* man? Tell *me* what to do! Quit being a weak-assed pussy and be the dickhead he appeared to be when I first met him.

No wait, I don't want that, do I?

I can't think straight, there's too much happening in my head. I have no idea what I want anymore, my conditioning in relationships has been all pain and anger.

"You want a man? You want a goddamn man? You want to be fucked like a whore, is that what you're asking for?" His green eyes are wild and blazing furiously. "What *is* wrong with you?" His voice shakes and his neck is beet red, the hue creeping up toward his face.

His anger turns me on, but at the same time it pisses me off. It reminds me of my ex, and I've missed this, but then I don't miss it. If that's not dysfunctional, I don't know what is!

I need way more alcohol in my system. Might help make some sense of this shit.

I can't do this sober, so I try again to reclaim the bottle.

He pulls away, and takes a gulp, then shoves it at me. "Drink up, Princess. You want to do this blooter'd? Then we do it together."

I take a few pulls savoring the burn, and shove it back to Maeson. "We ain't doing shit! Go home, let me be, *please.*" I plead, the last word is a whisper. My body wants him here, yet my head is screaming *'leave'!* And if he doesn't go soon, I'll break down in front of him.

"No, I am staying. If you don't want to talk fine, we can drink it out of you." He points to the couch. "*Sit down.*" His voice is stern and controlling, which excites me even further.

I'm royally fucked up in the head!

I crave the aggression, yet I hate being controlled.

So, what do I do?

I follow his command.

"There he is," I murmur, with a twinkle in my eye. I give him a drunken smirk and lick my lips suggestively.

"Oh, is that *man* enough for you, Miss Bennett? Or maybe *too* much? How much can you *handle*? Do you even ken?" His sarcasm snaps me back to reality.

I huff. "Oh, I can handle plenty, believe me, you asshole! You've *no* idea, no *fucking clue* the extent of what I've handled!" I ball up my fists, shaking in anger.

"Do tell." He smirks at me and casually raises the Grey Goose to his lips. He drinks straight from the bottle, gulping it down like water.

My mouth twitches with need as I watch the liquid slide down his throat. He licks his lips, those full sexy lips, ones that can make *any* woman beg for his kiss. I'm so tempted, the alcohol combined with my pills is creating an intoxicated fog and I long to press my mouth to his.

Damn, I'm pathetic, why do I let men get to me like this?

Ugh! I need to stop! My thoughts are all over the place. I need to drink my sorrows away in peace and quiet.

Get out! The silent scream echoes in my head.

"No! Now give that back and shut up! We'll drink in silence or not at all. My place, my rules, and if you don't like it, then you go bye, bye!" I wave my fingers at him, but he's not phased at all by my words.

He smacks the bottle down and strides to the stereo.

This world can be so cruel; the song is timed perfectly fitting the mood of this evening. Nick Jonas's sexy voice fills the speakers and just like him, one damn deep breath, and I'm locked in with the man standing before me.

The lyrics hit me, and I look up. Maeson's vibrant jade colored eyes stare at me with a palpable intensity, making my whole body quiver in excitement. The lyrics have so much meaning to both of us, and we know it.

"Close," Maeson sings.

I can't look away from him, the truth of the word affects all of my senses. His smooth, deep voice fills the room as he sings the rest of the song. He's visibly affected, as am I. Without losing the intensity of our eye contact, he throws his head back and drains the rest of the booze. Completely empty, he tosses it to the floor. His eyes become a dangerous deep forest green.

My mouth opens wide in shock.

How's he not wasted?

"Oh, Princess, don't look so surprised! I'm going to need a lot more than this tiny shot. Tonight, I plan to become the man I haven't been in years—the one you called out for, the one you pissed off by calling him a pussy. Now, where's the rest of your stash?"

Is that the same man I've seen glimpses of before? I'm in trouble now. Maybe I've pushed him too far?

The thought makes me feel guilty. What if he's like me and he keeps parts of himself hidden away for good reason, yet here I am egging him on by calling him a weak man.

Wait! Screw that shit!

I didn't ask him to come here or force him to drink. He's a grown man, I refuse to take the blame if he can't control his own punk ass.

"Top cabinet, on the right." I point a shaking finger to it.

With a few long strides, he grabs another, opens it easily and takes a long drink. I watch the muscles on his arm flex as he waves the bottle in the air.

What a sight he is for my sore eyes.

He flinches as the burn goes down his throat. "Got to love the burn! Oh, that burn, brings back memories for me, Princess. Many memories."

I raise an eyebrow and smirk. "Oh? Do tell."

"Och, Princess, *not* happening tonight. This is your time, you were the one screamin' bloody murder in your sleep last night. Yes, I heard you, and then you come home after that place, like this"—He waves his hand up and down, motioning at the wreck I must look like.

What? I had a nightmare and didn't realize it?

"No." I jump to my feet and fill a glass with vodka, then hand the rest back to him. "Ugh. Fine, let's go up to the roof, I need air." I badly need a smoke, and the fresh air might calm my nerves.

"Lead the way." Maeson steps aside letting me pass, and with the vodka in hand, he follows me up the stairs.

With this nut-bag of a show happening, I manage a sassy smile as my ass sways side to side in his face.

* * *

THE WARM AIR HITS MY face as I reach the top of the steps. I breathe in deeply, admiring the breathtaking sight of the brightly lit city.

Maeson sits on the couch staring out at the view as I head for the gas grill to grab my pack of Camel Crush Menthol Silver. The spinning has subsided, but the vodka coursing heavily through my veins is making me brave. I crush the little ball in the cigarette filter to enhance the menthol flavor and light up, blowing a puff of smoke as I drop onto the seat beside him.

"Why'd you do that?"

I laugh. "Extra flavor."

With a curious look, he shakes one out of my pack. "I'm intrigued, let's see what these are all about." He squeezes the end of it, like I did, then puts it between his lips. The lighter flickers and he touches the flame to the cigarette. He inhales deeply. "Holy shit, lass! That menthol is no fucking joke!" He chokes out the words, the smoke trailing out of his mouth as he speaks.

I burst out laughing and pat his back. "Oh, crapola! I shoulda warned ya, they're rough on the lungs!"

"You think? I could've died!" He gives me a huge dimpled smile and leans back, taking a smaller drag this time.

We sprawl on the couch and listen to the tunes playing in the background on my newly installed outdoor speakers. There's so much to say, yet neither of us speaks as we smoke and gather our thoughts.

Unable to stand the silence a second longer. I down the rest of my drink and turn to face him. Everything I've held back, each question in my mind, it all tumbles from my mouth in a drunken rush. "What I say to make him hurt me sooo much? Why he put me down? Make me doubt everything!"

My slurred voice brings Maeson out of his trance, and he glances over. "Who?" He seems confused, the concern is written all over his face.

"My ex! Bastard didn't even take the time to know who I *truly* am. Beat me every chance he got, made my heart n' body bleed for him. Never had an issue knocking me out cold, or shooting every want n' dream down. *Fuck!*" I shake my head, memories flashing behind my eyelids and I spring up from the couch. The head rush has me sinking back down, and I lean my head on my knees.

The world spins, and it takes several deep breaths to slow it down. I try to remember how much I've told Maeson about Ray, but everything is so fuzzy. I can't concentrate.

"What a fucking asshole!" He stands suddenly, towering over me as his voice rises. He shakes his fist, his eyes spitting green fire. "I wish he was alive so I could find him and break his fucking bones!" Now he's pacing, running his hands through his hair, his fists clenching and unclenching.

Wow! I wouldn't want to get on the wrong side of Maeson Alexander.

"Too late since he's gone, *permanent* like, so no changing that fact."

Maeson stops dead in his tracks and stares at me in dismay. "As far as I'm concerned, he escaped too easily. Then he left… you behind… like this…" He waves his hand in my direction.

Gee, thanks.

"I'm not so bad. I deal with it. I'm S.T.R.O.N.G." My tongue feels sluggish as I slur out each letter individually. "Don'tcha worry about me, I'm pickin myself up, dumb ass not gonna break me from the grave, no way!" I give a humorless laugh.

"Och, lassie! I have to say, I'm more than glad he's dead! No man should ever hurt a woman like that!" His eyes reflect his horror.

I ignore him and ramble on. "We been 'seeing' each other for some time now, and you can tell how broken I am, right? So, if my baggage is *too* much for you to handle, please run along." I give a little *'go away'* wave with my fingers.

He shakes his head vehemently and refills my glass. Maeson taps it with a clink, then tilts his head back, gulping down the liquid. The frustration vibrates from his tense body, his arms flailing around as his pacing picks up again. "Not leavin you, woman! Keep going, tell me everythin', *please*." His accented voice grumbles thickly and I laugh silently.

If only he knew! I could write a damn book!

I take a long sip of my drink, needing the extra liquid reinforcement before I continue. The burn as it trickles down my throat is heavenly and I smack my lips in satisfaction. "Always hadda be his way or *no way*, makin me wanna die, I *didn't* wanna live without em tho. He got off seein me beg n' cry, like the pathetic child I was." My fingers curl into a fist, and I wish I could repay every moment of pain, have vengeance for each and every bruise. I punch the cushion, wishing it were his disgusting face.

Too late and a few cents short for that now. Deep breath!

"You don't seem like the kind of woman who's ever been pathetic. Ruby? Gang back a second, what happened between you two for him to kill himself? How did it become so violent?"

I take a few long calming drags of my cigarette, and let the last of the smoke out in a rush. An impatient huff leaves Maeson and he roughly slumps onto the couch awaiting my reply.

Deep breath! Hold your shit together woman!

Inhaling once more, I concentrate on the words I want to say, doing my best not to slur as I speak. "The abuse started... after I asked to find my independence. Come to find out... he was cheatin' on me all along. Said, I nagged too much—deserved it. Then he... uh... killed emself in my living room, after... after, I told em I couldn't take it anymore n' wanted out." I emphasize this with a sharp upward gesture of my hand as I force out the words.

When I stop, Maeson reaches out and entwines his fingers with mine. "Fuck, Ruby. That's the scary kind of shit you hear on the news. Never expect to hear it from people you know."

"Yeah." Taking another soothing drag, the burn of it tells me there's barely anything left of it, so I stomp the butt under my foot, grinding it into the patio. "The asshole made it so I'd find his bloody body, the final straw, broke me mentally. Threw me in the loony bin for a time-the-fuck-out. Left there when I was ready, and then came to Dallas. Hadda start over. Thought you knew or at least figured it out, after the conversation you overheard with Mo, or from the articles you could've read bout me with a Google search."

"Aye, I did, but only from what you were telling Molly and what you told me yourself, the articles were not for me to research. I wanted to know everything from you and only you. Sorry, love, a bloody terrible thing for anyone to go through. Not only with him, but your foster home, and the loss of your parents—too much to survive through."

I look into those disturbingly beautiful eyes and see the pity floating within them, which frustrates the shit out of me.

Pity! I don't need his or anyone's pity!

"Ohhh, so, you felt bad for me n' let me live here? That why you didn't run screamin' the other way? I see the pity in your eyes, tell me different!"

He jumps to his feet. "Not for a damned second! We all have our breaking points and I can't use that against you. Just sorry you had to get to it so early in life. Your story intrigued me, it didn't push me away nor do I fucking pity you."

"I see," I say dubiously.

"I'll prove it to you in time." He wags a finger, then sits on the edge of the couch, his whole demeanor softening. "Tell me what brought it all back to you, upsetting you so much?"

"Uh... today wasn't exactly like the first day of volunteering

I anticipated. The girl I'm paired with reminded me of... *me.*" I motion to my chest, picturing the shadow of a girl who was me, not so long ago.

"Didn't I tell it was a bad idea? Why would you go to a place that's a trigger for you? You're not recovered yet either." His tone soft, filled with actual concern.

"I explained this already! It'll help me recover, workin' with Aria, it'll help me focus on somethin' besides myself."

"I have to disagree." Maeson shakes his head as he speaks. "Today was only your first day, and you're already drunk and crying. I don't see this helping. But it's your life, I don't control you—do what you want."

I can tell he isn't getting it at all. "Meetin' her took me by surprise, she's my age, an' so damaged. The pain in her eyes made the pain I feel inside push forward. Next time? I'll be prepared."

"I can't tell you what to do, but I think you need to take care of yourself *first*." He pats my knee, his large hand surprisingly gentle. "You're brave for putting yourself out there and trying, few would do the same in your position."

"I wanna help, you know? Not just give money, but make a real difference. I never had that so..." I give a half shrug. He needs to understand how important this is to me.

"You're doin' so much already. The project and the charities are more than enough. But, I get it, Ruby, you have a good soul with a damaged heart. Although you should be careful, your ex and foster family may not have broken you, but this jus' might. Anxiety meds and alcohol aren't the answer, *believe me*." His words are beginning to slur and a distant look appears in his hazy eyes.

"Wanna explain? Give this young bodacious woman some ole man advice?" I chuckle and he literally growls at me, his mood lightening.

"Donna tease a blooter'd cheil about his age!" He throws a pillow and it hits me in the face, making me laugh.

"Okay! Okay! My bad... *gramps*!" I push off the couch and

wobble across the roof, inviting him to chase me with a glance.

I love seeing the playful side of Maeson, his laughter fills the open space as he staggers behind me.

"You cannae outrun me, hen!" Even in his drunken state, he catches me and pins me against the wall. He bends his head down, bringing us face to face, our heavy breathing mingling together.

"Hen? Who calls a lady, a hen? I'm not a damned bird, Maeson!"

His smile deepens and he chuckles, "Hen is a woman, you need to brush up on your Scottish, lassie!"

"Oh, I've been workin on it, jus been busy figurin out this thing called *life*." Unable to handle the intensity of his gaze, I look down at my feet.

His lips are against my ear. "Jus' don't lose yourself, lass." He inhales deeply before he whispers, "Like I did."

Lose himself?

The revelation races through my mind, and I lift my head, ready to speak, but he doesn't give me a chance. His mouth locks onto mine, the tang of cigarette and vodka on his tongue. My thoughts jumble and I forget what I wanted to say. I slide my arms around his neck, pressing my body tight against him.

The alcohol is talking, and I'm losing control. My fingers slip under his tee, his skin hot to my touch. I work it upwards over his head, exposing the glorious tattoos on his body. My hands glide across his skin appreciatively, moving further south. As I touch the button on his jeans, Maeson's long fingers grasp mine, halting my progress.

"What do you want from me, Princess?" He nibbles on my ear, teasing me, driving me crazy.

What is with that question? Right now, it's quite obvious!

"Your di—"

"*That* I know!" He pulls away, sporting a devilish grin and he has an evil twinkle in his eyes. "You know what I mean, earlier you insulted my manliness, now explain what you want out of this, from me?"

His question sobers me, and for the first time in forever, I say exactly what I want. "You can be the comfort by my side, but I also crave the take charge part of you. I can't have one without the other, I'm used to the roughness of men. You being gentle all the time aggravates the shit outta me! I can't explain it, but it does." I shrug, all the honesty making me feel guilty. "I *want* the man I met at the hotel a few months ago."

"I get that, but I've only been holding back because I am unsure of what you want. My true nature has been hidden for many years. I let myself out fully once in my young twenties an' got burned. After 'at it was fuck em an' leave em." He grasps my face between his palms, staring into my eyes as he speaks. "I've preferred to stay away from relationships, till I met you. Now, I have no clue as to what I want or who I am either."

I reach up to cover his massive hand with my own. "I feel the same. I've no idea how to start over. My feelings confuse me, let alone someone else's. It's one day at a time, no rules or regs. I used to plan my future, now I can't think past today. What are... are you looking for?"

"I want us to try. I haven't truly been with someone in years so, try is all we can do. I'll be your man if you'll be exclusively mine. I want you to open up and tell me everything... so I can understand."

"Ok. I can do that, but you have to do the same."

"I will in time, I promise you. First, we need to take care of you before I unload my baggage."

We look at each other for a long moment, the tension is building between us, I can almost taste it. He strokes my cheek, and his eyes gleam wickedly.

"Maeson I can..."

"Shhh, Princess." His hands trail down my body, stopping at the hem of my shirt, and pulls it over my head, exposing my sheer black lace demi-bra.

A shiver runs down my spine as the rare cool night air hits my skin. I close my eyes, gathering strength and sigh. I will try again, trust again, and love again.

One. Last. Time.

-36-

MAESON

RUBY'S SO MUCH STRONGER THAN I initially thought. She's nothing like all the thin mints I've slept with in the last six years. She might be the only woman that'll truly comprehend me and my very own pain. She could be the one to open me up and stand by me, support me, unlike…

Not going there.

Mid-thought, I sense her shiver. "Cold?" I brush my lips against her ear.

"No." She shakes her head and runs her fingers across my bare tattooed chest. She stops above my heart, which pounds uncontrollably.

My thick fingers entwine with her slender ones and I tug her closer into me. Leaning down my lips touch hers, tenderly at first. Then I graze my teeth across the bottom one and surprise her by biting down, not hard enough to draw blood, but enough to get her heart pumping. She moans against my mouth and squeezes my hand. The sound excites the fuck out of me, and I can't get enough.

This is what I've been waiting for, waiting to show her, waiting for her to be ready.

I nibble my way down her neck, creeping lower until my hot mouth covers her hard nipples through the lace of her bra. My hands skim over her sides, grasping those lovely hips, and release the button on her jeans, slipping them down to the stone as my mouth continues downwards. She steps out of them, the breeze wafting over her skin, bringing goosebumps to the surface.

My muscles tighten and flex as I rise and desire shoots through me.

I need to make her feel good, to feel what I feel and can't express

She's not the only one with issues or fears.

I'm just better at hiding them.

I pull away grabbing the bottle on the tray near us and let the liquid flow into my mouth, I swallow and repeat, but hold it this time.

This one is for her.

Putting my mouth on hers, I let the vodka flow into her parted lips. She swallows the liquid, then sucks on my tongue, and I can't help the approving growl that escapes from deep in my throat.

In this moment, she's all I want.

It seems I'm not the only one in need, she boldly takes my lip between her teeth and bites down firmly.

I groan, the pleasure exciting me to no end. "Fuucckk, Ruby," is all I manage before our tongues entwine, my mouth rough against hers. I grip her shapely thighs and easily lift her.

Ruby squeezes my biceps and I flex under her fingertips.

Man enough for ya, babe?

As if she hears my inner thought, she wraps her legs around me, tight against my hard dick. She has no room to move with her back pressed to the wall, not that I'd let her if she tried.

I tighten my grip on her and stare into those molten lava colored eyes. There's so much passion swimming and swirling around in them. "You're utterly breathtaking." My hands knead against her soft flesh, and my hips push against her.

In response, she squeezes with her legs. "So are you," she whispers and her fingers wander through my hair.

Keeping her fully wrapped around my hips, I turn and take the few steps away from the wall. She doesn't let go as she plunders my mouth. Ruby's releasing the inner lioness I witnessed only a handful of times.

She's like a savage straight out of the wilderness.

I lower her to the patio and lay her down on the cool stone. Staring at her below me, I find myself enamored by the way her hair fans out in a mass of unruly curls and the desire to tug them grows.

She's exactly what my body craves.

Ruby works frantically on the button of my jeans, her fingers then fumbling at my zipper. "I want you naked." She rubs my cock through the pants.

"I want me naked too." I'm so hard, I need to have her bare body against mine.

Finally succeeding, she yanks the waistband downwards and I help by sliding them off the rest of the way along with my Calvin's.

"Magnificent," Ruby murmurs in my ear.

Her entire body is smooth and plush and the moonlight glinting off of her gives her an angelic look. Ruby sighs as I move over her, my lips blaze as I glide them across her skin.

"This"—I tear off her bra—"needs to go." Covering one breast, I tease the nipple with my tongue. It firms to a hard peak, and I feel the little shivers run through her.

"Yes. Oh—"

I move on to the other nipple, back and forth, teasing and nipping. I travel further south; my hands are rough against her soft skin as I slide her skimpy black lace thong along her legs.

"Oh, Maeson!" She whimpers as my teeth graze the sensitive skin on her thighs, behind her knees.

I want to devour her, revel in her luscious body and forget all of our fucking problems.

Obviously feeling the same sentiment, she wraps her fingers into my hair, pushing my head down firmly.

Oh, she wants more.

"You like it rough, do you?" I run my hands up between her thighs, testing the wetness, stroking her, practically driving both of us insane.

She wants and I please with… a taste or two.

My mouth follows to where my fingers are, licking the most intimate part of her, lightly at first. When she bucks, I increase the speed, then insert two fingers, intensifying her pleasure. In and out they go as my tongue circles around her clit, flicks it, and sucks on it until her pussy pulsates against my mouth. I'm tempted to stop and tease her, extend the tormenting need to orgasm. The idea of hearing her beg for more excites me so I purposely slow down.

"Please! More!" Her back arches further into me. "Don't stop! Ohhh!" The words tremble out of her mouth, a bare whisper, as the orgasm hits her and she thrashes under me.

Not anytime soon, Princess.

My need for her is close to boiling over but I hold back, this is for her. I slip my hands under her, scooping that plump ass into them. I squeeze roughly adding fuel to the fire between us.

"*Oh! Fuck!*" Her shouts and moans give away how good that was.

"Not so *mediocre* am I, *Princess?*" I growl low in my throat.

"No. You're. Not." She's quivering, gasping, and trying to catch her breath all at once.

My lips never leave contact with her burning flesh as I move upwards, adding a few nibbles, and nips on the way. "Och, lassie, you're so sweet." I wrap my fingers into her curls and yank firmly. "I love these."

"And I love thaaaat." Her long pointy fingernails dig into my back. "Oh, I need you, now, *now*," she whimpers.

"Your wish. My command." The first thrust is firm, and I pause briefly, peering into her almond pools of lust. Our mouths are so close our breaths mingle.

Ruby raises her head a fraction of an inch to nip at me, and my mouth descends on hers, one long deep kiss before I move again. Sweat dribbles down my back, our bodies slam against each other as I move faster, low grunts sounding from deep in my throat. This is all out primitive, barbaric fucking, and I thrive in it.

Just my kind of sex.

Ruby's pussy is gushing wetness, practically dripping, and I emit an uninhibited guttural growl. My hips buck wildly when the grip of her legs wrapped around me intensifies, allowing me deeper. I increase the pace, thrusting harder and harder, ever faster, my hand clutching her thigh. "Feels so damn good. Too damn good." Lifting her hips higher, I pound into her, our frenzied movements like wild beasts, our groans, and moans filling the night air. Our bodies slap together, our skin slick with sweat. "Princess, oh…" I grind out.

Time freezes, my toes curl and we both shout out as the orgasm slams us in unison. Ruby's whole body clenches around me, and mine shudders as the last of it hits me. A few last thrusts and I collapse onto her, my sweaty body covering hers. We both lay in a fog, neither able to move for a long moment.

"I'm fallin' for ya, lass." I roll onto my back, looking up the stars.

She's speechless for a beat but then surprises me. "Me too, laddie." A bare whisper, full of fear, all the what if's cascading from her in a few words.

I close my eyes, trying to fight the questions, my thoughts in turmoil. Her hot skin brushes against me and suddenly I notice the cool breeze around us. I stand.

Ruby jolts upright. "Where you goin'?" she says softly, as if afraid of my answer.

I smile deeply, knowing my dimples soothe her. "Doncha worry, lass, not far, I need a cig." I have a sense her gaze is boring into me as I turn away. A shiver runs through me, I'm sure she's inspecting my tattoo, and wondering why I chose wings.

Why? Oh, how can I even begin to explain, without having to relive it myself? Would she look at me the same?

I know exactly what it looks like, I designed every exquisite detail, each feather defined, with the name so intricately inscribed. Then there's the additional quote. *'For Those I Love I Will Sacrifice'.* Every fucking damn day, it's a fact and proven more so after... when it was too late.

But I tried so hard before... I would've sacrificed it all but I never got the chance.

I close my eyes and take a deep much-needed breath before reaching for the pack and lighter. After a moment, I dismiss my doubt-filled thoughts and turn, strutting back toward her. Dropping down next to Ruby, I produce my shirt and pull it over her head. "You look a mite cold, lass."

She smiles and sniffs the shirt. "Thanks. Whatever this cologne is, will forever remind me of you."

"Then *Jean Paul Gaultier—Le Male,* will be the only one I wear from now on." I place a cigarette between her lips and light it.

Smoke fills the space between us and she waves it off. "I'd like that. It's utterly delectable." She licks her swollen red lips and smirks with an evil glint in her gaze.

"You're the devil in a woman's body." Laughing, I slip an arm around her shoulders and she leans against me.

My heart pounds with her so close, I'm horny all over again. But I know she needs rest, between the breakdown, the yelling, the alcohol, and now sex, she must be exhausted. Though I must admit, by the way this night started, I didn't expect for it to end so... *perfectly.*

Something is changing between us. Bringing us closer. I can sense it deep inside.

We sit smoking and gazing out over the city in silence, no need for words.

My legs ache and tremble, and I'm sure she's in no better shape. Bruises will most definitely appear on her thighs, and she may have lost some skin off of her ass. Yet I'm as content as ever, satiated and satisfied in a way I've never been in my whole life. Not even with—

"Maeson?" Ruby's soft voice pulls me back to reality.

"Hmmm?"

"Why can't you tell me what you feel? How you act truly confuses me."

"I don't know how. I told you, I did once, and it scarred me badly."

"Oh. Understandable. Can you at least try? Like I am?" She pulls in her bottom lip, nibbling on it.

I look down at the tattoo on my thigh, the quote bringing things into perspective. "Yes, Ruby, I'd like to.

"Good." She scoots closer to me. "Someone once told me *'always remember where you are going and never forget where you've been'*. That's us, you know? We can be better people—we can learn to just breathe and let it all go. I mean not overnight, but in time. All we need is *time*." Her fingers unknowingly caress the hidden scars beneath my tattoos.

I flinch. "Time is all I have left, Princess." Kissing the top of her head and inhaling deeply, I memorize the sweet scent of her that never fails to calm me. Her warmth and breathing lull me, I close my eyes, savoring the moment.

What mattered abandoned me years ago.

-37-

Ruby

UNWRAPPING MY BODY FROM MAESON'S tight hold, I sit and orient myself.

Where am I?

It takes me a few moments to realize we're in my bedroom. The sheets are a twisted disaster, and Maeson looks like a hot mess. I probably don't look any better if the aches and pains shooting through my body are any indication.

Closing my eyes, I let the visions of last night replay through my head. Sex, lots of hot—not at all mediocre—sex. His hands and mouth devoured every inch of me, then I returned the favor tenfold, teaching him those *things* I promised.

I might like to take, but I've never been one to hold back when it comes to a man's needs—when he can handle it.

Maeson kissed the scars on my back so tenderly that I literally cried out, not in pain but in release. I'm freed of the shame, the agony, and I'm finally able to let someone *see* them.

Like my tattoo, these deeply embedded scars have stayed

hidden, covered by a shirt most of the time. During my one night stands it had been easy to play off my need to wear a top. They never asked questions if they got what they wanted, which included that first night with Maeson.

Then there was Ray. When he first saw them he was disgusted and only allowed me to undress completely if the room was dark so he couldn't see my naked body. But now, with the man sleeping soundly in my bed, it's different. Not once did he seem repulsed at the sight of them. Instead, he caressed each and every single one as if it would help ease the suffering they once caused me.

Just because he treats you well now doesn't mean he always will.

That's why I'm not letting go entirely with him. All relationships start off the same—you fall desperately for each other. You either stay that way, or the true nature of the individual comes out, ruining everything as quickly as it began.

Been there, done that. Never again.

Like Maeson's tattoo says, *'Never Settle'*, and I refuse to settle this time around. I've learned from my mistakes and know better now. I'm only twenty-five and have so much time to find something *real*—to find the man worth what I've got to give. That kind of man doesn't exist in the land of make-believe television and stories I used to believe in.

Today's a new day. Don't ruin it thinking about this shit again.

My mind has the right damn idea. I need to quit overanalyzing the details I couldn't control back then, and concentrate on what I can in the here and now.

Like, wake Maeson up with…

Okay, nope not that. Geez, didn't I have enough sex last night? Now I'm waking up with sex on the brain. There must be something else I can do. I peer over my shoulder at the lightly snoring Maeson.

I should wake him up with a tickle attack! Who doesn't love that?

An evil grin spreads across my face as I form a plan and prepare to pounce. Shifting my weight, I turn and lean forward, then slowly extend my hand closer to Maeson's ribs.

Closer, just another inch.

Right as I reach him, Maeson's arm shoots out grabbing mine, and I yelp. "Shoot! I almost got you!"

He chuckles deeply and those delicious dimples make an appearance. "You almost got nothing, woman. I hear and feel everything—nothing and I mean nothing escapes me, little lady."

"Ugh! You suck, old man!" I try to look hurt, and even put on the cutest pouty face I can manage just to make it even more believable.

"Stop with the puffy lip thing you're doing, you look like you're going to pass out." He lifts himself and rests his head on his hand. His hair is so wild and messy, some pieces are sticking out oddly, and others are stuck to his face, yet he's as sexy as ever. He had to be drunker than I was, so how does he manage to look this good afterward?

Bastard. I probably look like hell!

"This"—I point to my puckered lips—"is called an adorable—no—*the most* adorable pouty face you've ever seen. Don't you dare lie and act like you're not impressed, *buddy*." I wiggle my brows and unsuccessfully curl my lip like the great Elvis.

"You go ahead and tell yourself that, *missy*. Let me show you what a proper pout looks like." He demonstrates by jutting out his bottom lip and letting it hang while widening his green eyes.

"Now who looks like they're going to pass out? Better yet, you look like your lip is about to fall off or something. Kind of scary, actually." A giggle escapes me, and I hop off of the bed right as Maeson lunges, attempting to capture me. "Missed, *old man*. Those reflexes suck! Need some fish oil to lubricate those old bones? Or maybe some extra calcium supplements to strengthen them instead?" I back closer to the door so I can take off once I manage to rile him up enough. "Oh, what else could that almost forty-year-old body of yours need? Hmmm, maybe Ginkgo Biloba for memory? Wait! Even better… maybe a gym?

Your six pack is starting to look like an *ollldddd* wrinkly four pack! Oh look, is that a baby fat roll I see?"

Now that did it, he strikes, and I run down the hall, laughing all the way to the bathroom and lock the door behind me.

"Open up!" he bellows, his accent thick and sexy as always.

That's all I have to do to hear it? Rev him up a notch or two? I can do that all day long. It'd be a damn pleasure and a nice change from the shitty previous relationship I had.

"Nope. Not happening, *sweet cheeks*!" I laugh loudly and wholeheartedly, and it feels as if my soul is freeing itself from some of the pain and mending parts of it.

"Och, lass, you better, or I'll break down the fucking door."

"Go ahead, it'll be at your expense." I pause waiting to see what he does, but nothing happens, so I continue my verbal assaults on him. "Besides, I highly doubt you could even do such a thing. You're so old you might break your shoulder instead. You know weak bones and all at your age." Covering my mouth, I try to stop my uncontrollable laughter.

He pounds on the door this time and it rattles. "At my age, huh? *Seriously*? Oh, woman, you will come out of there soon enough, and there will be no escaping me. I have all the time in the world to wait you out. Don't underestimate an older man and the amount of patience he's learned."

"Bullshit, *Gramps*! You'll have to leave soon enough, business will come a callin' before you know it." For shits and giggles, and knowing I'll be in here a while, I turn on the shower and start stripping.

"Are you fucking kidding me? A shower, right now? Get out, *Woman*! Come out and play like the big girl you pretend to be!" He growls.

Lowering my voice, I make it as sexy as possible, knowing it will drive him up the wall even further. "Oh, but honey, I'm so dirty, I need to clean up. Wish you were here with me... Oh!" I can envision on the exasperated look on his face, imagining me naked—touching myself—and he can't even see it. "Ugh, oh

God, yes!" I moan loudly, adding it for effect.

He slams against the door and it shakes worse than before.

Oh shit! I've awakened the beast.

"Want to come and play?" I tease.

"Ru"—Pound—"by open the door!"

Turning up the hot water, I sway back and forth, letting the heat of it relax my sore body. "No way, Jose!"

"You will be the death of me, I swear it!"

"Or maybe it will be the other way around."

"Talk under your breath all you want while you're hiding, but wait till you get out here. Game on, baby!" he says and stomps away. His footsteps seem to be purposely loud.

Ah! He's faking it!

Stepping out of the shower, I don't turn off the water right away, instead, I lean my head against the door, listening for movement. Nothing, not even the sound of breathing.

Maybe he did walk away?

I'm not taking the chance of finding out yet. I take my time wrapping a towel around me, then combing out my unruly hair and that's when I hear the familiar ring tone.

Aria.

As I'm about to open the bathroom door, I hear Maeson's movements.

He was still there! Standing like a damn statue.

"Ruby!" Maeson's voice calls out from the distance. "Come here quick!"

Panic sets in at his tone, and I fling the door open, racing to him.

He's holding my phone out toward me. "It's Aria, she needs you. She's in some sort of trouble." He hands it over so I can see the message she left.

My heart races as I read the words.

HELP! HE'S AT IT AGAIN!

Five simple words and I understand exactly what they mean.

Below the text is a map of sorts, like her location or something. I click on it and a map opens, giving me the option for directions to where she is.

"Maeson, I have to go. I'm sorry. She needs me." I don't hesitate or think twice about the action I'm going to take, I simply do it.

He grabs my arm, stopping me. "You're naked, and I'll take you. You're in no state to handle this alone." Not a question, but a demand, and one I simply won't stand for.

"You do not own me. Let go... *now*." My voice is steel, as I fixate my eyes on his glowering face. "Play time over."

He drops his hand immediately and walks past me into the bedroom. I turn and watch him, fear creeping up my spine.

Is this Ray all over again? I pissed him off now I have to pay? I've already seen what anger looks like on this man.

There is a lot of rustling, and what sounds like drawers opening and closing. Then Maeson reemerges, clutching... my jeans, a tee-shirt, my bra, and underwear. My heart drops and my knees almost give out at the site of him holding them out to me. He sports a frown—another sad attempt at a pout.

"Please be careful." His accented voice is low and deep, almost remorseful.

My chest tightens as I approach him. "Thank you. I will."

Smiling sadly, he extends his arm and hands me my clothes. Our fingers touch in the exchange and heat courses through me.

He's just proven to me he's not at all like my ex, it seems this man does have some sort of restraint.

"Get dressed. She needs you." He turns and strolls back into the bedroom as I throw on the outfit.

"Thank you... for understanding," I say awkwardly to his retreating back.

He doesn't respond, and I can't afford to waste any more time. So, I rush to the kitchen, grab my keys, and hit the button to open the elevators doors.

As I step in, Maeson's voice fills the room behind me. "I don't want to own you, Ruby, so please don't throw me into the same shit pile as those scumbags you've dated."

Those are sweetest words a man has ever said to me.

Refusing to give him the opportunity to see the tears rolling down my face, I keep my back to him, and let the elevator doors close.

All the things I could've said—*should've said*—trample through my mind. The best answer of all?

Prove it.

Fucking prove you're not like those bastards who used, abused, and threw me away! But it's too late to get that off my chest, isn't it?

Why didn't you stop, take a damn second to tell him exactly that?

Because Aria needs me—*not* Maeson.

* * *

THE GPS TELLS ME I'VE arrived at my location, but what *location* is that? I'm surrounded by abandoned buildings, broken-down homes, and a few feet in front of my car are two filthy men sleeping on the ground, wrapped in torn blankets. How in the world am I going to find her when I don't even know which house she's in?

Well, you dummy, the only way to find out is by getting out of the car to search for her. Sitting here won't do Aria any good.

Conceding to my psyche, I reach for the door handle with trembling fingers and push it open slowly.

What's the worst that can happen? Someone puts an end to my misery?

That is a chance I'm willing to take if I can help Aria. My first option at finding her is asking the men before me. "Excuse me?" My voice shakes as I speak.

Deep breath. You can do this.

One of them stirs and peeks his head up. "Yeah?"

"I'm looking for a young woman by the name of Aria, have you seen her? I believe she lives on this street."

"Mikaels?" he grunts, and I nod. "She comes around from

time to time, seeing her man." The man lifts his hand and points across the street. "Blue door... down there."

"Thank you!" The corner of my lips quirk up into a smile, but I shut it down as I notice a familiar evil gleam in his eyes. Before I can find out the true meaning behind it, I rush back to my car and drive in the direction he pointed.

The house is tiny with a few broken windows and the front door is hanging on by a thread.

Great freaking place to be. What are you doing to yourself, Aria?

As I'm about to open the rickety door, I realize I have nothing to protect myself with, or her, or anyone else for that matter.

I should've had Maeson bring me here.

"Fuck that shit," I mutter to myself and pull back the cloth covering my tattoo. Seeing the black ink fills me with pride and it renews my strength. Puffing up like an irritated bird whose feathers have been ruffled, I slide through the open door, and into the house. Immediately, I cover my nose and take in the space around me, searching for the gag-worthy scent.

I'm in the kitchen. Dirty dishes litter the countertop, cabinets are cracked in half, and the trash bin is full to the brim. The smell in here is beyond horrendous, and if I don't leave this room I'll surely throw up.

Either way, nasty smell or not, I need to get moving.

The more I stand around the worse things can be for Aria. Not wanting to alert anyone of my arrival, I quietly tiptoe through the living room which is in the same condition as the kitchen—trash scattered around the floor, one of the two couches in the room is flipped over, and the other has torn cushions with the stuffing sticking out of them.

This must be where the struggle started.

Pain flares through my chest at the sight and my heart speeds up, as do my feet.

Fuck tiptoeing! I need to get to Aria!

Peeking through another open door, I find an empty bathroom, so I move on. There's one more door left in the hallway, but this one is closed. What if someone heard me moving through the house and they are hiding—waiting to pounce on me the moment I open that last door?

Shit! I'm going to die tonight. What the hell was I thinking? I'm no damn superhero!

"Aria?" I whisper.

Nothing at all, no movement, no heavy breathing, nothing but broken furniture, and foul-smelling trash. It's silent in this house... eerily so. I've felt this kind of silence before and it only means trouble.

"Aria?" I try again, but louder this time. I'm right in front of the door and my heart pounds erratically as I reach for the knob, but I stand as still as possible before opening it, listening for any sort of noise.

"Here." The female voice is muffled and if I wasn't listening so intently I would have missed it.

Pushing the door open, I spot Aria on the floor, covering her face with bloody hands.

I rush to her side and do a swift inspection of her body, searching for major injuries. "What happened? Are you okay?"

She pulls back her hands and the worst of it is on her face, it's swollen so bad she can barely open her eyes. The blood pouring out of her nose is running down her hands, and her leg is laying at an odd angle. "I'm... not... no... I dunno." Her voice is rough and broken.

What the hell did he do to her?

Peering at her neck, I notice the familiar finger shaped bruises and redness that can only come from a hand tightly wrapped around a throat.

Fucking bastard!

Aria releases a ragged whimper. "He was mad... so mad... he flipped... found out I'm going to the shelter. Thought I hid it, but the hobos ratted me out cause I wouldn't do them *favors*." Her shoulders tremble as she speaks and tears rush down her face.

Seeing her so broken shatters my heart. It rips my soul apart, but somehow, I find the strength to get past the sight of her and think clearly enough to form a plan of action—a plan to get her the hell out of here, and fast. "Listen to me. I will help you but you need to follow me, can you manage?" By the looks of her I'd doubt it, but a woman's power, when put to the test, is massive.

She nods between heartbreaking sobs. "He left me again! Bring him back, please!"

My legs almost give out at those shattering words and the sound of her hoarse voice.

Bring him back? Oh God, she sounds like I did.

How do I respond to that? Tell her the truth and say, *'fuck no, I'll never do that'*, or give her the only answer that will get her out of this place? "Okay sweetie, we will do that. Let's go." I muster a small smile and help her up.

She leans against my body and a gut-wrenching moan filled with pain escapes her. I give her a few moments to adjust, then with small and slow steps, we move toward the bathroom. I need to clean her face, her hands and anything else I can manage before we leave. Setting her down on the toilet, I give her a tissue to use on her bleeding nose, and I soak a ragged towel using it to gently wipe away the blood.

Aria stops my hand and tries to open her eyes, but fails and leaves them closed. From experience, she probably knows there's no point in forcing it, she'll only make the pain worse. "I love him."

"I know. Been there remember?" I rub her shoulder lightly.

Aria relaxes.

"Thanks." She hangs her head and begins to cry again.

"Hey, no more tears, please. You'll be alright, I told you I'll help you. Let's go."

She clasps each of my arms and rises to her feet. On our way to the door, I spot a blanket and wrap it around Aria's shaking body.

Where am I going to take her? The hospital?

No, she'll probably run and then never speak to me again.

My house?

That's a better alternative. Maybe once we're there I can convince her to go to the doctor. We should ensure she doesn't have any life-threatening injuries. Her leg is twisted, though probably not broken. I'm not a specialist, but I've experienced enough of my own injuries to know this one has to hurt pretty bad. However, she hasn't complained of any pain, all she's done is cry, sob, and cry some more.

As I'm driving down the highway, I find the courage to peer over at her, and it seems she's fallen asleep.

Thank goodness, she needs the rest.

This is just the beginning of her pain.

The first day is always the easiest.

-38-

MAESON

MY CHOICES IN THIS SITUATION were limited. Follow Ruby to make sure she didn't get hurt, or stay back and wait to hear from her. Both options sucked. One would piss her off for crowding her space and the other would make it seem like I couldn't give two fucks. So, what did I do?

Obviously, I followed her.

I watched as she ran into this shit shack of a house and waited until she came out with who I assumed was Aria. The poor girl looked badly beaten up and her clothes were stained with blood. When I saw them both rushing out of the house my body went into protect mode. I was ready at the drop of a dime to be by their side.

Guard them.

My mind screamed the words over and over until Ruby's car sped down the road and out of sight. Before leaving, I hung back for a while making sure no one followed them. That's the last thing Ruby or this Aria girl needed.

Now I find myself staring out of my bedroom window toward

Ruby's building, hoping to catch sight of her. No luck, though. What would be the right thing for me to do right now? Go and check on her? Call her? Or do what I do best and break into the penthouse?

Call first, you idiot.

Fine! Pulling up the contact screen on my phone, I scroll through the long list of names until I land on the only R. It rings three times before it goes to voicemail, but I don't leave one since it will take too long for her to listen to it, and call me back. My next option is to show up there, but not break in Oceans Twelve style.

Not giving it a second thought, I grab my keys and make the short walk to the building across the courtyard.

* * *

WAITING FOR THE ELEVATOR TO reach the top floor has to be the longest few minutes of my life. It seems most of my time is spent in one of these damn things, I swear.

Once the familiar, yet annoying sound signals the opening of the doors, I'm practically flying out of them, only to be frozen in place.

Maybe I should've stayed the hell home...

My eyes will never be able to erase what they are seeing right now. The young blonde girl is sprawled on the floor, passed out. Her face is badly swollen and red, marked with gashes across her cheeks. Then there's Ruby, sitting beside her, leaning over her body, and wiping her hands of what looks like blood. She's crying, swaying back and forth, muttering things I can't understand.

For god's sake, how do I fix this for Ruby? Aria needs to be in a hospital, not here.

She doesn't look up at me when I approach them and kneel beside her. "Can I help?" I say softly.

"She doesn't want it. I tried to get her to the hospital, but she swore she'd kill herself if I forced her." A gut-wrenching sob escapes her and she covers her mouth trying to hold another one back. It takes her a few moments, but she regains some composure and continues. "So, here we are, Aria knocked out, and me cleaning her up as best as I can. I had no other choice, Maeson, I *tried*."

"I know you did, wouldn't expect any less from you... considering..." I trail off not wanting to finish the sentence, the words would only bring back more unnecessary memories for Ruby.

"What should I do? Never had to take care of anyone but myself before. My... own—I had to clean my own." She takes a deep breath and closes her eyes, only to open them after exhaling. Her body seems to relax as if the smallest amount of weight has been lifted from her shoulders.

"I'll help you. Let's get her on the bed, maybe you can wipe off the rest of the residue, and manage to change her clothes?"

She nods and brushes away the remaining tears on her face, before heading into her bedroom. Maneuvering closer to Aria's body, I scoop her up—the poor girl barely weighs a hundred pounds.

With or without the current bruising, you can tell this wasn't the first time this young woman was abused. Her legs are exposed and so are the scars that never had a chance to heal properly. What is also noticeable to the naked eye is her inability to deal with the pain on her own, the track marks scattered up her arms tell me everything I need to know. The older ones have left permanent brown indents on her skin and the new ones are still a reddish-purple color.

Does Ruby even realize what she's gotten into?

Probably not, since she sees herself within the woman in my arms. To her it's helping—to me it's Ruby self-destructing.

Not my place to judge. That's how you end up on Princess's shit list.

Gently, I place Aria down on the mattress and back out of the room to give them privacy while Ruby finishes cleaning her up.

* * *

BY THE TIME RUBY REAPPEARS from the bedroom it seems like hours have past, but in reality, was only about twenty minutes. She looks exhausted, her eyes are shiny with unshed tears and red from rubbing at them so much. Her lips quiver as she approaches and I open my arms wide for her. She slumps onto me and I wrap my hands around her, holding on tight. It's the only way I can prove that I'm here for her.

"Will she be okay?" Ruby's voice is a soft whisper and I strain to hear every word.

"We can only hope, princess." I drop my legs from the couch, giving her more room.

She sighs as she stretches out and a small smile graces her beautiful face, and *of course*, my pathetic heart leaps in my chest at the sight of it. It's a small sign from her, but a sign either way that Ruby will be all right no matter what she's gone through and going through currently. She's a survivor at heart with the inner strength of a lioness on the hunt for her next meal.

Men might have physical power, but what they lack is exactly what Ruby has tenfold. I was weak, utterly weak, cut at the knees, and crawled my way back up—not all the way yet, but I'm getting there. Then you have Ruby who was dismantled at every turn possible and has managed to put herself back together each time. That alone makes her...

Worthy.

Or is it the other way around? Should a person be worthy to receive *her* compassion, attention, and devotion? Either way, she's proven her worth too many times to count it seems and everyone's simply too blind—too jaded to notice.

"You did a good thing, you know?"

She shrugs and closes her eyes. "I had to be there—like no one else was for me."

"Few would do that for another without gaining something from it or profit in some way. Very admirable of you."

"One thing people should learn about me is... I will never

expect anything in return. When I give, it's free willing, no compensation necessary."

"Noted, love. Noted. Though, no matter what happens with Aria promise you won't give up hope on your vision of helping others, okay? Especially if she becomes too out of reach and doesn't want to escape the life she lives."

"I know, but it's hard to see her as a lost cause. I just met her yesterday. There's so much I need to tell her and explain. One day, I know Aria will move on. All she needs is time, and that time *will* heal her. Then after her, I can move on to the next person who needs me, or maybe even take on extra volunteering." She shifts further down on the couch and lays her head on my leg. "Regardless, you're right, I'll never stop wanting to be there for these woman, no matter what happens to them. It's their lives and choices, I can't control any of that." She yawns and pulls a blanket over her body. Exhaustion taking over whatever is left of her energy.

"Good, because her lifestyle choices are more dangerous than you realize. Heroine is a hell of a drug, Princess."

"What!" Her eyes widen and her jaw drops. "So, she did lie to me…"

"Yup, I saw the track marks. You need to be careful. I'm not saying she's a bad person, but what I am saying is her choices of avoidance are terrible… fucking deadly if she over does it." I shake my head as my own memories start to swirl around in my mind.

"I'll… I'll talk to her about it. If I'm surviving without the hardcore stuff, so can Aria. I know she can."

Not wanting to upset or worry Ruby any further, I nod in agreement. "You're probably right. Why don't you get some rest? It seems you need it now more than ever. I'll watch over you both."

Her head bobs up and down, then she closes her eyes and begins to drift immediately. "Not always alone, am I? Saw your car." Her words are softer than a murmur.

She knew I followed her!

-39-

Ruby

LIFE HAS BEEN INCREDIBLY BUSY since my move to Dallas and the days have flown by! July suddenly turned into August—August swiftly was September, then October feels like it lasted a full day, not a month. And now, I can't even begin to process it's already the first week of November. This is in stark contrast to my old life, where I was at the whim of my asshole ex—Ray. My days moved in crippling slow motion, dragging by the seconds.

That was my old life and this is my new one, which is what matters now. Right?

Wrong. There wouldn't be a new if there wasn't an old. Lessons of the past help me prepare for my future and I need to understand that if I'm ever going to move on.

If I let go of everything, I'll have a chance at a good future, won't I?

At the thought of a future, my mind immediately goes to Maeson, which lately seems to be where my attention is at automatically. Our relationship is flourishing steadily even after

I've repeatedly broken down in front of him. We've developed a daily routine, starting with coffee every morning at our favorite café. We spend every night together, and alternate whose apartment we sleep in.

Surprising, I know!

But I'm learning to live day by day, to share my thoughts, and bits and pieces of my past with him. Although, there are no extravagant expressions of emotions between us, we enjoy the moments we do have and expect nothing more.

I do wish he would tell me more about his life, but he has yet to disclose any further information and it's beginning to irritate me. But this time, I refuse to rush whatever it is we have and I'm taking it all in stride.

I've already learned that lesson.

Still, a mild sense of unease nips at me and a niggling thought runs around in my mind. Things escalated so fast that night two weeks ago. We were both emotional and more than a little drunk. No time for thought, no time for anything.

Wait!

My eyes about pop out of my skull and my breath catches in my chest, I suddenly can't get enough air.

Deep breath! Breathe, Ruby, breathe!

Time freezes as reality hits me—we didn't even take time for a condom!

Shit!

Before I have a public freak out session, I force myself to think about something else, something good. What good has happened lately?

Oh, I know!

We decided to use the land Maeson already purchased for our project, instead of searching high and low for something else. That will end up saving us a lot of time in the long run. All we had to do is split the original sale price into three even shares. From what Axel told me it was a pretty fair deal out of a ruthless businessman like Maeson.

Then there is Molly. I discovered that Maeson plans to hand

over the reins to her so he can immerse himself into our new partnership. She will be promoted to the position of Vice President of Rose Gardens and has no clue yet. I can barely contain my excitement at the news, but I was sworn to secrecy. Keeping my mouth shut around her is becoming more than difficult—it's freaking impossible at this point.

Speaking of which, I need to call her asap. There is something else we need to discuss now.

My heart aches when I think of her and how close we've become no matter how busy work and life, in general, have been. Our lives are so hectic we haven't even had the opportunity to enjoy one of our weekly be lazy, vent, rant, and bitch sessions.

The good, the bad, and the ugly all transpiring in a remarkably short time without Molly by my side.

Maeson tries to fill in, but he doesn't get it. Nothing is the same as talking to my best friend.

You survived before her so why the theatrics? Because now I know what it's like to have a friend. She's the sister I never had.

I've even been neglectful on planning her thirtieth surprise party that's in a few weeks. I need enough time to sort out my ideas on making it as special as possible for Molly, especially now that I know Maeson's gift to her is the promotion. I sigh and fiddle with the strings on my purse.

I'm a terrible friend.

Glancing out the large glass window, I search for the sales lady who I hope will be returning with my online order soon. Sitting still like this allows me to think too much, and as always ever since that day I had to pick her up, beaten and broken, Aria comes to mind.

I've seen her numerous times this week alone, and it's as if she takes one step forward then two backward, repeatedly. I have no clue on how to help her break the brutal cycle.

She has to want it, I know, but it's difficult to accept that.

Our bond is strengthening and the trust is building, but when I think we've made progress, and the bruises are fading, she runs back to her piece of shit boyfriend.

When she returns, battered, and bruised, and looking worse than ever, I ask, *"Why do you go back? Give me a valid reason."*

Her response is always the same. Tears falling down her face, she bows her head, her hair hiding her eyes and whispers, *"I love him."*

The promises I made, to not push and to take it one day at a time are difficult to keep. I want to shake her, and make her listen to me. I want to tell her to run away from him and never go back. Sometimes, I'm tempted to track down this low life and show him the anger I'm harboring and teach him a lesson he'll never forget, but I recognize it will only make things worse.

For some reason, I can't stop comparing our similarities, which obviously doesn't benefit *my* sanity. I already have too much going on as it is—blueprints, permits galore, volunteering and meetings out the ass.

Deep breath.

That's it! I don't care if we're up till four in the morning, but some major girl talk with Molly is happening tonight. She *needs* to know about my '*oops*' with Maeson. Even thinking about accidentally getting knocked up makes my breathing uneven and my heart pound.

Ray always swore the pull-out method worked. He discouraged other birth control, and never used a condom. Luckily, I never got pregnant. At the time, I foolishly believed him and never took the Pill. And since Maeson's been good about using protection, I haven't started taking any other contraceptives.

No time better than the present to start.

My stomach rolls because pregnancy is a real possibility. The thought is always there, in the back of my mind. I've never wanted to be someone's '*baby momma*'. I picture myself happily married, then having little ones. The idea of being a mother doesn't terrify me, it's the thought of being mentally unstable and unprepared for the responsibility of a child.

I can barely manage myself, how could I possibly care for an innocent and dependent little life?

Molly is the only one who can help me deal and organize my thoughts, bring me down to reality. I need to hash it all out, get the what ifs out and accept what may or may not be.

Now on the top of my *'need to do list'* is to make sure Maeson doesn't get a whiff of my realization. I'll stay calm and cool, not wanting to start a fight and deal with the repercussions *if* I end up missing my monthly friend.

While I'm thinking of it, I call my new family doctor. Briefly, I explain my problem to the nurse and she schedules the appointment for the soonest opening—next week. Now I can breathe better knowing I will have answers soon... *I hope.*

Deep breath, girl!

* * *

IT'S NINE-THIRTY, I'M PREPPED and primed, ready for a fun night out with friends. I fuss with my hair one more time and as I'm slipping on my shoes, my phone rings.

"Molly! You ready?"

"Yeah! I'll meet you there." Molly's voice is high-pitched and filled with excitement.

"Sounds good. I'm waiting on *Maeson*. He should be here in a few. Wait outside for us. Oh, by the way, Jax is joining us. Hope that's cool." Unbelievably, my tone changed when I said Maeson's name.

Oh, no, am I that far gone already?

"Oh, okay. See you soon, Chicky!"

A firm knock sounds on my bedroom door, my heels click on the hardwood as I stumble across the cluttered room and open it. Unabashedly, my eyes wander up and down his body, hungrily taking him in, and as always, he looks amazing.

His hair is slicked back making him look like the sexy actor Jason Momoa with the addition of green eyes, dimples, and a sexy neatly trimmed beard. He's wearing a crisp black blazer with a black tee underneath and his dark blue jeans fit snugly, showing off his well-endowed package. This bum looks hot in anything he wears, whether it be a sleek professional suit, laid back sweats, or a sheet of aluminum foil wrapped around his body.

Show off.

I guess if you know you're working with excellent merchandise, you strut your shit. On the other hand, it took me hours to curl my long hair and pick out an outfit sexy enough for the lounge.

"Wow! You look sexy as fuck in those heels!" Maeson's eyes bulge, making my ego jump a few slots.

To get a look like that again, I'll wear heels more often, no matter how much I hate them.

"Not so bad yourself, for an *ole* guy." I smirk at him and he rolls his eyes and opens his mouth, but I don't give him a chance to retort. Grabbing my purse, I dash into the elevator.

He swats my ass. "You'll be payin' for such a comment later, *Princess.*"

Promises, promises.

* * *

As Maeson parks the car, I spot Molly walking toward us with a huge smile on her face.

She greets me with arms open and embraces me.

"Hey, sweetie pie. I've missed you. Been too damn long!" I give her a tight hug.

"Me too! No more, we'll make time for us soon. I promise!"

"Dontcha worry. It starts after we leave here, you're all mine!" We both laugh, knowing it's going to be a long night.

"You got it!" Her eyes flicker as the men approach.

Jax is casually dressed in a tight black button down shirt and fitted distressed jeans. With him standing next to Maeson, I notice he's shorter by several inches and appears to be no more than six feet. His eyes and hair are a deep chestnut brown, which contrasts his alabaster skin. There's something undeniably sexy about him.

"Hey, Mae Mae." Molly pulls him into a hug. "I miss seeing your grumpy face daily. You're too happy these days." She looks over at me and winks. Releasing Maeson, she extends a hand to Jax. "Hey, big guy. Long time no see."

Did she just call Maeson, Mae Mae? Now that's a nickname I didn't expect for him. Must be the one he mentioned hating a while back.

Maeson chuckles, his dimples are out full force. "Big guy, she says. Like *you'd* know."

I stare up at him and raise a perfectly arched brow, not expecting the tinge of protectiveness in his tone.

"People! Enough about my dick. Let's go inside." Jax laughs and starts for the door with Maeson following behind him.

I study the two men and notice certain features that weren't as evident in the handful of times I've seen them together.

Jax has a light sprinkle of white throughout his dark hair, giving him a distinguished appearance. I thought he was no more than thirty-five, now I realize he's much older.

My curiosity is piqued. "Jax!" I call out and he turns. "How old *are* you?"

"Forty-one." He smirks "The salt and peppa has to give it away, or do I actually look younger than this old fart?" He points to Maeson beside him.

"Holy shit! You *are* older than this bag o' bones!" I laugh, and Maeson swats my ass again playfully.

Everyone joins in on my true, and deep laughter that warms my soul. "Okay! Okay!" I hold up a hand, still giggling uncontrollably. "I've got to stop before I pee myself. Who's ready to drink themselves under the table?"

I know I am!

There's too much shit going on in my head and it's the only way I'll be able to enjoy myself tonight.

* * *

ONCE WE, WELL, I WAS **drunk enough to call it a night, we** ended up coming back to my place. Although, Jax and Maeson only stayed for a little while. Maeson claimed we talk too much and his brain was fried from it.

No sweat off my back!

That left us ladies able to have our much-needed girl time.

"Upstairs? It's beautiful out tonight," Molly calls out from the bathroom.

"That's good with me!" Before I follow Molly up to the roof, I grab two glasses and fill them with Vodka and apple juice.

After placing the drinks on the glass table, I settle on the lounger across from Mo and sigh. "What a night..."

"Tell me about it. Fun, right?" She tugs a cigarette from the pack, flicking the bic to light it. Taking one puff, she hands it to me along with the box. "Here. I can't smoke these anymore, they're making me sick. I think it's time to change brands or go to a lighter kind." She curls her lip and hands them both to me.

"Oh, that's happened to me before. Usually when I've had too many in a row." I take a drag and smile at her, understanding the feeling.

She returns the smile and leans further into her lounge chair. "Maybe that's why then." She shrugs. "Anyway... What do you think of Jax?"

"Well, it's the first time I really hung out with the man, but I have to say I like him. He's such a nice guy and he seems to have Maeson's back like a brother. Can't take a loyal friend like that for granted."

"He is, and honestly? They are brothers through and through—blood or not—they are as close as it gets. Maeson is the image, the talker, and the enforcer. Jax is the brains, the one who keeps everything going, keeps Maeson together, keeps him whole." She grabs her drink, then shakes her head, and sets it down. "They're both good men in opposite ways. Be around them long enough, and you'll see it too."

"I think because of Jax I saw a different side of Maeson tonight. He was less reserved, less bipolar." I laugh. "Anyhow, enough about them. What's new with you?" I inhale deeply, holding the smoke for a moment before blowing it out in a rush.

Molly avoids my eyes and looks down at her sparkly purple shoes which match her low-cut shirt. "Nothing much. Busy with work. My damn boss has me doing shit around the clock since he's so busy with the new thing ya'll are working on." She clears her throat. "I'm not complaining, but things are kind of crazy right now. And I'm so pissed, all of this stress eating has caused me to put on so much weight!" Molly grumbles and pinches her flat belly.

I throw my hands in the air, unable to believe she thinks she's fat. The woman looks like a goddess!

She's so clueless—what's a few added pounds?

"First of all, you look fantastic! I didn't even notice the weight change, so quit worrying over nothing." Laying my head back, I look up at the starlit sky, wishing I could be up there peacefully floating around. "On a serious note, I do feel terrible you've been thrown under the bus to handle the rest of the crap Maeson can't. I get it, you need a breather." The smoke from my cigarette billows around us, making it seem like we're lounging within a cloud.

Molly bobs her head and grins. "A fucking breather is right, maybe even a week's worth of them." She meets my eyes and the smile is wiped from her face, replaced by a thin straight line. "How have you been? Are *you* okay?"

I know that tone. She's worrying about me again and needs a play by play of my emotional status.

In a drunken stupor, a few night's after my 'breakdown' with Maeson, I divulged every gory detail of my past to her. And ever since then, her support, concern, and love have been unconditional, no matter how busy we've been.

Now that's a friend I shouldn't ever take for granted. I need to return the favor somehow. Like, plan the best birthday bash ever for her.

"I'm good. Taking everything in stride and not rushing things between Maeson and I by keeping it as *uncomplicated* as possible. Honestly, there is so much to keep me busy these days that I haven't even had much time to think or even deal with the past.

The nightmares come and go—some nights are better than others, but I can handle that. I just need to get my shit together first and I'll be fine."

She blows away the hair that's fallen in her face and frowns. "So, you're keeping the bad shit you should be facing on the back burner until a *better time* comes along?"

When I roll my eyes, refusing to answer her observation of my obvious and unhealthy attempt to avoid the disturbing portions of my life, she continues to speak, "Fine, evade all you want. I'll move on." She shifts and crosses one long, never-ending leg over the other. "I will say *uncomplicated* is *not* a word that goes well with *that* man. Shit, he looks at you like you're his fucking sun, moon, and damn stars! About damn time someone's managed to capture the asshole. Too funny because before you moved here I told him it would happen eventually, but of course, he didn't believe me! Bastard..." Oddly, her crystal blue eyes appear glossy. "He'll never admit it and I'll never shove the *'I told you so'* in his face, but we both know you make him happy and that means so much to me. I love him like a brother—yet another thing I'll never repeat—and the subtle differences I'm noticing keep him... going—*living*."

"Are you crazy? No one *captures* a man like him. Besides, we've been—whatever the hell it is we are—for all of what a few months? I couldn't have changed him much at all and I highly doubt he wasn't *living* before we met. From what I've seen, he was surviving *just fine* between the oh-so-many women hanging on his every word. There is nothing *that* special about me." I laugh at how ridiculous the idea sounds of Maeson being affected by me.

More accurately, I think it's the other way around.

"How can you not see what a great woman you are? Don't you dare think so little of yourself! That heart of yours is too big for your own damn good. What he did before he met you was barely considered living. He was drunk every fucking night, so much so, it was hard to even look at him anymore. He had good days and others were… worse than bad." She pauses, taking a long deep breath before she continues with her rant. "Oh, and those women? They mean nothing to him—*fucking playthings*—damn thin mints are what I call them! Clueless toothpicks!" She growls in revulsion and clenches her small fists, anger building so much she's fuming. "I'm sorry." She bows her head. "Those kinds of women truly disgust me. They make the rest of us who try so hard to be *good*, *kind*, and *caring* look bad and less fun to be around. For example, have a woman with shitty confidence witness some prissy little bee sting titty bit draped all over a man she's interested in and afterward how can she not compare herself to them and think… 'well, shoot maybe I'm not enough for the guy'?" Molly stops to finally take a breath and a small smile forms across her face. "Alright, tirade over. It's just knowing what I know about you and the way you speak about yourself made me snap… sorry."

A grin surfaces on my face, her protectiveness warming my heart.

I wish I had someone like her around when I was growing up in foster care.

"Believe me those women annoy me as well, but I do my best not to focus on them. I have to trust that one day I'll meet a guy who's not interested in *that* at all and will want me for me. Keep in mind, though, my confidence was lacking way before I even met Maeson. His nightly benders and seeing him with those—'*thin mints*'—as you called them, didn't make it worse for me, it fueled my fire to not turn into one of them. Which could've easily happened, but I rose above my hate for them and what they represent. Instead, I chose to stand out of the crowd of nobodies." I shrug. "Being with Maeson is fun for now. He's not anything serious nor do I want it to ever be between us. Too much emotion is involved in relationships. There isn't enough room in my heart for any more shattered pieces to float around in it."

"Well, as long as you keep a level head you'll be fine. I'm watching your back, Ruby and I'm starting to love you like the little sister I never had." She reaches over and pulls me into a hug.

"I love you too," I whisper and squeeze her back.

"Be careful, sweetie, somehow that man always finds a way into the hearts of those who need him."

"I'm being as careful as I can be right now. My eyes are wide open when it comes to Mr. Devil in Disguise."

We release our embrace and smile at one another, complete understanding in each other's gaze.

She has my back and I have hers just like... sisters.

"I'm getting too old for this much worrying. Why don't you tell me something good? Any new gossip?" She beams. "Or maybe gimme some juicy info I know you've been holding out on. Like how's the sex?" She wiggles her eyebrows and laughs.

I giggle. "Best I ever had, I swear! Never came so many times in my life!"

"That's what I wanna hear! I'm glad he makes you happy in *that* department. Even though, now as I'm hearing you say it out loud, it makes me want to throw up!" She sticks a finger in her mouth and pretends to heave. "Gah! I thought I could forget he's like a brother to me!"

I choke on the cigarette I just lit and shake my head at her reaction to the question *she* asked *me*. "You wanted to know, I simply answered. Hmmm... maybe it's time you block out the fact you know him, so we can openly discuss my amazing sex life from time to time.

She smirks. "Give me a day or two, I need to do a complete cleansing to remove *'my boss'* Maeson from my mind and replace him with the image of *'my best friend's sex partner'*."

"Seriously? It'll take that much work?" I raise a brow in question and take one more hit of the cigarette, then stub it out in the ashtray.

"Hell yeah, it will! Ruby, I've seen the man bare too many times to count for fuck's sake. I can't tell you how many instances he was too drunk to take care of himself, or I walked in on him with women—oh, even better—I showed up at his place unannounced once. Great fucking times! You know how much it damages a lady's vision seeing her brother naked?"

Molly revealing she's seen Maeson unclothed doesn't bother me in the slightest, especially knowing after all the years she's worked for him they've never had sex. Their relationship is purely a friendship with a touch of familial love.

"Nope and I don't plan on finding out—seeing as I don't have a brother. But since your irises have been utterly damaged by a man who has muscles galore and is covered with tattoos, I can understand needing a few days to mend your vision." I giggle.

Shit, even my eyes got damaged by the sight of him but in a better way than poor Molly's were.

"By the way, since we are on the subject of boss man, I'm noticing Maeson's accent more and more." She wiggles her thin eyebrows and laughs. "I assume it's your doing?"

"Not sure if it's me or not, but I think he's starting to let go, and not trying so hard to hide it anymore."

"Good, I'm glad. He shouldn't be ashamed. We're in a different day and age now."

"Exactly what I tell him daily, but you know he's stubborn as hell."

Molly bursts out laughing. "Oh yeah! That for sure I know!"

I pat Molly's leg. "He needs to get rid of that stubbornness and I need to get past the ghosts, but I know both will take time."

Her lips part and she exhales harshly. "I wish you wouldn't have had to go through so much—just thinking about all that shit makes me upset."

I know the feeling. I get the same way when I'm over processing my past.

"Me too. But it's fine. Remember, each new day of me living out here, in my own place, working on a new venture, and hanging out with friends like you are part of my healing and a step in the right direction for a better life."

"You're right... So right. You're such a strong person, sometimes I wish I had such strength." She closes her eyes briefly and when she opens them they're shiny again. "Anyway, damn it, my emotions are all over the place tonight! Back to our conversation of *your* man, what's new with you guys?"

"Well, I'm glad you ask. Boy, do I have some shit to load off on ya! You ready for it?" I pause for effect.

"I'm on the edge of this couch, spill it already!" She looks exasperated.

I open my mouth and spit it all out, pulling no punches. "We had sex up here a few weeks ago, or so, the kicker, though, no condom. I'm freaking out, Mo!"

"*WHAT!* Could you... be prego?" Her big blue eyes are full of curiosity and something *else* I can't figure out.

I shrug with a calmness I don't feel and my stomach rolls. "Not sure, waiting to see the doc next week."

She nods, that odd gleam still there. She's bursting to tell me something. She twists her long dark hair around a finger nervously. Her smile has disappeared and her face is scarily pale.

This won't be good.

"Does Maeson know? Okay, that's a dumb question—he should, he was there..." She's collecting her thoughts, tapping her fingers nervously on the arm of the couch. "Better thing to ask is did he realize he forgot to use a condom?"

"No. I mean, I don't know. If he did he didn't mention it at all or seem worried that it could be a possibility. We were both so drunk and it was only once, you know?" Now, I'm mentally preparing myself for the worst and my palms start to sweat.

"Yeah, that does happen. Those crazy wild night sex sessions get you every time and common sense flies out of the window. Is your period late?"

"I have no idea! For the life of me, I can't remember the last time I had it. That's why I'm panicking!" My heart is pumping so hard now, it's becoming difficult to draw in a breath.

The last thing I need right now is a pregnancy scare.

In the middle of my panic attack, a pain shoots right through me, stabbing into my body, and I double over. "Molly... somethings wrong!" More pain slices through me.

Molly reaches for me, steadying my body against hers and I close my eyes as dizziness sets in.

I feel like I'm going to pass out...

"Fuck! Shit! Shit! You're bleeding... *bad*!" She lays me down across the couch and through my half open eyelids, I see her grab her phone. "Hold on, sweetie! I'm calling an ambulance."

The pain is too much to handle and the last thing I manage to do is give Molly a small nod of acknowledgment before I faint and find myself surrounded by darkness... yet again.

-40-

MAESON

LEAVING THE WOMEN AT RUBY'S house was a damn fine idea.

Finally, some peace and quiet.

I'm finally able to lay down on my cooshy couch, but instead of relaxing, I get to watch Jax pace back and forth like a fucking maniac.

Holy shit! How did I find these misfits to hang out with?

Between Molly and Ruby's constant yip yap, Jax's sour puss face all night, and the amount of alcohol I managed to down, I'm surprised I'm still conscious.

Those women were serious gabbers.

If there's one thing men can't stand, it's fucking girl talk, the gushing over complete bullshit.

But who am I to judge, since people tell me I don't talk enough?

That's how it is when you prefer to take it all in versus taking over every conversation. I do enough of that at work amid business meetings, dealing with contractors, lawyers, and making sure the day to day flow is on the up and up.

Then there's Jax who was out of his element for some

unknown reason. Once we all started to drink, the fucker stopped talking altogether. He couldn't be more out of order if he tried.

"Hey, man, chill out and sit. You're making me dizzy." I clutch my head, hoping the spinning will stop.

"Shit. Sorry." He pauses. "Too much caffeine today." He begins to pace all over again.

"I see that, but I'm going to call bull fuckin' shit on that. Sit fucker. You don't want me to get up."

That being warning enough, he sits on the couch across from me. "Fuck man. I think I fucked up, ruined everything." He covers his face with his hands, rubbing harshly, and his skin turns beet red.

"What did you do?" I try to sit up, but I think better of it when the entire room moves and my eyes can't focus on a single thing.

"What would ruin our friendship? Our brotherhood?" He sighs and watches me intently.

"Having inappropriate relations with my woman, that'll do it. And lying to me could be a deal breaker, depending on the lie." I raise an eyebrow and frown.

I knew something was up! Please don't tell me he's sleeping with Ruby—I might have to kill him.

He shakes his head. "I'd never sleep with one of yours, you know that, asshole!" When he raises his voice the southern drawl mixed with a faint Scottish lilt peeks through.

"I know that, but you asked, so I responded." I pause waiting for him to spill the fucking beans already, but of course, he doesn't. I'm going to have to drag it out of him. "What. The. Fuck. Is. Up?"

"When I'm ready, I'll tell you, damn it." His arms fly up in the air and he launches off of the couch.

"Hmmm. You're off your damn rocker. Figure your shit out once and for all, you're freaking me out." I lay an arm across my eyes, shielding them from watching his sorry ass stomp back and forth again.

"I'm tryin'." After a loud huff and a few more stomps, he

freezes in place. "Look at me."

Removing my arm from my face, I look up at his rigid form.

"Know that above all, no matter what happens, I love her." With that, Jax storms out of my apartment. He doesn't even let me process, respond, or question what was just said.

Bolting from the couch, I attempt to catch up to him, but by the time I reach the elevator doors, they're closed and it's descending to the first floor. My head spins and my thoughts are all jumbled, so I trudge back to my comfortable spot and close my eyes, hoping sleep will take over.

What the fuck is he talking about? The fucker doesn't make any sense at all!

Maybe the woman he met is a complete mess, and he's ashamed to bring her by? Or she's like the other strays he's found and tried to fix? People are *not* always fixable and if that's the case, he knows I'll freak out.

No way am I going to stand by and watch anyone use him and tear him apart.

We've both been there and done that, and I'm never going to let it happen again.

Damn it! Why do I care so much? Being a dickhead is so much easier.

Fighting with Jax or Axel is something I despise, they're the only family I have here. My mom's been gone since I was eighteen. My dad, along with all my other relatives, are still in Scotland, so it's slim pickings. Jax is the brother I never had and thanks to his father, I am where I am today.

I'm alive because of that man.

Then you have Axel, who chooses to be a wreck. I guess that's what happens when people lose interest in each other and go their separate ways. Well... at least the man is a successful wreck, unlike Jax and I after our breakups, and his was a damn divorce. Although, Axel is smart, rather than dwelling, he's moving on and has bounced back into the singles game. And since he was back and chainless, we'd started to reconnect the three stooges we used to be.

Until of course, I met Ruby. Now I'm around less and less. Jax is no better, he's missing in action more than I am these days. I think the three of us need to start up boys' night again and keep up with the trend we started years before. It was our only outlet, the escape we needed from it all. Get wasted, play cards, pass out wherever you land.

Oh, how time flies by and our lives change.

Eventually, we're going to need that outlet again, what with the new project taking up so much of my time and energy. The idea is solid, but I know how difficult it is to get going. And it's not that I'm complaining, but having a few hours of guy time won't hurt.

During my arbitrary brooding, my phone vibrates in my pocket. Pulling it out, I lift it to my ear. "Yeah?"

"Mae Mae, she needs you. We're at the hospital." Molly's shaky voice sounds far away and muffled.

I lunge, sitting straight up in an instant. "What? What happened?" My heart is hammering in my throat and I struggle to breathe.

"I don't know! One minute we were talking and the next she's in so much pain. You need to come here, she asked for you a few times. We are the only family she has, but the doctors don't see it that way. Had to stay in the emergency waiting room. Maybe you can convince them to let you in. She's all alone, Maeson." She sobs on the other end.

"I'm coming." Ending the call, I slap some cold water on my face, grab a water bottle from the fridge, and race to the hospital.

I don't care how drunk I am, nothing is stopping me from getting to Ruby.

* * *

A BEAD OF SWEAT TRICKLES down her face as nurses' poke and prod her. My gut clenches at the sight. Her eyes are closed and she moans in pain.

Deep breath. It's going to be a long night. Or morning? I have no idea what time it is.

"Sir? We gave her some medication to help with the pain and the doctor will be in shortly," one of the nurses, a petite blonde woman, says before leaving the room.

At last, alone with Ruby, I approach the side of the bed and caress her arm which is connected to an IV. "Princess?"

At the sound of my voice, she stirs. "Hmmm?" She cracks open her lids and sighs. "You're here... they let you?"

"Yes, all I had to do is show off my dimples, tell them I'm your fiancé, and that you have no other living relatives." I hold my breath hoping the how I got in doesn't upset her much.

"Fiancé, huh? Never." She gives me a small smile and winces.

I laugh and use one of the terms she's repeated to me many times before. "I know, I know. No emotions allowed." When she grimaces again, I grab the wet cloth by the bed and wipe her forehead. "The pain will be gone soon. They gave you something for it."

"Working a little. Thank you for coming," she mumbles and another smile graces her beautiful face.

There's a knock at the door and I turn to see a new doctor peek into the room. "Hello, Ruby, I'm Dr. Sanders." Her eyes travel over me as she approaches the bed and pulls up a stool. She pats Ruby's shaky leg and smiles, the kind that comes with a calming effect to it. "I'm going to adjust the bed to lift you, alright?" She waits for Ruby's approval and presses the button for the bed to rise. Once it stops the doctor continues, "Let's discuss what brought you in tonight." She looks down at the chart in her hand and flips through a few pages, nods, flips another page, and nods again.

I clear my throat, wanting to demand immediate answers and solutions, but I clamp my mouth shut and adjust the pillows behind Ruby. Leaning in closer to her, I ask, "Would you like me to stay? Or should I go? Need privacy?"

Her bright brown eyes peer up at me. "Stay. Please." Then facing the doctor, she says, "Go ahead, Doctor, what's wrong with me? Am I dying?" Ruby's voice is soft and trembles.

"No, not at all. From my experience, it seems you had an ovarian cyst rupture, which would cause all the pain and bleeding. But I won't know for sure until I perform more testing and a thorough exam. Though I do have a question." She pauses waiting for Ruby to speak when she simply nods the doctor continues. "When was your last gynecological examination?"

"Never."

With one simple word, I could tell she's embarrassed but knowing what I do about her, she shouldn't be. Ruby was extremely sheltered by every single person who found a way to control her, and that is most definitely not her fault.

The physician's expression remains the same, unfazed by her response. "We'll take care of that. Also, as soon as you arrived, they made sure to take a pregnancy test—just in case—and it was negative."

Ruby sighs and visibly relaxes as if a weight is lifted from her chest. "Good to know. Thanks." Her voice is terribly weak.

The doctor's long straight blonde hair covers part of her face as she looks down at her paperwork. "I'd like to do your pap exam now since we've managed to stop the bleeding." Her face softens. I'm sure she sees the fear in Ruby's eyes.

"Okay," Ruby murmurs.

"Bring your legs up on these stirrups." She guides Ruby's feet onto the metal. "Now relax your legs, I'm going to insert the speculum, so you may feel pressure. Let me know if it becomes too much."

I stroke Ruby's hand while the doctor proceeds with the exam and she squeezes as it becomes uncomfortable.

This moment should be my worst nightmare, but I can't even begin to describe how much of a non-issue shit like this is when you see a person you care for in so much pain. That awkwardness I'd expect to be feeling isn't there in the slightest.

"Doing okay, Ruby?" Dr. Sanders asks.

"Yes." Ruby nods her head and seems to realize she can't see her. Her eyes meet mine and she grins.

That's the first sign of the Ruby I know and my heart swells.

"Next I'm going to insert this." She peeks up and presents the longest Q-tip I've ever seen. "And take a swab of your cervix." My eyes all but pop out of my head and she laughs. "I'll make it as quick as possible. Ruby, you might have cramping or nothing at all, it depends on how sensitive your body is."

"I'm ready." She tightly grips my hand, and suddenly her legs clamp shut.

"Open up for me, Ruby, almost there."

Ruby grits her teeth and holds her breath, not making a sound. There's such strength within her, not the *'I have muscles and can lift anything'* kind, but the *'I've been to hell and back'* hidden inside her soul kind.

"All done." Dr. Sanders removes the thing she called a *speculum* and pulls off her gloves, throwing them in the trash bin. "Wasn't too bad, right?" She helps guide Ruby's legs back onto the mattress and faces us.

Not at all, I almost passed out looking at those tools, but I'm fine. Thanks for asking.

Internally I'm laughing my ass off, but I keep that bit to myself and let the actual patient answer.

Ruby shakes her head. "Not too bad, cramps aside."

"There's some spotting, so you might have cramps for the rest of the day. Take Tylenol and it will help. Luckily, you only have to do this once a year." She pats Ruby's hand reassuringly. "And I'll call you with the results in a couple of days."

"Thank you, Dr. Sanders."

"Not a problem. So, I'm going to give you a script to properly kick-start your next cycle. You'll take it for ten days, then within a few days, it should start. On your day one, please call the office." She pauses, probably knowing how difficult this information is to process all at once. "Then we will schedule blood work, and ultrasounds so we can check your fallopian tubes, ovaries, and uterus. We'll monitor you for the next few months, and hopefully, we can get you back on track. How does that sound?"

Gah! So much nonsense, I don't need to know. Woman problems! Thank the lord I was born with a dick.

"Sounds like a lot to swallow, but a good plan. I wouldn't mind this *never* happening again." Ruby's beams and her sarcasm gives me hope all is well, for now.

The doctor appears amused by Ruby's words and smiles back at us as she stands, nearing the door. "I agree and we will try to avoid it in the future. Until then, please rest and once you feel comfortable you can go home. Though I do suggest taking a few days off, just in case."

"I sure will. Thank you for all of your help."

"My pleasure, dear. And whenever you're ready to go, the nurse will have everything ready for you, including directions for each testing. The regular business hours are listed on the card I left on the table with your things. If you have any questions before your appointment, please call or email me. I'm here for you."

"Thank you, Dr. Sanders." Once the doctor leaves us, Ruby grins evilly. "Hospital sex?"

"Oh, *not* happening, suddenly healed? You were rushed to this place remember? No way am I hurting you any further."

She pouts and pats the empty space next to her on the bed. "Come here, I'm fine."

"No, you little minx, that's all the medicine you're pumped with talking. Docs orders are for you to *rest*, so that's not going to work, sex is the complete opposite. How about we get you dressed and I take you home instead." I hand Ruby her clothes.

She continues to pout, but notices my stance won't change on the matter and begins dressing, all the while huffing and puffing the entire two minutes it takes her.

At the front desk, the receptionist hands Ruby a folder filled with paperwork and a script attached. "I've scheduled your next visit with Dr. Sanders and her office is upstairs on the third floor." She smiles brightly.

"Thank you very much." Ruby's smile is shaky as if the reality of her next steps is setting in.

I can only hope this is the end of her pain, but if I've learned anything in the last thirty-seven years? It's that pain never does stop—it simply fades into the background until it can no longer be contained.

-41-

Ruby

IN A MEDICATED DAZE, I find myself wandering through these hushed hallways. The death of the living spirits surrounds me. We're all mere shells of who we once were, driven to complacency by the world which stole our dreams.

I can't bear to witness so much of the same sadness and misery I have within myself. It's reflected in their eyes as I slide past. There's no joy here, not in a place as dark and dreary as this. No smiles are seen or laughs heard, no one has energy, we're barely alive.

My gown flows and waves between my legs as I drag my unwilling feet back to the safe-haven of my room. Subconsciously I know I haven't always been this way, I used to be happy.

How much more can I handle? For the rest of my life, I'll be burdened by my physical and emotional scars, I highly doubt I can take much more.

* * *

MY PHONE RINGS, STARTLING ME out of my dreadful daze.

"Hey, Molly. What's going on?" I clear my throat and force my voice to sound normal.

"Not much. How did your follow-up visit with the doctor go?" Her voice is somber and isn't filled with the usual chirpiness.

"I just left the office. She said everything is good and she put me on BC. Now I can relax on that subject. Where are you at?"

"Actually, I'm on my way to your place. I don't want to be alone right now. Maybe… you can call Maeson so we all can hang out for a bit?"

"Ummm. Sure, if that's what you want. What's wrong, though?"

Something is not right with her for sure.

"Nothing. Just having one of those moments, I guess."

Like one of those—I'm depressed I'm almost thirty and single— moments she's had a few times before.

But I don't say that aloud, I won't shove it in her face when she seems to be having a hard time with it already. "I get it. You want Maeson and me to make you smile after working so much this week."

"Exactly!" She laughs, sounding more like herself.

"Then come on over. I'll be home soon."

Within ten minutes, I'm riding up the elevator and when the doors slide open, Molly is already in the foyer waiting for me.

"That was fast!" I say and stride over, pulling her into a big hug.

"Yeah." She pulls away and smiles sadly.

"Then you seriously didn't want to be alone. Come sit." I motion for her to relax on the couch. "Want a drink?"

She nods. "Some tea?"

"Sure. One sec." While I'm prepping the kettle, I peek over at Molly, and she's fast asleep on the couch.

Wow, she must've really been tired!

I wander over to her and tap her shoulder. "Hey, sleeping beauty. Why don't you go into my bedroom and rest? I'll call

Maeson in a little while and have him come over."

"Okay," she smothers a yawn.

Once Mo is settled in my room, I call Maeson.

"Well hello, Ruby." His smooth, deeply accented voice flows through the line, making my whole body come alive.

"Hey," I whisper.

"Why are you whispering?" His own voice drops down a notch.

"Because I don't want Molly to hear, she's resting. Can you come over?"

"What's wrong, lass?"

"Nothing, but Molly seems to need us right now. You've known her a long time, maybe you can help get her out of the rut she's in lately."

"Oh, she admits it! I'm amazing and you both need me. It's about time you ladies see it." His laugh is so deep, the huskiness of it pulsates through me.

It always surprises me how a simple thing like a laugh from this man affects me. "Hush, you nut! Stop talking and bring that ass here! Now, *Mae Mae*." With that, I cut the connection and grin.

He despises it when I end conversations abruptly. But I can't help myself because I love ruffling his perfect feathers, and my incessant teasing has an added bonus. Like how he makes me pay for pushing his buttons.

Promises, promises.

Ones he never forgets and keeps *oh so well*. My body is hot and ready for him before he even gets here. The effect this man has is absolutely ridiculous and should be illegal.

Damn, he's good.

Teacup in hand, I peek in on Molly and she's fast asleep. Setting the tea down on the side table, I cover her with my favorite red plush blanket.

Poor thing. A nap will do her good.

Making sure I don't wake her, I tiptoe out, and settle on the couch in the living room. Leaning my head against the cushions, questions begin to trickle into my mind.

What's wrong with Molly? How is she going to manage a promotion if the current load of work is too much? How can I help her out?

Times like this, I miss my parents desperately. I wish I had my mom to talk to about… everything. As if she heard me, my gaze falls on my precious photo album, tucked in the bookstand.

You're with me, aren't you mom? Always with me, right?

I pluck it off the shelf, and carefully turn to the first page.

Ruby,

Our most precious gem. Our blessing from above. For you, we fought. For you, we lived, and because of you, we believed in miracles. As we watched you grow into a beautiful young lady, pride filled our very being and kept us going.

These pages are filled with our love for you, and no matter where we are, our love will always be with you. Remember us, Ruby. Remember the special moments. Remember to love those around you.

Be strong. Always be strong, sweetheart, no matter what, have strength. Continue to fill these pages, baby. Fill them with everything you love and cherish, as we did.

Love Always & Forever, Mom & Dad.

Tears sting my eyes. I miss them so much, each day it's a struggle to see the book lying there, let alone opening it. I turn the page. *Ruby- Newborn- September 26th, 1991*

My mother holds me in her arms, smiling brightly down at my red face. Even then, her hair was short and fragile. My dad on the other hand—always the jokester—makes bunny ears behind her head, his eyes crossed. The next photo is black and white. I'm in a diaper laying on their bed, my dad's kissing my small feet, my mom's kissing my forehead as tears slide down her face. My gut clenches. Seeing their faces hurts worse than being lashed with the whip by my foster father. I vehemently slam the album closed.

I can't do this right now. I need to get out of here.

Fresh air will do me good. I take my cup of tea along with my smokes, and trudge to the roof.

My phone vibrates in my back pocket as I reach the top step. It's the grim reaper. "Hey, old man. Where you at?"

"First floor, *princess.* I'm coming up."

Oh, yes, he's agitated and I couldn't be happier.

"Okay. Mo's still sleeping, so come up to the roof. Bye." I cut him off again and laugh out loud.

I'm such a rebel and love it!

Within minutes, I hear heavy footsteps and brace myself for Maeson's onslaught.

"Woman!" His bellow is loud enough to wake the whole damn building.

"Shut up, asshole! I told you Molly's sleeping!" I giggle, trying to wipe the grin off my face.

Anger emanates from him, his eyes flashing dark green, and lips pressed into a thin straight line. He wordlessly stalks over and grabs my arms, lifting me effortlessly into the air. The forceful kiss takes my breath away. "Don't you ever"—his mouth presses to mine again—"hang up on me."—lips roughly devour mine—"ever again! And that name you called me? A big no, no."

His kisses leave me immobilized, and unable to respond. My body tingles in excitement as his hands roam and grope me roughly. He's aggressively sucking, licking, and nipping my lips, and my insides practically burst into flames. During sex, Maeson becomes a different man, the aggressor I desperately crave. I melt into him, my body limp. I've totally forgotten why he's here.

Oh, shit, Molly!

Reality strikes and I push at his chest, gasping for air. "Woah!

Stop!" I press my fingertips to my swollen lips, dragging in several deep breaths.

"What?" Maeson's eyebrows go up. Confusion clouds his eyes as he pants and reaches out to grab me.

"Woah there, handsome! There's a reason why I called you remember?" I wink and skip to the stairs, letting him watch my ass jiggle. "We can revisit my punishment later."

* * *

WE REACH THE DOOR TO my room, and Maeson huffs loudly. "What is going on?" He growls in my ear.

"Honestly, I have no clue. She's been working so much, she might be overly exhausted. I have a feeling she's going to ask you to either hire someone else or lessen the amount of work she has to do."

"She's that tired? The only reason I left everything up to her was because she said she could handle it."

"Well, after a while weren't you tired of doing everything alone? I assume that's why you hired her in the first place. The girl needs a vacation, Maeson."

"All she has to do is ask, damn it! I'm such an asshole for not noticing!"

"It's never too late to offer her some time off. Now shush, she might still be asleep." I peer into the room and Molly is sitting up at the edge of the bed, full on crying.

What the hell?

She doesn't look up at us as we walk in, but she knows we're in the room with her. "Maeson. Mae Mae. I fucked up. I fucked up bad." Covering her face with both hands, she bursts into loud, heartbreaking, soul-wrenching sobs.

Oh God, this is worse than a tired, overworked friend in need.

Maeson doesn't falter nor misses a beat as he rushes to her side. Fear is written across his face, the creases in his forehead, and the frown he's sporting clearly expresses it. "What did you do?" He pulls her hands away from her tear-filled, mascara smeared face, and caresses it with a tenderness I've never seen from him before. "It can't be that bad, sweetie. I'm here, you know I am, always have been. Tell me. I can fix it like I fixed everything else."

Molly shakes her head vehemently and cries out, "I can't. You'll hate me forever!"

As I stand in the doorway watching them, fear creeps up and something seems off. What's being said throws me, how could he hate her? She's the closest thing he has to a sister, unless she did something unforgivable? But even then, that's hard to believe.

I bite down on my lip and stay quiet, this is their moment. I'm the bystander watching what seems like a moment in time which could, quite possibly, change their relationship forever. My palms begin to sweat as Maeson's expression changes to confusion, and who knows what else he's feeling.

Regardless of what she says, he continues to hold her hands, and support her trembling body. "Nothing you say can make me hate you. Tell me and we can deal with it. You're starting to scare me, so get it over with. *Please, please,* sweetheart."

My gut clenches at the note of tenderness to his voice. It's something I'm hearing for the first time, a deeper insight into the man I'm falling for. The man I barely know the ins and outs of.

There's so much more to him than I even thought. So many secrets, stories, memories, and emotions this man is hiding. I need to know more.

There's obviously so much I don't know about either of them. Molly's said many times, she has no family, but not once did I ask why. Not once did I push to know.

Fuck, I'm a terrible friend. Lately, all of our conversations revolved around me and my life, never hers.

Same goes with Maeson or *Mae Mae* as Molly calls him. I'm beginning to realize I have so much to learn and it seems this might be the time that starts.

My head buzzes as I wait, on edge, for Molly to speak up between her sobs. Her lips quiver uncontrollably, hair stuck to her face, stains of black dripping all over her shirt.

Suddenly, her shoulders stiffen as if a moment of sanity hits her. Her mouth starts to move, but no sounds escape, she tries again, this time she screams.

A hysterical, full of every possible emotion scream. The kind when you're at your wits end with nothing left to do but yell out all your frustrations and fears. The ultimate release known to anyone who's hit rock the fucking bottom.

Rock bottom. That's where it all started for me and now Molly's reached hers. How did I not notice something was wrong with her?

This is the moment when I *know* she needs me. It's my turn to provide her comfort and lend her a shoulder to cry on. I'm the one person in this room that can be there without judging her choices.

I push Maeson aside, giving Molly space and pull her into my arms as I whisper in her ear, "Shh. It's okay, baby girl. You can do this. You're a strong woman. Tell us what's wrong. We are here for you." My hands tremble as bad as hers at this point. Being right in the thick of all this, unbearable emotion messes with my head. My own memories bombard me and I fight to push them aside. "Look at me." I bring her face up, peering into those deep pools of pain. I see the rawness of what she feels and my eyes water. "Let's sit against the wall. I can't hold you up for much longer."

In the haze of it all, she manages to bend her knees but falls to the ground. Maeson's strong hands are on her immediately, helping her sit between me and the bed for support. She lowers her head between her knees, deeply breathing in and out. Maeson and I watch her silently with grim expressions spread across our faces.

It takes her a few minutes to gather some strength and the sobs subside. The biggest, bluest eyes I've ever seen look up at Maeson, tears cascading down her beautiful face. "I'm three months pregnant," she whispers sadly.

Oh, my god! How did I not notice it wasn't stress weight she gained? Was I that self-involved? She's freaking pregnant and never said a word!

I'm mentally freaking out and processing her revelation. Maeson, on the other hand, doesn't move an inch, not one muscle flinches at the news. "Lass! You about gave me a heart attack! You're upset over that? Women get pregnant all the time. I can help you if the man won't. Ruby and I are here for you." He moves toward us, but Molly puts her hand up, stopping him in his tracks.

"With Jax's baby."

Simultaneously, Maeson and I reel back. Time freezes, shock ripples through the room, and an unsettling silence sets in.

This is bad, very bad. Jax? Shit! They've kept this kind of secret from Maeson for this long? Three whole months of knowing, three months of lies, and going behind the man they both consider a brother's back.

My eyes meet Maeson's blazing ones, the expression on his face—indescribable. All over again, he looks like the man I first met, anger thumps off of him. The moment he opens his mouth, I tense up. "My *brother*... my *best friend*... Jax?" His voice is hard as stone, his body is stiff and rigid.

I close my eyes, unable to bear looking at him any longer.

I think I'm going to lose the man he's become.

Molly flinches as if she's been slapped in the face. "Yes," she says in a small, shattered voice.

The green in Maeson's eyes darkens until they're almost black and he takes a deep breath. Releasing it in a rush, he turns and stalks out of the room, slamming the door behind him.

"Maeson wait!" Molly yells out after him.

After a silent beat or two, realization seems to sink in—he's not coming back—and her body collapses into mine. I hold her tight, grasping for something to say—anything to make it easier for her. Really, there's no need for any more words, enough have been said tonight, but I try anyway. "Let him go, honey. He needs space right now. I'm here for you. It's okay. You'll be okay." In an attempt to comfort her, I squeeze her shoulders tighter.

Instead of answering me, she cries out, hysterically yelling at the closed door. "*Please*... come... back... *not* Jax's fault! Mine, all *mine!*"

This time, I don't speak, simply because she's too far gone to comprehend that it will be all right, *eventually*. It's all about finding that strength we all have buried within ourselves. But she's not ready to dig that deep inside for it. I close my eyes again and listen as she screams, over and over again.

Misery loves company they said. Of course, it does… it's found me yet again.

STAY TUNED

Thank you so much for reading the first book of Ruby and Maeson's story! I truly hope you enjoyed it but their story is far from ending... 'The Beginning' is behind us, awkward formalities are over and we get to move into 'The Middle' section of this trilogy. Please stay tuned for book two which is titled—Scarred Wings.

Until then, my dear readers, remember to... *Take a deep breath!*

I love to hear from my readers!

Feel free to contact me on the following social media:

FACEBOOK- AUTHOR KATERINA BRAY

www.facebook.com/authorkaterinabray

INSTAGRAM- KATERINABRAY

www.instagram.com/katerinabray

WEBSITE - www.katerinabray.com

DON'T FORGET TO PLEASE ADD A SHORT REVIEW ON **AMAZON** AND **GOODREADS** TO LET ME KNOW WHAT YOU THOUGHT! THANK YOU!

SPREAD LOVE!

ABOUT THE AUTHOR

When I'm not at my full-time job, I will often be found at my laptop, writing. For that, I thank my loving grandmother. Her strength was my inspiration.

My husband and I had experienced a devastating loss after endlessly trying so hard to have our own family. Shortly after, we learned our journey would be a long one, and we are still hoping for our miracle.

Writing became an outlet, allowing me to express my feelings, and turn around a difficult situation. My loving husband reminded me daily of everything we share—our love, our health, and most of all—each other.

During this time, I was inspired to write this tale about Ruby Bennett, a woman who holds on strong even during her own times of adversity. I hope that others who read this story will be reminded that no matter what they are going through, it too shall pass and that it will give them strength to endure. As many of my favorite authors did for me, perhaps I can provide that small escape from their troubles.

CPSIA information can be obtained
at www.ICGtesting.com
Printed in the USA
LVOW11s0412060717
540382LV00001B/232/P